Before the Roses Wither

H. L. Chandler

A Wings ePress, Inc.
Futuristic Novel

ings
ress, Inc.

Wings ePress, Inc.

Edited by: Jeanne Smith
Copy Edited by: Heather O'Connor
Executive Editor: Jeanne Smith
Cover Artist: Trisha FitzGerald-Jung
Images: Christelle PRIEUR, Willfried Wende - Pixabay

Wings ePress Books
www.wingsepress.com

Copyright © 2022 by: Louise Chandler Guffy
ISBN-13: 978-1-61309-507-2
ISBN-10: 1-61309-507-4

Published In the United States Of America

Wings ePress Inc.
3000 N. Rock Road
Newton, KS 67114

Dedication

To fiction readers who enjoy imagining 'what might have been,' or 'what might be.'
Thanks for spending time with this story.

* * *

Before the roses wither and the fields become dust,
Gaze upon green hills and watch them turn to
rust.

If you survive the hunger, the riots, and the storms
Remember Eden, where life from dirt was formed.

Out of the mystery we came, to it we shall return.
Until the great mysteries of time and life we learn.

Prologue

It is two days after leaving the withered and stricken town of Garden City, Oklahoma, that I am starting this journal. The hours of bumping along dust-clogged back roads, being hungry most of the time, and finding Evan and Simon in no mood to talk leaves me bored and restless. This alone is enough to make me seek diversion, but I also realize that where we are heading and what we intend to do might someday be important. I should keep a record, and count it lucky that I have a pen and paper. Simon, being of an older generation, packed a tablet, and he is kind enough to let me use it. To begin with, my name is Ryan Lanier; I am sixteen-years-old. I am traveling with Evan Hunter and Simon Taylor toward the Canadian border. The date is November 15, 2197.

Staring at this first entry, I see there is something missing. It can't simply start with our odd, traveling trio: Evan Hunter, a fiery-eyed twenty-seven-year-old evangelist, Simon Taylor, an eighty-four-year-old relic, and me. None of it will make sense without telling what has gone before, why we are fugitives from the Church and state. I need to start two and a half years ago, when the three of us were part of a disaster that might have helped topple an already shaky world system.

It sounds as if we were instigators of some sinister plot, but actually, it was more like being one of the pebbles in an avalanche. Events came crashing down, dislodging and sweeping us along, small rocks gathering speed and mass, rearranging the face of the prairie and sending tremors and shock waves around the world. There will be accounts written in government records, giving dry details and numbers, yet they can never present the true picture of how it hurled and flung us, like tiny gravel, pebbles, and rocks, out of our normal places.

It caused more disruption than even the year of the Great Solar Flares. I capitalized those words because people make much of how the event changed the world. I was five years old and it didn't mean a lot to me. People were frantic over the loss of their electronics, nuclear plants, satellites, and other conveniences they had grown accustomed to. I never understood the concern over losing instant connection...bad news travels fast enough. People learned to cope. They started reconstruction, but older people complained because it was never the same. The biggest problem was depleted natural resources that had nothing to do with solar flares. Wood, oil, minerals of every kind were scarce, because the world population was around sixteen billion at the time. These things are still in short supply, and electronics never returned to the pre-Flare period. The good news is, with population control, and a couple of plagues, earth's population has decreased to twelve billion. It is a number most experts believe we can sustain, if we are careful.

That is in the past. Now we are running from a current disaster.

There is no way to tell the future, but I can record the actions and reactions of those we left behind. It will occupy me on this long trip, and perhaps give me an understanding of human nature. For whatever part I may play, the knowledge should be useful. I am lucky to be with Evan, who was in the thick of it, and Simon who, old as he is, has sharp eyes and a good memory. From time to time when I'm able to divert Evan's attention from driving and watching for anyone trying to stop us, and when I can keep Simon from nodding off, they fill in whatever I've missed. They knew these people better than I did.

As we talk, they seem worried, almost in shock. I have noticed older people have trouble adjusting, and the older they are the more trouble they have. It must be that the changes come too fast for them. One thing piles on another and the world spins faster until they are entirely off-center. I don't intend to lose my balance; things have moved fast most of my life and I am used to it. Evan is still young, yet a small look of doubt and confusion sometimes flickers across his face. It makes me wonder if he is as strong as I first thought.

Simon has given in completely, professing to know nothing, giving everything over to God, saying, "He has a plan, formed before the foundation of the earth, and every last detail will come to pass, exactly as He has ordained. He deals on a scale too large for us. We can do nothing but trust and obey."

Simon may be right about there being a plan, but I'm not certain it is beyond our understanding. We should be in control of our destiny. The day will surely come when I can do my part. Until that time, I will learn from Evan and Simon. Neither of them has said as much, but I think they expect me to follow their footsteps, carrying the message to which they are dedicated. I find no fault with their sincerity and enthusiasm. Their deep faith that God alone will control this world is touching; yet, they are a bit short on the practical side. It is one thing to have visions of eternal peace and a destroyed earth returned to Eden, and rather another to take the steps necessary to accomplish it. I don't flatter myself that I will ever actually have the strength and power to bring about the greater good for the greatest number; still, if I am single-minded and willing to sacrifice, I shall find some way to serve.

Perhaps writing about how it was in Garden City will be worthwhile; other affected areas must be much the same. As Simon once said, "You need to know where you've been or you'll find yourself there again."

I'll start with the Brockman family, as they were one of Garden City's prominent families. I didn't know Diana Brockman personally, but Evan's description did much to reveal her character. A third-hand account cannot be completely accurate, but I'll try to be objective, although I have to admit my imagination will fill in the bare spots.

If it were not for Evan and the calamity, I doubt I would have known these people. They are the ones who always had everything, their comfortable positions shielding them from the hardships that were routine for the rest of us. I take no pleasure in their loss, but it was necessary if a new order is to come. That it should start with the land and those closest to it seems fitting, for the earth and the fullness thereof should belong to everyone.

One

By eight o'clock, the June sun was climbing in a cloudless, turquoise sky. Golden rays filtered through the huge oaks on Fern Brockman's expansive lawn. Her granddaughter, the elegant Diana, stepped through the French doors onto the flagstone terrace and surveyed a perfect world. She let her head fall back and her sea-green eyes closed as she breathed in the magnificent morning. For twenty-three summers, she had come to Fern's home and found the perfect setting for her own delicate beauty. The fact that there were few of these oases left pricked her like a thorn. Early summer flowers, standing firm and crisp in the coolness of morning, bordered the fresh green lawn, bright with dew. Behind her, the great stone house, filled with things made of silver, crystal, and velvet from days past, created an imposing fortress against an inelegant world.

Diana walked across the terrace and moved along the flagstone pathway to the rose garden. As she neared the dusky pink- and lush wine-colored flowers, a clean, sweet smell saturated the air, clouding her vision with a rosy mist.

Outside her world, people were busy with things that didn't matter; none of it would affect her. In a few short days, she and Clay

Sanderson would be married. Her life would continue as gracious and beautiful as it had always been.

"Diana," Grandmother Fern called.

Diana turned and strolled to the terrace where Clarence, in a crisp white serving jacket, was putting breakfast on a glass-topped table. Clarence and his cherubic wife, Nora, had worked for Fern since Diana was a child. Between them, they kept the fine old house on Grand Avenue running. It was a well-oiled, very silent machine. Diana never questioned the loveliness. It simply existed, as rightfully hers as the shimmer of her light brown hair. She was aware of, but uninterested in, the family holdings of Oklahoma wheat land and the office building at the other end of Grand Avenue where Uncle Avery and her father practiced law. These things were like the mulch under the roses, necessary, but not worthy of attention.

She viewed the breakfast setting and smiled at how different the mornings were in her parents' home only three miles away. Her forty-five-year-old mother, Glenda Brockman, epitomized the strident feminist ideals worshipped by her mother, Grandmother Baker. The Brockman home was an equal opportunity battlefield filled with sharp angles, glass, chrome, and stark colors. Diana deplored her mother's taste and viewed her lifestyle with revulsion.

At every turn, Diana fought to upright the pedestal her mother had foolishly kicked over. If Glenda had her way, even Diana's wedding would be one of those ghastly equitable affairs resembling a courtroom procedure. However, Diana's icy stares and shrill protest had prevailed. Her wedding would restore grace, dignity and elegance to the ceremony.

As Fern poured the rich, dark coffee, her hand shook slightly, one of her few signs of age. There had never been a time when Fern was not perfectly groomed or serenely composed, even last year when her husband, Thomas, died. She went through the services, graciously accepting the condolences of friends and family. Diana admired her grandmother's regal bearing and felt that one day the mantel of family matriarch would fall upon her own shoulders. If anything, her sensitivity for the finer things would surpass her grandmother's taste. While Fern's bravery was admirable, Diana's reaction had been more refined. Death was hideous and ugly, a violent assault on life's beauty. The talk of how natural Thomas looked had made her rush to the bathroom, where she retched until her stomach ached. In Diana's opinion, the entire family had gone temporarily insane with their calm acceptance of his peaceful death.

Thomas had passed away in his sleep at seventy-one. It was as if he and Fern had planned it that way. An easy end to an easy life. The harvest made possible by the hard labor of Brockman generations that had gone before. Anyone in Garden City who mattered knew the Brockman family history.

Daniel Harris Brockman had been the first of his line to arrive on the Oklahoma plains. He had made the run in 1889, even though he was sixty-two at the time. He had with him his wife Delphie and their youngest child, twenty-two-year-old Henry Tyler. They had left three married daughters in Pennsylvania. Perhaps if Henry had married and settled in Pennsylvania, no Brockman would ever have seen the plains, but Henry had a wild streak and old Daniel wasn't ready to give up on adventure either. They staked their claim and dug in. Henry, true to his wayward nature, married an Osage Indian girl called Rising Star. When the later generations had to acknowledge her as an ancestor, they told stories about her beauty and gave off-handed hints that she was the daughter of a chief. That made it, if not acceptable, at least bearable.

Henry and Star produced two sons and secured three sections of land. When the brothers, Samuel and Tyler Harris Brockman, decided to study law at Oklahoma University, the family began to take on its present shape of land and law. Tyler married a cattleman's daughter, bringing more land into the family. The brothers were hard workers; the future looked bright...until the stock market crashed, and the prairie began to blow away.

Through those desperate years, Samuel and Tyler watched the land turn dry and they became as tough as the desert plants, pulling into themselves and growing slow to retain the juices of life. The entire country was in financial trouble, but nature as well plagued the plains. The grim-faced plainsmen knew they had two choices: tough it out, or pile their belongings on a rattletrap truck and become one of John Steinbeck's Okies.

Day after day, Samuel and Tyler watched their friends and neighbors load up and pull away, joining one of the most pitiful parades in the country's history. Half of the people looked as if they couldn't physically make the trip and the other half looked dead already. These were first- and second-generation pioneers, a sturdy tough breed. They had to be to survive the damage done to their bodies and spirits. The sun scorched the ground and the constant wind blew. It came out of the southwest like the breath of hell and blasted the dry topsoil into the air, carrying it for miles, blackening the sky. Tight-lipped men who would rather joke than cry talked about plowing the sky if they could get their tractors to run upside down. By 1935, worse yet was upon them and no amount of rough humor could help them grin and bear it. The blowing, swirling dust sifted through the tiniest crack and sandblasted their skin. People became a grayish brown and children hopped around whimpering as the sand stung their legs.

During that time, women's eyes took on the haunted, desperate look of trapped animals preparing to face death. At that point, many a man said to hell with it, swallowed the last of his pride along with a mouthful of grit, and left his land. The Brockman brothers stayed, managed to form a law practice, and used it to acquire more land. Samuel never married; he was too practical to take on a family in bad times, and when times changed, he was content to remain a bachelor. Tyler's children carried on. For another five generations, the practice of advantageous marriages continued.

By the time Diana's grandfather, Thomas Daniel, was born, few remembered the dust storms and the country that had nearly collapsed over two-hundred and forty years before. Thomas stepped into a preordained position, head of a centuries-old law firm and thousands of acres of prosperous land. Thomas married Fern Hillard, another suitable marriage. They had two sons; they named the first one Thomas Hillard and called him Tom to avoid confusion.

Both Tom and his brother, Avery, continued in the law. The brothers took nothing for granted; the Brockman work ethic was in their blood. Now that Grandfather Thomas had passed on, Diana's father, Tom, along with Uncle Avery, continued the law practice. Diana supposed her brother Tyler, in his turn, would manage the family's considerable land holdings. There was no reason to think things would ever change.

Fern sipped her coffee and smiled. "I'm glad you decided to stay with me these last few days," Fern said. "I know you won't be far away, but it will be different. You'll have your own home and if that gleam in Clay's eye is any indication, I'll be a great-grandmother before long."

Diana laughed. "I think Mother is keeping her fingers crossed that we put it off as long as possible. I really don't understand her; she could have been a grandmother by now if Tyler were married."

"Well," Fern said slowly. "It has something to do with how she was raised...women's freedom, and the rest of it. For years, women have boasted of their total equality. Poor Glenda, she expected more than it produced."

"I suppose. It aggravates me how Jan Mary clings to that nonsense. I don't know why it made an impression on her; maybe she listened to Grandmother Baker too much."

Fern patted Diana's hand. "Don't let your sister's ways upset you. She is only nineteen and if her willfulness didn't take this form, it might be something worse. She'll fall in love one of these fine days and it will make her forget these passing fancies. Isn't she going with some young man from Tulsa now?"

"Yes, but if he weren't Indian, I don't think she would look twice at him. It is ridiculous, her obsession with equality. The anti-discrimination laws have been in effect for over two hundred years. She does these things to humiliate me."

Diana's chin quivered and her temples throbbed, causing her eyes to blink rapidly as they did when things disturbed her. Quickly she steadied herself and smiled faintly.

"You're right. She'll outgrow it in time. For now, we've called a truce, at least until the wedding is over."

"I'm glad, dear. Now finish your breakfast. Your mother will arrive shortly. Glenda isn't happy about having to make these wedding arrangements as it is. You know how she scolds us if we cause any delay."

Diana and Fern shared a sly smile as they leisurely continued their breakfast. Diana wondered how she could have survived without Fern; the rest of the world was insane. Her father turning red and screaming at every press conference President Morris held, yelling, "What's that man doing to us?" It did seem that with every new policy, inflation climbed another few points, but that had been going on since before she was born and it hadn't caused starvation in the streets. It was simply something people learned to live with. Thank the stars Clay wouldn't be involved with those things. He was a farmer and as long as he had the land, he would be content.

It was funny how their two families had started the same and yet had grown in different ways. Now, this marriage would unite two of the largest landholders in the state. The Sanderson family had arrived in Oklahoma about the same time as the Brockmans and suffered the same hardships. They too had stayed, their sons attending O.S.U. in Stillwater and majoring in agribusiness. Clay had followed the same pattern, and for the past three years had managed near seventy-five thousand acres with his father. It pleased Diana that Clay was a farmer; they were a stable lot, not given to joining in labor and union squabbles and touring about the country fighting first one issue and then another. At least they always had been. Diana frowned as she thought of how Clayton seemed to be changing. It was only in small ways and she didn't want to think about it. Once they were married, he would settle down, the same as his father, Mark, had done. He'd be too busy with the land to be involved in the turbulent churning of the times.

She and Clay never discussed their financial future. That was his responsibility. Mainly they talked about the home they were building in the lake section to the southeast of town. At first, his parents were angry over Clay's building a home in town, but Diana had gently pointed out that her idea of gracious living was not a sun-baked prairie without a tree in sight or getting her face and arms sunburned while scratching around in a vegetable garden.

Clay's mother, Eva Sanderson, had laughed and said, "Really Diana, it's not that way. The only reason we have a family garden is because the quality is superior and we do have help, you know. You could hardly call our place a homestead."

Diana grudgingly agreed. The Sandersons' home was quite nice, if you cared for the style. Still, Eva's appearance defeated her argument for living there. The woman was round as a barrel and wore her long hair drawn back, leaving her broad face brown as a field hand's. Some people liked farm life; Diana was not one of them. For a while, Clay took his parents' side in the matter.

"It would be more convenient. No sense in driving fifteen miles each way every day. You pick the spot and we'll have the same house built on the farm."

With a slight flutter of her silken eyelashes, Diana had overcome his objections.

"I guess your family has been living in town too long," he'd laughed.

With that settled, they purchased five acres close to Prairie Lake and Diana proceeded to direct the contractor in every step of the construction. This house was to be the fulfillment of her dreams. No detail escaped her notice. At first, the contractor, Mr. Johnson, was most agreeable, then for some reason he turned surly and for two days, Diana's temples throbbed. By the third morning, she would tolerate no more, marched onto the site, and in her coolest manner delivered an ultimatum.

"Mr. Johnson, as you must know, there aren't many people financially able to have homes built. I understand the construction business in general is struggling. If you can't give better service, I'm sure someone else can."

His face had turned a deeper tan, and his jaw clenched. He had tried to smile. "Miss Brockman, we are doing everything possible to accommodate you. There are building regulations, permits...some materials are extremely hard to find. You can't believe the state and federal forms we are required to file at each step of construction."

"Those are your problems, Mr. Johnson. Things will go along faster now that we have had this understanding. Don't you agree?"

Evidently, Mr. Johnson did agree, because after that morning things went along nicely. She wished Clay would show more interest in the house. It didn't excite him half as much as his heated discussions with her father over the future of farming. Still, she passed it off as simply his being male.

Men were always concerned about business; perhaps they needed a reason to complain. New government regulations, the high cost of borrowing money, and the increasing cost of machinery were Clay's department. If he chose to let those things upset him, that was none of her concern. As far back as Diana could remember, the men of the family had fumed over the state of business and government regulations. It amounted to the same thing, and life continued on as it always had. There was no need to worry, let the skeptics chew their fingernails and predict gloom and doom. There was no way for it to touch her.

Diana glanced across the table at Fern. She was living proof that even in troublesome times there was a way to live a gracious life. It simply took some thought, planning, and being certain to make the right choices, as she had in deciding to marry Clay. For a time, she had considered someone else as a possible mate. Now Evan rarely crossed her mind. She was certain that, even if Clay had not come along, she would never have married Evan. She had no objection to becoming a minister's wife, if that minister held the proper position in the Church's hierarchy, but there was a flaw in Evan that would limit his future. Underneath outward calm beat the heart of a rebel. Diana almost laughed. A man of God and yet a rebel...a contradiction, wasn't it? In her world, the two definitely did not mesh. Certainly, it was a noble calling; too bad he took it literally. Praise the stars, she was able to keep her good judgment and recognize the affair for the pure physical attraction it was.

Evan Hunter was one of the handsomest men she had ever seen. The proportions of his face and form were what might be an artist's concept of man perfected. There was a most remarkable thing about him; it was as if the sun were always shining on him. His skin looked burnished to a golden sheen and his blond hair seemed alive with glistening lights, while his eyes projected a piercing crystal blue. An extremely striking man. For a moment, Diana let her mind linger over his beauty, and then quickly snapped the lid on the unproductive thinking. Clay was not without attractions of his own.

Evan was almost too exotic to endure day after day, while Clay was as dependable as the earth he worked. A sturdy man of nature, brown as an oak leaf in fall and with eyes the deep, solid blue of woodland violets. The merger of Sanderson and Brockman lines should produce healthy, beautiful children. Children were not of particular interest to Diana; still she supposed they would be necessary at some point. Clay's family would expect it and they could be used to an advantage in certain circumstances. While Diana looked with disdain upon many modern customs, and definitely preferred the more refined days of her grandmother's younger years, there were some advantages to the current lifestyle. The law limiting family size, for instance. When it became time for her to fulfill her maternal duty, she need not produce more than two children. A wonderfully sensible piece of legislation, to her way of thinking. The quality of life was slipping fast enough without bringing more pink, damp, squalling bits of humanity into existence. Diana smiled as she finished the last of her coffee.

"Having pleasant thoughts, my dear?" Fern asked.

"More like wicked thoughts." Diana smirked.

"In that pretty head?" Fern teased.

"I was thinking about having children and it brought to mind how close I came to not having a sister. Jan gets furious every time I mention it. If mother had waited a year longer for her third child, Family Law would have been in effect. Jan wouldn't be here."

Fern's eyes twinkled. "Oh, you are a wicked girl. Come now, let's get dressed, we're already late."

Two

Even in the early morning with dew still lingering, the dirt road was ash dry and dusty. It ran straight along a section line of the Sanderson land. The red-brown road seemed a strip of desert between the lush wheat stretching away on either side. The scene was a chalk drawing of flat-blue sky and a yellow-ball sun plastered above green fields cut into mile squares by ruler-straight roads. There were no hard ruts in these wheat land alleys. It had not rained for months, and the silt-fine dirt lay inches deep. The truck Clay drove rattled in the silent plains. Dry, red dust clouds billowed from beneath the wheels and fanned out over the fields. The man riding with Clay was dressed in cotton work clothes and wore a wide-brimmed straw hat. His skin was dark and creased from many seasons under the sun. The deep perpetual frown lines between his eyes matched the grooves holding his mouth in tight-lipped silence. His eyes were the kind that could twinkle with merriment, but this morning they were clouded and grim.

"Come on, Jeff, cheer up. The fields look good. See how fat those heads are." Clay pounded the steering wheel with the palm of his hand. "By God, I bet we get over eighty bushels to the acre. It's going to be one hell of a crop. A few days ago, I was with Jim Durbin, our manager in the south—you remember Jim, don't you?"

Jeff nodded.

"Anyway, they are two weeks into harvest and it is one of the best we've had. There'll be a big bonus for everyone."

"Maybe not after what I got to show you."

Clay shot a sidelong glance at the man beside him and a small twinge of apprehension pricked the back of his neck. He knew it was important or Jeff wouldn't be dragging him to the far side of this five-section tract. From long experience, Clay respected Jeff's judgment, but Jeff was a worrier. A cautious man who could have started in business for himself, still he had worked for Mark Sanderson for thirty years, preferring the security of employment to the risk of farming. The Sanderson Company provided lodging at the main compound, there was always transportation, and Mark paid his hands well. Clay didn't begrudge a penny spent in running the huge operation. It was a tremendous job and without men such as Jeff, it wouldn't be possible.

The day of the small farm was long gone, but there were still farmers, men as enduring as the land itself. They loved the Southern Plains with a love that came from being part of them. Clay and his father, Mark, shared those feelings. Clay's earliest memories were of standing on the edge of a field with the wheat swaying before him, and the smell of warm green rising from the stalks. The heat from the soil burned the bottoms of his bare feet, and the hot, dry wind wrapped around his body. He knew the land was a thing alive, only tolerating men that they might tend it. When the fields were ripe and the wind quickened, ripples and swells rose and fell across the land, some said like the ocean waves. To Clay, it was the earth breathing. A cloudless blue stretched above the prairie from horizon to horizon. The point where sky and land met was distant enough to make his eyes grow wide and burn with the effort to see. There was something unexplainable about its hold on a man. It was not an easy land, yet once the fine-textured soil was under a man's fingernails and filled his nostrils, if he were a certain kind of man, the land claimed him.

Still, Clayton was different from Jeff and his breed. He had to be. Times were different. Long ago, the smaller farms had been absorbed into corporations and companies with holdings running into the hundreds of thousands of acres, managed from boardrooms located in the East. Their on-the-site management teams were highly specialized experts who calculated soil conditions, weather forecasts, and types of grain on computer systems. Information was at their fingertips, and with the press of a button, they could put troops of men and machines into the fields to carry out their orders. To survive and compete, Clay and his family had to run their farms in the same manner. Years ago, Mark recognized the trend, stayed abreast of each new development, and increased his landholdings at every opportunity. Some others had done the same. Now, worked in among the absentee landowners were a few family-owned and-operated companies.

Jeff was silent as they bumped along and it was useless to try talking with him about whatever he had found disturbing. They'd had the same discussions in the past. Jeff was strongly against the use of pure technology in managing the land. He was convinced that in the end it would fail. No matter how Clay argued, explaining improvements and higher crop yields, Jeff would never believe otherwise. Jeff's deep-seated beliefs were a legacy from his father, Simon Taylor. Simon combined farming and preaching, instilling love of God and of nature into his son. Simon also kept alive the over two-hundred-year-old stories of a 1929 dust bowl.

Raised on those stories, Jeff swore by the creed of dry and wet seasons, each following the other in uncontrollable cycles. Some land you could plow, but some you should not turn. It would cause an imbalance man could never put right. There was only a certain amount of life in a stretch of land. After the demanding wheat, corn, and cotton bled it dry, the land died. It needed healing crops and a time of rest to restore and repair the soil. The longer you worked the ground, the longer it took to rebuild the nutrients and minerals.

Clay knew this was true in what seemed ancient times, but now they were not at nature's mercy. From what had once been forestlands west of the Mississippi to the foot of the Rockies and from Canada to the Gulf, every inch of the Northern Heartland and Southern Plains was under cultivation. It had been for Clay's lifetime and it was working fine. America's power base sat firmly upon the broad, bountiful farmlands, and despite his grumbling over government interference, Clay was proud to be part of it. His faith in scientific means of soil regeneration and moisture control were as strong as Jeff's distrust of it.

Jeff pointed to a spot beside the road. "Stop here," he said.

The two men stepped from the truck and Jeff led the way to a patch of wheat, then stopped and put his hands on his lean hips.

"There, what do you see?"

Clay quickly scanned the area. At first, he was puzzled, but something was different about this particular spot. It took him a second to recognize it. In a strip about ten feet wide and stretching far into the field, the wheat seemed shorter than the stalks on either side.

"What the hell?" Clay muttered. "Am I crazy or is this shorter than the rest?"

Jeff nodded. "Sure is. Not more than an inch and I'd never noticed except it's together in sort of a band. But that's not the worst of it."

Jeff squatted on his heels, pulled a narrow blade, and handed it to Clay. The puckered leaf had a yellowish tint with mingled spots of brown. In the brownish patches, the leaf was thin, nearly transparent, akin to a mosaic leaf mold. Jeff stood up and walked through the wheat, often stopping to pick a blade. Clay watched a minute then motioned him to return.

"Is the whole strip this way?"

Jeff walked back with his handful of leaves. "No. If you weren't looking real hard, you wouldn't notice. It's only a blade here and there."

Clay turned the unhealthy leaf over, examining it carefully. He bent down, broke off one of the heads of wheat, and rolled it between his fingers.

"Whatever it is hasn't seemed to bother the grain. This feels firm and full to me."

"I don't think it's going to hurt this harvest any," Jeff mused. "If the field had of turned full ripe before I saw this, we wouldn't have known something was after it."

"Insects?" Clay ventured in disbelief.

"Not been a bug in these fields for twenty years."

"Maybe it's some new microscopic organism at work. Is this the only place you've seen it?"

"There's four more spots about a mile apart. Long strips that reach far into each section."

"I'll get these off to the experimental station in Amarillo. The fellows there will explain it soon enough. I don't think it's anything to worry about. If it doesn't affect this crop, we'll find what it is long before next planting."

As they walked to the truck, Jeff kicked at the ground. "Wouldn't hurt to get some rain once in a while."

Clay laughed and shook his head as he climbed into the truck. Couldn't argue with Jeff on that one. They never hurt for water because of the irrigation system. However, it was expensive and rain was free. It would be ideal if every winter brought heavy, wet snows that stayed on the ground and slowly melted, letting the nitrogen-heavy moisture penetrate deep into the soil with no driving wind to sweep it away. Then some long, gentle rains in April and May, tapering off into a hot summer giving the grain the heat to come to full, ripe maturity.

In Clay's lifetime, there were only two or three years when conditions were perfect and one of those had been marred by cutworms. He'd been a small boy when it happened, but he remembered his father's reaction. Mark had cursed the sky, the earth, and every living thing on it. It was the disappointment. However, that would never happen again, for the next year they eradicated cutworms along with other insect plagues. Finally, every landowner made use of the proper pesticides at the same time and in one sweep, the entire mid-section was clean, leaving only wind and water with which to contend. The wind still blew, but since many crops reseeded themselves, there was less cultivation. By keeping most of the land covered, it held the soil firmly in place.

Even water was no longer a problem.

When the big corporations came on the scene, big solutions came with them. Men who controlled thousands upon thousands of acres were not going to depend upon something as capricious as the weather. Their investment was far too great to risk failure. They had the money and the technology and, of course, the bottomless pit of federal aid to assist them. For years, the vast Ogallala aquifer had served to irrigate the arid land. The first settlers dug as deep as they could to find water for family and livestock. Salvation came in the form of super-powered drilling rigs that gave farmers the means to water miles of cropland. By the 1980s, more than 150,000 wells pumped away at the life-giving liquid, but still it was not enough.

The demand increased and they drilled more wells. The level of the ground water dropped, making it harder to reach. The drills went deeper and deeper until the quality of the water and the cost of reaching it made it a losing proposition. However, the agribusiness conglomerates had no intentions of giving in easily. Their next move was in the northwest along the Rockies, trapping the spring runoff, eventually moving high enough to divert some from its natural course down the western slope. This brought about a near water war with the states to the west, but as in most emergencies, an answer came.

Clay was ten years old at the time and he remembered his father's excitement over the news. There was a great subterranean water source running from west to east. It originated somewhere around the foot of the Bighorn Mountains in Wyoming and collected in the southeast corner, forming a giant underground lake. From there it seeped through a wide band of pure white sand hundreds of feet below the surface under part of Nebraska and Colorado on its silent underground route. It didn't take long for the farming corporations occupying the dry, thirsty lands of the Southern Plains to see that any amount of money would be well spent in creating a massive underground reservoir and bringing the flow to the south. What they constructed was a mammoth irrigation system with thousands of miles of underground pipe. The controlling companies were in a position to irrigate their own land and sell water to independent farmers. The initial charge to connect to the main line was expensive, but it would have been insane not to take advantage of the system. The Sandersons were still paying against the loan they had obtained. Yet the comfort in knowing they were no longer dependent upon the whims of the weather made it worth the cost. With a call, Clay could order the amount of moisture he wanted and at the proper times.

Still, Jeff grumbled, fearing the great reservoir would run dry, or that a pipe would break farther along the line, or perhaps National, the corporation they bought from, would raise the price too high. Earlier that month, Jeff had gone into a gloomy slump when they received news of the latest earthquake along the Canadian border.

"Ground don't take to having tubes and pipes forced into it, pulling out water that's supposed to stay where it is, and pumping in chemicals along with it," he muttered, referring to the fertilizers and soil conditioners injected through the water lines.

Thus far, the life-supporting water system was an answer to nearly every farming problem. Clay had stopped trying to convince Jeff. He was simply grateful that by keeping the soil moist below, the grain would forever grow above. As for this blight, or whatever it happened to be, some new spray could take care of it in short order. He would send the sample in this afternoon and that would be the end of it. Jeff was still frowning as they climbed into the truck.

While Clay drove along the dusty section-line road, he wished he could solve some other problems as easily. Sometimes a small steel hammer of worry pounded in his head, or maybe it was more a pressure building behind a valve about to blow. No, he decided, it was both; the tiny hammer tapping away as he studied the reports from their accountant and the pressure steadily pushing as he struggled to make the right decisions. Mark still helped, but several years ago he had developed a heart condition. Now, Clay tried to protect his father as much as possible. At times, he wished there had been a brother to help shoulder the load. He loved his sister, Tracy, but the farm didn't interest her.

When Tracy married Frank Ivers, Clay thought there might be some help from that quarter, but even then, he knew it was an idle dream. Frank's carefully styled coal-black hair and manicured fingernails weren't the equipment a man needed for farm work. Frank's specialty was talking faster than a man could listen. The uncertain economic times seemed to work to his advantage. Frank managed to slip into one deal after another, fast enough that the losers in the schemes didn't have time to catch him. A couple of times, without Mark's knowledge, Clay bailed Frank out when the squeeze got too tight. He had to for the sake of Tracy and her two kids. Why she didn't leave the bum Clay would never know. She said it was because of Frank Jr. and Robin. Clay could do nothing for his sister except hope for the best.

The only thing Clay could do for his family was keep them solvent, even if he had to fight the entire government. A farmer's life had never been a bed of roses, but things were getting ridiculous. In the past five years, the government had enacted two federal laws that concerned all farming. They in effect nationalized every piece of farmland in the country. The first had to do with the selling of crops. It left open two markets for the independent: sell directly to the government or to the four huge grain conglomerates, who in turn sold to the government, which used food as a bargaining chip in dealing with other nations.

It was getting to the place a man couldn't go to the bathroom without checking a regulation first. For a while, Clay and the other independents fought, formed their own marketing group which accounted for millions of tons of grain each year, but they simply didn't have the power to pull it off because of the second law. It was a new regulation that governed credit. After establishing the markets, the government, in what Washington called the biggest boon to farmers since the tractor, took over the debts.

It wasn't a matter of going to your friendly local banker anymore and saying, "Hey Charlie, I've got my eye on this fine new piece of equipment." Now it was form 29A, and if you answered lines five and nine in the proper manner, three months later the amount you applied for would appear on your local statement. It was a wonderful thing; no end to the credit. The catch was in line five, asking who you sold to last year, and in line nine, asking for a commitment on the sale of your product for the entire term of the loan. The pincer laws gripped the farmer in his two most vulnerable areas: source of credit, and a market in which to sell. Farmers used to grumble over tight-fisted bankers, Clay thought, but at least you had the right to go to hell in your own way.

The agriculture department even dictated the type of crops a farmer could plant. A whole office full of men and computers spewing reams of statistics determined which crops would best serve the national interest. The only thing left to the farmer was title to his land and the mortgage on it. The earth Clay drove over was indeed precious; it was all he could hope to own. Even if he found the money, there was never land for sale. If a parcel came on the market through a farmer's death, an individual bidder didn't have a chance. The corporations always came in with the highest offers, backed by the government, which held the mortgages along with the right of approval on assumption. There were no two ways about it...Clay had to make it on the land his family now owned.

As they pulled into the compound, Clay drew a deep breath, expanding his ribs against the sides of his form-fitting shirt, and before he could stop it, a heavy sigh escaped his lips. Jeff gave him a sharp look.

"What's the matter, boy, you more worried about them fields than you let on, or are you having second thoughts about taking a wife?"

"Course not. Neither one is going to be a problem. Diana will be a big help. She's going to bring class to this old farm family...besides, I love her."

"Oh, she's got class. Maybe a might too much for our kind of living. Brockmans don't go in for lean and good years. What I hear, they want things nice and even. Still don't know how you're going to live in town and work the farm the way you should."

"I'll manage."

"It'd be good to set some rules right off. Maybe not taking a honeymoon in the middle of harvest."

"You can get by without me for a few weeks. Besides, no one is that hard to reach. If you and Dad can't handle it, I doubt I'd be any help."

It was no secret Jeff was displeased with Clay's choice of a wife. Others probably were too, but they didn't express an opinion. He hoped that when they knew her, things would be different. Besides, the Brockmans weren't that far removed from the land. A large part of their income came from grain sales, too. 'Course it was in a different way. They had their holdings leased to National Grain Producers; therefore, they had nothing to do with management of the land. Mark Sanderson could have done the same thing. NGP made repeated offers to either buy or lease Sanderson's one hundred seventeen sections which sprawled over Oklahoma and spilled into Texas. Sometimes Clay wondered how smart it was to keep on fighting. It would be easier to let the land go, quit struggling with the problems. Yet, Clay knew, as long as he lived, he would keep trying.

When the day came that the last independent was gone, Clay had the feeling something horrible would happen. Not only to him and his family but the entire country as well. A gut-wrenching certainty told him he must hold the line. Maybe it had something to do with the reoccurring dream he'd been having. Most nights when it woke him, there would be sweat across his forehead, upper lip, and running from his armpits. Actually, the dream wasn't too terrifying; it always started happy and pleasant. The fields were green and Clay was walking through them. He would feel a surge of joy and begin running, the stalks slapping around his legs while a blue and gold sky stretched above. He would reach the very center of the field and suddenly stop because men or some strange machines began to approach. They would come nearer in a wandering zigzag pattern searching for something. Suddenly Clay would know that they were coming to cut out the land's beating heart and it would jolt him awake.

It always took him a while to get back to sleep. In the light of day, he chided himself for remembering the dream. Dreams meant nothing. Maybe he was nervous about getting married, but that was only natural. Things were bound to grow calm after the wedding. Clay had objected to the date. He had to agree with Jeff—the timing wasn't great, but Diana had been insistent.

"Clayton Sanderson, I will not be married in any other month. I've wanted to be a June bride since I was...well, forever."

The wedding date, and the new house, were his presents to her. It might be a problem living away from the farm. Still, if it didn't work, they could always sell the house by the lake and build on the farm where they really belonged. Let her have what she wanted for now. Later she'd see it was impractical. No use trying to force the issue. Besides it would take care of itself after the children came.

Three

On Thursday evening, with the last of the sun's amber rays streaming through the tall dining room windows of the farmhouse, Clay and his father sat at the big oak dining table. Its surface gleamed, as did the matching china closet, buffet, and sideboard from years of oiling and rubbing. Clay's mother, Eva, had kept the furniture from the first house Mark had built, and inadvertently, had a collection of priceless pieces. Year by year, she'd added rich carpeting and bits of china or crystal that caught her eye. At first, it seemed a hodgepodge of mismatched styles, colors, and textures, but at last, it came together in a fashion deep with meaning and more beautiful than the most carefully decorated room. Eva had woven her slow but unerring pattern throughout the entire house. The large kitchen had a quarry tile floor and gleaming stainless and copper fixtures. The room was distinctly Mexican in design, with bricked arches over the doors and open fireplace. The dining room also carried traces of the Southwest in the woven wall hangings. Upon entering the living room, the setting changed to a New England sparseness with the muted colors of a coastline in the rain. From the slate floored foyer rose a rich mahogany stairway leading to the upstairs rooms.

The house unfolded room by room like a well-planned banquet, something to surprise and pique even the most lagging appetite.

As Clay had watched Diana in a frenzy of picking and choosing furnishings for their new house, he became more aware of the one he was leaving. He tried to tell her it took years to shape and mold a home, but she had tossed her head and laughed.

"Nonsense, Clay. I'll have this completed before we leave on our honeymoon."

As the charges for her purchases rolled in, his stomach churned. The price of a small velveteen chair was staggering. Still, maybe she was right in buying it now. With labor disruptions and shortages of materials, it was hard to find some products at any price.

"Seems we'll eat alone tonight, son," Mark said. "You know, it's funny. I miss your mother even when she is gone for only an evening. The house isn't the same without her."

Clay nodded as he started on his salad. He ate hungrily in anticipation of the chicken he could smell roasting in the kitchen. Strange how things had come full circle. When he was small, everything on the table had come from their own garden, henhouse, or slaughterhouse. Then, the time came when everyone's energy went into producing cash crops and it was more efficient and economical to buy food from stores. Now again, the farm was self-sufficient; hardly an item came from outside and Clay liked it that way. Yet, it was disturbing to think of how expensive and scarce foodstuffs were in the market. He pitied anyone depending upon those limited supplies. Of course, he and Diana wouldn't have that problem, for they would obtain what they needed from the farm, the same as his sister, Tracy, did. That crazy Evan Hunter might be right with his dire warning of impending disaster. Evan only needed a flowing beard and white robe to complete the image. Still, despite the man's wild notions, Clay liked him. Clay knew that, for a short time, Diana had been attracted to Evan, but it didn't bother him. Diana had come to her senses. She wasn't the type to commit to a man hell bent upon self-destruction. Evan was embroiled in some dispute with the Church and, from what Clay had heard, he was on shaky ground. Clay helped himself to a slab of white meat from the platter Tillie, their housekeeper, had placed on the table. The steaming, juicy chicken with its crust of golden brown skin gave him a warm satisfaction. Let Evan fight his theological battles. As for Clay, what more could he want other than to enjoy the fruits of his labor and rest confident in his ability to keep providing for the family?

"You're pretty quiet over there, Clayton." Mark spoke as he buttered a hunk of home-baked bread. "Not getting cold feet over this marriage, are you?"

"No, but I have a lot on my mind. I do wish it were over, though. I'd a hell of a lot rather stay home than go to this bachelor party tonight. You don't suppose we could forget it; they probably won't even miss us."

Mark laughed.

"No. I think we had better attend. I don't think Diana would be too pleased if we didn't."

"I guess, but with the women over at Tracy's having that shower for Diana, you'd think it would be enough. But no, they had to go organize something for the men, too." Clay shook his head. "I can't understand why Diana had to have these old-fashioned trappings. We could have gone to the municipal center and had it over in an hour."

"I know. Tell you the truth, I haven't seen such a wedding in years. But that's Diana for you; I don't think Garden City will forget this wedding for some time." Mark paused a second, studying the baked potato on his plate, then lifted his head. "How's everything going in the field, Clay? I was in the office when you and Jeff drove in. From what I could see from the window, Jeff looked glum. Nothing wrong, is there?"

"I doubt there is. You know Jeff gets upset over anything that even looks suspicious. He found some kind of withering in a few places and course he thinks the whole crop is going to die."

Clay saw the concern in his father's gray eyes and the flush to his ruddy skin, making it the same tint as his coppery hair. Mark looked sturdy and solid; it was hard to believe his heart was fragile as a fluttering moth's wing.

"But don't worry," Clay hastened to add. "It's not much of anything. Certainly won't cause a problem with this harvest. I sent a sample in and should hear something shortly. Could be we got some defective seed in that spot; can't be anything wrong with the soil. We've done everything by the numbers."

Clay and his father ate on in silence. He knew his father was pondering the mystery the same as he was. Bad seed indeed. That rarely happened; ninety-nine percent of the seed was perfect. It was a specially grown hybrid guaranteed to be disease free and -resistant. As for the ground, it was as controlled as if it were in a laboratory. However, they both knew what rode on this and coming harvests. Each year had to bring in enough to pay existing debts, operating expenses, and future capital outlays for new equipment. There was no question of borrowing for those things. With interest running at thirty percent, it was the sure road to ruination. Taking on more debts was foolhardy, which made him think about the new house by Prairie Lake. Damn, he wished he hadn't weakened on that point. He'd told himself they could always sell it, but who was he kidding? No one had enough money to buy anything right now. Still, things were bound to turn around. If they lived there long enough, he might even sell it for a profit.

That night when Clay and his father walked into Prairie Hills Country Club, they found most of the guests had already arrived. Girls in tight black tunics that stopped at mid-thigh were scurrying about keeping glasses filled, and the air hung heavy with the smell of burning hemp.

Through the haze, Clay recognized a few of his friends, but since Diana had made the guest list, many of the faces were only vaguely familiar. For a minute, seeing the rich food, fine clothing, free-flowing liquor, and drugs, Clay rebelled. He had no moral objection to gatherings, but the waste of limited food and energy offended him. Looking at the grinning faces, some already bleary-eyed, he wondered if they understood the delicate balance of the country's economy. Perhaps being part of the nation's most vital industry made him more aware. The fuel that propelled their cars, the clothes on their backs, everything bought and traded for with the precious golden grain. It was a harvest-to-harvest situation. There were no huge reserves to rely upon...too many hungry bellies the world over had taken care of that. The coin of the day was not gold or oil, it was corn, rice, wheat, and soy. Still, the world had survived worse. Crises came and went, but he didn't take a wife every day! Smiling, Clay lifted his head and decided to join the party. Maybe Diana was right. Perhaps that rosy glow on the horizon was the dawn of a new day and not the fires of hell, as Evan had fiercely put it.

Mark said a few words to his son and headed for a group of older men that included Diana's father, Thomas Brockman, and her uncle, Avery. Soon a gathering of Garden City's successful young men surrounded Clay and began the good-natured teasing that he supposed was the purpose of the party. He took one of the smooth, yellow capsules offered by a smiling dark-haired girl. Shortly he was drifting among his friends and dreaming of long nights between satin sheets with Diana beside him, smelling of deep red roses.

When the party ended, Clay and Mark drove toward Tracy's home. In the rearview mirror, Clay saw Frank following them. As Frank's car weaved along, the bright headlights first pierced the dark side of the road, and then flashed blindingly in Clay's mirror.

"Damn that brother-in-law of mine. If he can't handle it, he ought to stay sober," Clay muttered.

"Take it easy, son, don't be angry when we get there. Your mother and Tracy will sense it right away. We don't want to spoil things."

"Did you see him?" Clay continued. "He had Avery Brockman cornered for over an hour. Trying to sell him on some stupid scheme, I suppose. No wonder Tracy has trouble holding up her head in this town."

When they pulled into the circular driveway, most of Tracy's guests were gone. Eva's electric town car stood beside Glenda Brockman's Silver Star, and Clay stopped beside them. As Clay and Mark opened their doors, Frank's car roared into the drive and slid to a halt, spitting gravel in every direction. Walking toward the front door, Clay looked back at Frank.

"I don't think anything I say will upset Tracy any more than getting a look at Frank," he said to Mark.

Inside, remains of what had surely been a successful shower littered the house. Paper streamers decorated the living room and the bountiful buffet table looked well picked over. In one corner on a table were mounds of gifts stripped of their silver paper and white satin ribbons. In the middle of the disarray stood Diana, her glowing face telling Clay how much the parties and elaborate wedding preparations meant to her. After an exchange of polite conversation, Eva and Mark left. A bit later, Glenda Brockman kissed Diana and departed, leaving Clay, Diana, Jan, Tracy, and Frank to review the presents and compare notes on the two parties of the evening. Tracy hurried about the room removing glasses and ashtrays and putting pillows in place to make room for them to sit down. Tracy's movements were quick and nervous and her brown eyes kept steady track of Frank's every action. Clay ached for his sister; it shamed him to see how desperately hard she tried to be part of the town's higher society. Tracy's delight in the alliance with the Brockman family was hard for the Sandersons to swallow. Eva had been particularly stung by it, feeling her family was every bit as good.

"You make a spectacle of yourself," Eva had scolded her daughter. "Running after those Brockman girls, trying to dress like them, getting things you know Frank can't afford."

Tracy had tossed her dark, close-cropped curls and answered tersely, "You don't know what you're talking about, Mother."

Diana and Jan politely offered to help with the cleaning, and Tracy equally politely refused, waving her hand toward the remaining clutter.

"I wouldn't think of it; Carrie will put it right in the morning."

Tracy mentioned Carrie, giving the impression a maid was a permanent fixture in the Ivers household; however, Clay knew they could only afford Carrie on very special occasions.

Diana pulled her sister toward the towering pile of gifts and they bent their heads together sorting through the stack, praising some, and giggling over others. There wasn't much in their appearance or personalities to suggest the two were sisters. The seed of Rising Star had surfaced in Jan's dusky skin and snapping dark eyes, giving her the energy and dazzle of a sunbeam, while Diana was delicate as moonlight. Their interests were also different. It was a treat to see them enjoying each other's company for a change. Clay shifted his weight from one foot to another until Frank offered him some wine and poured himself a large glass as well.

"Here's to wedded bliss," Frank slurred. "May your dreams come true."

Clay took the glass and stepped closer to Frank.

"What were you trying to sell Avery tonight? Not some of those worthless mineral rights, I hope. You know it isn't legal to sell something you don't own."

Frank flashed a beguiling smile. "Forget that, Clay. I have something much better going now. You should be in on this yourself. Gems, Clay, think of it. Handfuls of emeralds and rubies, not scraps of paper that aren't worth the ink on them. How long do you think people will keep giving anything in exchange for our credit notes?" Frank leaned toward Clay. "I have this contact in South America; you should come in on this."

"Does Tracy know what you're doing now?"

"Your dear sister doesn't know or care what I do. As long as I keep her in the style you Sandersons wouldn't turn loose of a penny to do. What's that hundred and seventeen sections worth now, a little over a billion?"

"I don't know. Since we have no intention of selling, I don't keep track."

"You better start. The squeeze will get tight; you won't have the price of seed. Remember my offer, let me do the bargaining. I can get a deal that'll set you up for life."

Frank tilted his head and lifted his glass. "And what the hell, after that, what do you care?"

"You make me sick, Frank. I don't care how much we could sell for. You're right about one thing: a truckload of paper won't be worth the match to burn it. Which makes me wonder...what are you thinking of using to buy these gems, if you really have a deal with anyone."

Frank's ebony eyes glittered. "Now if I told you that, it might get around. I could lose my whole setup, right?"

Clay put his glass down, walked across the living room into the den and opened the sliding doors onto the garden. Starlight danced across the smooth surface of the pool while the white lawn furniture stood bleak against the shadows, like the skeletal remains of some strange animals. Clay stepped into the cool predawn with its blue-black sky and mint-sharp air. He was still foggy from the pills and drink, but his head was clear enough to find Frank's conversation troublesome. Frank talked about many things. Was this only one more gossamer web or did he really have something working? What could Frank possibly put his hands on that would be valuable enough for that kind of trade? Keeping the family afloat was similar to treading water, without sight of land or ship. He didn't need Frank creating waves, no matter how small they might be.

He'd have to keep Frank away from Mark; no sense upsetting him with this latest folly. Thank God, Mark was no more susceptible to Frank than he was. The only time Mark even came close to taking Frank's advice was when he'd had the first heart seizure. With the diplomacy of a mortician in a sickroom, Frank had sat by Mark's bed and inquired about his method of passing the farm on to Clay and Tracy. Clay, with his teeth clenched, had ordered Frank to leave, but Mark said no, Frank was right; it had to be talked about. Mark had a conventional will leaving everything to Eva and upon her death, his children shared equally. Frank mentioned the unnecessary estate tax and that Mark should see about a trust, something irrevocable to secure the passing of the land. Mark was ready to agree and have it done immediately, but the rest of the family was too disturbed and shocked by the illness to consider letting him make changes.

"Things are fine the way they are," Eva had said. "You concentrate on getting well!"

Clay studied the tiny flashing ripples on the pool's surface, making the water dance. The motion almost hypnotized him until a tiny hammer started tapping in his head. He didn't want to think about Mark dying any more than Eva did. Still, they should prepare for it. Maybe not exactly as Frank suggested, but with things the way they were, he knew they were not putting enough aside to cover inheritance tax. He and Mark would have to talk about it soon. Suddenly, Clay felt a soft arm slip around his waist and Diana was standing beside him. She lifted her face and began to nuzzle his neck.

"What are you doing out here? You know I can't stand it when you leave me alone," she murmured against his skin, sending chills down his back. "You don't want me to be lonesome, do you?"

Clay took her in his arms and pressed the length of her soft, curving body against his. He bent his head, burying his face in her scented hair. "Mm, you feel good," he whispered. Then he kissed her, their lips melting into a warm, soft dampness that drove other thoughts completely from his mind. He moved his head lower, his lips caressing the smoothness of her throat, and she gently began to pull away.

"Later, my love," she said.

Clay tightened his hold and began moving toward a poolside lounge. "They won't miss us, stay a minute longer. Later may be too late."

Diana giggled and pulled back stronger. "Come on, Clayton."

"That's what I'm trying to do."

"Not now, darling. We have to help keep the party alive. Or at least keep Tracy from killing Frank."

"What do you mean?"

"Oh, Frank was getting too friendly with Jan. Harmless, but you know Tracy. I don't think she would care if he were discreet about it, but it was embarrassing her, you know."

"My God," Clay answered with disgust as he took Diana's hand and strode into the house.

Upon finding Frank still alive, with Tracy and Jan chatting quietly, Clay suggested one last drink and then perhaps it would be time to go.

"Can we take you home, Jan?" Clay offered.

"Was Evan at the Country Club?" she asked.

"Come to think of it, I didn't see him. Why?"

"If he was, I thought he might be coming to meet me. But since he wasn't, it won't be any trouble to drop me off, will it?"

"Of course not," Diana cut in. "I didn't know you were seeing Evan. That's an interesting combination."

"It seemed to be for you at one time." Jan's reply was curt, but then she quickly turned toward Clay. "I'm sorry; I didn't mean to hurt you."

"Think nothing of it, Jan. That's the past. We're broad-minded, aren't we, Tracy?"

Clay hoped his sister would get the point, but as they started toward Clay's car, the argument in the house behind them grew louder. From the years of living on the wide, open land, Tracy's voice rang clear as crystal in the cool dawn.

"You are an ass, Frank. A complete ass."

Clay hurried Diana and Jan toward the car, his expression struggling between a frown and a laugh. It seemed Tracy was well capable of holding her own with an unruly husband.

Four

The day before the wedding, the last of the furnishings arrived at Diana and Clay's new home on Prairie Lake. Diana dashed through the house, adjusting a picture in one room and straightening a drape in another. By afternoon, Diana seemed satisfied that at last her domain was complete, and she led Clay to the dining room where she ceremoniously made him sit.

"Now, don't look until I say ready. I have a surprise for you," she said mischievously.

He could hear the clatter of silverware and the tinkling of glass, and shortly Diana came from the kitchen and set a large silver tray on the table. It held fresh, tender asparagus spears wrapped in thin ham, blue-veined cheese, glistening strawberries, and a bottle of champagne.

"There, isn't it lovely? Our first meal together. I simply couldn't wait until we moved in."

As he filled the glasses, Clay smiled. She seemed a small girl playing house. The setting was charming, and when he stepped into the dream with her, the rest of life melted away. It was an escape from the heat and dust and worry in the fields.

"I hope our future meals will be heartier. You may not realize it, but I live mainly on meat and potatoes," he teased.

"I'll tell cook that," Diana answered.

"I thought I was talking to the cook."

"Oh, Clay. I'd poison you in the first month. I know we can't get anyone right away—it is hard to find someone that will fit in—but Fern has fixed that. She is letting me have Nora for a while until we are settled. Isn't that wonderful?"

Clay took a strawberry and sank his teeth into the tart sweetness, while wondering how to explain things to Diana. He swallowed and reached across the table to take her hand.

"Listen, Diana. This is beautiful, the house and everything, but about getting help, well, I don't see how we can do that. Maybe you haven't noticed, but everyone doesn't live the way Fern does, and I don't think we can either. At least not for a while."

Diana rose and came to sit in his lap. "Clayton, how serious you are. Don't worry about it, you take care of your fields, and I'll make sure everything is nice for you at home."

He wasn't convinced, but he accepted her kiss. Jeff was right... Diana never would be a real farm wife, but she had other talents. While Diana's lips lingered on his, the doorbell chimed and Diana jumped to her feet.

"That must be Jan. I asked her to stop by and bring Evan. I want them to see everything while it's brand new."

Diana ran from the room and Clay slowly followed. As Diana took her first guests on a tour of the house, proudly pointing to her prized possessions, she seemed not to notice that Jan viewed the house with a critical eye and Evan was unusually silent. As Diana dragged Jan away to the kitchen, Clay and Evan went into the recreation room. Clay looked around, still himself a stranger in the house. When he walked to the bar, Evan followed.

"Well, what do you think?" Clay prompted.

"It's grand, Clay. It is really grand." Evan continued to survey the room. "Diana seems to have thought of everything. I see you have the latest in audio and visual equipment, and what's this?" Evan pointed to a lounge recessed into the wall and surrounded by lights and buttons.

"You got me." Clay shook his head. "Some sort of Pleasure-Sensor Unit, I think they are called."

Clay felt a wave of embarrassment which gave way to defensiveness, but as he studied Evan's face, he found no reason for either emotion. Evan's expression was calm and friendly, clearly holding no condemnation.

"Let me fix you a drink," Clay said quickly. "It appears the bar is completely stocked. What will you have?"

"Some wine will be fine, thanks."

The two men held their drinks in awkward silence, until they slowly began to smile and in a minute were laughing.

"Very civilized, isn't it?" Evan ventured.

"Oh hell, Evan, I've wanted to talk to you before. Seems there are things we should say, but I don't know what they are."

"Don't worry about it. I know what you mean. If it will make things easier, there was never anything serious with Diana. We were friends for a while; I wasn't the right husband for her. Things usually work out for the best." Evan grew solemn as he said this last.

"Seems you might be hoping the same for some other things, too," Clay offered.

"Yes." Evan nodded. "Sometimes I think people are right, maybe I am crazy."

"Are you still fighting them over at the Church?"

"I wish you didn't have to put it that way," Evan said with a crooked smile. "But that's about it."

A sudden rush of compassion swept Clay as he put his glass on the bar and looked at Evan. They were about the same age, yet Evan seemed older, something to do with the set of his jaw and the haunted glare of his eyes. He didn't understand Evan's struggle; still he was sympathetic to the signs of a man laboring for something he believed in. It was easy for Clay to read this in Evan, for he fought the same battle. He wished there were a way he could help. Evan seemed alone in his fight.

"Listen, Evan, if things get too tough, I know it isn't much, but I can always use another hand on the farm. Leave and tell them to go to hell."

"You have a way with words." Evan laughed. "Thanks, but I'll stick with it. I have to do what I know is right."

Suddenly interested in Evan's problems, Clay leaned forward.

"I don't want to be nosy, but I don't understand. What is it that bothers you about the Church?" He'd heard bits and pieces and it was beginning to sound dangerous for Evan.

Evan sighed. "I'll put it this way. What would you do if you saw a train rushing toward a bridge that you knew was no longer there? Wouldn't you try to stop it?"

Clay nodded.

"That's what I'm doing. It's hard to make people understand. The Church looks healthy on the outside, with the quote 'good works,' but it's a shell. A highly organized institution that has nothing to do with the standards set forth in the Bible." Evan smiled sadly. "See? The word shocks even you. They don't say Bible anymore. We have a completely revised, updated, standardized manual now.

"Ten years ago, when the last major denomination joined the Unity Council, they had agreed to devise something that would encompass the diverse doctrines and beliefs. Something to satisfy everyone. Do you know that I hold a management position in the most powerful organization in the world? They don't want that advertised, but that's what it is."

"How can you fight something that big?" Clay thought of his own struggle against the giant grain companies and the government. "Sounds like they have it well put together. You might have a great future if you went along with company policy. Why don't you?"

"Because no one is hearing the truth anymore. The truth is that the real Church is not an organization, it's individuals. No matter where a believer is, they are a piece of the Church. When Christ comes for His Church, it isn't going to be that highly polished shell that is sucking everyone in. He'll gather it Himself, the way He calls individuals now. Salvation doesn't come with that gold-edged certificate they present. The crime is that good people are misled, made to believe that mankind, through his own efforts, can bring about the peace and unity we desperately long for. They are shifting the emphasis away from the concept that God is in control to the idea that we determine the future."

"Aren't you being hard-headed, Evan? You have to admit there is far more respect for religion now with the bickering between denominations stopped. What can you hope to accomplish by causing trouble?"

"I don't want trouble, Clay. However, I can't renounce what I believe for the sake of peace with those I know to be in error. There isn't another way for me. I appreciate your interest. If you want to know more there is a small group that meets at my apartment each week. Jan has started coming; you and Diana are welcome to join us. We're studying some important things."

Clay laughed. "Well, I'm not surprised that Jan is getting involved. She likes a good fight and the greater the odds the better. But seriously, if this thing starts to get out of hand, I hope you'll keep her clear of it."

"That will have to be her choice. That is part of what we are trying to teach, that commitment to God is highly personal, something no one can do for you. Faith is a gift of God and only by believing in the Lord Jesus Christ can a person find true salvation."

Evan's gaze was sharp and piercing. A fire seemed to burn behind his clear eyes, making them feverishly bright. Clay cleared his throat and shifted from one foot to the other. He was beginning to see why people labeled Evan a fanatic. He was almost sorry for his earlier offer of assistance. Clay had enough trouble, no need to add some religious lunatic. Much to Clay's relief, Diana and Jan entered the room. His discussion with Evan had become uncomfortable.

Evan and Jan stayed another fifteen minutes and when the front door closed behind them, Clay put his arms around Diana and breathed a huge sigh. Diana raised an eyebrow.

"What's this about; did you find Evan that tiring?"

"A little," Clay answered.

Diana looked at him, her pink satin lips in a rosebud pucker.

"No more than I found my sister, I'll bet. You know she practically called me a heathen. And we were baptized the same Sunday. Oh well, it's another of her crusades; it will pass. Although I did find the human rights issue more interesting. Too bad she can't separate her sex drive from her moral convictions."

~ * ~

The next day, Diana Lee Brockman and Clayton Sanderson were married in the gleaming marble congregational hall of the All Souls Unity Church. Mark was right...Garden City would remember this wedding for a long while. The plush velvet pews were crammed with relatives and the town's leading citizens arrayed in their finest. Large baskets of crimson roses banked the altar. Even bigger arrangements of spectacular white gladiolus softened by lush pink and wine-dark iris sat beneath the glowing stained glass windows lining each side of the hall. Diana seemed to float down the aisle wrapped in the misty, white lace of Fern's wedding gown. The ceremony was over much faster than Clay had expected. Suddenly his new mother-in-law was kissing him, followed by men and women he scarcely knew shaking his hand or kissing his cheek. The crowd began to thin as the guests drifted toward the banquet room for the celebration that would soon begin. A group of admiring women chattered their congratulations as they surrounded Diana. While Clay watched Diana, Fern came to his side, a happy, yet wistful look resting softly on her face.

"It's simply lovely," she sighed. "And Diana looks beautiful."

Clay nodded as he continued to gaze at his new wife.

"Same old slippers, same old rice, same old glimpse of Paradise," he heard Fern whisper.

"What's that, Fern?"

"Nothing, dear." She patted his arm. "It's an old quote I was remembering. Oh look, Diana is coming over."

~ * ~

The honeymoon in Acapulco lasted a short ten days and Diana was surprisingly sweet about it. She had wanted a tour of Europe, but harvest was a month away. It had already started in the southern district. As the ripening grain spread northward, he needed to arrange housing and feeding for the harvesting crews, and securing fuel allotments for the machinery took time. It was a matter of pride; he couldn't let anything stand in the way of his responsibilities. The first day home, Clay felt he had been gone for much longer, but he soon finished the reports from their operations to the west and farther south. One line in the report from the western manager caught his eye and he read it again. "Looks like a good go on the harvest, but some samples show slightly underdeveloped heads."

Clay quickly pushed the call button that connected him with Jim Durban in the southern region. The Texas harvest was almost over and Jim's reports were normal, but he needed further assurance concerning the quality of the grain. Satisfied with Jim's positive answer, Clay took the western report to his father's office and put it before him.

"I just spoke with Jim. He said things are okay in the south. But I'm slightly concerned over the western report."

"I saw this yesterday," Mark said. "I called Chuck to find out how serious it might be. Seems it is only a smattering, nothing to worry us for now."

"I called the testing station before I went to Mexico. Did Amarillo send a report on the samples from our fields?" Clay questioned.

"Not that I know of. They must be busy, though."

"Why?"

"When I talked to Chuck about the report he sent us, he said they sent samples in several weeks ago and aren't getting any answers either."

The rest of the day, Clay puzzled over the two delayed sample reports. It was highly possible the station was simply too busy, but they were usually faster than this. It was strange having two incidents in fields where crops were otherwise near perfect. It was either two different things causing it, or one thing in two places. Thus far, it was only in the west and central areas; nothing to the south. By late afternoon, he was still troubled, and he decided to get in touch with a couple of independent operators he knew, one in Kansas and the other in Colorado.

Several years ago, they had been involved with Mark Sanderson in forming the independent marketing agency. Since its demise, they had drifted apart, but still shared information and saw one another occasionally. First, Clay called Doug Hansen in Russell and after a few pleasantries got to business.

"I'm surprised at your question, Clay. But yes, we've seen a bit of what you have described. I didn't think much of it, though; it wasn't enough to worry me. Everything else is going along okay, but what you're saying does concern me."

Clay's second call to Harvey in Colorado brought similar news, except they had taken samples to their agency in Springfield.

"Have you received a report with the results?" Clay asked.

"Yes, they didn't say what caused the problem, only that it wouldn't hurt this year's crop. Like I didn't already know that," Harvey said with some sarcasm. "Seemed an evasive answer to me."

By evening, Clay's worry had grown into a full-blown threat that needed to be dealt with, and fast. Something was happening in those fields and two separate agencies hadn't responded responsibly. One gave no answer and the other seemed evasive. Before leaving for town, Clay stopped at the main house to talk with his parents. Eva was busy in the kitchen helping Tillie with preparations for the next day's canning operation, and Mark, freshly showered and wearing a clean shirt and pants, was coming down the wide staircase.

"Thought you'd be off to your new home by now, son," Mark greeted him.

"I have to talk to you first."

"You look mighty serious. Come into the den."

Clay built his case slowly using the lean facts to support his suspicions.

"I'm sure there has to be something strange happening there."

Mark frowned for a minute, and rubbed the back of his neck as he usually did when considering something.

"Maybe you're right. Damn, I hate to think I'm getting old and can't spot trouble. What do you want to do about it?"

Clay shrugged. "I don't know. Guess I hoped you'd say I'm making a mountain out of a mole hill."

"Tell you what, tomorrow I'll get in touch with old Ed Hillard over at National Grain; he's still in their Oklahoma City office. If something is wrong, it isn't going to skip their fields. I think Ed would let me know if they noticed anything."

"Hillard, isn't he Fern's brother? Why, he must be over eighty by now."

"Take it easy, there's still a lot of knowledge in these old heads, least those of us that haven't gone mushy yet. Besides, how much do you think they are going to tell us if I don't get to someone that's halfway friendly?"

"You're probably right. If there is nothing there, guess I'll forget it, go ahead with the harvest, and make plans for fall planting. Are we going to get the same fertilizer and soil conditioner allotments we did last year?"

Mark put his hand to the back of his neck again. "Far as I know we are. Those forms went in about four weeks ago and we haven't heard any kicking about it. I guess Jeff and I have something in common. I can't get used to working dead ground either. It's nothing but a growing medium. Without pumping this stuff into it, even Buffalo or Grama grass wouldn't grow."

"I know. It is scary to think of what would happen if we tried planting without those transfusions. Maybe nature would correct it in time."

"Not in our lifetime, Clayton. We've drained the land of everything; it can only produce because of what we put in now."

When Clay left his father, he made a stop at their fueling station and filled the truck's tank. Every time he did this, he thought of his good fortune. The farming industry was in a high priority class where fuel was concerned. The country had been on rationing for years. Some people were sure it was a political maneuver, but the government staunchly maintained it was to conserve its reserves. There was constant work on alternative energy sources—solar and wind had held promise, but eleven years ago, electromagnetic impulses (EMP) fried most everything. It destroyed extra high voltage transformers around the world. None of the power grids could operate without them. With no way to cool the nuclear plants, many of them had failed, causing death and destruction. Rebuilding took time and materials. Other nations were no better off, and horded their natural resources. The Middle East was too unstable to count on, and with America still supporting Israel, she had few friends in the area. How long should it take a small nation to become secure? Clay wondered. It had been well over two hundred years. There had been short intervals with no conflict but without any real peace. Evan had certain theories about that part of the world—otherworldly theories, in Clay's opinion.

He chuckled as he sped toward Garden City. One thing about Evan, he was a persistent cuss, still trying to get Diana and him roped in on some of those meetings. It was a damn shame for Evan to keep wasting his abilities; he should be in politics, or some kind of public speaking. He could make a fortune even in these times. The truck window was open and the hot dry air whipped against his bare arm, turning the skin to parchment. Although he professed no fear of drought because of faith in the irrigation system, he still sighed with relief as the blistering, angry sun slipped below the horizon. If it weren't for the dark semi-cool nights, the ground might finally burst into flames, irrigation system or no. The flat land lay in deepening gray and lavender, giving a false sense of cooling. It was almost dark as the blinking red neon star above Jay's Tavern on the outskirts of town came in sight. For a second Clay considered stopping...his throat was tight and cottony; an icy beer would sure taste good. The image of Diana rose before him and he pushed on the gas pedal, speeding past the tavern. He was hungry, thirsty, and tired. No use making trouble by being any later than he had to.

Five

In the Brockman living room, Thomas and Glenda were having after-dinner brandy, when Jan breezed through and quickly dropped a kiss on her mother's cheek. She waved at her father and started for the foyer. Thomas looked up from his paper.

"Where are you rushing off to?"

"Don't you remember? Evan has a meeting tonight."

"Wait a minute, young lady. We need to talk about this."

Jan frowned and cast her mother a beseeching look, but Glenda kept her head lowered, staring into the amber liquid in her glass. This was the signal that Thomas would handle the situation. Her mother was bringing out the bigger gun. Jan was familiar with Glenda's irritating habit of switching from independent woman to deferential wife, depending upon which suited her needs. During several arguments, Glenda had made it plain that Evan's cause was not the type of active involvement she endorsed.

"Sorry, Dad. I'm late. We can talk another time." Jan started toward the tiled foyer.

"Afraid not, honey," Thomas called. The recessed lighting above his head turned the gray in his dark hair to shining silver threads. "Come and sit a minute," he ordered.

Jan bit her lower lip and looked at her watch. She did have some time before the meeting. Whatever her father said wouldn't stop her. Might as well get it settled now; he would insist on it later. His file-cabinet mind never lost an item, simply stored it on a follow-up calendar and the matter kept reappearing until it was resolved. Jan sat on one end of the curved couch and waited.

"You know," Thomas began, "we have never put restrictions on your social life and we wouldn't be interfering now except we feel this thing with Evan could be dangerous."

Jan set her face in neutral, showing no emotion. She had learned the trick from her father. A blank expression left people guessing your thoughts and feelings.

"We are only thinking of your welfare," Glenda interjected.

Thomas gave his wife a "let me handle this" look. "We don't mean you can't see the fellow once in a while," he continued. "You can invite him here; there is always the privacy of your lounge and bedroom. Perhaps when this attraction wears thin, you'll understand that it's better not to see him in public, and you'll know what we are talking about."

"And exactly what are you talking about?" Jan's tone was level and cool.

"Jan, we've been over this." Glenda hurled the high-pitched words at her.

"Please, Glenda. Let's keep calm about this," Thomas cut in. "I'm sure you didn't explain it to her properly."

Thomas carefully folded the paper and placed it on the chrome and glass table beside his chair. Jan watched with amused detachment as he built the mood to present his argument. He stood, walked to the huge stone fireplace, and turned to face her. Jan almost smiled at his striking a pose. It was always better to stand when trying to impose your will upon another person, and taking a relaxed posture to give things a friendly air.

"You're a highly intelligent girl; I'm not going to play games with you."

Marvelous, she thought, he's using a trusted technique. Compliment your opponent; let him know he is smart enough to see your point.

"I would appreciate the same consideration from you," he continued. "I've been hearing disturbing things about Evan, and today they were confirmed. I lunched with Reverend Warwick. He is the state coordinator for religious activities. He usually handles everything from his Tulsa office, but some pressing business brought him to Garden City today."

Jan shrugged. "Well?"

"He said it was to make a revision to the child care in the area, but that would hardly involve seeing me. They have their own competent staff of attorneys. I'm no pillar of the Church; he wouldn't feel obligated to pay a social call. Halfway through lunch, the purpose of his visit was clear. According to Reverend Warwick, Evan is on his way out of the Church. They have been extremely patient in trying to salvage this particular dissenter because of his abilities and personal magnetism. He could be a great asset."

"Personal magnetism." Jan laughed. "He irritates practically everyone he speaks to, except the few that understand his teaching."

"Please, Jan. I'm trying to explain. Evan has repeatedly violated Church laws, especially the one governing unapproved meetings. Tomorrow he'll be called before a special council and if the differences can't be resolved, he is to be sanctioned and removed."

"He knows that," Jan said wearily. "He wanted to work within the organization as long as possible, thinking more could be accomplished that way. If they eject him, it won't make any difference. He will simply continue teaching wherever he can. I have no problem with that. I don't care if he holds a high position in a church or not." Jan stood and tucked her purse under her arm.

"I think you better hear the rest of what your father has to say." Glenda gave Jan a riveting look.

Thomas clasped his hands behind him and stood with his feet apart, assuming a more commanding posture.

"There are some fine points of law involved with this, my headstrong young daughter. One of them being that they could send Evan to prison. I thought you better understood how things worked. The Church pays a tremendous amount in taxes, state and federal; they also have one of the most powerful positions in Washington. Besides that, they are a strong arm of the worldwide Unity Council. Built upon this foundation, they have secured laws that are nationally enforced. The Church has the government behind it. This prevents dangerous cults from starting. Those foolish enough to encroach upon Church territory will be punished."

Jan's cheeks grew hot and her skin tingled. It was almost impossible any longer to control her expression. "What about freedom of religion and freedom of speech?" she nearly shouted. "There are certain individual rights at stake."

"Neither of those is infringed upon." Thomas held his voice low and calm—another tool Jan recognized—but she was too angry to play the game in kind. The carefully calculated moves her father and such men used to get what they wanted were revolting. None of them held beliefs of their own. Quicksilver men who changed with the times, automatically slipping into the most advantageous position. She wanted to scream, to shatter his smooth, slick exterior that hid the decayed values and putrid morals. Thomas flashed his most persuasive smile.

"Evan is free to teach or speak on any subject he chooses, as long as he goes through the proper channels. There's nothing repressive in that. Ordered societies must have laws. They held a vote—every denomination agreed to join the Council—it protects each of their particular doctrines. It's a wonderful thing; it stops dissension. Any fool can see it's the only way to handle an emotional religious issue. The important thing for you to understand is that these laws will be enforced, make no mistake on that, and along with Evan, those supporting him can be punished. Now, are we clear on this subject?"

Slowly Jan nodded. They were extremely clear. She relaxed her face, drawing a shade over her expression; from now on, no one must read her thoughts. She hadn't believed Evan when he told her what might come. She thought he was overstating the Church's opposition to his ministry. Maybe the rest of what he had said was also true.

"It's really quite a compliment." Glenda smiled. "Don't you see? Reverend Warwick made a special effort to speak to your father; if you were some day laborer's daughter, he wouldn't have considered your welfare."

Jan managed a smile. "You're probably right, Mother."

Thomas went to his chair and took the paper, giving it a firm shake. "I knew you'd understand once it was explained." He gave Jan a playful wink. "Evan is attractive, we understand that, but the town is full of handsome young men. Don't pick a controversial one next time."

Jan's stomach burned and a bitterness stung the back of her throat. The whole room seemed distorted, everything larger and brighter than it should be, and somehow disgusting. Even Thomas and Glenda looked different. They seemed hard and metallic like excellently groomed robots, the sound of their voices clanging cymbals.

"Well?" Glenda said.

Her mother's words broke through Jan's thoughts. "Were you speaking to me?" she asked.

"Of course I was. I said, slip into something soft and comfortable, and spend an hour on the Pleasure Lounge. That always refreshes me."

"No, I think I'll drive around for a while. Maybe stop and see how the newlyweds are getting along."

Once outside, Jan's heart pounded as she fumbled, trying to start the car. The drive across town to Evan's apartment seemed to take an eternity. Her mind churned in confusion. It was time to make a decision, to decide exactly where she stood in the scheme of things and where she wanted to go. Usually, her goals were clear and she was able to cut to the heart of a matter. On the surface, Evan's cause had merit, but was it worth total commitment? There was never any question of her committing to something, for a person had to have ideals and fight for them or life was nothing but an empty sham. Still, a crusade simply for the sake of involvement was worse than doing nothing. The action would be as worthless and senseless as the lives of her pleasure-oriented family and friends. She remembered Grandmother Baker saying that a person had to be good for something to justify their existence. She picked issues that seemed noble and worthy and she tried to contribute to improving conditions. Still, a missing something loomed beyond her vision, elusive and tantalizing.

Even though there were volumes of laws ensuring equality, abuse remained. The laws made things worse because there was no platform or basis for a fight. Legislators wouldn't listen, the argument being that the laws were in place, channels were open; people only need take advantage of them. However, it was a joke. Evan was right. Morality could not be legislated. No amount of organization or governmental pressure could erase prejudice. People simply went around the laws or turned them to their advantage. That was why Evan's message was interesting. It taught that an inner transformation was possible; individuals could rise above their circumstances.

It would be wonderful if this movement caught on. It would make the laws as superfluous as they were ineffective. Yet, Evan was starting from a weak position; chances of his succeeding seemed slim. Startled by this last thought, Jan grimaced. She was acting the same as her father, weighing the chances of success before committing. The possibility of failure was holding up her decision. How ignoble to only want association with winning causes. If she truly believed Evan's message would reach one heart, there should be no question over her being involved. Excitement replaced the doubts. She had abilities Evan needed. She could make a definite contribution to this movement.

In the parking lot of the red brick building where Evan lived, Jan recognized a car belonging to one of the regulars who attended the meetings. She hurried up the concrete steps; the meeting was probably in progress. Still, whatever lesson Evan was presenting could not be as important as the news she was bringing.

They would need to give this evening over to making plans on how to proceed in the face of Reverend Warwick's threat. They might take the Council by surprise, have a group of marchers outside the hall while Warwick, or whoever, questioned Evan. It was short notice, but they could spend the rest of the night making calls, speaking with some of the less devoted followers.

Evan was standing in his shabby front room, an open Bible in his hands. Seated in a semi-circle before him were ten people. Jan found a kitchen chair and sat on it. She waited until Evan came to the end of a sentence before standing to gain attention.

"I'm sorry to interrupt," she began, "but I have some important news."

Evan and the others turned toward her and she proceeded to tell them what her father had said. "...therefore, we must do something," she concluded.

Jan searched their faces for some response. One very old man, Mr. Taylor, who lived in Evan's building, sat calmly watching her. They couldn't expect much help from him as he probably came to the meetings more for the companionship than anything else. The others, they were younger; there should be some support from them. A few looked frightened, but no one spoke. Jan turned to Evan.

"You were expecting something to happen. Surely you have a plan."

There was a tightness around Evan's mouth, but he smiled. "You're right. I didn't think they would let me go on forever. We'll continue with our meeting. Jan, do you have your Bible with you? As you know, we have been studying the book of Matthew and we are in the twenty-fourth chapter."

Evan laughed and some of the others smiled. Jan opened her purse and took out the small New Testament Evan had given her. Puzzled by Evan's reaction and thinking he would unfold some strategy as he spoke, she quickly turned to the chapter.

"Strangely enough, we are up to the ninth verse," Evan went on. "As we read, the disciples had questioned Jesus concerning the future and the signs that would accompany those times. In verse nine, Jesus is saying, 'but then shall they deliver you up to be afflicted.' Those predictions sound awful; none of us wants to suffer this. Yet, we have His promise that He will never leave us and will see us through our trials."

Evan looked up from his notes. The feeble light from the one lamp was a weak reflection of Evan's own radiance. It made Jan think of fire burning inside a crystal globe. For an instant she wondered what would happen if the heat cracked that pure exterior. Although Evan's voice was soft, it carried an undercurrent of excitement.

"Those of us tonight, studying and sharing the Word, can spread it further by telling your friends and relatives what we are learning. Throughout His teachings, Jesus gives us great comfort by letting us know we are not alone, He will provide, and we can be confident in that. Our text is timely, but it goes beyond what Jan has mentioned. We can apply this to our lives every day. Many people look for signs of the end times, but each of us will have his own end. Therefore, it behooves us to live each day as if it were our last."

Jan listened in amazement; Evan was going on with his prepared lesson. As he ended, he asked them to kneel and form a circle holding hands. After Evan prayed, the meeting ended.

Ryan Lanier, a stocky, brown-haired boy who attended every gathering, threw his arm around Evan's shoulder.

"What can we do? Will they really stop our meetings?"

Evan patted the boy's back. "Now, Ryan, it will be okay. We'll keep going the best we can. We may have to find a new location, but we'll try to keep it close enough for those with no cars to still attend."

Some of the others had gathered around and were offering weak suggestions of possible plans. Jan's heart sank. What a pitiful ragtag group. There were three middle-aged wives of refinery workers, Ryan, a young Indian girl, two men that worked for the city street department, a young couple that Jan didn't recognize, and old Mr. Taylor. Maybe that was why Evan hadn't made more of her news. What could they possibly do to help? Not one of them was in a position to put pressure on the Council. Even as a group, they would be powerless. Why, oh why hadn't Evan attracted some of the more influential people in town? At least that would have given him some chance of success.

Evan stood at the door and shook hands with each one, saying he would keep them informed as to where they could attend future meetings. When the last had left, he turned to Jan, the fire behind his shining eyes now a soft glow.

"I know you're upset, but believe me, there isn't anything to do but take each day as it comes and do the best we can."

Too angry to speak, Jan threw her purse on the table and stared at him. After a minute, the words came.

"Evan Hunter, I don't understand you. Do you mean to say you're going to let them walk over you?"

"No, I'll stand firm in what I've said and done."

"And you think that will stop them?" Jan sneered.

"Maybe not, but they won't stop me either."

"What about the small matter of arrest if you don't stop. Doesn't that bother you? Is that what you're really after? Maybe you have some kind of martyr complex."

Evan looked at the worn carpet and a shadow fell across his face. For a second, Jan thought he was angry, but when he lifted his head there was only a pained expression.

"I'm no hero, Jan. I'm scared. I don't want to face Warwick, Dewberry or any of them tomorrow. I sure don't want to find myself in one of their confinement cells. If I do, I won't be the first. Paul was in prison, but it didn't stop him. He told the guards about Jesus and the plan of salvation."

"Oh, Evan, will you stop sounding like some pre-recorded religious message. This is the real world; you're going about it wrong. If you believe in what you're teaching, try to present it in the right way. I've watched people get what they want often enough to know you need a power base. Work behind the scenes until you have enough followers or enough support in high places before you start to fight. I believe in what you teach; I know you have to reach inside of people to bring about real change. And the rest of the world will learn too, if you bring it in the right way and don't get stopped before you start."

"Jan, this isn't the type of struggle you're used to. You still see things from the natural side, not the spiritual. This battle is in an unseen realm; we fight to tell people about the choice they must make. The urgency is that the war is almost over and the outcome is certain. The story of mankind will unfold exactly as God has determined."

Jan lifted her hands and looked toward the ceiling. "Well, let's sit and wait for Judgment Day. Why do anything?"

"Because," Evan began in a measured tone, "when God sets a fire in your heart, you can't keep still. It's another of His mysterious workings. I've known it could be dangerous, but since I've made my decision, I have to play it to the end. If it comes to physical pain, God will have to support me or let me die, for I have no natural courage in that area."

Evan stopped, seeming reluctant to say more.

"Come on, Evan. The world has progressed further than that. I'll go with you tomorrow. I can wait outside."

"No, there's no reason for you to get into trouble over something you don't understand. Perhaps it is better this way. If your awakening comes later, when they think we've been stopped, you'll be a new shoot growing in a new area."

~ * ~

The next day, Jan stayed home, not because Evan said to, but because she saw an advantage in not calling attention to herself. If things went against Evan, she would be of more help on the outside. It was always the same...the ones with true dedication, the ones who stood in the vanguard, usually had no organizational ability.

As the morning progressed, Jan wandered aimlessly through the Brockman house nervously twisting her short, sturdy fingers as she plotted. Still, her planning ended in frustration. She was unable to make decisions until she heard what action the Council intended. It would be better to keep busy with other things. Maybe Diana was home. She needed to see her anyway and ask her to cover for last night. She doubted her mother would check with Diana, but it wouldn't hurt to have an alibi.

When she arrived, Diana opened the door and threw her arms around Jan.

"I'm glad to see you. Have you had lunch yet?" Diana pulled Jan into the entry hall and through the living room toward the kitchen, calling as she went, "Nora, Jan is here. Set another place for lunch."

Always a bit suspicious of Diana's motives, Jan wrinkled her forehead and wondered why the exuberant greeting. Since Diana did look honestly glad to see her, Jan decided she might be wrong. Perhaps Diana was lonesome. The sisters walked arm in arm into the stone-floored garden room off the kitchen. A small fountain splashed cheerfully in the center and sprinkled the red geraniums blooming in the planters at the base of the fountain. Around the glass walls were taller plants, some actually small trees, that grew to the latticed ceiling. With the sunlight filtering through the leaves, the area glowed with a soft green light, creating a small-cultivated jungle.

"We'll eat here. It's restful, don't you think?" Diana asked.

Jan sighed and sank onto a wicker chair. "Fine, I could use some rest."

Diana took a watering can and began pouring at the base of a tall fig tree. As Jan watched, she noticed Diana's movements were quick and rather nervous. She looked impatient or aggravated about something. After watering two plants, Diana set the can on the floor and stepped to the kitchen door.

"For goodness' sake, Nora, is it going to take you forever? I thought lunch was ready." She turned to Jan. "I can't understand it; Fern never has any trouble with her. You know what Nora told me this morning? That she would only stay until the end of the week. Can you imagine that? Fern promised her to me as long as I needed her. I don't understand these people."

Shortly Nora brought two luncheon plates containing chicken salad, wheat wafers, and orange sections decorated with mint leaves. Jan began eating in silence as Diana picked at her food and rambled on about the difficulty of finding someone to replace Nora.

"Clay is no help whatsoever. He actually thinks I can handle this house myself."

Diana looked demandingly at Jan, indicating she expected a sympathetic comment. Jan blotted the corners of her mouth with a linen napkin.

"You should have known that would be his attitude. Even with household help, Eva takes an active part in the work. Clay naturally expects his wife to do the same."

Impatiently, Diana put her fork aside and shook her head. "It isn't only that, Jan. Oh, I'm glad you came over. I need someone to talk with. Clay comes home tired and he doesn't want to do anything. I have tickets to the Harvest Dance at Prairie Hills and he won't go. We haven't been anywhere. You'd think he was actually in the fields doing the work himself. He's worrying about some bug or fungus or some damnable thing chewing at the wheat. He simply doesn't pay any attention to me."

Diana threw her napkin on the table, stood, and began pacing. It didn't bother Jan; she was accustomed to her sister's hysterics.

"Trouble in paradise already? Well, don't worry; it will work itself out."

"It's boring and dull," Diana said angrily, her chin quivering slightly.

"Look, Diana, you can't expect a rosy pathway the rest of your life. There must be something you can take an interest in, other than Clay's inattention."

"Maybe." Diana raised a finely arched eyebrow. "I talked to Tracy the other day and Frank is playing his usual tricks. He wants her to help him with some deal. She didn't say what it was, only that when she questioned him too closely, he got angry. He actually hit her. A sordid low-class mess. Makes me wonder what kind of family I've married into."

"Why don't you get pregnant? That would give you something to do and probably make Clay a lot more attentive."

She was being sarcastic. In her opinion, Diana would make a terrible mother. Instantly, she was sorry she had mentioned it. Jan had known her sister to go through worse things to get something she wanted. Diana tried to grab every richness life offered. She reminded Jan of a greedy child sitting before a huge chocolate cake, never stopping to consider it could make her sick. The soft skin of Diana's temples pulsed lightly and her finely molded chin trembled as she frowned in thought.

"I don't know," she said slowly. "Clay does want children, but I had thought of delaying as long as possible."

"I was teasing," Jan said quickly. "You really should wait and make sure this marriage is going to work."

Diana's eyes blazed; her temperament changed in a flash. Jan was also used to the sudden changes.

"Of course it will work," Diana declared. "Why would you say that? Clay can give me everything I want."

"But do you want Clay along with it?"

Diana's eyes narrowed; her face tightened, the softness gone, leaving sharp angles, and blue throbbing veins. She was close to one of her unreasonable explosions. Jan ducked her head and tried a reconciliatory smile.

"I'm sorry. I shouldn't have said that. Forget it, okay?"

Diana gave a curt nod and the fire in her eyes faded. Better than anyone, Jan knew Diana's mercurial moods could quickly rise and fall.

"Besides," Jan continued in order to distract her. "I didn't come to upset you. I want a favor."

Diana's face brightened with interest as Jan told her about Evan's meeting.

"If anyone should ask, I was with you last night, okay?"

"That should be easy enough. Clay was in bed and snoring. He'd never know who was here. It was one of the few nights he's been home before eleven. He stays on the farm later than he should. But tell me, Jan, I'm dying to know, have you been to bed with Evan yet?"

"If it's any of your business, no. We're working on things that are more important. Evan's ideals are not located in his pants."

Diana threw her head back, a harsh chuckle deep in her slender throat. "I thought not. If I couldn't do it, I was sure you couldn't. Don't worry over it; he's not worth the effort. I know you, Jan, you'll be intrigued for a while with these noble aspirations, but then when there's no action forthcoming, your interest will dwindle away."

"We'll see," Jan answered grimly.

By late afternoon, when Jan left her sister, a sick feeling had settled in her stomach, souring the chicken salad. The beautiful wedding, the gorgeous house, and the marriage were beginning to decay. Diana's values were empty and base. Jan loved her sister, and when she wasn't angry with her, felt sorry for her. It was a sure path to an unhappy life. She should caution Diana against becoming a younger version of their Aunt Wanda: divorced, and remarried enough times that the family lost count. Always searching and never finding the certain something that would make her happy.

Jan drove straight to Evan's apartment, and seeing his car, parked and ran up the steps to knock on his door. Evan opened it; he looked exhausted. The lines around his eyes were deeper and his shoulders slumped. Jan rushed in and put her arms around him. He was still for a minute resting against her, and then they sat on the faded couch.

"Was it terrible?" she asked.

"Pretty rough."

"Well, go on," she urged.

Evan sighed, stood, and walked to the window. He pushed the sagging woven curtain aside and stared at the street.

"They can do more than I thought. I am to stop any unauthorized meetings and teach strictly from the Church manual. If I don't, they will issue a directive barring me from every denomination. I could never work in any capacity for any church in the world. My pay would stop immediately; I would lose my gasoline card. I couldn't purchase any until I had another job that issued me a new card. They would call in the loan that put me through seminary immediately with full interest due, even for the unused years of the loan. They made it clear they will watch me. One more infraction will bring legal action. They demanded I sign the agreement to stop the unsanctioned activity."

As she listened, nothing he said dimmed her hopes. Evan looked worried by their threats, but her quick mind saw something else in their words. It was only a warning. They were not ready to take a hard line with Evan. Perhaps they didn't have enough proof, they still valued him as something useful to the Church, or were fearful of making him a martyr. If they were not afraid, they would have arrested him today. Jan stood and hurried to him.

"Don't worry, Evan. I've been thinking. Pretend to go along with them and we'll find a way. We'll go slowly and build a following they can't ignore. We'll surface with enough power to make them listen to your doctrine."

"It isn't my doctrine, Jan. It's the Word of God they don't want spread around."

"I understand, but…"

"No, you don't." Evan's jaw was tight and the words harsh. He took her by the shoulders and looked directly into her eyes.

"I haven't told you everything. When they asked for my affirmation of the Church's position and presented me with the agreement to sign, I refused. They are sending the transcript to the high council in Rome. Within a few days I'll be penniless, immobile, and in debt. If that doesn't stop me, and I hold another meeting, they will arrest me."

"Evan, how foolish. There are other ways. What would it have hurt to sign the stupid paper?"

"I have a few days before they have authorization from Rome. I'll use the time to see what I can find, maybe somewhere outside of town. I'll have to do it alone; I can't put you at risk."

Jan stayed with him until midnight. She studied him closely as they talked and she cooked them something to eat. He was a puzzle… the qualities of a leader and yet never ordering any direct action. He seemed to feel his way along, a blind man trying to maneuver a dangerous obstacle course. There was power in him, Jan could sense it, and see its effect on others. He was like the wind, an unseen force, stirring and swaying whomever he touched.

Even Diana was compelled to react. First by finding him interesting and now irritating. Clay seemed drawn to him, but Diana would probably influence him. Jan thought of her mother's strong response. Glenda's attitude was definitely one of aversion, possibly fear. Her father's words told her that even he recognized something potentially dangerous. Jan sighed. For someone wanting to go quietly about the business of teaching love and peace, Evan certainly caused a storm.

As she prepared to leave, she hesitated.

"Let me stay with you," she urged. "I could help in many ways. At least tell me what you're going to do."

"I will." A smile softened his face. "Next time I see you."

Jan hugged him and kissed his cheek. "Have it your way. I suppose I can wait a day or two."

Six

For the entire month of August, Garden City, the central and southern plains, baked under a blazing ball of fire. Every morning the angry sun burst forth in a cloudless sky and set about scorching an already parched earth. By noon of most days, the temperature reached a searing one hundred and ten, leaving the long afternoon to climb even higher. People moved as little as possible, doing necessary chores early and taking to the relative coolness of a darkened house to escape the worst of it. For the last two weeks of the month, showing there was no limit to the awesome fiery power in the sky, temperatures rose to one hundred and eighteen. They would teasingly slide into the nineties during the night, giving the faint hope of a cooler tomorrow.

Midwestern people were accustomed to this periodic searing. They had witnessed these cycles as many summers as there had been inhabitants of the vast, flat land. In the decade before, when faced with physical discomfort, the touch of a button brought to life millions of relief-giving air conditioners. However, the failure of seven massive nuclear plants put a final nail in the coffin of an adequate energy supply. Radiation containment took every resource, leaving nothing to spend on restoring creature comforts. It threw the nation back into the 1800s, only worse, because of severely limited oil, coal, and hydro, and the demand being much greater.

The heat alone was almost bearable, but when the wind rose and pushed it against trees, animals, and people, they wilted and died, none of them able to retain much moisture in the path of nature's blast furnace. Only the scorched, brittle vegetation kept the powdery dirt anchored to the earth. Over the years, every patch of bare ground received some type of cover. Lawns in the towns and cities, tough buffalo grass along highway rights-of-way with honey locust and green ash backing it for windbreaks while fields were kept in crops or resting under a cover of vetch. Still, the wily, ingenious wind found bits of loose grit to swirl through the air. The dust became tiny blotters; it absorbed any stray drop of moisture. Some days the only dampness anyone saw was the sweat of his body.

The Sandersons' harvest around Garden City was over, completed a month earlier. The crews had moved north to reap the next ripening grain, leaving a tired sheared land to once again accept and nurture seed. For some years, Clay and his father had followed the practice of stubble mulching, leaving the plant residue of the previous year as a protective mulch on the soil when preparing for the next crop. This worked fairly well in hiding the soil from the searching, drying wind. The perennial corn crops were excellent ground protectors with their short, matted root system clinging to their patch of ground. It was a long-standing feud as to who would retain ownership of the land, the farmer, or the wind. For well over two hundred years, the farmer had been winning. His ground was staying put because of his constant vigilance. The farmers left no land bare and unprotected. If a cash crop didn't cover the ground, the dust-eating sudan grass, kefir, or millet did, but with the high demand for grain production, few fields had a chance to rest.

It was becoming harder for the country to feed its population and still produce enough for valuable export trade. It was no longer feasible to let cattle roam across acres of grassland. It was more expedient to bypass this stage of turning grain to protein and use the product of the fields as food for people. There were still huge cattle operations, but the hooves of the beef never touched ground. The same as poultry and pork production, beef was a factory operation with a calf proceeding from pen to pen and coming at last to the slaughterhouse and packing plant, with the entire process taking a minimum amount of land. The resulting product was an expensive item. In most households, it made sense to eat the more available and less expensive grain.

Despite the worldwide measures to curb population, the number of people needing to eat continued to grow, while farmers the globe over hurried to stay ahead of the storm. America had been more successful in its efforts, and therefore had the added advantage of enough basic crops of wheat and corn to use in the world markets. However, nature was still an uncontrollable force. Even with the irrigation systems and advanced technology, it was a constant fight. Clay could not make Diana understand that a farmer's wife lived on the slim balance of wind, water, and soil. She argued that Clay could always sell to the corporations if he got tired of fighting. The suggestion repulsed him, and a sale price that seemed good might later find them starving as inflation continued.

"You could lease the land to someone," she had replied. "Daddy did and it works for him."

"It wouldn't make any difference," Clay answered patiently. "Corporations have the same problems I do in working the land. I would rather be there doing it myself. That way, if we have a bad year, at least I'll know why. I won't have to look to some company to tell me what went wrong with my income."

Despite everything—the drought, heat, and the strange findings in the fields—the Sanderson land turned in a bountiful harvest. Clay and his father were happy and optimistic as they went about arranging for the fall planting. Clay guessed it didn't much matter if Diana understood or not, as long as the land produced. Still, he hesitated to mention an even touchier subject. A few weeks earlier, Evan Hunter had come to Clay's office in the compound. And as Evan had explained his circumstances, Clay shook his head.

"I don't know, Evan. Seems you've got yourself in a fix this time. Don't worry, I made the offer, and I'll stand by it. You can work for me. The living quarters aren't grand, but the men seem to enjoy the lodge we provide. Each man gets a bedroom and they share the common areas."

"I'd be most grateful, Clay. I'll give you an honest measure of work in return. But there's something you need to know. I'm going to keep on with the meetings. I won't hold any of them on your property; I'll use the homes of different members, several have already offered. If we move often enough, I think we'll get by."

Clay frowned. "Damn it, Evan. Why do you have to keep on with this thing? You can bring trouble to other people. What about those who come to your get-togethers, what about them?"

Evan raised his hands and stepped back. "It's okay. Believe me, I understand how you feel. I won't hold you to your offer now that you know what I intend to do. As for the others, they feel it's worth the risk. But before I go, I need to talk to Jeff. Is he around?"

Clay studied the man before him. It was crazy but he couldn't seem to turn away. He knew he should kick Evan off the place and have nothing more to do with him. Still, Clay felt compelled to stand by him. Perhaps it was still the thing of seeing a man facing overwhelming odds alone. Clay struggled to let his reason keep the upper hand. Yet, Evan's calm manner and constant determination influenced him. Evan was like one of the towering rock monuments of the land to the west, standing silent and alone while the elements whipped around it.

Clay shrugged. "Oh, what the hell, if a man can't stick by his friends, I guess he's not much good."

In that instant, Clay realized he did indeed think of Evan as a friend. A strange one, to be sure. Still, he had the definite feeling that should he need him, Evan would be as relentless in helping a friend as he was in standing firm in his beliefs.

"Take the job. We won't discuss what you do in your free time. I insist; I want you to. Now, you said you wanted to see Jeff. What in the world for?"

Evan seemed to breathe a sigh of relief as he said, "Thank you, Clay."

A strange kind of joy fluttered in Clay's breast, a feeling of reward far greater than what he deserved for what he considered a small act of kindness.

"Jeff is probably at the equipment shed," Clay said as he went to the door to point the way. "Do you want to see him alone, or shall I go with you?"

He wondered what Evan and Jeff could possibly have to discuss. Could Jeff be one of Evan's group? Evidently, Evan read the bewilderment on Clay's face, because he laughed.

"Why don't you go with me? We have no secrets, no dark subversive plans; we aren't plotting anything."

As they neared the building, Jeff came through the door into the bright, blinding sunlight. He stopped as the two men drew closer and squinted at them. Clay thought Jeff probably didn't know Evan, but when a wide smile brightened Jeff's face, Clay changed his mind. If not friends, they certainly weren't strangers.

Jeff wiped his hand on the side of his jeans and then extended it to shake Evan's hand. It was a warm greeting, and Clay wondered how well they knew each other.

"You're going to be working with us," Jeff said after Clay gave him the news. "That's good, glad to have you. We'll take the kinks out of him won't we, Clay?"

Jeff's manner was a surprise; it wasn't his way.

"I'll try to keep up with you," Evan was saying. "You may have to be patient until I catch on."

Jeff clapped a hand on Evan's shoulder. "Lord a' mercy, you're a strong fellow. You won't have any trouble. 'Bout time we got some good honest help. Half these other fellows come and go, same as tumbleweeds."

Evan cleared his throat and his expression turned serious. "What I've come to see you about, Jeff, is your dad. You know he's been attending the meetings, but I'm not sure you know they are trying to stop us."

"Well, I sure hope they don't," Jeff cut in. "Those sessions mean a lot to him. He can't get around much anymore and the meetings are a blessing for him. He's an old-time preacher man himself. He never could adjust to the Church's new ways."

Evan nodded. "I know, Jeff. Your father is a courageous, Bible-believing Christian. Not many of them around these days, but we have a problem. Much as I want him to continue being with us, we're going to have to be on the move."

Evan continued to explain the situation, while Jeff wrinkled his leathery forehead and chewed a corner of his mouth. Jeff nodded slowly and seemed to study the distant fields.

"There's a boy named Ryan who has offered to drive Simon to wherever we might be meeting. I thought I should talk to you and let you know what's involved."

"I appreciate it, Evan," Jeff answered. "To cut him off from associating with other believers might kill him. He can't quit standing for what he knows, any more than you can. He was a powerful preacher in his time. We'll have to manage something. Maybe I can drive him. If anyone asks, I'd say I was taking him to the store, nothing suspicious about a son driving his old dad around."

After Evan left the farm, heading for town to finish his business there, Clay walked slowly to the office and wondered what he had gotten into. Still, it wasn't anyone's business who he hired. Evan wasn't exactly a fugitive yet, but from the look in his eyes, he would be shortly if the Church kept pushing. Maybe they'd drop the whole thing once Evan left town. Besides, what harm could a puny group of ten or twelve do? Clay put Evan and his problem aside. There were other things worrying him. He still had a nagging suspicion that something was wrong in the fields, something deep in the soil, lying there waiting to attack the next crop. Finding out what had caused the infection was turning into a major operation.

He had talked to several people at the experimental station and they were polite enough, but wouldn't even acknowledge knowing of other farms reporting anything amiss. This made him even more apprehensive, because he trusted Doug Hansen and his friend in

Colorado more than the government agency. The farmers had no reason to lie. Maybe the experts didn't want to admit they couldn't find an answer, or perhaps it was exactly as they said, there was no problem. Still, the mystery preoccupied him. It was also making things worse between him and Diana. He'd have to remember to stop talking about it at home.

By the end of September, the Southern Region, under the management of Jim Durbin, had seed in the ground and things seemed to be going well. Planting had started on more Sanderson land to the northwest, while Clay and Jeff were seeing the last of the seed into the ground in their area. Each day Clay scanned the weather reports looking for relief from the heat. Sometimes, summer's searing temperatures lasted into September, making it a scorcher. Clay looked to October for even a slight relief, a small shift in the wind, and a drop in the temperature. Yet October passed and the heat continued. Clay punched order after order into the central irrigation control office. From the looks of things, it might be a dry winter and he had to keep the soil moist or the sprouting wheat could wither.

Jeff, still mistrustful of the system, added his complaints.

"I see where National Grain is getting ready for another rate increase. They must think they got gold running through those pipes instead of water."

Clay's worries about having Evan on the place faded. Evan was a good worker and Jeff seemed to enjoy having him there. If there was more trouble with the Church, Clay was not aware of it.

At the end of November, that changed. Two Unity officials paid the farm a visit. The minute Clay spotted them on the farmhouse veranda talking with Mark, he knew something was wrong. He almost ran across the yard separating the working compound from the residence. Mark had been in total agreement with having Evan work for them, but if there was trouble, Clay didn't want his father upset by it.

"Here's Clay now," Mark said as Clay stepped onto the wide wrap-around porch.

"These gentlemen are checking on Evan. I told them he's doing fine, far as we're concerned."

The men were dressed nearly identically, both in black suits with blinding white shirts and black ties. The smaller of the two, Mr. Carter, had a thin mustache that looked drawn on with a black marking pencil. He kept fingering it in a nervous manner. The other, Reverend Dewberry, was the minister who had performed Clay's wedding ceremony. Without the colorful robes he had worn at the wedding, he looked less imposing, but still carried himself with a great deal of authority.

"Well, good morning, Clay," the reverend intoned. "I see you have survived the first six months of marriage."

Mr. Carter chuckled softly, encouraging Clay and Mark to do the same in appreciation of the reverend's generous attempt at humor. Clay and his father only smiled slightly. Reverend Dewberry cleared his throat.

"I know you are both busy men; we'll get right to the purpose of our visit."

"Please do," Clay said. He hoped his firm tone indicated that any business on Sanderson land didn't concern them.

"It has come to our attention you have Evan Hunter working for you," Mr. Carter put in.

Clay didn't care for the hard sparkle in Carter's eyes, or the prissy sound of his voice.

"That's what I was telling your father, Clay," Reverend Dewberry added as if trying to subdue the small snappish man. He gave Clay a concerned look.

"I don't believe you are aware of Mr. Hunter's position. The man brings trouble wherever he goes. A few months ago, the Church found it necessary to sever connections with him. In fact, he still owes the Church a large sum we advanced for his education."

"You want us to start holding it from his pay, is that it?" Mark asked sternly.

"Oh, my dear man." The reverend smiled. "The Church doesn't intend to burden its members with these details. No, what we want to do is advise you it would be wiser not to have this person on your property. We also understand Mr. Hunter may still be conducting unauthorized meetings. Now if you knew anything about this and didn't report it, I'm afraid your family's standing with us would suffer."

Mark hesitated a second. His look at Clay seemed to give him permission to handle the matter. Clay shifted from one foot to the other while his jaw and back stiffened.

"It's this way, Reverend Dewberry," Clay began. "We don't give the Church any trouble and being long-time members, we make the required donations. But you making suggestions about who we hire, well, I'm afraid that's too much."

Clay tried to sound firm, but not too harsh. It was true he and his family were Church members, but had long since stopped regular attendance. In the past, the Sanderson family had belonged to a small Baptist congregation in Garden City. Clay's grandparents had been staunch supporters. When the denominations consolidated under the blanket coverage of Unity Council, the Sandersons were more or less lost in the shuffle. Their names remained on the rolls, and they continued the required financial support, but that was the extent of their involvement.

It had rankled a bit when the directive came governing the required tithing, but they had gone along, believing it was perhaps sensible to put the Church on a more business-type basis. Otherwise, how could they continue the charitable work, without knowing what income to expect?

Mr. Carter drew himself to his full height. "Now look, Sanderson..." Reverend Dewberry made a motion with his hand as if stilling a small snapping dog.

"Clay, my boy, we mean no interference. It is for your own good to settle this small matter. Once you understand the subversive actions of this man, I know you and your father will want no part of him. Further involvement with this man could affect your family's religious standing, to say nothing of business matters."

When the two men left, Clay and Mark stood on the porch watching the dirt cloud rise behind the departing car. They watched until the dust settled and was only a small plume in the distance.

"I'll swear," Mark muttered under his breath.

Clay looked sharply at his father and noticed he was pale under the dark tan of his deeply creased face. A fine sprinkle of sweat stood on his forehead. Clay took his arm and turned him toward the front door.

"Come on now, let's get inside and see if Tillie can get us something cool to drink."

Clay could see the Right Reverend Dewberry had definitely upset his father. They went to the kitchen and when Tillie saw Mark, she gasped.

"My land, Clay Sanderson what have you been doing? You know your daddy isn't supposed to get overheated. What if Eva comes in and gets a look at him?"

Tillie held a kitchen chair and Mark eased down upon the seat.

"I'm fine, Tillie. You don't need to call Eva. We'll take some lemonade, or whatever you have. Damn, it's way too hot for this time of year."

Indeed, the outside air was too hot, but Clay knew it had nothing to do with Mark's condition. When Mark seemed to be breathing easier, Clay relaxed.

"The way I understand it, if we don't fire Evan, the Church fires us. No more marrying, burying, or baptizing Sanderson babies. Far as I'm concerned, that's not much of a threat, but I'll listen to how you feel about it, Dad."

Mark waved his stocky hand. "First time in my life anyone has tried to tell me who I can keep on my own land. What the hell's wrong with everybody? First, I don't get doddle squat from Ed Hillard over at National; he keeps putting me off with a bunch of double talk. Now these two butting in." Mark shook his head. "Maybe things are getting too much for me. Clay, you do as you please about Evan. When your mother and me pass on, we don't need their graveyard. There's a pretty rise of ground over in the western section that will do us fine." Mark laughed gruffly. "Maybe you can get Evan to say a few words over us. Seems to me that will do as well as the mumbo jumbo the Church goes through."

That afternoon when Clay went to his office, something his father had said was bothering him more than what to do about Evan. Ed Hillard's behavior was strange. It was a simple request. Mark had asked Ed to check around and see if National Grain reported any slight crop damage similar to what they and Doug Hansen had experienced. Hillard didn't answer yes or no, only kept saying he'd watch, that he really didn't have access to those reports. Clay didn't believe him. It should be easy for Ed to find the information. Clay's best guess was that Ed knew something and couldn't bring himself to outright lie about it.

The reports from the experimental stations were equally unsatisfactory. Their assessment was that conditions were fine and the farmers could proceed with the normal routine. Clay even sent in some of the new seed to make sure it was okay before planting, and they confirmed it was top grade. Yet none of the answers satisfied him. If something had been wrong last year, why would it be different now? Clay's hope was that this new crop would be fresh and green. That there would be no sign of the wilt Jeff had found the year before.

Driving home that evening, Clay rehearsed the talk he would have to have with Diana. He had definitely decided to let Evan stay on the farm. There was no doubt Dewberry would follow through and bar every Sanderson from further services. There was no way to keep that from her.

When he walked into the house, he found Diana in an extremely happy mood. She was wearing a pale aqua gown with scarlet roses around the neck and on the edges of the sleeves. Her brown hair, brushed to a high sheen, curled softly around her glowing face. Clay couldn't remember when he had seen her looking this lovely. Since Nora had left, there had been a procession of cooks and housekeepers, none of them meeting Diana's standards. The current one had been with them for a month. Clay still considered them unnecessary, but perhaps this one was going to stay. At least, Diana had not met him at the door with a barrage of complaints. If this were the result, it was worth it. For tonight, Diana was a joy. A rare treat. He hoped his news wouldn't destroy their evening.

Clay showered and changed and as they went in to dinner, he was pleased to see a delicious looking roast on the table. There were small browned potatoes and a boat of rich dark gravy. This, along with a fruit salad and homemade rolls, was the sort of meal that made Clay's mouth water. The meal was as good as it looked and he ate more than enough.

After dinner, Diana directed the latest cook to bring their coffee into the living room. As they rested on the couch, Diana curled against him.

"Isn't this wonderful?" She sighed. "You, relaxing and well fed. Don't you absolutely love our home? I told you I could make it perfect with the right sort of help."

Clay smiled and nodded. He had to admit it was a nice evening. Diana leaned forward to pour their coffee, and he sat straighter to take the small china cup she offered. He drank a bit and then set the cup in its saucer. He hated to break the mood, but she would know soon enough. It had better come from him.

"I hate to mention something unpleasant, particularly after a great dinner, but I have to tell you about Evan Hunter."

Diana arched an eyebrow. "Oh, really? What is he doing now? I haven't heard much about him since he left town. I know he is somewhere close because Jan is still seeing him. She acts like she's playing some spy game. She's driving Mother and Daddy crazy with her evasiveness. They have absolutely forbidden her to have anything to do with him. We know she is, but can't catch the sneaky little thing at it."

"He's working on the farm, Diana. He has been for some time."

Diana's sea green eyes grew stormy. "And you didn't tell me?"

"There didn't seem any need. I knew it would upset you."

"Why are you telling me now?"

Clay set his cup and saucer on the marble end table. He noticed Diana shifting into a stiffer position, having lost her earlier softness. It was beyond him why she looked angry when he mentioned Evan.

As he explained about Reverend Dewberry's visit, a definite chill descended upon the room. Diana stood and walked to the tall narrow windows, where she stared into the dark night for a minute before whirling to face him.

"Are you are determined to keep him on, even after what Reverend Dewberry said?"

Clay nodded.

Diana straightened to her full height while the rose trim on the front of her gown trembled.

"How could you do this? I may be a Sanderson now, but I'm still a Brockman and you are tainting both families." Diana threw her hands in the air and began pacing before him. "I don't understand it. Jan and now you. What hold does that man have on you?"

"It's the principle of the thing. I can't believe you are as dedicated to the Church as to care about not being a member." He knew his words would displease her, but her anger irritated him. Diana rushed to him and sat at his side.

"Put him off the place, Clay. Please, I'm asking you for my sake. I know you have these high ideals about independence, but think of our position in town. The Church is active in many areas. This would ruin me with the Ladies' Society. When everyone learns what has happened, none of the better people will have anything to do with us."

Clay nearly softened at her pleading, but when he thought of Evan standing firm, his resolve grew stronger.

"I'm sorry, Diana, but I gave the man my word. It wouldn't be right to refuse him because of a few self-righteous hypocrites."

Diana glared at him, her face dark with fury. "Maybe you don't care where your parents are buried, but I want my baby baptized, and to grow up respected by its peers."

He patted her arm. "Look, by the time we have children this will have blown over. They won't ban you from the Ladies' Society; they'll still think of you as a Brockman."

A sly smile curved her lips. "I hope they don't. They had better think of me as a Sanderson, considering my condition."

As Diana's news sank in, Clay was shocked and then elated. Nothing could please him more. A boy, he thought. Maybe we'll have a son, but a girl would be fine, too. At the prospect, an explosion of joy brightened his mind. Then he thought of his parents and the happiness this would bring them. He could already see a tow-headed, sturdy little boy tagging after him. And Mark a grandfather. It was fantastic. Clay grabbed Diana and hugged her. Even the certain knowledge that he would be at odds with her over keeping Evan couldn't extinguish the glow of excitement. It kept him awake far into the night.

Seven

Clay talked Diana into one of her rare trips to the farm in order to break the good news of her pregnancy. After his initial elation died down, Clay was a bit peeved that Diana had taken it upon herself to start their family before consulting him, but he was too happy to object. Diana patiently explained how she had wanted to surprise him. She knew he would want a son. Therefore, when the first embryo proved to be female, she had disposed of it.

Diana squeezed his hand and smiled as she explained. "You see, I thought of everything. I know you don't think I am very capable, but in this area, I'm the expert. I didn't want to tell you until I had our son well on his way."

"But we lost a little daughter," Clay said thoughtfully.

"Oh, Clay. Leave it to you to put it that way. The next one will be a girl."

"And what if it isn't? We throw away another boy, simply because we want a girl?"

Diana ran her hand through her hair, an impatient look on her face.

"Next time it won't be a surprise. You can go in with me and have the sperm isolated, that way the only conception will be female, or if you want, we'll make it two boys. Does that make you feel better?"

Clay drove on toward the farm wrinkling his forehead in thought. He knew about the various systems of producing children, determining the sex and physical characteristics. Cattlemen had been using the same methods for years to get the desired results. It was selective breeding carried to the ultimate and for livestock it was fantastic. Still, no matter how he tried to talk himself out of it, the idea of doing it for people didn't sit well. He was thrilled about the boy child Diana was carrying, yet the faint image of a tiny girl kept floating in his mind. He knew she was only a speck of matter when the termination took place, but still she had been alive. Clay supposed he was hopelessly old fashioned. He guessed it came from his nature, which was to make things live and grow.

His parents were as excited as he knew they would be and the day went smoothly, or at least smoother than the usual meeting between Diana and Eva. Clay couldn't understand the tension between the two women. He tried to be fair in judging each of them and he honestly felt it was not his mother's fault. Eva did everything possible to make Diana welcome. She always invited Diana to accompany her as she went about her work, and maybe that bothered Diana. In her family, when company arrived everyone stopped what they were doing and gave the guest undivided attention. Eva did, too, with some friends, but with old and close friends, Eva went about her business, chattering as she worked. It was her way of drawing them into her life, making them a part of family. Diana didn't understand, probably because in her family, servants did the work. If Eva sat politely making small talk, she was keeping the person at arm's length. Diana should be thankful for the way Eva accepted her. Instead, when Eva asked her to help, Diana seemed insulted.

After lunch, Clay and his father left the table and Diana immediately got to her feet and started for the living room. Clay put a hand on her arm.

"Dad and I are going to the office for a bit. We won't be gone long. There are some reports we want to study. Why don't you visit with Mother until we get back?"

He caught her stone-cold stare and hoped his parents missed it. Eva had started helping Tillie clear the dining table, a practice Diana thought disgraceful.

"Yes," Eva called. "We can have a nice talk about my new grandchild, and I want to show you the Christmas cakes Tillie and I have started."

"Grandson," Diana corrected tersely as she reluctantly followed Eva. "It is a boy; you'll be having a grandson."

Eva laughed. "Oh, that's right. In the past, they took what came and felt blessed with either one. Maybe the modern way is better. Mark and I didn't avail ourselves of it, and look what we got!" She laughed again and Tillie joined her.

Once in the office, Clay and his father studied the morning's report that had come from their accounting firm in Tulsa. The figures looked good. Both men smiled and Clay knew Mark was as relieved as he was. No matter how good the crop yield had been, there was the hanging question of how much it would bring on the market. It always depended on selling the product. Even though prices had been at an all-time high for the past five years, there was the outside chance the price per bushel could drop. It was hard to understand how the market had stayed high this long. Usually, in the world of selling, supply and demand were the two sides of a giant balance. When the supply was constantly high, prices went down, but for years, both had seemed in perfect balance. It was a strange phenomenon, one that Mark especially had trouble accepting. Of course, there was a lot of artificial support for those prices, the government controlling foreign sales and domestic regulations. Still, Clay hoped the balancing act could go on forever, while Mark was sure it couldn't.

Sitting at the desk, Mark pounded his fist on a stack of record books. "Well, there it is again, son. Another profitable year. I don't guess I'll ever get used to it. I keep thinking we are going to do ourselves in. We keep improving and producing more and more. Yet the market keeps absorbing it, almost faster than we can shovel out, it seems," Mark said, gazing out the window.

Clay understood the feeling, but he also understood world conditions. America, Canada, Australia, and Argentina were feeding the rest of the world. It was an excellent position for the food producers, and no doubt, it saved millions of lives, but with expanding populations, the hunger continued. Small nations ravaged by rebellions and wars were too devastated to even transport the grain to the starving once it reached their borders. War kept the famines going, and in a ripple effect, kept the Sandersons going. Mark considered it an unhealthy situation.

The whole globe was into specializing. There were the energy producing countries, nations that made nothing but machines, others that provided virtually every household item and clothing. The system originated in the United World Assembly, the reasoning being that each nation, due to natural resources and abilities, could supply certain products cheaper. Another benefit was that it made nations interdependent; none was able to stand completely alone. In theory, the reliance upon one another would in time bring complete unity.

Clay watched his father and could almost read his thoughts. Independence was at Mark's core. He was sure there was no security when an individual or a nation had to depend upon someone else. Restricting a country to one type of product for export seemed a sure path to destruction. It limited the bargaining power.

"I still don't trust some man in Washington doing my trading for me," Mark said.

"I know," Clay answered. "But there's nothing we can do."

"No, and I can't see why farmers over a hundred years ago thought it was a good idea. They should never have handed over our individual rights."

"Yeah, but they did. We have to deal with it the best we can. We still own the land!"

Clay's remark made his father smile, but he knew it didn't make the situation right with Mark. He was firmly of the opinion that individuals' striving and succeeding, in the end, proved best for humanity as a whole. That there was something unhealthy about having men in official positions make choices for everyone else. Clay respected his father's beliefs and hoped that some of his more dire predictions didn't come true. They had been through several cycles of inflation and had managed, but it made him nervous.

For one reason or another, a nation would decide a trade agreement was unfair and raise prices on their products. Before any governing body could react, a price spiral started. In response, the other countries would raise their prices to protect their interest. The situation always worsened before high-level meetings of unions, cartel leaders, and government officials agreed upon a solution. It usually involved reduced trade, a worldwide boycott that brought offending nations into line. However, it left prices at a new high. Putting a good face on rotten deals, presidents, ministers, and premiers would declare that we were better off than before. They'd say a new age was on the doorstep. Mark never trusted the speeches or proclamations. Clay didn't either, but his approach was different. He held an unshakable faith that no matter what happened, the grain they produced would save them. He only had to hold onto the land and keep it productive.

There would always be a need for Sanderson grain.

From the office window, a magnificent view unfolded. The flat land stretching to the west in its winter colors of heavy brown and brick red wore stripes of tender green sprouting wheat. Far to the north, the olive-gray lines of windbreak trees were barely visible sentinels. Overhead, the sky was a cloudless crystal dome. Clay never tired of the scene. As the sky and land interacted, it changed constantly. On bright days, golden light bathed the land, making the crop leaves shimmer emerald green. When the heavens were host to running gangs of clouds, swiftly moving dark shadows mottled the ground below. It was a pulsing, living, breathing thing and, oh God, thought Clay, how he loved it. He and his father never spoke of their shared love of the land, yet they each understood the other's feeling. He supposed it was simply too deep for words.

Mark was sitting at the desk again reviewing the records. He looked healthy, but his heart condition was never far from Clay's mind. He couldn't imagine life without his father. Still, something Frank had mentioned the last time Mark was sick had stayed with Clay. They should discuss Mark's will. He wasn't sure this was the time to approach Mark, but would there ever be a right time? The family knew about Mark's will, but they didn't discuss it. It was easier to pretend things would go on forever, and if something happened, Clay would manage in his father's absence. The family talked about the farming operation and their health, but not much about death. Still, times had changed; the old will wasn't sufficient. The land grew dearer with each passing year; they needed to protect the family's interest. Perhaps Frank's suggestion of a trust was the way to go.

Clay touched Mark's arm. "Dad," he said.

Coming from somewhere far away, Mark turned. "Yes, what?" he said softly.

"I've been putting this off, but I think we should talk about your will." Clay's words were halting but clear.

Mark smiled. "I see. Now that you're going to be a daddy, you're going to get real serious on me."

"I meant to say something even before Diana told me about the baby. I mentioned it to Tracy; I thought she might want to be included when we discussed it. She and Frank both acted offhand about it. It didn't much matter to them, that whatever we decided would be fine."

"It shows how much your sister trusts you." Mark chuckled. "At least I don't have to worry about my children fussing and fighting over this business. Even Frank seems to have enough sense to leave the farm in experienced hands."

Clay took a seat on the other side of the desk and relaxed. It was going to be easier than he had thought to talk with his father.

"You know what I'm worried about, don't you?" Clay began. "Even with things going well, I don't think we'll ever get enough ahead to pay inheritance taxes. It would mean selling part of the land. If we do that, it will cut the operation to the place where we can't stay in business. I think we should see Tom Brockman and arrange some kind of trust. Even if it was Frank's idea. Tom would know how to ensure a smooth passing."

"Mine or the lands?" Mark's eyes twinkled.

"Dad," Clay protested.

"It's okay, boy, don't worry. I'm going to be around probably a lot longer than I should. I didn't say anything, but I've already talked with Tom. We took care of it; you can rest easy. It made me feel a lot better. I should have said something before. I'll give you and Tracy each a copy. I couldn't stand the thought of losing the place to a stranger."

Clay looked at the floor and cleared his throat. "This trouble about keeping the land in the family. If you would stay with us longer, we wouldn't have to worry about it for who knows how long."

"Don't start that again. When this heart problem showed up, I made my decision. Two weeks in the hospital, I had lots of time to think and I haven't changed my mind since. What does it say, 'three score and ten?' well, that suits me. Lord knows with this stuff I'm taking, it will probably be a lot longer than that."

Mark's expression matched the firmness of his words. He had clearly come to terms with how he intended to manage his life. Again, as many times before, Clay marveled at the wholeness of him. He seemed to accept whatever happened and remain calm; he and Jeff were much alike. He supposed it was a generational thing. It was hard for Clay to put time in perspective. He felt young, yet old and ancient as the distant western hills. His father looked strong and healthy, with only occasional spells of weakness. At sixty-six, Mark looked younger, but his attitudes and an ingrained weariness gave him an age beyond his years. Perhaps years didn't matter. He had listened to Mark tell stories of his past, the years crammed with startling events making the sixty-six years seem a hundred or more.

Before Clay's grandfather, Joseph, had died, he told stories of world wars, the last one ending with an atomic bomb. It happened long before Joseph was born. Several generations knew only police actions and cold war. No nation had used their most powerful weapons for years. For a while, nations suffered electronic attacks against their commercial and civic facilities. There were uprisings of some small nations against one another, but no world wars. After the devastating effects of the solar flares, warfare decreased. Countries were too busy trying to survive to attack their neighbor. However, one of the first things the larger nations did was to rebuild their weapons of defense. One of the most effective was an anti-personnel ray.

Clay had seen pictures of Egypt where they had used the ray eight years earlier. It was amazing...the land looked normal and the cities stood with no visible damage, but there was not an animal or human in sight. Pictures showed an eerie looking place. The experts weren't sure how long it would be before the land was habitable because of the destroying rays' lingering effects. From the north to the south, Egypt was lifeless. The forecast was that the land might remain barren another thirty years.

The past three generations had witnessed medical advances that affected birth and extended life, and modified behavior...the list was nearly endless. The countries that could afford it were rebuilding the space stations destroyed by solar flares. Less prosperous nations were still struggling to restore lost technology. Despite the years of political and religious upheaval, the nations were trying to come together. The religious community seemed to be succeeding, except for a few dissidents, such as Evan. Still, no movement ever had total support. Perhaps the Church could lead the way to a better political situation; there was hope they would.

The nations were too dependent upon one another to remain separate. The churches were setting the example of what cooperation could accomplish. It hadn't made the United States happy when the shift of economic power came about, but now there seemed to be the feeling that perhaps that too would work to some advantage. It made sense that the more densely populated portions of the world should also be the center of commerce. It lifted a burden from America. There were no longer accusations of its taking unfair advantage of underdeveloped countries. It was an open system with the World

Trade Board in Rome making the decisions. Yes, the globe had been spinning faster and faster during Mark's lifetime, but it bothered Clay that his father would not take advantage of the new medical developments to stay alive longer.

Mark was shuffling some reports on the desk. Clay stared out the window, until he turned to Mark and tried once more. "Isn't there anything I can say to change your mind about the heart replacement?"

"Nope," Mark answered. He handed Clay a report. "You want to go over this again?"

Clay took the report and glanced at it. It was inconclusive about the blight Jeff had noticed during mid-summer.

"No, I don't need to see it again. What do you think happened with old Hillard? He was no help."

Mark nodded. "Only thing I can figure is that he really didn't know anything. Hate to think he was covering something that might hurt us."

Clay shrugged. "Probably nothing anyway. The new crop seems to be sprouting okay. Have you given any more thought to using National Grain's new perennial strain? It would cut operational costs."

"Maybe I'll let you give it a shot." Mark grinned. "I don't know if I could handle any more miracles. Come on, we better go to the house. Eva will have Diana's ear talked off."

Clay closed the office door, and hurrying to reach his father, impulsively threw his arm about Mark's shoulder. It was a wonderful, beautiful day. The farm was in fine shape, Clay had his family around him, and better yet, a new soul was on the way. More than enough to make a man glad. Even the earlier concerns over something wrong in the fields and the lingering drought slipped from Clay's mind.

~ * ~

On the way home, Diana sat with her arms folded and her jaw in a firm line. She glanced at Clay once or twice. It irritated her even more to see the contented look on his face. He knew she didn't enjoy these visits to her in-laws. How could he have left her with Eva and

Tillie for the entire afternoon? It was unforgivable. They nearly drove her frantic with the talk about cooking, bargain hunting, and babies. She wanted no part of the world in which those two women lived.

Clay turned and smiled at her. "You sure are quiet. Did you get too tired today? Guess I'll have to take better care of you from now on."

His talk made her sick. If this was how it was going to be, what had she done? The baby had seemed a good idea, but now she wondered. It could be a trap. Certainly not from her point; she could carry it with no inconvenience. After delivery, a nanny would handle things. Still, a strong suspicion was beginning to set in that Clay and his family would use this child to tie her to them. Bind her more and more to the type of life she abhorred. If she had wanted drudgery, she would have started a career.

The sun had slipped from view and the western sky was a backdrop of deepening blue streaked with pink that swiftly changed to purple. The trees along the road pointed their bare, dead branches accusingly at the dry winter sky. With the coming of fall, the temperatures had dropped slightly, but the different season brought no moisture to the thirsty land. The bleak stretch of prairie made her shiver.

"Are you chilly?" Clay asked, seeming surprised. "It's plenty warm for me, but maybe your chemistry is changing."

Diana clenched her teeth and shook her head. Clay was trying to be considerate, she was aware of that, but each word he spoke made her resent him more. She definitely didn't care for the way things were going. The disappointment put a bitter taste in her mouth, and it made her angry. It was the same as biting into a luscious looking piece of fruit only to find it tasted of gall. The most disgusting part was that she had chosen it. Could she have been this far off in her judgment? It infuriated her. She had thought her father and Uncle Avery were bad about bringing their work home. Still, they did let go of it long enough to attend parties, and their interest did extend to things in the community, but Clay? The farm never left his mind. She was sure his dreams centered on it. Clay reached across the seat and held her hand. He smiled, his teeth bright in the dim light.

"You really made the folks happy with the news about the baby. If I know Mother, she will want a big Christmas, but watch next year when there is a baby in the house."

"I hope she doesn't make too much of Christmas. I plan to have the main party at our house. They can come into town, can't they?"

Clay was silent for a minute. "Well, I suppose. Christmas at the farm has always been special. Frank and Tracy bring their kids. We invite the men and those with families bring them."

Diana tried not to groan. She could imagine the Sandersons' type of party. Strange children running through the house, spilling punch and grinding Christmas cookies into the carpet.

"Can't they give the help a party of their own, maybe in the men's bunkhouse before attending ours? I'll call your mother and arrange it."

She noticed Clay's smile had disappeared. She would not give in on this issue. It was enough that she had gone along with the visit today. She also reluctantly conceded that she would have to make another one sometime around the holidays, but as to the celebration arrangements, there was no way she would forsake her plans. She didn't want to talk, but when Clay didn't answer, she continued.

"I don't want to upset your family, Clay, but we have our own life and it hasn't started very well."

Clay turned sharply. "What do you mean by that?"

"For one thing, we might as well be living there for the amount of time you spend in town."

"I'm home every night. You know that."

"But your mind isn't here. You never want to go anywhere. We don't have any friends in town. Even my best friends have stopped calling since we never accept their invitations." Diana shrugged and turned her head toward the dark window. "I feel buried alive."

"I see," Clay said glumly.

Angrily she turned toward him. "No. You don't see. That is the point. No more than you see my side of things concerning Evan."

"Would you please tell me what Evan has to do with any of this?"

Clay seemed angry, too. Inwardly she smiled. If he thought being aggressive would win him anything, she could show him how wrong he was. He had nothing to complain about; everything went his way. She was the one put upon by his family and humiliated by his association with Evan.

"First, thanks to your stubborn insistence about having Evan on the farm, we certainly won't be welcome in church this Christmas."

"Oh, I didn't realize religion meant that much to you," he said sarcastically.

"If you will let me finish. I seriously doubt anyone else will invite us either. More importantly, if you don't end this nonsense, they won't baptize your son. I had the pleasure of seeing Evan today, while you and your father were busy. The only reason I tolerated him was that Tillie and your mother were about to drive me wild with their revolting dribble. He came to get a chocolate cake Tillie had made for the workers. I thought they had a perfectly capable cook in their own quarters, but it seems your mother can't stop trying to feed them herself."

"That's enough, Diana. It would make things easier if you tried to cooperate with her. I hope you didn't make a fool of yourself saying something stupid to Evan."

She wanted to scream. "What is it with you and Evan? You're taking his side against me. How dare you?" A dark cloud of fury rose in her. She spoke through clenched teeth. "Get rid of him, Clay. Do it by Christmas or..."

"Or what?" Clay snapped.

Diana refused to answer. She wasn't sure what she would do, but she never made idle threats. She would find some way to make Clay take heed when she spoke, or he would be extremely sorry.

Eight

The night of December twenty-fifth found Evan and Jeff driving away from the Sanderson farm in Jeff's truck. Evan sat silently watching the darkness of the roadside. The illuminated dashboard clock read seven-thirty. Evan was holding a meeting tonight, and he was a bit concerned for the safety of the ones attending. He and Jeff were on their way to pick up Simon, Jeff's father, before going to the Christmas gathering at Ted and Laurie's. Evan had told Jeff he didn't need to go, but if his father were there, Jeff insisted on being there, too. Ted and Laurie were a young couple who had attended every meeting since the beginning, but Evan still worried about having the celebration in their home. The couple lived with Laurie's parents; an older brother and his wife and children lived there, too. The housing shortage made this arrangement necessary. Individual homes were far beyond the reach of young families and the luckier ones had parents with large houses.

Evan didn't know how the members of Laurie's family would react to the fifteen people coming to their home this evening. Ted had assured him it was okay, that their family had agreed to having the meeting. There were many parties in town that night...who would know that theirs was any different from their neighbors? Evan hoped it would seem the same as the rest, but he hated the risk that came with their generosity.

He glanced at Jeff, who was staring straight ahead, his face set and expressionless. Since coming to work on the farm, Evan had gotten to know Jeff better. He was a strange man. His Christian beliefs ran every bit as deep as the older Taylor's did, but Jeff didn't talk about them. He didn't attend church in town and as far as Evan knew, he didn't associate with Christians other than his father. Except now, he accompanied Evan and attended some meetings for his father's sake.

At first, Evan could not understand how Jeff could survive without the support and comfort of being with fellow believers. He had asked Jeff about it one day as they were working in the barn.

"It might be easier, I guess," Jeff had said. "But I'm content the way I am."

Evan had let it drop. There was something to Jeff's way of thinking, and the calm, steadfastness of the man proved it. A person should grow and bloom in a way natural to him. Many nights as Evan lay in the darkness of his room, he pondered his own growth. Sometimes he came dangerously close to questioning God, and the strange circumstances in which he found himself. Why couldn't he simply hold to his faith and march on silently through the years of his life, the way Jeff did? Wasn't Jeff's witness as strong as his was? Maybe it was stronger. Jeff stood solid in his belief and nothing swayed him. He was rooted in the firm soil of eternity, while Evan, a wanderer, felt rootless. Deep in the silent nights, his soul cried, begging God to show him the way. Some comfort came from the certain knowledge that the Church was not on the right path. Occasionally, there was a feeling of shame. For didn't his wondering and questioning show a lack of faith? He prayed for guidance and the faith to follow, even if he could not see where he was going. Sometimes he laughed at the strangeness of his calling.

He had no special talents. When he taught the lessons, his words seemed too unexpressive and inadequate for the great message. It was a mystery why he had received high marks at the seminary, and a greater mystery why this storm should brew around him. He was only one man against a huge institution, yet they needed to stop him. Several times, he'd caught a trace of fear in their faces, and it puzzled him. He couldn't challenge or harm the order and power of the religious world. The laws in every nation were behind them. It was laughable that they should take notice of him. It caused Evan to closely examine his motives: was he doing this because it was forbidden? Did something in him want the notoriety caused by his maverick actions? The answer was always a swift no, because his fear was far stronger than any desire for attention. He would rather hide in the shadows, cling to his faith, but bear none of the responsibilities. His cowardice shamed him. No true Christian feared death. Neither did he, but physical pain frightened him.

Again, he looked at Jeff and saw no fear hidden in this man, nor in his father, Simon. He wished he could talk to Jeff about it, but he didn't have the courage to make the confession. His consolation was in remembering how sometimes God picked weak, poor vessels, that His strength and richness might better show through. "Well." He spoke silently to God. "You will undoubtedly make a wonderful showing in me. There is surely not a weaker container of the message."

Jeff began to chuckle softly.

"What's funny?" Evan asked.

"You are." Jeff's lined face cracked into a wide grin. "You think you're silent. I can hear the wheels of your mind grinding. I can hardly hear myself think. Kind of reminds me of when I was a boy."

Evan was puzzled. "I don't understand."

"Not sure I do either, but it's the same feeling I used to get around my dad. He'd never utter a word but his thinking created a lot of noise."

"I'll try to keep it down." Evan laughed. He didn't know what Simon Taylor's mind had clattered on about those years ago, but suddenly there was a joyous kinship with the older man. Maybe he'd talk to Simon, who might understand the fear.

As they drove into Garden City, every light pole, street sign, and tree had colored lights covering it. Above the streets, silver banners and decorations reflected the red, blue, and green lights. Music blared from speakers on every corner. Groups of merrymakers in fancy clothes gathered beside lamp poles singing and sharing drinks. Others were slumped in doorways, a bottle of pills or a needle in their hand. A knot of anger tightened Evan's chest. The decorations were expensive, yet the reality behind them was cold and hollow. A bitter taste flooded his mouth. The mockery was hard to bear. The display cost more than the struggling community could afford, but the men in power were clever. Throughout the year, people had scrimped and fought to feed their families; now they needed a release. Let them have a celebration, approve of every form of festivity, encourage the people to indulge in riotous behavior. What better way to ease the tensions? And to relieve any sense of guilt, do it in the name of God.

It was diabolical.

The word *sin* seemed inadequate; it was beyond that...it was deception on a grand scale. They sanctioned the sinful behavior and at the same time declared forgiveness under the guise of celebrating the birth of Jesus. More than that, there were banners proclaiming human achievements, and government posters promising a better tomorrow. The glitter and celebration were as false as the religious teachings.

Jeff stopped in front of Simon's apartment and found the old man standing on the curb, waiting. Evan got out and carefully helped Simon into the cab of the truck.

"Too warm for winter, isn't it?" Simon said to no one in particular.

Jeff simply nodded.

"Yes, it is," Evan agreed. "I don't mind being warmer, but Clay isn't happy. The heat and lack of moisture aren't good for his business."

"That's the truth," Jeff said. "'Course it probably won't make much difference because of the irrigation system provided by National Grain. There is water enough. I expect Clay is worried over the cost. Rain is free."

Simon seemed to study Evan's face. "You look pale; what's the matter, boy?"

Evan tried to smile. "Nothing, I'm fine."

"Well, you don't look fine." Simon snorted.

"Come on, Dad. Don't pick at Evan," Jeff said. "Maybe you think we're working him too hard, but this isn't the farm work you remember. He's okay, aren't you, Evan?"

Evan nodded, but Simon still frowned.

"Farm work isn't what I was thinking about," Simon insisted. "It's tonight that's bothering you, isn't it? Nobody has stopped us; I don't think they know we're still at it. Bet they think they scared you off. But going into a stranger's home, you're wondering what's going to happen." Simon didn't wait for an answer.

"Well, I'm telling you, don't wonder and don't worry, you go ahead and tell those people the truth. You had planned on giving the message tonight, hadn't you?"

For a minute, Evan caught a note of uncertainty in Simon's voice. He gave the old man a sharp look; it was hard to fool him. When Simon first came to the meetings, everyone thought what a comfort it must be for him. Evan quickly learned that Simon gave much more than he received. More than once, he had drawn on the older man's strength. Again tonight, he felt Simon's support and was grateful for his presence.

"Yes, I will give the message. Although I wondered how smart it was to accept Laurie and Ted's invitation. I appreciate them opening the house for us, but I wonder about the rest of the family. I don't want to bring trouble to bystanders. How obliging will they be if they find themselves facing a court?"

Simon put a withered hand on Evan's shoulder. "You're confused, son. Don't spread your thinking too thin over the whys and wherefores. You have one duty and that is to preach the true Gospel. Don't give more importance to yourself than is due. You don't cause these things to happen, and you don't bring one soul to salvation. Took me a few years—I was some older than you—before I got the idea of how things are. God is running this show. You and me, we follow orders. He knows what He's doing."

As they parked in the driveway, Evan didn't see Jan's car and it brought a small pang of regret. It was his own fault; he had discouraged her from attending. Still, the disappointment was there. The house was decorated the same as others on the street and Ted welcomed them at the door.

It was a large, old-fashioned house with a fireplace. Although there was no need for it, someone had set a few small logs ablaze. Any form of wood was hard to find. It was encouraging that the family felt the event important enough to splurge, for cheerfulness' sake. In the dining room, a long table was set with ham, a turkey, and the trimmings. Each person had brought something to contribute, lessening the burden on the host. Evan looked around and found his small congregation was there. Ted introduced Evan to his in-laws and Laurie made an apology for her older brother.

"He really wanted to attend," she said. "But he works at the power company, and someone had to take this shift. His wife is gone, visiting the other grandparents."

Evan smiled and nodded. There was a measure of relief over the brother's not attending. One less family member in danger. When Jan came through the swinging door between the kitchen and dining room, it startled him. She was smiling and holding a large plate of cookies as she looked over her shoulder, talking to someone in the kitchen. When she turned, her gaze locked on Evan, and for an instant, it seemed they were alone. She came forward and set the plate on the table.

"You look surprised to see me," she said.

"I didn't see your car."

Jan frowned. "But you had to know I'd be here."

He had to admit he was glad to see her. Jan stepped to his side and slipped her arm through his.

"It seems weeks since I've seen you. How have you been? Are you okay, Evan?"

"I'm fine. You are looking well."

"Telling me to stay away was useless. I understand you think I'll be in danger if I follow you, but that is my choice."

Evan took her to a corner at the foot of the stairs.

"How can I make you see?" he said. "No one comes because of me. They are at this gathering because they are true believers. They don't blindly follow me; I'm not what you think. There will be no great uprising because of what I preach. What I'm trying to do is get the Word to as many people as possible before it's too late."

Jan looked into his eyes, her face void of expression. "If what you preach is true, I'm in more danger by going along with the rest of the world. I'm not stupid; give me time, I'll learn. However, how can I with no teacher? Don't you think I'm worth saving?"

He didn't know how to answer. Of course, he wanted Jan to be a Christian. As he looked at her, he realized how much, but maybe he was a distraction. She could pay too much attention to him and never see the One he preached. He looked across the room and saw Simon watching them. A wave of humiliation hit him as Simon's words rang in his ears. It was true; at least in his dealings with Jan, he put more importance upon himself than he should. The Holy Spirit did the convicting of sin, not him. Evan took her hand and pressed it between his own two hands.

"I'm glad you came. May God grant you more understanding than I have."

At that minute, Ted waved from his place beside the fire.

"If you're ready, Evan, you can begin. We'll have our dinner afterward."

The group gathered in the living room and Evan stood before them. He bowed his head and first prayed in silence for guidance. Aloud, he offered a prayer for each of his listeners. He knew his sermon well; it seemed written in flames upon his brain. It was the old story of Jesus' birth, life, and death. It was Christmas, but he carried straight on into the Easter message. This was the heart of his belief. He preached Christ risen.

"For—" Evan's voice rang in the silence, "—this is our hope. If He did not arise and ascend into the realm of God, He was merely another prophet. We would, as others do, be following a man. He left us with a wonderful promise. 'In my Father's house are many mansions: if it were not so, I would have told you. I go to prepare a place for you. And if I go and prepare a place for you, I will come again, and receive you unto myself; that where I am, there ye may be also.' We come together to celebrate His birth, and we remember His departure, but what fills us with joy is the promise of His return."

Evan was absorbed in his message, searching each face as he spoke. He barely noticed the front door opening and the two men who stepped inside. If any thought of them crossed his mind, it was to think that one of them might be Laurie's brother arriving late with a friend. He ended with a prayer and the listeners stood and began to talk among themselves. As the two men entered the room and started toward Evan, the conversations turned to sharp exclamations and startled cries. At the same time, Jeff, Jan, and Ted drew close to him. In a flash, the truth of the situation became clear. The men were dressed in plain clothes, but their faces were uniform masks of authority.

Evan's first impulse was to run, but faster than he could even reject the idea, the men stood before him. The only distinction between them was that one had dark hair and the other light. The blond one spoke. "Evan Hunter?"

Evan nodded.

"In direct violation of the Council's warning, you are conducting an illegal meeting. You are therefore to be placed in containment until the Council meets to bring charges against you in a criminal court."

As the man spoke, a couple of people edged toward the door, perhaps hoping to slip away. Some of the men gripped the backs of chairs hard enough to turn their knuckles white, almost as white as the faces of the women standing beside them. Evan wanted to shout at them to leave, run before the men charged them as well. The air in the dry room crackled with electricity, and the people looked frozen in place. A static moment, the instant before tinder leaped into flame. Yet, instead of exploding, the men and women in the room shifted silently between Evan and the two men. Smooth yet forceful, the same as a flowing river, they pushed Evan aside, and moved the two men farther away, mixed in with the guests. Jan pulled Evan toward the kitchen while Jeff shoved him from behind. He started to protest, the same as the two Council representatives were doing. Within seconds, Jan and Jeff had him through the kitchen and into the black night.

Evan struggled, trying to turn back. "We can't leave everyone." He fought against Jeff's hold on him as Jan pulled him farther along. Just when he thought he might break free, Jeff's fist caught him under the jaw. His teeth snapped together and the night swirled with tiny stars. He remained conscious, but not enough to protest. He was dizzy and nauseous, whether from the blow or the near arrest, he couldn't say. As they put him into Jan's car, he heard her speaking to Jeff.

"I thought this might happen; that's why I parked in the alley."

"Can you get him to the farm, or shall I come?" Jeff's voice sounded hollow and far away.

Jan settled behind the wheel and Jeff leaned through the window. Evan raised his head and reached for the door handle. Jeff knocked his hand away.

"I'm sorry, Evan, but you move and I'll clip you again." Jeff looked anxiously at Jan. "Maybe I better come with you."

"No," she said. "You have Simon to see about. Why the farm? That's the first place they'll look. We should go to my house. It's large, and no one ever comes in there."

Jeff shook his head sharply. "No, the farm is better. We could hide an elephant there. Now get going."

Jeff turned, sprinted across the darkened lawn and disappeared around the corner of the house. Jan started the car, and without turning on the headlights, drove from the alley onto the street. They were soon out of town, speeding along the empty highway toward the farm. The headlights illuminated one fence post after another and then lost them again in the blackness while the tires whined against the pavement.

Evan's head began to clear and he gingerly touched the lump rising under his jawbone. The relief he felt at escaping brought shame and sadness. Shame for allowing his rescue, and sadness for the people left behind. He hung his head and his stomach churned while his eyes stung with tears of disappointment. The moan that escaped his lips broke with a sob; his chest felt ready to crack open. Jan jerked her head toward him.

"Are you okay?"

"No, I don't think I am," he muttered.

"Shall I pull over?"

"It isn't that kind of sick. Keep going."

They drove on for several miles, Jan turning every few minutes to study him. He felt her gaze and each look seemed to brand him for the coward he was. He would have done better to knuckle under to the demands in the first place. Maybe he could have found a way of working within the system. To make a stand and run at the first confrontation seemed beyond cowardly. His thoughts were too dark to speak.

"Stop it, Evan," Jan snapped at him. "I know what you're thinking and it is all rubbish, unproductive rubbish. We did what we had to. If you were taken away, who would hold the meetings?"

He didn't answer, but if he were gone, someone would take his place. Ted or maybe even Simon would carry on; the message was much larger than any one man.

"Nothing is going to happen to anyone there." Jan spoke crisply. "They will be issued warnings. Nothing more. The Council isn't going to risk undermining their authority by going against their own laws. One of their biggest proclamations is the settling of differences by peaceful means. I made it a point to check it in my father's library. There are two warnings before a hearing. Only chronic offenders are tried, and that is in civil court. It is the teacher who falls under criminal prosecution."

Jan stopped for a breath, and continued. "The Church wants followers. If they arrest everyone, it might cause a backlash. I think they would rather use reconditioning drugs than imprison people. No, Evan. We did the right thing. Besides, haven't you ever heard about running away and living to fight another day?"

Evan nodded. "I suppose you're right."

Jan smiled, an air of excitement rising around her. "What's the next move? I don't expect you to do anything this minute. You can stay at the farm a few days and make your plans. I'll go into town and see if I can find anything there."

"I don't have to make plans. I'll keep doing what I've always done: preach to anyone who will listen. This isn't a war, Jan. At least not the kind you understand."

Jan tilted her head and gave him a knowing glance. "You say it isn't a war, 'at least not the kind I would understand.' Your words betray you...it is a war. I'm surprised at you. The world knows nothing but wars of one kind or another. I know one when I see it."

His jaw was aching, but he managed to mutter, "There haven't been wars for generations."

Jan laughed. "No, they don't call them that, but it is still one nation subduing another."

They turned off the highway and were driving across Sanderson land as Evan tried to think of what to do about Jan. She expected him to do something, retaliate in some way, or take the cause into the courts and wage a battle there. She saw things purely on the secular level. His struggle was in the spiritual realm. Trying to make her see was useless. It was the same as finding hidden images in a puzzle. Difficult to see until it suddenly became clear. There was only one course open...he would continue preaching as long as anyone would listen.

Jan parked beside the lodge and he looked toward the main house. There were a number of vehicles parked in the driveway. The house's windows cast yellow shadows on the winter ground. The farm was silent and the flat land stretched on, seemingly endless under the dark sky. The big house stood as if it were the last abode on the edge of a lifeless, barren land. He saw Clay's car and considered going inside to tell him that he would be leaving. He could no longer burden the Sanderson family, but decided his talk could wait until he was not as rattled.

Jan took his arm and they started into the farmhands' lodge. She began to laugh.

"What's funny?" he asked.

"I saw Clay's car. Diana must be boiling; she swore she wouldn't spend Christmas at the farm. I say good for Clay. Someone has to be firm with her."

Once inside, they went into the large kitchen and Jan started making coffee. When Jeff and Simon came through the door, Evan was relieved to see them. They appeared in good condition.

"Is everyone okay?" he asked.

Jeff grinned and patted his shoulder. "It was nothing. Those Council officers gave us a warning and sent us on our way. They said since it was Christmas, gatherings were allowed."

Jeff tilted Evan's chin to one side to inspect the damage. Evan winced.

"Ouch, it still hurts."

"Hey, I said I was sorry. You're too stubborn for your own good. Better a sore jaw than a jail cell."

"I thought because they allowed Christmas parties, we might get away with it."

"I suspect they made an exception in your case," Simon said with a chuckle and took a drink of coffee.

It was common knowledge that Evan was staying on the farm. There was no doubt that someone would be there shortly to look for him. As he and Jeff discussed what to do, Simon held his coffee cup between his thin hands and studied the steam rising above it.

"You could flee to the wilderness," he offered. "It has been the refuge of many a disciple. Out to the barren lands. The place of rocky crags and dry blowing sand, where a man can stand under the empty sky and the only movement is his own clothing flapping in the wind. In the day, the bright, burning sun bleaches the color from the ground and fades the sky until they are both a glaring bone white. A man can't tell where the one ends and the other begins."

The old man's eyes grew bright and intense, lit by a vision. His hands holding the cup trembled slightly.

"I stood once on a rise with the desolate land going on forever, not a creature in sight. No bird flew above and not even an ant crawled below. The silence was intense; I could almost grab a handful. When I spoke, not even the sound of my voice could penetrate it. It was strange to cry aloud and not hear my words; I stopped trying to speak and became a dumb being. I stood there empty as the land around me, an emptied clay pot. Until I heard another voice.

"It came like sweet spring rain washing the dryness from me and filling me to the brim. The words were love, comfort, faith, and trust. 'You can trust me.' That's what I heard." His shoulders began to shake like he had a sudden chill. He reached for Evan's hand.

"I heard it, son. It was a voice more real than yours or mine. It was solid, but still not having substance. It was real; it didn't need any of the stuff we call matter."

Jeff put his arms around the old man and helped him to his feet.

"You're tired, Dad; I'll help you to bed. Evan and I will figure out something. Don't think about it anymore." Jeff led his father from the room.

When he returned, Evan and Jan were sitting quietly waiting for him.

"Will he be okay?" Jan asked.

"Sure," Jeff answered. "He gets that way when he thinks about the desert. He did go there once years ago. We thought he was lost. It was right after Mother died. He preached her funeral, and after that, he changed. You could talk to him and he wouldn't hear you; there was some terrible war going on inside him, but he finally got over it. Some said it was the heat and no food that caused him to hear things."

"What do you think?" Evan asked.

Jeff shrugged. "I'm not sure, but I know my father and if he said he heard God, I'd never be the one to say he didn't."

"Wait a minute," Jan exclaimed. "Simon may have the answer. Why don't you go farther away? We could bring you anything you need."

Jeff rubbed his chin. "She's right. You could go to the same place Dad went. I never told anyone because the land is worthless. I wanted to do something for him, but he only wanted to own that piece of badland. We even put an old shack on it."

They both watched Evan expectantly. It was a kind suggestion; no one would think of looking for him there, but hiding was not his purpose. To continue giving the message, he must be in the midst of people. Hiding would put an end to the work.

"Thanks for the offer, but I can't quit. I can't stay on the farm, either; I don't want to cause Clay trouble. Maybe I can find some place in town." He started toward the door. "I'll tell Clay now. I don't want to leave before thanking him for being good to me."

Jeff grabbed his hat and jammed it on his head. "I'll go with you."

~ * ~

In the main house that night, Clay was having his own problems. Despite what Diana might have thought about being able to alter Eva's Christmas plans, the entire family was at the farm, gathered in the living room. The other guests had left and Clay began to relax. Diana's icy attitude had been embarrassing; he hoped most everyone overlooked it. As usual, Frank was drinking too much and talking even more. It surprised Clay that Frank was still going on about the same business deal he had mentioned the night of Clay's bachelor party. Usually, Frank was in and out of his schemes much faster. It was also surprising that Tracy let him ramble on; she normally tried to stop him. Maybe Frank was actually putting this deal together.

Clay had to admit it sounded more legitimate than most of Frank's deals. According to him, the South Americans were coming into the country to conclude the transaction. The only point Frank was completely silent about was what he'd use to purchase the gems. Maybe Frank had found a backer.

Mark and Eva entertained Tracy's children and listened patiently to Frank's endless line of bravado. It was an old story by now, but no one worried about Tracy or the children's future. Clay would provide for them even if Frank failed. The family had finally accepted Frank as he was and not much he did surprised them. Diana, on the other hand, was a new member. Clay could tell his parents didn't know how to take some of her remarks.

Diana was sitting on a bench close to where Mark was showing Frank Jr. how to operate a toy the boy had received for Christmas. Eva was on the couch near Diana, and Clay caught bits of their conversation.

"I don't understand how you can be content on this farm. You miss everything," Diana said to Eva.

"But I love it," Eva answered.

"Well, I'd be bored senseless in two days."

Eva smiled. "Not when you have small ones, you won't. There is a lot to do. It must be instinct, but you'll find yourself striving to make a home for your husband and children. There is a great deal of satisfaction in the whole process, you'll see."

Diana's smile was almost a sneer. "I think the rest of you will be the ones to see. I hope none of you expect me to stay tied hand and foot to this child. There are a number of studies that show children are far better adjusted and able to cope with the world when raised in an environment similar to the outside world."

"What do you mean?" Eva looked puzzled.

"Simply that the child should be taught, managed, and controlled by experts. Not by Clay and me; we are too inexperienced."

Eva looked toward Clay, her face wrinkled in bewilderment. Clay came across the room and put his arm around Eva's shoulders.

"Don't worry, Mother, we're not going to put the kid in some institution. I think what Diana means is that we'll get the best teachers possible. Right, honey?"

Diana lowered her head and leveled an icy stare at Clay.

"Surely I won't have to get a consensus before raising this child in my own way, will I?"

Before Clay could find an answer that would dispel the building tension, Frank ambled toward them. For once Clay was glad to welcome him.

"Tracy tells me you're getting nervous about the arrangements for passing the farm on..." Frank cleared his throat softly and continued. "...after Mark's departure, to put it delicately."

Clay frowned at Frank and jerked his head toward Eva.

"For goodness' sake, Clay," Eva said, "I'm not touchy about it. Your father explained and I agreed. No one lives forever, despite modern miracles."

"A very enlightened view, Mother Sanderson." Frank bowed slightly. "I'm not condemning you in the least, Clay. I was telling Tracy she should be more practical. She doesn't want to think about this sort of thing, but it must be done."

As Eva didn't seem to object to the discussion, Clay didn't see why Frank shouldn't know Mark had taken his advice.

"I've talked to Dad about it. He had already done as you suggested."

Frank tilted his head and smiled. "You don't say?"

"I don't have the details. I didn't read it closely, but I'd take care of the place same as I do now. He'll give you a copy for Tracy."

"Mark went ahead with the irrevocable trust, didn't he?"

"Yes. Tom fixed it so we don't have to worry."

"Sounds great. With everything in a trust for you and Tracy, I'm sure Tracy would always want you to manage for her. There is no doubt you'd take care of your mother."

Frank smiled pleasantly and went to join Tracy at the buffet table. Clay watched him walk away. Frank wasn't that bad. He probably couldn't help being the way he was, but at least he seemed to be thinking straight about protecting Tracy's interest.

It was after midnight when Mark and Eva told their children good night.

"Your rooms are ready for you," Eva said as she took Mark's arm. "Tracy, you and Frank will be in your old room and the children's beds are in the playroom next to it. Clay, you and Diana should be comfortable in the guest room."

"See you at breakfast," Mark added. "Don't stay too late, now."

Clay smiled, thinking how hard Eva tried to please Diana. They could have stayed in Clay's old bedroom, but it wouldn't suit Diana.

The guest room, on the other hand, had a private bath and Eva had redecorated the two rooms last year. Yet Diana was unhappy about spending Christmas at the farm, and he doubted having a nice room would help. He was right.

They stayed a while longer with Frank and Tracy until Diana, pleading weariness, marched upstairs. The look she gave Clay made him know that he should be right behind her.

He did intend to, but the arrival of Evan and Jeff delayed him. Frank and Tracy stayed downstairs long enough to be polite before excusing themselves and going to their rooms. Clay was happy to see Evan and Jeff. He knew they had been in town attending a Christmas gathering at the home of one of Evan's followers. He didn't fully understand Evan's persistence in defying the religious orders, but in a way, he took pleasure in seeing someone stand against any overpowering authorities.

"Come on in the living room, sit down, and tell me about your evening," he said.

As they seated themselves, Jeff coughed and kept shifting his hat from hand to hand. It meant there was a serious purpose to the visit.

"Here." Clay reached for Jeff's hat. "Give me that before you twist off the brim."

Instead, Jeff grinned and tossed his hat onto a chair.

"Better tell him, Evan. I know this boy; he gets impatient."

Clay nodded in understanding as Evan related the incident.

"I guess I want to say thanks and goodbye," Evan continued. "If I can ever do anything to repay you for letting me stay, let me know."

Clay was shocked, despite knowing this could happen. Now that it had and Evan wanted to move on, he didn't want him to. He felt that if he let Evan leave, he would be losing something. It was a strange emotion, for if Evan stayed, Clay knew trouble would come. Why the crazy desire to make him stay? It would be better for Evan to find a new place. Clay looked at the rug between his boots and tried to make sense of his feelings. It was bad for the Sandersons and it was bad for Evan, but Clay clung resolutely to wanting Evan to stay.

"I don't want you to go," he said.

Evan and Jeff's expressions said they didn't expect this from him. The look irritated Clay. Did they think that because of some trouble he'd back down? It made him even more determined.

"This is private land, and a hell of a lot of it. We know when strangers come on it. There's no better place for you. They'd find you in town in two days. You can go to the far side of the farm when we see them coming. Besides, I won't let you go."

"Clay," Evan began. "What about your family? Do you want to cause them trouble? You know I'm going to keep on with the meetings, and that means I have to leave."

Clay stood and began to pace. "Jeff, you understand, don't you? If I let Evan go, I might as well roll over and play dead. That would mean this place doesn't count for anything...owning it would be only work, no pleasure. This life has always meant a man was free—anyway, as free as a man could be. Now with the regulations and controls binding you every which way, to turn a friend away because of some stupid rules of an organization that don't mean spit to me anyway, I won't take it. Evan, you stay or you'll be robbing me of my right. My right to have anyone I please on my own land. It isn't often a man gets a chance to take a stand. Don't take mine away from me."

Clay sat down, feeling tired and somewhat surprised at his long speech. But he meant every word.

"I know what you're saying." Jeff spoke softly. "We can hardly do a thing without someone having to put a stamp of approval on it."

Clay could see Evan wanted to move on, but he had made it a matter of principle. Evan was a man to honor principle before practical considerations.

Evan nodded. "Okay. I'll stay for a while, but the minute it causes trouble, I'll leave."

Jeff looked pleased with the decision.

After they left, feeling satisfied by asserting his rights, Clay poured a last drink. As he drank, he thought of the baby and smiled; such thoughts always made him happy. A baby needed a strong man for a father, one that fought for his family. Mark was a good father, and Clay hoped he could grow into the role. When he remembered Diana and his unspoken promise to follow her to bed, he quickly finished his drink.

When he entered the bedroom, Diana was undressed and wearing a velvet robe.

"I'm not going to forgive you for this, Clay," she said softly.

He pulled off his shirt, sat on the bench at the foot of the bed, and began removing his boots.

"I don't know what you mean...don't start with me. It's been a long day and I halfway enjoyed myself." He wondered if she had overheard his late visitors, but didn't think she had. He certainly wasn't going to mention it.

Diana stood with her hands on her hips, glaring at him.

"You think you have me right where you want me, don't you, Clayton. Don't think for a minute I'll stay away from town because of this baby. But I must admit that today in the kitchen with Tracy and your mother, I learned something."

"Hope it was something about cooking." He stood and stretched his arms above his head. He was trying to joke in hopes it would derail an argument. He was relieved she wasn't talking about Evan, another sore spot with her.

"Don't be ridiculous, I don't need to know how to cook. Eva said you won't raise children anywhere but on the farm. She wouldn't be surprised if you tried to sell the lake house. You aren't thinking of doing that, are you?"

He didn't miss the threatening note in her voice. He had thought about moving, but it wasn't the right time to talk about it. Diana sat on the edge of the bed watching as he finished putting on his pajamas.

"My dad had some business with Tom lately. Guess it's handy having a lawyer in the family. Did you know your dad created a trust for us?" he asked, in an effort to change the subject.

"What? What does that have to do with what I asked you?"

"Nothing, I only wondered if you knew any details concerning it." Clay walked to the window and looked over the compound. He never tired of the scene and now in the hours before dawn it was a study in silvery-blue, black, and gray.

"You can ask Jan that question. She's the one that should have gone to law school."

Thinking of Jan seemed to distract Diana for the moment, and Clay continued looking out of the window. He turned and motioned to Diana.

"Come look," he said. "Speaking of Jan, isn't that her car over by the lodge?"

Diana came to his side. "Where? I don't see it."

Clay pointed. "There, next to Jeff's truck."

"Yes, it is." Diana whirled and swept across the room and immediately got into bed. Clay followed her.

"Now what are you mad about?"

Diana didn't answer and somehow Clay felt it was for the best. He really was too tired to argue. Whatever Jan and Evan were doing was none of his business. He had more than he could handle in convincing Diana they would be happier on the farm. In the dimness, Clay smiled. His mother knew him well; he did want them to live on the farm. It was the best place to raise healthy, happy children.

Nine

Clay was relieved they had come through Christmas with no major arguments, but he had no hope of New Year's being the same. Diana stubbornly refused to leave their house. There was nothing to be done short of physically dragging her, and Clay didn't think that would help matters. After Christmas, Diana had delivered her last word on ever living on the farm.

"I absolutely forbid you to think of selling this house," she had screamed at him.

He let the matter drop and attributed her behavior to being pregnant. On New Year's Eve, he dressed to go out by himself. Diana watched from the bedroom doorway.

"Give the old folks at home my best. Tell them I'm not feeling well."

"I'm not going to the farm," Clay answered as he buttoned his shirt.

Diana came into the room and raised an eyebrow. "No? Where are you going?"

"The Country Club maybe. I don't know."

"Why didn't you say that? Wait while I get dressed."

For an instant, he almost hated her. Too sick to spend time with people who cared about them, but full of sparkle and brightness to go where they could impress a bunch of worthless people. Clay quickly grabbed his jacket and hurried through the house with Diana close behind him.

"I'm going alone; maybe you'll feel better when I get back," he called over his shoulder.

Diana's face was red with rage.

As Clay headed for the Club, he marveled at how angry Diana was. Each time they fought, he didn't think she could find greater fury, but lately it seemed she might come close to bursting. Maybe he was being hardheaded about moving to the farm, but they might not have a choice. It was true the harvest had been good, but that year was behind them. Every year was a new game: success or failure waiting there in the fields. He was almost inclined to pray to the earth, the wind, and the water. Primitive people did, and he understood why. No matter how a man contrived and planned, there might come a vicious whim of nature to destroy a whole crop.

Tomorrow was a new year, and battle lines were already drawn. The weather was always a threat but the mighty hand of government was also busy. They had sent revised regulations and controls, particularly about money. Clay tried to keep abreast of every development: local, national, and international. For the past ten years, the international news had had more bearing upon the course of action than even the local weather conditions.

As he drove through town, he chewed his lip, wondering where to turn for help. He'd heard the older men talk about the past and everyone agreed that times were always bad, but Clay couldn't help thinking it was worse now. It had to be, with the increased interference. The last bulletin made him want to rip the console from the wall. He was accustomed to flash communications; information came and went as fast as a man could think. The messages appeared on the screen as the audio blared. If that were not enough, it made printed forms in case no one was in the office.

Sometimes Clay was upset enough to send a protest that reached the center as quickly as their message reached him. However, he knew it was useless. The automated control answered incoming calls and sent an appropriate reply. The first response was always sympathetic, followed by a lengthy text explaining the new order. There was no provision for questions. It didn't matter what the individual thought. It was easier to accept and adjust. However, this time, Clay desperately wished there were something he could do. The International Currency Regulators' latest dispatch had devalued the U.S. dollar again.

It didn't make that much difference if you traded only within the same country, but the conglomerates they sold to had binding contracts with the foreign markets. Now the Sanderson account would be credited with X number of I.C.R. scrip, which in turn would be translated into the corresponding value of his country. It simply meant that no matter what the selling price, by the time their account held the profits, it would buy less than the year before. It was the same old game of inflation, but played on the international scale. The idea was that with a worldwide regulation board, stability should set in. They expected that some countries would suffer before the conversion was complete. The International Currency Regulators' officials assured the world it would finally work. He had agreed it made sense to deal in one currency. However, it wasn't going to be easy while the adjustments took place.

Already Clay was facing reduced profits in the coming year. He wished he could find a way to make Diana understand the problem, but that didn't seem likely. She wouldn't even listen to something as simple as his being worried about the weather. The winter was unusually warm and the prairie wind was dry. Every day he watched the weather station reports. They came in by the minute, if a person had a mind to stay and watch. Each day he hoped for better news. However, no cloud made an appearance over Oklahoma or any surrounding state, and the wind continued to blow. Sometimes, the forceful gusts hit as hard as the aftershock from an explosion. Other times it came in a river-like flow, steady and moaning, curling around people and buildings, but never stopping.

Sanderson land was carefully matted and protected against the sucking, pulling of the wind, but with everything this dry, he wondered how long the best ground cover would hold, even with irrigation. There hadn't been rain since May...only the irrigation system helped the winter wheat to sprout. Clay faithfully sent orders to keep the water flowing at the proper setting. He was glad to have National Grain's water system. They could not survive without it, but the charges were mounting. Something else to whittle away at smaller profits in the coming year. No matter how he tried to control everything, it was like chasing straws in the wind. The few he could grasp slipped through his fingers, and went swirling away with the rest. He had thought life, if not easy, would be simple: marry Diana, make a home for them and work the farm. Their children would grow up on the farm and someday own it. Nothing came easy, but it wouldn't hurt to catch an occasional break.

Even Jeff was acting unpredictably lately. It had something to do with Evan's problem. It rankled him that they didn't trust him enough to explain.

"It's for your own good," Jeff had told him. "The less you know, the less you can be held accountable for. You understand."

Clay had nodded, but he didn't understand. When Jeff didn't leave and shuffled from one foot to another, it was clear something more was on his mind.

"What is it, Jeff? Something else I shouldn't know?" He was being sarcastic, but he was hot and tired.

"I hate to ask, Clay. It's my dad. Simon is getting older and can't get around as good as he once did. It worries me, him living alone in town. There's room in the lodge. Maybe we'd find some chores he could do."

Shame settled over Clay. He liked Simon; there *was* room in the lodge. And Jeff was nearly indispensable. He shouldn't even have to ask if his father could live with him.

"I'm sorry I didn't think of this. Of course, Simon should move in. We'll be glad to have him."

Clay wondered if there were more to it than Simon needing to live with someone. If there were, he wished Jeff would tell him. On the other hand, Jeff might be right; Clay had trouble lying with a straight face. The day after Christmas, when the Council's men came to inquire after Evan, Clay had spoken roughly to them while trying to keep from lying.

"I can't keep track of every man wanted by the Church. I'm too busy to bother with that. Don't waste my time. I'd appreciate it if you'd leave."

Evidently, his method was successful. The men departed, saying they didn't believe Evan would come there, anyway.

As expected, Diana was livid over the trouble Evan had brought to the farm. Patiently, Clay explained.

"There isn't any problem. They don't think Evan is on the farm. They looked around and left. I doubt they will be back."

Several times, Diana tried to catch Clay in an unguarded moment.

"Where do you think Evan went?" she'd ask. "Do you think Jan is hiding him? Could he be hiding on the farm, and you not know?"

It didn't seem right to keep a secret from his wife, but Diana was the last person who should know where Evan was.

Clay tried to think of something to make the New Year worth celebrating, and he didn't need to think very hard. He was going to have a son. The trouble with Diana would pass, and the farm would survive. Things were not that bad; this baby would make it worthwhile. Even though he celebrated the New Year alone, Clay was optimistic for the future.

~ * ~

By the end of January, Clay wondered if he hadn't been whistling in the dark, hoping things were okay. Diana was more sullen than before, but he had no time to worry about it. A mystery had developed in the fields that demanded all his attention.

Not only was the wheat growing slowly, it was dying. The seed sprouted and the ground became covered with tiny, green shoots that grew to about four inches in height before slowing and barely growing. When the blades finally neared eight inches tall, they turned yellow.

Mark, Clay, and Jeff stood on the edge of a field. For a long while no one spoke. Clay's mind churned with questions. Still, what could he ask? His dad and Jeff were also as confused. It was enough to turn a farmer's blood cold. The field was a ragged patchwork. Some areas were a sick brown already wilted to the ground. At this rate, in a few weeks there'd not be a sign of the fall planting.

Mark shook his head. "Never seen such a thing as this in all my life," he mumbled.

Jeff squinted, making the lines of his face even deeper. "Looks dried out," he said. "But there is plenty of water. Nothing wrong with the irrigation."

Clay didn't say anything; he felt sick. It scared him to see the two older men at a loss. In the past, he had used every new technique and worked with the county agency to solve problems. He could always depend on Mark and Jeff's experience. If he mismanaged, they were there to put things right before true disaster struck. Now that security was gone. Years of experience seemed useless in the face of this situation.

Clay shoved his hands in his back pockets and cleared his throat. "Might as well head to the office. Nothing we can do now."

Mark climbed into the truck and Clay helped Jeff load the samples they had taken of the soil and plants. They had brought along large flats and shovels for scooping sections of the wheat in its various stages of deterioration. They used a bore to reach deep into the ground and lift dirt samples.

"Maybe the station can give us an idea what's going on when they examine this," Clay told Jeff as they lifted the last of the flats into the truck bed.

"Maybe," Jeff agreed, but he didn't sound optimistic.

When they returned to the office, Clay poured three cups of coffee and they sat silently drinking. The next move was obvious, but no one spoke of it. Finally, Clay stood.

"No use putting it off any longer. I'll get in touch with the western and southern divisions and get the news from there."

Still, he made no move toward the communication center. Mark set his cup on his desk and looked at Clay.

"I suppose you'd better. Don't worry too much; we got good men there. They would have shot a message to us if they were in trouble."

Jeff nodded in agreement. What Mark said was true. Yet maybe they were trying to handle it themselves. Well, Clay thought, we won't know until we speak with them.

He crossed the room and sat in front of the large video console. He punched in the code for Jim Durbin in the southern district. In an instant, the image of Jim's assistant appeared on the screen.

"Hi, Clay. What's doing?" His cheerful voice made Clay's shoulders relax.

"Is Jim around?"

"No, but I'll patch you through."

The screen went dark and in a second, Jim appeared. He was standing beside a large storage shed, looking into a handheld screen. "Hey, Clay. How are you?"

"We've seen some wilt in our crops. How are things there?"

Jim frowned. "Fine. Is there something I should worry about?"

"I guess not, but keep your eyes open."

As Clay signed off, there was a collective sigh of relief. Mark laughed.

"See," he said. "I knew Jim would have scorched the air if he saw what we saw in a field."

With more optimism, Clay struck the code for the western region.

Chuck Masters quickly appeared, but he wasn't smiling.

"Clay, I hope you aren't calling about a problem."

"Why, is something wrong there?"

"Two days ago, I sent samples of some strange wilt to the lab. I didn't want to contact you until I knew what it was."

Clay described what they had found in the central section and listened as Chuck told the same story.

"I've rechecked the quality of the seed, and done everything I can think of. I won't know more until the report comes," Chuck said.

"Keep us informed," Clay told him. "And we'll do the same. Our samples will go in today...you will know sooner than we do."

As both men signed off, their smiles were weak. Disheartened, Clay swiveled his chair around to face Mark.

"Looks pretty bad, doesn't it?"

"Seems it does," Mark answered. He stood and headed for the door. Jeff started to follow, but Mark turned again to Clay.

"Call Jim and tell him the story. He'll need to keep a sharp eye from now on. There's no reason this thing won't spread. I'm going to the house and pack a bag."

Clay was puzzled and Jeff looked the same. Mark shook his head.

"Don't get upset, I'm not running out on you. Jeff, pack some of the samples. I'll fly them to Amarillo. I'll wait there until someone gives me an answer."

Jeff nodded and hurried away. Worried, Clay frowned. With his heart condition, Mark didn't need to be running around.

"Dad, I'll go. I can wait on answers as well as you."

"No, you stay home and think. Go over every inch of the ground. Study our records, talk to anyone who will listen. You play detective while I'm gone. One of us is bound to find something."

Mark left that afternoon and Clay started searching. He went through the entire operation looking for an answer. At the same time, he gave orders to replant the worst hit areas. It could be throwing good money after bad, but there wasn't any other way. The timing was off, too; still with the crazy weather it might work. Jeff suggested they switch crops in some of the fields; maybe only wheat was susceptible to the strange malady. Clay thought about it for a while; it was a big decision. In the first place, wheat was the best selling, bringing the highest price, and secondly the Sandersons' growing permits were for wheat only. They had been for years.

It would take time to get the permits changed and a new crop assignment. A band of tension tightened around Clay's forehead. He pounded his fist in anger. They were in serious trouble and the regulations were hindering something that might help. He was thankful Jeff was silent. He didn't need any discouraging comments. Jeff had never liked the restrictions and regulations. However, it had seemed the only thing for the agriculture department to do. They accounted for every acre of producing ground. Projections of the number of bushels of wheat, corn, or soy helped stabilize prices. A farmer couldn't simply decide to plant soy when his papers stated wheat. Yet, these were special circumstances. They would surely grant a reassignment, but that could take weeks, maybe even a couple of months. A different crop could mean less profit, and there might even be some sort of government fine, but that was better than no crop.

"Okay," he told Jeff. "See what you can buy on the side markets... corn, or soy, I don't care which. If this mild weather holds, we can get in an early crop."

He couldn't order seed from the regular agency...there would be endless questions and outright denials. By the time the proper forms were processed, they would have lost precious time. The only thing Clay could do was send Jeff to scavenge for seed while he filed the new request. Planting before the permission arrived was risky, but these were unusual conditions. If the agency leveled a fine, it shouldn't be much.

The first three days Mark was gone, no one thought much about it: the testing station was probably busy, and it could easily take a week to determine what was wrong with the samples he had taken in. When the first week stretched into two, Clay began to worry. Every day he spoke with Mark, and he could see the concern in his father's eyes. Mark kept his voice strong and confident, but it didn't fool Clay. Mark repeated the excuses the officials at the station gave. Clay knew it was for his benefit when Mark tried to make them sound reasonable. On the first day of the third week, Mark told Clay he was coming home.

"No need for me to stay any longer. I guess they'll find what the trouble is as well if I'm not there."

Clay agreed. The strain was too much on his father. Waiting was hard enough, but to do it away from home was worse.

"I'll be home tomorrow. Tell your mother to make something special for supper. The food I've been eating isn't anything to brag about." Mark hesitated; he looked tired. "Sorry, son. Seems I didn't do you children much of a favor making that trust. The farm may be more of a burden than it will be worth. Still, if the garden patch isn't affected, you'll always eat."

Talking with Mark further depressed Clay. It was clear that if the experts hadn't given an answer while Mark was there pushing, they wouldn't later. There was nothing to do but wait.

Jeff continued to care for the fields the way he always had, even though it was the wrong time for planting. Still, they had no choice. They crossed their fingers and hoped. However, hope didn't help; the seed Jeff managed to purchase did no better than the original planting. They had to face the fact that this year was a total loss. Clay stayed at the farm night and day during February and lived in a total daze. The world had turned upside down. February was warm and dry and the wind blew from the wrong direction. It came out of Texas, bringing sand and grit the farm didn't need; they had plenty of their own, as every bit of cover died, leaving the ground more exposed than it had been in over two hundred years. Even the thousands of dollars Clay spent on irrigation didn't help.

Simon Taylor walked around the compound and shook his head, pursing his dry, wrinkled lips. "Might be it's a happening again," he said to each farmhand he met. They knew what he meant; Dust Bowl stories were ancient history, but too frightening to forget.

"Simon," Clay said. "Times are different now. When we find what is wrong with the land, we will correct it. After that, the weather won't be a problem. The irrigation system will provide all the water we need just as it always has."

His explanation didn't remove the faraway look in Simon's eyes as he continued to wander on, studying the sky. Simon was easy to dismiss, an old man with old ways. Clay wished his problems were this simple. The dead fields were painful to see—not only a practical farming problem, but also an emotional burden for Clay. When Diana appeared on the office screen, he smiled. A call from his wife should be a nice break.

"Clay, when are you coming home?" Her frown and tone startled him.

"I don't know, sweetheart. Things are no better."

"I see. Never mind. If you aren't here by this evening, you don't need to bother coming home. I'm doing well enough alone."

The screen turned dark and Clay wanted to smash his fist through it. If she thought she could issue an ultimatum, he'd show her he had a few demands, too. He had tried to make excuses for her—she wasn't used to farm life—but there was a limit to his patience. He left the office and headed for town.

When he stormed into the house in Prairie Lake Estates, he found Diana in the living room with Jan and Glenda, the three of them with tall drinks in their hands, smiling, and no doubt gossiping. The sight brought a wave of resentment and anger, along with the possibility that this marriage had been a mistake. The problems on the farm were real; a less selfish wife would be at his side helping.

Clay fought to keep the rage from building. He swallowed hard and forced a smile as he entered the room. "Good afternoon, ladies," he said.

The three turned toward him. Jan's face was a mixture of fear and questioning. She probably thought he was bringing news of Evan and feared it was bad. At least she cared about someone other than herself. He crossed the room to stand before Jan.

"How's my sister-in-law getting along these days? We haven't seen much of you since Evan left. But you could come to visit with the rest of us once in a while."

Jan smiled, seeming immediately to relax. "I've been busy. I hear you have, too."

He tried to stop frowning, and turned toward Glenda. "I hope you'll forgive my appearance, but as Jan says, I've been too busy to give much thought to how I look."

"Never mind, Clay." Glenda set her glass on an end table. "Men seem to get too involved with their work. Sometimes they tend to forget there is anything else in life."

With her last words, Glenda gave Diana a meaningful look. Diana had avoided meeting Clay's eyes, but her mother's words seemed to encourage her. She lifted her head and glared at him.

"That does seem to be the way of it, doesn't it, darling?" She threw the words at him. "Why don't you shower and dress? We can have a nice long visit after that."

Clay wanted to settle things immediately, but it was clear Diana would have her way. Jan and Glenda made no move toward leaving, and even though he was burning with resentment and anger, he kept his head enough to know he'd gain nothing by making a scene. As he left the room, he heard Glenda saying, "As I was about to say, you remember Henderson, the one whose son is a senator? Well..."

Disgusted, Clay entered the foyer and started for the stairs. The world could be falling apart and these women would expect to carry on the same, he thought. Except for Jan maybe; she did seem to care about Evan. He wondered if she knew where Evan was, or if had he kept her in the dark, too. Jeff might have spirited Evan off to one of the crumbling line shacks left over from the days when Mark ran cattle.

Clay stripped off his clothes, letting them fall in a heap on the bedroom floor. He walked into the expansive bathroom...for a second, the whirling water in the sunken tub enticed him, but if he submerged himself into the relaxing waters, he might fall asleep despite his tension. He quickly stepped into the glass enclosure with six revolving showerheads. A tingling spray fell on his body, followed by a flow of soap.

The shower was a good idea; it gave him time to think before meeting Diana head on. He needed to decide what he wanted to accomplish. Clay waited impatiently for the wash to finish and the rinses to begin. The automatic shower made him wonder if people had any choices left...everything was pre-programmed. After the rinse, he was sprayed with an invigorating liquid that set his skin tingling as the drying cycle wrapped him in warm air. When he stepped out, he knew what he would say to Diana. He'd decided to start with the basics. He did love her; she was spoiled, and sometimes bitchy, but maybe it wasn't her fault. It was the way Glenda had raised her. It was a puny love that couldn't stand a few flaws in the loved one. Besides, Diana had a bonus in her favor: she was carrying his child. He wanted them both and he wanted them with him. He finished dressing and started for the living room.

Jan and Glenda were gone, and he hoped Diana was ready to listen to reason. She was lying on the couch, her arms above her head. The area below her waist caught his attention. It was the beginning of March, the fifth month of her pregnancy, and he was impatient for it to show more. He sat across from her and leaned forward, clasping his hands between his knees.

"Do I look better now?"

Diana tilted her head, giving him an appraising look. "I guess, definitely more human. I don't understand why you get grimy. You wouldn't have to leave the office, you know."

Clay ignored her small complaint. "First, I'm sorry for not being home more," he began. "We have a lot of trouble and I couldn't leave while Mark was gone."

"What about after he returned?" she snapped.

"Diana, I'm not going to argue. I talked with you every day and you were more than welcome to come stay with me."

"Ha!" She snorted. "That will be the day."

"We might as well get right to it, Diana. Now is that day."

Diana stiffened. "What do you mean?"

"You remember I told you, or tried to, sometime ago about our financial situation. If the farm has a good year, you and I have a good year. This house and the things you love to buy, they depend upon what comes from the ground. This year there won't be anything. Nothing, because the second planting is as dead as the first."

"Are you trying to tell me we are broke?" Diana laughed as if it were a joke.

"Not broke; we only need to stop spending and wait, work through it. I hate to tell you, but we can't pay the mortgage on this house. I never should have let you talk me into it. If there are a few good years on the farm, we can try for another house. If things go well, I'll build you a new and even better one. The only thing we can do for now is move to the farm."

Diana stood and began to pace, tossing her head in defiance. He almost expected her to roar. She opened her mouth several times, but didn't speak. She seemed too angry for words. She whirled to face him.

"You did this on purpose. You want me pregnant and on that farm. I was a fool; I played right into your scheme. I thought giving you a son showed you how much I love you. That should be concession enough on my part. I know you want to live there, but the baby should compensate for that."

Clay went to her and put his hands on her shoulders. "Stop this; don't say things we'll have trouble forgetting. I didn't do this on purpose. I wish we could keep the house, but we can't spend with no income. Now, go pack. I'm taking you to the farm today. There is trouble enough...don't make a fuss."

Diana glared at him and stormed from the room. He took a deep breath and wondered if he had done the right thing. Diana didn't understand, but things would be okay once they were living on the farm. Clay went into the lounge and mixed a drink. His hand shook, and in the mirror, his face looked pale and drawn. He hated being harsh, but he'd take Diana to the farm by force if necessary. Once she was settled, she'd see it was for the best.

After his second drink, Clay decided he might as well go on with his plan to sell the house. The longer he waited, the more time Diana would have to find some way to forestall it. He put his glass on a nearby end table and stepped to the small communication console. After Clay placed his sell order with a broker, he pressed the button to connect to Diana's bedroom. He wanted to tell her to hurry—patience was not one of his virtues—but a light came on indicating that the unit in her room was in use. He went to the bar and downed another drink. She was probably talking to Glenda, complaining about his brutish manner. It wouldn't do her any good. Her father, Thomas Brockman, was a sensible man and once Clay explained the situation, Tom would uphold his decision.

Finally, Diana stepped into the room. "I'm ready. My bags are in the bedroom. I'll be in the car."

Clay shook his head in wonder. Her elegant tunic trimmed in brown fur wasn't suitable for the weather, or the farm. Nothing she owned was. Only the best suited her. Her clothing, the house and furnishings, most made of natural fibers. Those materials were expensive and in short supply. Clay gathered her luggage and locked the house. As he turned the car around and drove along the sweeping driveway, he glanced at Diana. She was staring straight ahead. He doubted she'd want to talk, but she should know he was selling the house. It would be better to get it over with quickly.

"I've listed the house; I had to. I need to drop the key by the sales office on our way out of town," he finished.

She didn't look at him while he was speaking; she sat straight and stared ahead.

"If you are making one stop you won't mind making another," was her only comment.

"No, of course not," Clay said.

"Fine. I spoke with Dr. Kruger before I left the house and explained my situation to him. He has some pills for me. We can pick them up at his clinic on Fourteenth Street."

Somewhat optimistically, he started toward the clinic. Since Diana had called Dr. Kruger, and not her mother, that could be a good sign. She was making provisions for her stay at the farm.

"What kind of pills?"

"It's some extra vitamins," Diana answered.

Ten

Frank Ivers paced the thick bedroom carpet of his heavily mortgaged home and between deep drags on his cigarette yelled at his wife, Tracy.

"For God's sake, Tracy, hurry."

"In a minute, Frank," she called from the dressing room. "In a minute."

Frank continually glanced at his gold watch and stopped pacing long enough to stub out a half-smoked cigarette. He took a white linen handkerchief and blotted the perspiration from his forehead and upper lip. His stomach quivered with the need of a drink...for an instant he thought about taking a tranquilizer, but rejected the idea. There would be no liquor on his breath with the pill, but it might relax him too much. No, he decided, there was nothing to do but go this round dead sober. He needed sharp faculties to deal with the situation. It was too important to risk even the slightest chance of getting the short end of this transaction. He desperately wished Tracy didn't have to be at the final meeting. He had coached her for hours, telling her to say nothing. Simply smile and be agreeable; he would do the rest. He was nervous, but that was perfectly normal. Realizing it helped him summon his self-control.

He would be fine.

As Frank talked to himself, he did gain some measure of control and it brought a rush of confidence. It was in one's attitude, he decided. Assume the attitude of a successful, forceful individual and other people would see you in the same way. He had to make those two men from Colombia realize they were not dealing with some hayseed fresh off the farm. Frank almost laughed at the thought; the closest he had ever come to a farm was when he visited his in-laws. Still, for some reason Señors Matoes and Salvatierra had the idea he was knowledgeable in matters of land. He had never told them he was a farmer; they seemed to assume it when he contacted them in reference to farmland. Since it might help, he didn't bother to correct them.

It was strange that he was this nervous over the deal. There had been shady transactions in the past where his creditability hung by a spider's web, and he had walked into the meeting with the confidence and composure of a king. Yet now, his palms were damp and his mouth kept going dry, but it didn't take him long to understand why he was having palpations. This time, success was only an hour away. Once they signed the papers and put the payment in his hand, Frank Ivers would have more capital than he'd ever dreamed possible. He marched across the bedroom and jerked open the dressing room door.

"Come on, Tracy, you're giving me a heart attack."

Tracy threw him a threatening look, and fastening the clasp on her gold bracelet, brushed past him. She stopped in the middle of the bedroom and stood before him.

"Well, do I pass inspection?"

Frank looked her over carefully and slowly nodded his approval. Her dress was tasteful and subdued: the right look of prosperity, but not overly excessive. Now, if she could manage to act like a lady, they might make the impression Frank desperately wanted. He quickly checked his breast pocket, making sure the document he needed was there, and hustled Tracy to the car while giving her last-minute instructions. As they drove to the attorney's office in Oklahoma City, Tracy fidgeted in her seat and kept fussing with her hair.

"Leave your hair alone," he snapped. "It looks fine. You keep messing with it, you'll be bald by the time we get there. Sit still; you're making me nervous."

"I can't help it," she whined. "You made me this way, harping on how important it is that I look right and say the right things. If you'd keep calm, I might, too."

Frank knew she was right; he had put the pressure on, but he didn't think Tracy realized how much was riding on this meeting. It was their chance to be on top of the heap. In the past, he had never had enough backing, not enough capital to operate the way he wanted. It was the age-old story...he had to have money to make money. Frank remembered the times when good opportunities came his way, excellent investments. He would spend days trying to interest backers, trying to convince them of the merits of the plan, but nine times out of ten they sent him on his way. However, with five hundred million in gems, he'd at last be in the running.

It had taken him nearly a year to bring the parts together. He had tried to find partners: Thomas and Avery Brockman had been high on his list of prospective investors, but for some reason he couldn't get them excited about it. Maybe it was because of the last gold purchase he had put them onto, but that had been fifteen years ago, and not his fault. He had warned them of the risk. The year after their investment, owning gold became illegal because it was a disturbing element in the world economy. The only legal tender used in buying and selling was that of each country and the scrip issued by the International Currency Regulators. The official regulations on gold made it simply another metal, used only for practical applications suitable to its physical properties. In addition, the regulators barred it from the commodity markets. Possession of the metal required an international permit.

Frank had been a young man at that time, yet he knew human nature. Precious metal had an allure, and no law could make a difference in the way men felt about gold. He had established contacts among men that traded a shade into the darkness, past the light of prevailing laws. There were places to make purchases and safe havens for storage. When a client wished to convert to some other medium, he knew the transactions necessary to accomplish that. It was hardly his fault that Thomas and Avery didn't take his advice on storage facilities. For now, gems were an entirely different matter. Precious gems were still legal if you were a jeweler with a special permit.

Currencies were unstable, suffered constant adjustments with new directives issued nearly every month. It caused a swift traffic in gems, *objets d'art*, and even the forbidden gold. Trading swirled around the globe through a careful and select channel of investors. When Frank had first heard about the men in Colombia wanting to dispose of their collection, it was clear they did not want currency in exchange. They wanted something of higher and more dependable value. This type of transaction suited Frank. First, because if the Colombians wanted scrip or account credits, he was in no position to provide them. Even if they offered the gems below market value, he didn't have the funds. However, he did have access to something that would never lose its value.

As Frank drove on in silence, he grew thoughtful. It was a funny world they lived in. The more regulations and rules governments passed, the worse things seemed to become and the more opportunities there were open to men who operated outside the laws. Guns, for example...any firearm was illegal. Only law enforcement had a few for certain policing actions. The reasoning seemed excellent, and for a while, the crime rate did drop. Until the underground network built their stock of weapons and anyone could obtain whatever they wanted. For a price. The world seemed to operate on two levels. Most of the people were oblivious to the lower one. They praised the new order, saying that things were getting better. Of course, there were a few rough spots, but soon the world would become a second Eden.

In a way, Frank was sorry they were wrong; he honestly wished the bulletins and directives fed into the citizens' homes were accurate.

That with total cooperation, the world could become paradise. But he was a realist and knew it would never happen. Instead, there would be a greater gap between the controlled citizenry and the lawless ones.

Frank shook away the reverie and tried to concentrate on his situation. Even with the gems, it wouldn't be easy. He could not trade them for houses, cars, or even food on the open market. He'd need to convert them to cash, which he'd have to spend quickly before the cash lost value. The only legal place to sell them was to jewelry makers, but there the government controlled the price and amount of each sale. It was a safe way to go, but not the one to make a big profit. The profitable way was to deal with men who still recognized their value as a hidden source of security, an asset that would hold its worth when all else failed. It would take him a long time to peddle them piecemeal, but he would get a good price. Perhaps he would take cash for one small stone to cover immediate expenses. For the rest, he'd stash them away until he found someone willing to deal on his level. The only time it was wise to accept cash was if he could quickly buy some valuable commodity.

What he and his fellow traders engaged in was the ancient form of commerce, bartering. This eliminated the heavy tax that went with every legal transaction. It kept a man's business his own, no record of his every move. It also prevented the loss suffered with every new round of inflation. The trick was to have something others valued to keep its worth high. Frank supposed the time might come when food would be the commodity with the most value. He had seriously considered a hidden stockpile in case things reached that level. For now, the gems were safe enough.

After what seemed an eternity, Frank parked in the lot next to the Ravenswood Office complex that housed the law firm of Bruster, Sherman and Krupp.

"I don't see why we had to come here," Tracy said. "Couldn't Thomas have handled the papers if it's as simple as you say?"

Frank sometimes wondered about Tracy's mental condition. Occasionally, she seemed clever, but at other times, she completely missed the point. What they were doing was legal, but it wasn't something he wanted Garden City to know about. Especially anyone connected with the Sandersons. Of course, it would come out someday, but better later than now.

As they walked through the glass doors into the reception room, Frank put on a confident smile. Señors Matoes and Salvatierra rose from the leather couch where they had been waiting. Frank strode across the maroon carpet, hand extended, to give them a proper greeting. It was hard to keep from staring at the black briefcase held by Señor Salvatierra.

"Gentlemen," Frank said, shaking each of their hands in turn. "I'm sorry to have kept you, but you understand how a wife can cause a delay. Have you been waiting long?"

Both men flashed Frank an understanding smile and glanced appreciatively at Tracy. Frank made the introductions and was satisfied with Tracy's demure response.

Señor Matoes kissed Tracy's hand and turned to Frank. "A beautiful wife is indeed worth waiting for. It has been only a matter of minutes. And Mr. Sherman is with another client, in any case."

Still smiling, Frank sat trying to make small talk and wished Sherman would get his rear in gear. He was certain he would not draw a proper breath until this was over and they had put Matoes and Salvatierra on an airplane to South America. Finally, the receptionist stood and led the four of them into the spacious inner office. They took the offered seats, and Mr. Sherman reviewed the papers on the desk before him.

"I believe these are in order, but we will go over them to make sure there is complete understanding by the parties."

Mr. Sherman handed each man a page for them to follow as he read from the fourth copy.

"This is a simple loan agreement. You gentlemen are, in effect, making Mrs. Ivers a loan against her future inheritance. This is secured by the irrevocable trust established by her father, Mark Sanderson." Mr. Sherman turned to Tracy. "You understand, Mrs. Ivers, by signing this agreement that when you come into possession of your share of the farm, this loan will become due and payable immediately. Otherwise, Señors Matoes and Salvatierra will be the legal owners of your inheritance."

Tracy nodded. "Yes, I understand." Her smile at Frank seemed to ask, how am I doing?

Frank rustled the papers in his hand. "I am sure my wife is aware of the terms. We have discussed them fully."

"Fine," Mr. Sherman said. "If everyone is in agreement, I'll call in my receptionist and secretary to witness the signing."

Frank watched as Tracy carefully signed each line Mr. Sherman indicated. Matoes and Salvatierra put their signatures in the proper place. It was as legal and binding as an agreement could be, and the Colombians seemed satisfied. The only bad minute for Frank had been when Señor Matoes carefully read the copy of Mark's trust. Mr. Sherman assured Señor Matoes that the trust was indeed binding. Tracy was as good as in possession of the land at that moment. The only clause in the contract that gave Frank any worry was the paragraph making the loan payable should Mark in his capacity as trustee of the estate, dispose of the farm. However, Frank was confident the moon would fall from the sky before Mark sold any of the land.

Essentially, this was a sales contract with Matoes and Salvatierra taking possession of half the farm upon Mark's demise. In his previous conversations, Frank had made it as clear as possible that there was absolutely no chance that Mark would ever consider disposing of the farm. Señor Matoes had assured Frank they understood. They were satisfied to commit their assets for the undetermined length of time. It was a good bargain for them. They were getting a sizable piece of farmland that in years to come would be worth a great deal more than what they were advancing now. They were also securing their position in the event things in their own country soured more than they already had. It was the best possible type of contract, one in which each party was happy with the agreement.

The four of them left the office with Frank carrying the copies of the contract. They told Mr. Sherman the final stage of the transaction would take place at a bank with the transfer of funds into Mrs. Ivers' account. Instead, Frank drove to the new, busy Mid-Continent International Transport Center. The Colombians had a room there in the hotel that serviced the travelers passing through the center. They went to Señor Matoes' room. He unlocked the door, let Tracy enter first, and turned his head toward Frank.

"Now we get to the real business, right?" He smiled.

Frank laughed. "That's right."

When seated, Señor Salvatierra for the first time took his hand off the handle of the black leather case he had been carrying. He placed it on the top of the desk, and taking a key from his vest pocket, unlocked the case. Frank held his breath as Señor Salvatierra's slim fingers deftly snapped the catches and lifted the lid. He removed four brown velvet pouches, and setting the case on the floor, put the small bags on the table.

"Go ahead, Mr. Ivers," Salvatierra said. "Open them."

Frank looked at Tracy with a nervous smile. His heart was racing and he hoped to hell it didn't show, and then he found something more embarrassing to worry about. His hands simply refused to stop trembling. It was no time to become unglued and appear unsure in front of these men. Frank hesitated a second and stepped to Tracy's side.

"You do the honors, dear. They are yours."

Tracy looked at him in disbelief and he gave her a small nudge toward the desk in front of a window.

"Why not," she said and took the first pouch in her hands.

One by one, Tracy carefully opened and emptied the velvet bags until four piles of emeralds lay before them. Tracy gasped with pleasure and Frank could scarcely take his eyes from the gems. Their glittering facets caught the pale March sunlight, making them flash between a deep forest color and a sparkling spring green. For a moment, Frank was lost in the wonder of them before he regained his composure. They were only part way through the ordeal. He held the signed papers, the gems were there, but the exchange would not be complete until an appraiser had certified the gems.

Frank had made the arrangements with a man whose knowledge of gems he respected and whose honesty was widely known. Possibly the best quality of this man was his tight-lipped manner. Frank doubted that even the man's wife knew what he did for a living. Harvey West was the great-grandson of a jewel merchant. He was four generations deep in expertise. In Frank's opinion, he knew more about gems than any man alive. However, some jewels had flaws, and so did Harvey, a flaw serious enough to dismiss him from the family firm in New York City. His addiction to drugs made him an embarrassment and a liability. With a liberal settlement, they sent him away from the city and forbade him to return. Frank considered it a stroke of luck to have this man tucked away in the center of the country. Harvey fit in perfectly with his clientele, they accepted his condition, appointments were made and Harvey always managed to appear clearminded and able to perform perfectly.

Finally, Frank felt in control enough to keep from shaking. He scooped up the emeralds and put them into the pouches. He and Señor Salvatierra, with the gems, started for Harvey's apartment. Frank explained that Harvey preferred to see as few people as possible and it would be better for Tracy and Señor Matoes to wait at the hotel.

~ * ~

As the door closed behind Frank and Señor Salvatierra, Tracy sat in a chair by the window and self-consciously smiled at Señor Matoes. He returned her smile and walked to the bar.

"May I mix you a drink? It may make the time pass a bit quicker if we relax."

He gave her a questioning look and lifted a bottle of scotch. Tracy nodded in agreement. He turned away and began putting ice into the glasses.

"I hope this has not been too great an ordeal for you today."

Tracy twisted her gloves in her hands. "No, what makes you think that?"

Actually, Tracy didn't feel any more nervous than she ever did. Life with Frank kept her on the brink of flying apart. Yet, through their married years, Tracy had mastered the art of keeping herself together. Admittedly, others might view her as unstable, but in her own way, she was steady. Instead of facts and reality holding her sanity in place, Tracy had devised a web-like system, strong but flexible. She might appear weak and uncertain, but the ties held. It was a safety net. If she had tried to be a solid immovable thing, Frank's constant chipping would have broken her years ago. By being loosely constructed, Tracy moved and slipped away from the blows, a shaky suspended thing, yet remaining in possession of her parts.

Señor Matoes crossed the room and handed the glass to her.

"I didn't mean to pry, but you seem under a strain. Even now your hand trembles. Is there something about this transaction that disturbs you?"

He moved to a chair on the other side of the room and sat, crossing his legs in a relaxed manner. Tracy wished Frank had not left her alone with this stranger, but she trusted Frank as she always had. She remembered what Frank had told her concerning this deal and how he had cautioned her to watch what she said. She studied Señor Matoes for a minute and tried to find something threatening about the man, but he was calm and smiling. His face and manner seemed friendly. She certainly couldn't sit there and say nothing until Frank returned. She didn't want to appear stupid, or worse... make Matoes think something was wrong with the arrangements. Tracy shifted in her chair and set the drink on an end table.

"Maybe I do seem nervous," she began. "But I usually don't have much to do with business. I leave that to Frank. We have two children; they keep me busy." Tracy was pleased with her answer; it was good to mention the kids. Home and children, that was a safe topic.

"Ah, I see," he said. "And the managing of the land is left to your brother. I understand he is a capable man. I look forward to meeting him someday."

The mention of Clay unsettled Tracy. She had not counted on anyone bringing him into the situation. Yet, it would appear odd if she avoided talking about her own brother.

"Yes, he is." She lifted her glass and took a drink, hoping Señor Matoes would go on to some other subject.

"How does he feel about your decision to divest yourself of your holdings in the family land?" His voice was smooth, but his words put her on alert.

Tracy waved her hand airily to cover the feeling. "Oh, Clay and I have a good relationship. We don't interfere in each other's business. The only thing he really cares about is tending the land."

"I see." Señor Matoes smiled as he stood and took the glass from her hand. "Let me freshen your drink, and you can tell me about your children. I am sure they must be as beautiful as their lovely mother."

Finally, Frank and Señor Salvatierra returned. Tracy could see by the glow in Frank's eyes that Harvey West had confirmed the value of the emeralds. She was growing tired and wished he would hurry and finish with the two men. They each had another drink, Frank's first of the day, she noted with pleasure. Maybe the meeting was ending. She watched as Frank handed over two copies of the agreement, and Señor Salvatierra gave Frank the jewels. To her surprise, Frank acted as though half a billion came into his hands every day. In minutes, Frank's glass was empty. He refilled it and pressed another drink on the two men, which made her nervous. After longer than Tracy thought necessary, Señor Matoes glanced at his watch and announced that, pleasant as the company might be, they must leave to make their flight. When Frank gave Tracy the gems to put in her purse, she hoped no one noticed her sigh of relief.

She was even more relaxed when they accompanied Matoes and Salvatierra to the lounge area of the combination hotel and airport. While they waited for the boarding signal, she felt almost friendly toward the two men. They had seemed nice. Much better than Frank's other business partners. Señor Matoes seemed sincerely interested when she had told him about Robin and Frank Jr. It helped confirm her belief that this deal was the right thing to do.

After the airplane took off, lifting smoothly into the dry, almost white sky, Frank grasped Tracy's elbow and hustled her to the parking lot. When they were in the car, Frank opened her purse and took out a velvet pouch. As he studied one of the emeralds, his eyes glowed.

"We did it!" he cried.

His voice was high and his face pale. For a minute, Tracy was afraid he might pass out. After a bit, he carefully replaced the gem, started the car, and drove from the city. For some time, neither of them spoke. When Tracy judged that he had finally relaxed, she patted his arm.

"You know, I thought they were really nice."

"Who?" Frank asked.

"Señor Matoes and Salvatierra, of course. I got to know Señor Matoes better. Did you know he has three children? Three girls. I think he wanted a boy, but the selection technique was not in use in their country when Mrs. Matoes conceived."

Frank frowned. "I hope you didn't give him our entire family history."

"I didn't say anything wrong! We had to pass the time somehow. Besides, he knew about Clay and my parents anyway."

Frank quickly jerked his head toward her, his eyes narrowing. "What did he ask you about your family?"

"Nothing," Tracy snapped.

Frank's former jumpiness returning made her suspicious. Maybe Frank hadn't been entirely truthful with her.

"Frank," she said hesitantly. "This isn't going to hurt anyone, is it? You told me it wouldn't make a bit of difference to Clay or disturb things at the farm. That's true, isn't it?"

Frank reached across the seat and patted her leg. "Now don't start that again. I promised you this doesn't change anything. The farm belongs to Mark and will until he is gone. Even after that, as long as Eva is around, things will be the same. When it passes to you and Clay, the only difference is that Clay will have a couple of partners in Colombia. He will have exactly the same thing. He'll still have his half. How could that hurt anyone?"

Tracy thought a minute. "Well, why would they want part interest in some land this far away from where they live?"

Frank sighed. "They are very wealthy men and they stay that way by planning ahead. It may be an investment for their children; I don't know. Smart people understand that farmland is the only investment worth anything in the long run."

Tracy's heart began to pound. "Why did we give ours away?"

Frank stopped smiling and the lines deepened around his mouth.

"I told you before. We can't wait that long; we need the money now. If it will make you feel better, I'll buy some land with part of the money. Stop thinking about it, and if you don't want a family war, keep your mouth shut around Clay and your parents."

Frank stopped for a minute. "And anyone else, as far as that goes. Now, where do you want to go tonight? Soon as I get these gems tucked away, we are going to celebrate."

Everything Frank said made sense, Tracy again decided. Now she could redecorate the house, or maybe even buy a new one. She had been wanting a million things. She could take the shuttle to Dallas and do some real shopping. The stores in Garden City or Oklahoma City, for that matter, didn't have much anymore. Still, she'd heard from Diana that Dallas wasn't in much better shape. Everything was scarce and stores couldn't afford to spend money on inventory. Businessmen were foolish... how did they expect to keep customers if they didn't stock the store? They should put the stuff on the shelves, no matter what it cost.

It also seemed unnecessary to keep what they had done from Clay. He would be glad for them; at last, Frank had put a real deal together. He did it on his own; no one helped him. It was ridiculous to wait for years for something that belonged to her anyway. Riding along, Tracy considered the past hours and smiled over how strange men were. They were always willing to gamble; the South American men betting on a profit far in the future, even Clay, for he knew farming was risky. If it never rained again, the land wouldn't be worth anything. Having the jewels was better.

She would do as Frank had said. It would be their secret, because there was a chance it might upset Clay. With the strange weather this year, he probably had enough worry. However, the warm dry weather pleased her. Early spring storms wouldn't delay her shopping trips.

Eleven

Diana spent most of March in the upstairs rooms she and Clay shared at the farm. Pregnancy was her excuse to stay clear of household or farm activities. Sometimes she even managed to beg off appearing for meals. Tillie brought her a tray. Even though she acted concerned, saying how she hoped Diana would feel better soon, Diana heard the disapproval behind the kind words. Tillie's knowing eyes studied her in a way that enraged her. What right did a fat housekeeper have to pass judgment upon her? What did she know of the abject boredom and discontentment? To say nothing of the absolute revulsion Diana felt every time she looked in the mirror or ran her hand over her swelling abdomen. She was a prisoner in her own body. She no longer took pleasure in dressing, and the coddling, condescending way Clay treated her brought on more nausea than morning sickness had. She had to correct the situation, and quickly.

Her very existence was threatened.

Diana reclined on a lounge by the bedroom window, an unread book open on her lap. She could see the bunkhouse and office building, and farther away, the equipment sheds, warehouse, and barns. Beyond that stretched the barren fields, which were producing nothing but misery. The only thing she and Clay agreed upon lately was the land's terrible condition. If she believed in spiritual things, Diana would say there was a curse upon the ground. It had a sickness, and now the disease was spreading to everything. Clay was completely absorbed in finding a cure. As were his father and the other men on the farm. Eva and Tillie went around faithfully doing their chores, trying to keep the atmosphere in the house cheerful, but their efforts made the seriousness of the situation more evident.

She didn't need anyone to help her realize the depth of the problem. She was married to a man that, if a solution were not found, would be nothing but a poor dirt farmer, reduced to scratching for a living on the fringes of what were once lush fields. He might even need to work for the giant corporations that were still in production. Diana had never been poor, and she never intended to be.

She remembered the time she had spent with Fern before her marriage. The memory of her golden dreams and the example of Fern's gracious life were a reproach to her now. Thinking about it brought a bitterness to the back of her throat. Tears stung her eyes, but she set her teeth, clenched her eyes closed, and stopped them. For despite her dreams, Diana was capable of facing reality. Everyone said or implied that she lived in a world made of gossamer and silk...they were constantly trying to bring her down. Yet, deep within, where the real Diana lived, the hard rocks and dry grit of life were more than real. No one understood, except perhaps Fern, that you had to cover life's ugliness with beauty and smooth the roughness with elegance. Most people were fools; they never faced life's harsh reality.

It was knowing how empty and futile life actually was that made her this determined. She accepted the brutal existence squarely, and openly defied it. She would have a lovely house, beautiful clothing, eat nothing but the finest food, and associate with people who appreciated the same things she did. Confined to this bedroom, she was light years away from a gracious life, but this was only a waiting period. There was a way, a way back to her father's house; it would be a small matter to obtain a divorce.

She would start over.

This time she'd make sure her dream would come true. First, she needed to wait a bit and find out exactly what was fermenting in those fields. If it were a slight disorder, easily corrected, it could be better to stay with Clay. There was also the matter of the child she was carrying. Thinking about it, her lips curled in a smirk. In a way, she was the same as the fields. If they didn't produce, neither would she. Diana let her head fall back and she almost laughed, but the laugh was too dry to form an actual sound. Instead, it rattled in her chest, the sound of brittle bones in a wooden box. She detested the waiting and the discouraging reports Clay gave each evening. Perhaps she was foolish to wait, but a small hope lingered. Knowing there was an escape from this trap made her patient, even generous toward Clay. She recounted his good qualities. He was handsome and never failed to satisfy her sexually, and most of the time he could be maneuvered into indulging her.

However, remembering the Prairie Lake house, she frowned. Moving to the farm was abrasive, but losing the house was worse. When they had left, she wasn't too worried, not even when Clay told her they would have to sell it; no one could afford to buy it during these times. She had felt sure it would go unsold and be waiting when Clay resolved this ridiculous farm thing. Who would have thought Frank would find the money? There was something strange about that. Although it was not strange that Tracy should want the house, but that Frank somehow was able to pay for it. How stupid they were to think she would take it any better because the Iverses had bought the house rather than a stranger.

"It will still be in the family," Clay had argued. "If you can't live without it and things turn around, they'd probably sell it to us."

She doubted that. She understood Tracy. The girl always wanted anything she and Jan had. Tracy was a tasteless, unrefined product of farm life. Her pretensions at graciousness were pathetic. Even if Frank would sell the house back to them, she'd not want it. She would hold Clay to his promise of a new and better one. Clay had been delighted with Frank's offer; it relieved him of one worry.

Yet, Diana was revolted at the idea of Tracy using the lovely things she had carefully selected. It was the same as putting a pig in a velvet pen. Still, perhaps that was the only way Tracy would ever be in elegant surroundings.

Diana shuddered as she remembered the last time Tracy had visited the farm. Her hair was straight and cut even shorter, a new style but completely unbecoming, while her makeup screamed in colors too vivid for daytime. It was plain that her dress was expensive, but the cut and vile green material were as tacky as her hair. She had bought the dress to match her new ring, she said. Tracy had extended her hand to display the large emerald set in platinum. Its size was stunning; it took a second before anyone recovered enough to comment on its beauty. They congratulated Frank on his good fortune. Diana wondered if she were the only one who caught his tenseness as Tracy talked about her ring. Yes, there was something more to this than Frank's getting lucky, but that wasn't what concerned her now.

She was anxious to discover where her own fortune and future lay.

Later in the afternoon, when long shadows stretched behind buildings and trees, she heard Clay's heavy footsteps in the upstairs hallway. She quickly grabbed her book and pretended to be reading. He entered, walked to her side, and bending down, kissed the top of her head.

"Are you feeling okay?" he asked.

She shrugged, still reading.

"Well enough to dress and come to supper, I hope."

"Maybe."

"I wish you would," Clay said. "It may be my last night at home for a while."

The idea of his going away irritated her. Not discussing it with her was even more irritating. She stared at him.

"When did you decide this, and where are you going?" she snapped.

"Wyoming, and I decided just this afternoon."

Clay was sitting on the bench at the foot of the bed removing his boots. Diana swung her legs to the side of the lounge and started to stand. She felt a pulling in her leg muscles and a tightness in her back; sitting around was definitely not doing her any good. If this continued, she'd never regain her shape. She pressed one hand against her side and crossed the room.

"I want to go with you."

"No, there won't be any place for you to stay."

"If there is a place for you, there will be room for me."

"Don't you want to know why I'm going?" he asked.

"Why would you need a reason to get away? I know I don't; any place is better."

Clay rubbed the back of his neck and held his head to one side as he studied her. The gesture irritated her. Mark always did the same thing. Clay even held his head at the same angle. She had never noticed Clay doing that before they moved to the farm. It was one more reason for them to leave quickly, before Clay became a living, breathing replica of his father.

"And will you stop that?" she demanded.

"What?" Clay continued rubbing his neck.

"That. Rubbing the back of your neck. You're getting that from your father. Next thing I know, you'll be picking your teeth the way Jeff does."

Clay threw his clothes on the bed and stomped toward the bathroom. "Oh, shit," he said, slamming the door behind him.

Diana shrugged at his vulgarity and went into the hallway to a storage closet, where she pulled out one of her suitcases. If Clay thought he was going on a trip and leaving her at the farm, he was mistaken. She lugged the suitcase into the bedroom, heaved it onto the bed, and opened it. Next, she went to the closet and began studying the clothes hanging there.

"Clay," she called. "What should I take? Will we be seeing anyone of importance?"

She waited a minute and when he didn't answer, she went to the closed door and called again. Her only answer was the sound of the shower. Impatiently, she returned to the closet and began selecting a few things.

Clay emerged from the bathroom looking clean and refreshed, his damp hair neatly combed: a boy ready for school. The look suited him; the longer they stayed at the farm, the more she saw him as a boy rather than a man.

"Well," she began. "What should I take?"

"Nothing. You're not going." Clay took a clean shirt from a drawer and put it on.

Diana flung the blouse she was holding onto the bed. "Why not?" she shouted.

"I'm going there to look for something. We will be sleeping on the ground; I doubt we will go into a town."

"You can't be going hunting. There is nothing to hunt outside of the preserves. And if you are going to one of them, they have perfectly lovely lodges."

"I'm not going hunting for game. I'm hunting for some answers to our problems with the fields. If you had been listening to me, you'd know it isn't only us. Some of the men from the old association have found the same thing in their fields. They aren't getting any help from the agencies, either. Jeff and I are going to meet Doug Hansen in Russell and do some digging around on our own. The problem started farther north and is working its way toward the Gulf. Seems a logical way to see what's going on. Is this a trip that I could take you on?"

Unhappily, Diana had to agree, but she didn't feel any better about his leaving. Maybe she should have paid more attention to what Clay had been telling her. If it were this widespread, it must be something awful, and maybe they couldn't restore the fields.

"What if you don't find anything?" she asked pensively.

"Don't even think that." Clay shuddered. "If we don't find something soon, we'll be in deep trouble."

"You mean the land will be worthless," Diana stated flatly.

"Perhaps. Come on, get dressed and try to act halfway decent at the table. You know everyone tries to be nice to you, but you don't make it easy." Clay stepped into the hallway. "I'll be in the den...don't be too long."

Diana dressed slowly. Things were worse than she had thought. She was smart enough to know that if the ground were dead, they were, too. She sat on the edge of the bed for a minute and put her thoughts in logical order. Her guiding principle was that she would, under no circumstances, be the wife of a penniless man. She'd mostly ignored the conversations she'd heard. Now, she recalled them. Mark had used every contact he had to get answers from the government agencies. Clay had called their old friends, but none of them had any information. The authorities denied knowing anything. However, if they did know, it was something too disastrous to reveal.

Diana stood and went to the dressing table and carefully began arranging her hair, while her mind clicked with facts and conclusions. The Sandersons might be able to lose one year of production, and it was clear they probably would, but more than that would ruin them. They couldn't sell the land because everyone would know it was useless. Diana bit her lower lip and slowly pushed a hairpin into place. She might be able to weather one year of no harvest, but it certainly wouldn't be the time to have a baby.

At the dinner table, she encouraged the conversation. Clay seemed pleased, but she didn't do it for him. She was trying to learn more. Everyone seemed in good spirits, but it was simply their way of putting on a brave front. That evening as Clay packed his gear, he explained more about the trip.

"We're going to take the truck. Flying would be faster, but we'd have to file with the aviation authority and account for the fuel. Besides, we agreed it would be smarter to keep this trip as quiet as possible."

Alone in their rooms, after Clay went to help Jeff load the truck, Diana dug to the bottom of her lingerie drawer and reached for the pills she had gotten before leaving town. She slowly read the instructions and returned them to their hiding place. She had heard Clay promise his father he would call the minute he knew anything. That was the call Diana would wait for, too. If Clay found the reason for the crop failures to be as terrible as she suspected, that call would make the decision for her. She would use the pills in the drawer and be free from the Sanderson entanglement.

When Clay came to bed, Diana was especially sweet. She wanted to send him away confident of his marriage and unsuspecting that he might not become a father. He kept explaining how much he was counting on finding a reason for their trouble in the fields.

"The truck is loaded and we'll take off early in the morning. One hell of a lot is riding on this," he told her.

Diana patted his arm and thought, more than he realizes.

~ * ~

Clay had been gone for two days when Diana heard the commotion of someone bursting through the front door. She hurried to the stairs and to the landing to listen. It was Jan, and she sounded short of breath.

"I have to find Evan. Right away. Where is he?" Jan asked Eva.

"I honestly don't have any idea. You'll have to check with the men. Although I doubt they'll know. Jeff is the only one that keeps track of him."

For a second, Diana was furious. Evan was still at the farm. It shouldn't surprise her. What could she expect from Clay and his family? It was one more reason to break the connection. She continued down the stairs and entered the living room.

Jan's appearance surprised her. She hadn't seen her sister for a few weeks and Jan seemed to have lost as much weight as Diana had gained. Jan's face looked drawn, with deep lines framing her mouth. Her clothes looked like she had picked them in the dark. Diana went to her sister, put her arms around her, and kissed her cheek.

"What's this about? Now, now," Diana soothed. "Has Evan left you? Well, it's no big thing; he never will amount to anything but trouble. I hope this will put an end to your involvement with him."

Diana turned to Eva. "Could you have Tillie bring us some tea? We'll be in the den."

For an instant, there was a tiny flash of resentment in Eva's eyes, but the usual smile replaced it and she started for the kitchen. Jan frowned, but she followed Diana into the den. As they sat down, Jan took a breath, closed her eyes, and appeared to regain control. It was amusing to see Jan in this state. The logical, controlled sister with the answers to the world's ills, undone by a lover. Diana remembered what Fern had said about Jan changing when she found a man she really cared about rather than pursuing her noble crusades. Diana smiled...maybe now Jan would show some sense and start thinking about her future and securing a position in the world.

"Sit and relax for a minute," Diana told her. "You look perfectly awful. Nothing can be this bad. Once you get over these ridiculous feelings about Evan, you will see the wisdom of picking your men on more than what they are involved in."

A confusion of expressions passed swiftly across Jan's face. Finally, a calm seemed to settle there, and she leaned back in her chair and smiled.

"How have you been feeling? Everything going okay with my nephew? I bet Clay is still walking on air; I know the whole family is thrilled. Even Mother and Daddy have seemed to catch the enthusiasm over this baby."

Diana waved her hand in disgust. "I really don't know why everyone goes crazy over a baby."

Tillie brought in a tray with the steaming teapot and two cups and saucers. There was also a platter with some small cheese sandwiches and dainty chocolate cookies. Tillie smiled at Jan and set the tray on the table beside Diana.

"I fixed you a snack to go with the tea. Eva said you looked tired. Relax and drink that tea; it will help. It's my own special herb blend, make you feel fit in no time."

"Thank you," Jan said. "Maybe you're right. I should rest a bit."

Diana frowned and started to pour the tea. "Tillie, you may go now. We don't need anything more. And close the door as you leave, please."

Tillie's heavy jaw set in a hard line, and her eyes lost the softness they had when looking at Jan.

"Certainly," she said, leaving the room.

Diana clicked her tongue. "How impudent she is. It's Eva's fault. She treats Tillie like one of the family. Now, tell me about it. Did you and Evan fight? When did you see him last?"

Jan lifted a cup and slowly sipped the tea before answering.

"We haven't argued," she said. "It's something much more serious. I don't expect you to be very sympathetic; I know how you feel about Clay hiding Evan on the farm."

Diana's chin quivered and her eyes blinked rapidly. Now everyone knew Clay had defied her wishes. She fought to keep the anger down. She would never learn anything by letting Jan know how angry she was.

"Oh, Jan, I don't have anything against Evan; it's the trouble he creates. You know the Church brought sanctions against the whole Sanderson family and unfortunately, that includes me. I could never understand Clay's attachment to him. What is going on with him now?"

Jan set her teacup on the table. "Each week we meet in a different place. It really has been hard on some of the members, but it is amazing how they find a way to be there. Jeff has been attending... he brings Simon. I can't tell you what an inspiration that old man is. He's been through a lot in his life and still he holds firmly to his beliefs."

Jan's face took on an intensity Diana found disturbing. She picked up the platter of sandwiches and held it toward Jan.

"Maybe you should have something to eat," she said.

Jan waved the platter away. "No, the tea is fine." She leaned toward Diana. "Have you ever really thought about God? I mean about our beginning. Where the human race is heading. Don't stare at me, Diana. I know what you think, that I'm always off after some cause. It's because I'm looking for the answer. A way to help people, bring them a better life. The world is in trouble. When you use the Bible as a guide, it makes everything fall into place."

Diana drew a deep breath. Jan hadn't changed a bit. If anything, she was more involved in this current fad. The only thing Diana could agree with her sister on was that things were a mess. The situation could turn dangerous. Evan running around the countryside...such a lunatic could bring ruin on them. She wished they had never heard his name. For an instant, she remembered she had introduced Evan to her family. The thought swiftly vanished; she had had the good sense to distance herself from him.

Diana reached across to pat Jan's arm.

"Jan, it hurts me to see you this way. Can't you forget Evan? Go away for a while. Daddy will send you anywhere you want to go. If you don't want to take a trip alone, I know Mother would be thrilled to accompany you; I'd go if I weren't in this disgusting condition."

Jan looked away for a minute before turning to smile at her. Diana wasn't sure she understood the smile...it seemed a bit sad.

"I'm sorry, Diana, I didn't mean to upset you. You don't understand, but I'll pray that someday you will." Jan stood. "I should go, it's getting late, and I must find Evan before this evening."

"Don't go," Diana pleaded. "Clay is away and this place is only bearable with him here. Stay and have dinner with me. Why is it important to find Evan today? If you insist on this madness, I'm sure he'll be around tomorrow," she said sarcastically.

"Maybe he won't, if I don't find him. I have to warn him he'll be walking into a trap tonight. Somehow the agents have found out where this meeting is and they are going to be waiting there."

"What about the other members?" Diana asked. "You can't warn everyone. How far does your righteous concern go, only to save Evan?" Diana studied Jan to see how she would get around leaving Evan's followers to walk into trouble.

"I thought about that," Jan said. "But if Evan isn't there, the agents will have a hard time proving it isn't a simple social gathering. Everyone knows the risk. I'm doing the best thing possible by finding Evan and keeping him away. Besides, I've notified several of the members and they are getting the word to the others."

As Jan and Diana walked through the foyer toward the big front door, Eva came in from the dining room.

"Oh, Jan, are you leaving?"

"I'm sorry but I have to find Evan. I've already seen Simon; I guess I'll ask Mark next. Do you know where I can find him?"

"He might be in the equipment barn; there's not much to do right now but work on some of the machines. Let me call him for you."

Diana stood silent as Eva called Mark. Were they crazy? It would be better for them to have Evan put away. Evan's teachings blinded Jan, but why had the rest of them fallen under his spell? Clay was willing to risk their standing in the community, and Mark and Eva were evidently willing to go along. It was easy to understand Jeff's involvement. He was an uneducated farmhand. His father had preached the same brand of insanity. Jan should know better. Perhaps her advantages had given her a perverted sense of guilt. That could account for her self-destructive desire to provide for the rest of humanity.

They waited in the living room for Mark. When he came in, Jan explained about the need to find Evan.

"Maybe you should go with her, Mark," Eva said. "With two looking, you'll stand a better chance. Too bad this happened with Clay and Jeff gone."

Jan looked relieved over the suggestion. Mark patted Jan's shoulder.

"Don't worry, we'll find him."

As Mark and Jan left, Diana and Eva stood at the window and watched. Mark drove his truck toward the long driveway with Jan's car close behind. Diana cast a sidelong look at her mother-in-law. Eva continued to stand at the window, the afternoon sun bringing into sharp focus each line on her round face. The wisps of gray hair that curled around her face turned silver in the golden light. Eva wouldn't take the pills to keep her hair its original brown. It was an unattractive shade, but certainly better than the gray streaks of age.

"Why did you suggest Mark go with her? Isn't it bad enough that Jan's associating with Evan? Aren't you afraid Mark could be getting into more than he can handle? Hiding Evan is one thing. I tried to make Clay see reason, but I can't fight the whole family. You are taking a big risk in interfering with the Church's actions."

"Mark can take care of himself. Besides, he needs something to do, and Evan is a friend. We don't desert friends."

"Oh, Eva, you know Evan is slightly crazy, and a troublemaker."

Eva frowned. "He hasn't caused any trouble. They won't let him alone. They aren't very smart; keeping after him is fanning the sparks. If they would drop the matter, it might die. Take me, for instance. I haven't thought of the things Evan talks about for years. But now, if they're trying this hard to put an end to his teaching, there might be something to it."

"Well." Diana sighed. "I'm going upstairs to try to forget the whole thing. Please let me know the minute Clay calls."

Diana left her mother-in-law standing at the window and trudged up the stairs. The rest of them seemed to have lost their minds. They obviously couldn't see that, other than this problem in the fields, world conditions were getting better. Yes, some countries were unsettled, but there were wonderful achievements. According to the latest reports, two thirds of the world had adequate food, clothing, and housing. She had heard endless boring conversations between her father and his brother, Avery. They were sure the new system would finally put an end to hunger. It was only a matter of time until the backward nations came into this new era of plenty.

They admitted that the world was in the throes of a monetary upheaval, and annoying aggressions kept breaking out between nations, but these were simply growing pains. Anyone could see things were heading toward peace and a world of plenty. The only things delaying it were a few deranged dissidents such as Evan. However, they couldn't stop progress.

The Church had been the first to realize the only way was to unite. There were churches in every town, city, and country. It only took uniting every type of religion. After that, it was simple to distribute food and other benefits. If it kept the troublemakers in line, and the poor satisfied, it was surely to her benefit. She had a plan and didn't see why the Church's business should affect her. She might even find a way in which it could assist her ambitions.

Clay had called every evening since leaving, and Diana eagerly awaited his calls. Sometime very soon, she hoped, he would have some news. At that time, she would know what to do.

Twelve

By six-thirty, Evan had completed his chores in town. It was the first time since Christmas he had moved freely in Garden City. Because of the search, he had remained on the farm, moving from one spot to another and not letting anyone know exactly where he slept. He'd come into town only after dark and under Jeff's protective cover. Jeff and Simon would sit in the front of the car and Evan always kept low behind them. He hated the arrangement. He felt a bigger coward than ever, but it seemed necessary and it had been successful. Now, with Jeff away and Simon not feeling well, Evan came alone. He left the farm in the afternoon, making time to visit with Ted and Laurie before the meeting. Laurie was pregnant and not doing well; Ted had asked Evan to come see her if possible. He only stayed a short time, but it had been good seeing Laurie again. She had missed the last six meetings and Ted was worried about her.

After leaving Laurie, Evan went into Simpson's Department Store in the middle of town and bought a pair of pants and a shirt. He only had two changes of clothing and they were almost threadbare. It gave him a feeling of confidence to openly walk in and make the purchase. Not one head turned to look at him, and he wondered if his sneaking around had been necessary. Maybe Church officials thought he'd left the area after the first raid. He laughed softly as he thought how he would feel to find he was running and no one was chasing. When next he saw Jeff, he'd tell him they didn't need to be as cautious. Perhaps they had nothing to fear. If he kept telling himself this, in time he might believe it.

Driving along Seventeenth Street, Evan was happy; it had something to do with making the trip alone, which restored some of his self-esteem. Still, it was a relief to see the sun sink lower; the night would give him more cover. He wished he knew himself better. He'd even settle for understanding the fear that he kept deeply hidden. Were other men this afraid and simply clever at concealing it, or was he abnormally apprehensive? He despised the emotion and considered it an affliction. He had other faults, but they didn't produce the disdain this one did. He was determined to overcome it.

In the dead of night, Evan would pray for God to remove this feeling or to give him the courage to handle it better. Yet, at the thought of prison or other punishment, his skin went icy and crawled with terror. He read the Old Testament prophets, searching the ways in which they handled adversity. The old Book of Martyrs should have been an inspiration, but it only made him shudder in fear and pity for those poor souls.

There was still an hour and a half until meeting time; the prepared lesson was in a folder on the seat beside him. He couldn't drive around that long; instead, he headed for the park by the lake. It would be peaceful there and perhaps he would go over the lesson one last time. He parked behind the clubhouse to hide the car from the park's entrance, and lowered the window. Yet, as he opened the folder with his notes, his mind wandered. A small breeze fluttered the papers and he placed them on the seat.

He enjoyed teaching. Even if he had not found this urgent, important message, he might have gone into secular teaching. It was a pleasure to help people expand their minds, and it was a great privilege. Despite the turmoil and trouble, the world was a wondrous place. He would have felt this even if he were not a Christian. Knowing that it was God's creation made it even more awe-inspiring. Perhaps that was why teaching was important to him. He knew something simply too glorious to keep to himself. His need to speak was akin to a compulsion. Despite the fear of where this might lead, the driving force was constantly with him.

The wonderful news about Jesus filled his every waking minute. He could not keep still; he must tell helpless, lost people that there was hope. The world was searching for someone to bring order and end the chaos. That was one of the reasons Unity Council had an easy time bringing the denominations together. They offered the hope of harmony and peace, the elusive dream of a near perfect world. The Council presented itself as an organization willing to take on the responsibility of caring for mankind. National leaders were quick to see the advantages in doing the same thing. Unity would finally bring about a world where hunger and pain were gone, providing each person with every necessity, leaving them free to pursue happiness.

The stage was set. The props were in place, awaiting that one magnetic personality who would bring the parts together. Newscasts made Evan want to cry. People were willing to surrender personal freedom for the impossible promises made by a few men. Couldn't they see that once the chain was around their ankle, nothing could break it? It seemed people mistook evil for good. Their vision clouded, they constantly wanted to believe others actually had their best interests at heart. Evan admitted that he saw the worst in people, and still he loved them. It was a tug of war: condemnation with the offer of salvation.

As a small boy in California, he had questioned people's motives.

His mother, Lilla Zellmer, had been a beautiful woman. He always thought of her in the past tense as if she were dead. To him perhaps she was. Certainly the haggard, thin gray woman of today bore no resemblance to the round, shining blonde his mother once was. For years, her physical beauty resisted the damage of drugs and the degrading misuse by lustful men. In the end, her outward image became a portrait painted by every self-destructive device.

His earliest memories were of the women who cared for him. Most of them were kind, but none lasted long when subjected to his mother's harsh demands.

Hung over, wearing some flowing silk robe, she'd call for her son. "Bring him to me," she'd cry. "Where is my baby?"

The current nanny, who had washed, dressed, and combed him to perfection, quickly presented the small boy to his mother. Standing near her chaise longue, he'd stare wide-eyed at this queen on her throne. She'd beckon him with long fingers tipped in red.

"Come to Mama, darling."

Hesitantly he'd walk to her side. The fifteen minutes or less she'd spend fawning over him usually ended with a harsh critique of the nanny.

"Is he eating well? He seems too short for a four year old. Where did you get these pants? They are awful."

After she'd smother him with kisses, she'd send him away until the next command appearance. Along with the women his mother employed, there were tutors. Some were good and some were not. He knew no other life. Yet he sensed that something was terribly wrong. He was never sure if it was something he'd done, or the whole situation.

When he was five, Evan came to know that his parents were in the entertainment business. His father, Harmon, was as handsome as his mother was beautiful. His hair, a few shades darker blond than hers, merged with the honey tint of his skin. Women grew weak in the presence of this tall, bronze Adonis. Their circle of friends called them the Golden Couple. Indeed, it seemed to be true, for not only did their looks resemble the precious metal, but also everything they touched turned to gold. The films they made played around the world on every type of viewing device. His father was the first to take Evan to a film studio. Harmon produced movies and his mother was usually the star. People smiled and almost bowed as he and his father walked the wide hallway to a stage where his mother was working. His father put a chair off to one side and set him on it.

"There now. Watch and learn. The human body is beautiful and every function of it is an act of creation. Pure art," he had said.

What Evan saw in the studio was the same as he'd witnessed at home where various men were in constant attendance, performing with both his parents. Sometimes, young girls were involved. He wondered why they didn't simply film that rather than repeating it on a stage across town. When he had voiced this observation, his father had laughed.

"The difference? One is pleasure, the other business. You'll understand in time."

By the time he was fifteen, Evan knew everything about his parents. They never denied themselves anything. Money was never a problem. Harmon and Lilla Zellmer were constantly in the news. Evan's teenaged friends were openly envious.

"It must be heaven to have your parents," one girl had said.

He'd answered her with a shrug. Having everything somehow felt wrong. It made him ashamed, angry. He confronted his mother.

"Why do people pay to watch you do things they can do themselves?" he'd asked her.

She'd tossed her head and laughed. "But, darling, they can't do it half as well. Besides, they lack nerve and imagination. To say nothing of beauty."

The Zellmers were the brightest, most innovative of young moviemakers. Occasionally critics accused them of encouraging immorality. Harmon took advantage of the attacks. He produced what he called a documentary showing that repressing natural urges brought on mental illness. The film started with the story of Adam and Eve, the parts played by Harmon and Lilla. Everything was perfect in the garden until, in this version, the couple's conscience became corrupt, causing them to consider nudity sinful. Their heads bowed in shame, they covered their bodies with animal hides. The killing of animals the first evil. From there, the film portrayed mankind's downward plunge. It recounted the horrible chapters in history and linked them to a lack of personal freedom.

As the film ended, it returned to scenes of the Garden, making the argument that men could once again have this life. The answer was simple and completely natural: remove the false emotion of guilt and set the human spirit free. Forbid it nothing. A dark, repressive way of thinking was what had brought on the world's problems. Whatever a person desired, since it sprang from within him, could not possibly be wrong. It was perfectly natural. Thus came the title: *Nature Perfected.*

In the six months immediately after the film's release, a flood of reporters, doctors, psychologists, and clergymen spent hours extolling its virtues. They examined mental illness and criminal activity in the light of repressing natural urges. If allowed to develop unfettered by conventional morality, the person would remain sane. He'd have no reason to commit criminal acts, which were manifestations of suppressed anger and rage. People given freedom to act on their natural urges would not go mad or use harmful ways to express themselves. The film clearly showed that to defy nature caused man's ills. A few voices throughout the country asked, what is the function of the human conscience? They received a firm, swift answer. The mistake was in thinking the tyrannical voice was a force for good. Instead, this oppressive, guilt-ridden part of man created evil.

The proof was within any man's grasp. Deny the voice of guilt, make it a habit to indulge any natural urge. This practice would soon silence the harmful restrictiveness. Using this method proved mankind could overcome the dark force we call conscience.

An innocent child is unblemished in thoughts and actions until taught to obey a restraining conscience. Evan had listened to his parents' teachings. Everyone he knew agreed with them, yet he became more confused. If what his parents did was natural, where were the good results? He had watched their bodies fail under the strain of liquor and drugs. His father went first. Perhaps his indulgence was greater, or maybe Lilla was less susceptible to destructive elements. Not that they didn't try to save him, but it was past human doing. The lean, hard body that had once sent hearts racing looked bruised and bloated. Small red veins streaked his piercing eyes and finally they became gray and dull. Harmon tried every known medical treatment. Nothing helped.

After they buried him in a velvet-lined, silver casket, Evan was certain his father had been wrong. Harmon and Lilla had gotten everything twisted, and he desperately wanted to know the truth. He continued to live with his mother, who pretended she was still a blazing star. She refused to acknowledge what had killed Harmon. If anything, she grew more indulgent. She spent large amounts on lavish parties, supplying her guests with the latest mood-enhancing drugs, and new sexual entertainers. Lilla's friends continued to insist that she only grew more beautiful with each passing year.

When his mother remarried, the man proceeded to lose the family fortune. Faced with hard times, Lilla tried to work for other studios, but her one talent was gone. The loss of her beauty and position turned her sullen and bitter. She blamed the men at the studio for using her and burning her out too early. The vileness of her wrath spread to the world at large; there were scenes in famous restaurants and airports. Unflattering pictures appeared in every news media. Evan was past feeling ashamed...public opinion didn't matter. He tried to talk to his mother; he asked her how their lives had come to ruin. She sneered at him and turned away. He felt torn between love and revulsion. As he grew older, it tested his loyalty. It was hard to feel anything but disdain for Lilla, which brought on attacks of guilt.

Even Evan's body drove a wedge between him and his mother. At eighteen, he was more beautiful than either of his parents had been. Everything had doubled in Evan. His coloring was between the delicate platinum of his mother and Harmon's brilliant bronze, producing a true shining gold. Perhaps that was why his mother could not stand to look at him. He was a mocking reproach in her eyes. This hurt him until he learned to sear his feelings and seal his expressions. He became what many called him: a golden statue. Yet safely hidden away was a desire to find the truth, the meaning of life. It had to be more than the tangled, pain-filled lives of his parents and their friends. He supposed he would have stayed at his mother's side longer, but the pressure to take her place in films grew too great. His constant refusal enraged his stepfather and turned his mother further away from him. Evan was far from finding the answers he sought, but he was positive that following his parents' example was wrong.

"What are you going to do with your life?" his mother constantly harped.

For a while, his answer was always the same. "I don't know."

"You'll never know sitting around the house or staring at the ocean. Four producers have made offers; the least you could do is bring in a bit of money! I suppose you are too good for that. You might as well be a monk, the way you live."

"A monk? What do you know of how they live?" He had laughed.

However, her chance remark seemed to have bounced around and hit an unseen target. His mother had unintentionally knocked over a first thought and sent the others click, click, clicking in his mind. He had already rejected the material world. With nothing to replace it, his days were void; he lived in a place where there was no time or defined space. It left him suspended in emptiness. A monk's bare cell could not be emptier. In his world, where nothing existed, the idea burst like flame in pure oxygen. Why hadn't he thought of it before? It was everywhere. Unity Council was constantly in the news. There were conferences and seminars. In every country, national leaders met with religious representatives, uniting to solve problems that beset the world. The lives of those people had meaning. He tried to remember what he had heard about the Church and had paid scarce attention to.

Timidly, he made his way to the closest church. As he spoke with Reverend Mathews, his unworthiness made him hesitant and fearful. How could he expect to be welcomed into the religious community, considering the world he came from? Reverend Mathews had laughed kindly and put his hand on Evan's shoulder.

"You are a true innocent, my son. Haven't you ever heard that Jesus came to seek and to save that which was lost? Our doors are wide open. Your inquiring mind has brought you to us, and we will not turn you away."

His last year in high school, Evan studied the Church more than his secular lessons. Reverend Mathews was elated over his newest convert. He spent hours explaining Church doctrine to Evan. Many evenings they sat in the small garden behind the rectory where Mathews opened a glorious world for Evan, a world of peace and prosperity where each person achieved to the limit of his abilities. The Church's duty was to teach everyone how to reach this spiritual realm and create heaven on earth. Evan had been lost in a spiritual desert, dying of thirst; the message was as life-giving as a cool, crystal-clear spring. He could not get enough; he would make this his life's work. In a world crowded with conflict and shifting values, it was the only worthwhile endeavor. He would spread the message of hope for a better future. Serving in this manner was worth any sacrifice. Yet, far from his making a sacrifice, the way was extremely easy.

The Unity Council was actively recruiting young people to serve in The Army of God, a great movement to enlist workers in God's vineyard. Lilla had cried and pleaded.

"If you want to help someone, stay with me, where you're needed."

"I can't. The work is too important. We have to spread the message."

"You are a fool, Evan. They will use you and throw you away."

As he'd walked from the house, she followed him, her face twisted in anger.

"Go and be damned! When you crawl back, you'll know I'm right!"

Her pleading and threats did not move him. He was deaf, dumb, and blind to everything other than the new creed he had found. When Evan boarded the flight for a seminary in Dallas, his spirit flew higher than the ship that carried him. There was a bright, shining future for the human race and Evan would help bring it in.

The only ripple upon the smooth voyage into his new life came when he announced that he was changing his name. The divinity school's disapproval shocked him. The dean called him to his office. As Evan entered the room, the thick carpet muffled his footsteps. Leather-bound and gold-lettered volumes filled the tall mahogany bookcases. The dean sat behind a polished desk. Light pouring in the windows behind him put a shine to his halo of white hair, while leaving his face in shadow. Looking around the room, Evan felt it was the center of virtue and knowledge.

"Sit down, my boy," the dean said. "It has been brought to my attention you are contemplating a name change. Can you tell me why you want to do this?"

Evan hesitated. The dean's question gave him pause, but he still knew it was the right thing to do.

"I want to break from my past. You teach we are new creatures in Christ. That is what I want to be, a new creature. Keeping a name my parents made famous seems wrong."

The dean listened silently, studying the tip of the gold pen he held. Evan watched his face, trying to judge what effect his answer had. The dean raised his head, fixing his gaze on Evan.

"Did you ever consider the good your family name might do? It is a name recognized by a great many people throughout the world."

"Yes," Evan broke in. "But that name doesn't stand for the right message."

"Ah, but perhaps it does in its own way. Their universal message was one acceptable to people of every faith. They too were striving to bring enlightenment to a dark world."

Evan frowned and looked at the floor.

"You mean the film about man's nature."

"You must admit they exposed the human condition. They were seeking to raise expectations, to show the possibilities of a perfect world."

"That was show business. Done for money."

"Does that matter? How can it when the goal is this important? Through the ages, religion and entertainment have always had things in common...spectacle and pageantry. Both endeavors need many of the same qualities. Keeping your family name will draw people. Think of the ways to advertise your ministry. For instance"—he spread his hands as if displaying a banner—"famous producer and actress produce their finest work, a son dedicating his life in the service of the Church."

"I don't mean to be impolite, but what harm will it do to be called by another name? I intend to do this."

The dean sighed and stood, shaking his head. "If it means that much to you. What are we to call you?"

"Evan Hunter. I am a hunter, searching for the truth. It suits me."

The dean escorted Evan to the office doorway.

"Interesting. We'll see what can be made of that. You may not see it, but a bit of drama from your background seems to linger."

Evan wasn't sure what to make of the dean's last remark, but it didn't matter. He'd taken a name that meant something to him and it would help put his past behind him. It pleased him that Unity accepted his new name.

However, he hadn't expected the notoriety.

The college gave a twisted press release that made him sound pious, which was not his intention. Items in the secular media and the religious publications highlighted the decision he had made. None of the reporters spoke to Evan, and he was grateful they didn't. The stories made him appear noble and self-sacrificing, and showed the Church upholding the highest spiritual goals. They portrayed him as a young man renouncing his advantages in favor of taking a place among less well-known workers.

The dean gave reporters a statement. "We respect this young man's pure motives and feel he brings honor to this place of higher learning."

Alone in his room, Evan had puzzled over where he had gone wrong. He never intended to call attention to himself. Finally, he dismissed it as a misunderstanding. He had evidently failed to make the dean understand why he wanted to be Evan Hunter.

Soon the novelty wore off and Evan spent days and evenings in study. There was required reading of selected religious writers of the past and present. Studies of history highlighted civilizations' past failures, with outlines to map the needed changes. Along with this, the students carried a full schedule of economics, political science, literature, and psychology. The seminary produced well-educated young men and women. If they were to be leaders, they must possess the knowledge and ability to compete with other highly educated individuals.

The first two years passed swiftly. He had completed the required subjects plus two electives in Greek and Hebrew and a bit of Aramaic. Latin had been required, but the course gave the student only a passing knowledge of the language. In the third year, to some raised eyebrows, he continued with Greek and Hebrew. Over the objections of his professors, he gained the ability to study the Bible in the original languages. His teachers told him the study was unnecessary; the currently revised edition was more to the point and needs of the present day. Unconvinced, Evan continued the study and discovered discrepancies in some interpretations. Not being able to reconcile some of the Church's teachings with the Word puzzled him. Finally, his concern turned to anger. Was there no truth to find?

He'd come to the school believing it held the answer and was willing to commit totally to its work. God's Word was infallible and to be taken literally. His problem with the Church's teachings was similar to the situation he'd had with his parents. What they advocated did not bring the results they promised. The Church preached a religion based on truth, but twisted it enough to shift the emphasis from God to man. The Church and his parents promoted the idea of an earth perfected by man's efforts. Yet, he was new to the Bible; others had studied for years...perhaps he was wrong.

One morning as Evan sat at his desk, tired and scarcely able to read the words before him, he threw his pen down and pulled open the window shade, letting in a pale gray light. The clouds on the horizon were pink with an apricot under-glow. The sun would soon rise, and though he had pondered the puzzle through the night, he had no answers. The passages and commentaries he had read did nothing to dispel the confusion. Paul writing to Timothy came to his mind. Paul was warning Timothy of false doctrines, "having a form of godliness, but denying the power thereof: from such turn away."

Evan grabbed his Bible, and with the eagerness of a scientist on the brink of a great discovery, he quickly turned to the third chapter of Second Timothy, where Paul told Timothy that in the last days perilous times shall come. Evan's eyes devoured each sentence. "For men shall be lovers of their own selves." The chapter continued, "No natural affection, trucebreakers. Traitors, lovers of pleasures more than lovers of God: Having a form of godliness, but denying the power thereof: Ever learning, and never able to come to the knowledge of the truth."

Evan stayed in his room the whole day, missing his classes. Something was slowly forming in his mind. The truth was finally coming through. Never once did he entertain the idea that he was receiving any great revelation. He was no prophet. God was not putting a fiery finger on his shoulder; he was simply beginning to understand the mystery.

"I am Alpha and Omega, the beginning and the end." As Evan reread the life of Jesus, it became a consuming fire. The reality burned itself into his mind and heart. Something his instructors never spoke of happened to Evan. He believed that Jesus Christ was the Son of God and that His crucifixion provided a way back to God. With tears streaming, Evan prayed. He never remembered the words he spoke, and he didn't believe they mattered. God could read his heart; He saw the loneliness, the weariness of a homeless wanderer, the ache of living a half-life. As Evan prayed, it lifted a great burden from him. He gave his life to God and felt he had shed a suit of iron, bringing wonderful relief.

He repeated the Lord's Prayer and as he said, "Thy will be done on earth as it is in heaven," he realized this was not a request or invitation for God to have His way on earth. It was stating a fact. God's Will would be done on earth as it is in heaven. He wanted to laugh and shout. This was the Rock of Ages, a safe place to put his trust forever. Man would suffer and struggle until the end of time, but the sure and steady plan of God rolled on toward completion. Man could continue on his own poor, sad way or he could come home to his creator. It was simple, not the complicated doctrine presented by his teachers. Salvation was a gift of God. It was clear to Evan that believing in Jesus Christ would save him. No deep study, no amount of good works, no striving with clenched teeth to rescue the world. Once he took the leap of faith, God took over from there. The Church twisted the ladder to heaven, putting works first, when it was faith that saved. His parents said humans could follow their nature and create a perfect world. Religious teachings said much the same; only instead of nature, they said works.

Evan had intended to be the best Christian he could by following the teachings. He intended to feed the hungry, clothe the poor, work for peace, observe the rituals, and turn the other cheek. No one could deny these were good things, but not one of them would save a soul. Only the Spirit of God speaking through a yielded being could do that. He felt small and inadequate; he could do nothing of himself but speak the truth as revealed in the Bible.

In his last year, he thought about leaving the seminary. Many others did, but by staying he had access to the manuscripts and books he needed. It was difficult to keep his newfound faith with the constant barrage of twisted teaching, but he managed. His teachers weren't bad men; they were simply misguided. Despite these differences, he decided to stay. It would enable him to reach more people; maybe some of them would come to understand the true plan of salvation.

Gazing across the lake in Garden City, Evan recalled the past eight years. He had no more idea where he was now than when he had first begun. He had no big achievements, no great spirit-filled congregation. Only a small group meeting in apartments and houses, hiding from those bent upon extinguishing this small flicker of faith. Maybe he had made a couple of mistakes. He should have left the seminary as soon as he became a Christian. He had been mistaken in believing the leaders were good but misguided. Power not prayer was their goal. It was hard to accept that not everyone who cried 'Lord, Lord' were in truth Christians. Still, he harbored a fear of judging people. It was definitely not his place to judge...only God could read hearts and spirits. Yet, it was hard not to judge. He constantly brought the matter before God, praying for guidance. His walk with God followed a narrow path. He often lost the way, but he trusted God would stop him when he went astray.

The park grew dark, the trees making charcoal sketches against a fading sky. Evan glanced at the dashboard and noted the time. The folder on the seat beside him brought a twinge of guilt for daydreaming instead of reviewing the lesson. Still, the past helped give meaning and reason to the present. His attitude toward his mother had changed. There was sorrow for her wasted years and the abuse she'd suffered, even though much of it was self-inflicted. It was the reason she was a bitter, shattered woman. He tried to make contact with her, but she wanted nothing to do with this strange son. He should have done more, but what? He wasn't sure. Now she lived in a state-operated home for the aged. When he inquired, they told him speaking to her would do no good. Her mind had become a wilderness filled with mythical beasts and screeching birds.

Evan started the engine, backed out of the gravel parking spot, and headed toward tonight's meeting place.

Thirteen

When Clay and Jeff arrived at Doug Hansen's place outside Russell, Kansas, they found him packed and anxious to leave. Being polite, Doug invited them into the old farmhouse, although it was clear he would rather be on the move. Doug was a tall, thin man, and like a reed in the wind, constantly in motion.

"If you fellows aren't too tired," he said, shifting from one foot to the other, "we can get started right away. I have my plane ready."

"But I thought we'd drive," Clay answered. He didn't know what they were looking for. It seemed better to creep along inspecting fields and stopping to talk with farmers having the same problem.

"This is too important to waste more time than we have to, Clay," Doug said. "We can fly to Ira Thompson's near Harrisburg. He has a big all-terrain vehicle waiting for us. Said we could keep it long as we needed. What's more, his ground is dead as a doornail, too. No use checking ground between our place and his; it's the same. Hit him spring of last year, cut his corn crop in half and now the perennial growth is dead."

Clay looked at Jeff while Jeff studied the carpet beneath his feet. Clay turned to Doug.

"What in hell is going on? When did you know about your friend, Ira?"

Doug ran his hand through his thinning brown hair. "I should have called him sooner. The reason I finally called him was to see if he'd loan us transportation. That's when he told me he had trouble, too. I liked to died. He's even had people testing his fields and they don't know what it is."

"Did he check with his local agency?" Clay questioned.

"'Course he did. They told him they'd call when they had more information. Wouldn't admit that others had reported the same thing. If it's this widespread, it's worse than bad."

Jeff unclenched his jaw long enough to give his opinion. "When there's not a word of it made public, you know for sure we're in trouble. We should have been talking among ourselves. Too cussed independent."

Doug nodded. "Yeah, guess that's what caused the Association to fall apart."

The three men fell silent as the enormity of the problem settled over them. Clay was stunned, but more convinced than ever that he was on the right trail. If things started going haywire in Ira's part of Nebraska in the spring, with Doug's crops affected in early summer, and their place by late summer, it was clear the problem had started in the north. A couple of months later, Jim Durbin in their far south region reported trouble. Clay could only guess how far it had spread to the east and west.

The big questions were why had it been kept secret, and who was keeping the lid on it? The who part wasn't hard to answer: the only one big enough was the government, the agriculture department, but the why didn't make any sense. The government shared the same interest as the farmers. With the entire world system shaky, food was as important as defense. That was why ten years ago the government had tightened regulations. In the public interest, they said. The industry was too vital to leave in the control of the large companies and the very few remaining independent farmers. Clay was certain the big companies must be having trouble, too. He didn't see how the disease would affect only independent farmers. One thing about the weather, or problems with the land...nature made no distinction between corporate or independent.

"Instead of taking off on our own," Doug offered, "we could go right to the agriculture department. I can get through to D.C. in a matter of minutes. I've always thought Milton was a straight shooter. Maybe he could put some pressure on our local agencies and get some answers."

Clay frowned. "Let's not. Least for a while. You know damn well the local agencies haven't been keeping this to themselves. I'll bet you anything they have orders to sit on it."

Jeff moved around restlessly. Once he set his teeth into a thing, he didn't let go until it was finished. He jerked his thumb toward the door.

"If you two are going to stand around talking, I'll get our stuff into the airplane."

Doug laughed. "Okay, Jeff, I'm with you. I hope you don't mind, Clay, but I've asked Boyd Crawford to go along with us. He's a young chemist about your age. When I couldn't get anything from the testing stations, I called him. His folks said he was away for a while, but he called me yesterday and is interested in our problem. He's bringing along some of his equipment."

"Fine with me," Clay said. "We can use any help we can get."

By the time Boyd arrived, the other three had the gear loaded and were standing in front of the hangar. Boyd Crawford's appearance didn't inspire much confidence, but Clay knew better than to judge hastily. Boyd was a big, loose-jointed fellow that folded himself onto one of the rear seats as neatly as a paper accordion and sat silent during the take-off.

Doug seemed as at home flying as he would have been on the ground driving one of his big combines. For a while, the flight was interesting, but soon the monotony of the sky turned their talk to the purpose of the trip. Clay explained the situation to Boyd. As Boyd listened, he chewed one corner of his shaggy mustache. He gazed through the plane's window with eyes as pale blue as the April sky.

The few questions he asked, Clay couldn't answer. He could only tell him what they had seen, but Jeff had something to offer Boyd.

"It's no living thing we're looking for," he stated. "I've seen every kind of bug going, and the ones I can't see, I know their work. I don't know what this is, but I don't think it's in the fertilizer, insecticide, or the seed."

"That leaves the air and water." Boyd's voice was as disjointed as his body.

"That's the way I see it." Jeff nodded.

Clay watched as the two men lapsed into thoughtfulness. Jeff rubbed his leathery chin and Boyd resumed chewing the sparse hairs at the corner of his mouth. Clay was sure what Jeff was thinking: if it were either air or water, he knew Jeff would go for the water. It could be some airborne virus, but to the best of Clay's knowledge, the infection had not followed the prevailing wind currents. They had sent in samples of everything they could get their hands on except the water.

He didn't know why they hadn't thought of that, except that it came through the system of pipe straight from the huge underground reservoir. Nothing could get in to contaminate it. Clay's mind whirled on, mentally tracing the great sprawling network, vessels under the earth's skin carrying water instead of blood. Maybe there was a break along the line and some strange substance had seeped in, but that didn't make sense. If it had, the pumping stations would have noticed a loss of pressure. Besides, the force of water escaping should block anything entering the pipe. By the time they reached Thompson's place, it was too late to go on and they accepted his hospitality for the night.

The following morning, they piled into the rugged Landmaster and headed northwest. None of them knew what to look for, but they had agreed that tainted water was a good beginning.

Clay had seen pictures of the site where the irrigation system originated and it wasn't much to see. From the looks of the area, no one would suspect that a gigantic underground lake was dark and hidden in the bosom of the land. The main station, a big square concrete plant, was about the only thing to mark the site. The water from the reservoir went into a holding tank and from there into the system. The only other facility was a small electrical plant designed for the station's use. It took a great amount of power to deliver the water into the above-ground storage, but once there, the pumps handled it with ease. With small booster plants at long intervals, water could reach as far as the Gulf.

Last year's earthquake in the region had caused some concern, but the Water Division of National Grain had quickly checked the system. They had assured subscribers that it was in fine working order. After the initial worry, no one gave it another thought, as the system continued delivering the precious water. Clay was surer than ever that nothing could be getting into the pipes. The company would have found it in routine inspections. The distant Laramie Mountain Range stretched a long line of purple foothills to the west of their route, and to the east, the North Platte ran on into Nebraska. In the years long before Clay's birth, the river had been an important part of farm life in that area. However, as farmers plowed more and more ground, even using conservation methods, the river was unequal to the task. It was not until the great underground system came into operation that the plains really bloomed.

Farther on, they crossed the Platte and took a straight northern course. They drove for hours not seeing a town of any size, and for two nights, using the equipment they had brought, slept on the ground. Clay chuckled thinking how Diana, had she been along, would have rebelled under these conditions. This trip would be enjoyable under less serious circumstances. As they neared the turn-off toward the plant site, a large red and white sign with the NG logo of National Grain pointed the way. Jeff looked at the sign as they sped past.

"That big red NG stands for 'no good' far as I'm concerned," he muttered.

"Come on, Jeff," Clay chided. "Where would we have been these past years without their system?"

"Not in the mess we're in now, I'll lay odds," Jeff replied.

What a predicament, Clay thought. Not for a minute did he want anything to be wrong with the water supply, because next month would mark a year since it had rained. On the other hand, if the water was pure, they'd be no closer to solving the problem. As they moved along, the scenery never changed, flat land stretching to the horizon. They rode as four men suspended in a capsule, sealed away from everything except the air they breathed. For a minute, Clay felt he was in a dream, in a different place and time. He should be on the farm tending to business, although there wasn't any business to tend. He turned to Jeff.

"This whole trip is probably a waste of time; we should have taken samples from one of the pipes at home."

Jeff didn't answer but Boyd did.

"I don't think it's a waste. If they found anything in samples from your pipes, it might have originated in your lines. We need water from the source, and witnesses that it came from there. Otherwise, they can discount our findings." Boyd fell against the seat; perhaps the long speech had exhausted him.

Clay reluctantly agreed and nodded. He hated to think the water was poisoned, but even worse, that people in authority would hide it. Doug leaned over the steering wheel and squinted.

"What the devil is that?"

At some distance farther along the road, two trucks were blocking the way.

"Could it be a wreck?" Clay asked.

As they approached the trucks, Doug slowed. Two uniformed, armed men were standing in the road. Another man, using a red flag, signaled them to stop, while a fourth man leaned against one of the trucks. Doug pulled to the side of the road and stuck his head out of the window. The guard with the flag came toward the Landmaster and seemed to be inspecting the four men inside. He stopped several feet from the vehicle.

"I'm sorry, this road is closed. Please turn around, and leave the way you came."

Clay opened his door and started to alight, but the armed men came to attention and moved closer. The one with the flag took a step to the side.

"Do not leave your truck," he ordered.

Clay glanced at the two approaching men and eased back into his seat.

"Hey," he said. "I want to stretch my legs and talk about why the road is closed."

"There is nothing to talk about. No unauthorized personnel are allowed beyond this point. Please turn your truck around and leave."

"Now wait a minute," Doug sputtered. "We are on our way to take an inspection tour of the irrigation system plant. You can check with National Grain; we're subscribers. I don't know how many bulletins they've sent inviting customers to come and have a look. Far as I know, they never put a stop to it. What's the matter? Something wrong?"

The guard took another step and seemed to assume a defensive attitude.

"We have no additional information. Please leave. If you persist, we will be forced to take you into custody."

Doug's face grew red and angry. "Maybe you should do that. We'll get to talk to someone who will make some sense."

Jeff reached forward and put his hand on Doug's shoulder. "Doug," Jeff said softly. "Do what the man says. Let's go while we still can. Come on."

Doug obviously struggled to remain calm, but he managed a smile. "Okay fellow," he said as he started the Landmaster. "You win. No trouble from us. We'll be going."

Doug turned the truck around and sped away. Jeff, Clay, and Boyd looked back and saw the guards still watching them, and one of the guards went to a truck and retrieved a speaker which he held to his mouth.

"See that?" Boyd said. "He's calling someone. Still think you'd have gotten a straight answer through the regular channels?"

"What do we do now?" Doug asked.

"Circle around and come in on their blind side," Jeff muttered.

Clay twisted toward the rear seat. "You really think they have one, Jeff? If they've gone to this much trouble, they'll have the roads blocked. If we did get close to the plant, how do you think we could get in?"

Jeff's face darkened. "Clay, if you say go home, you're no Sanderson I ever knew."

"I didn't say that," Clay answered. "I'm pointing out we may have a few problems to overcome."

Boyd was chewing his mustache again. Then his eyes brightened. "Jeff's right. Look at that country; they can't have every bit of it covered. Let's get as close as we can. We'll decide something."

Doug slowed the Landmaster and began searching the roadside until he found a spot where the drainage ditch was shallow. He eased the truck off the pavement and into the open field. He glanced at the compass on the dash and pointed the truck in a northwesterly direction. He turned to Clay.

"You think maybe we should call someone and let them know what we're doing? This open country isn't anything to mess with. We could get in a fix if we break down."

Clay thought for a minute. "No, I don't think we should. Somebody we don't want might overhear. We should keep quiet for now."

As they bounced across the dried fields, there wasn't a living thing in sight the entire day. That night they made camp in a spot they believed to be north of the water system's plant. Clay made a careful check of their supplies and figured they had plenty for at least another three days. He didn't see how they could be away any longer than that. If something didn't happen by tomorrow, despite the challenge Jeff had thrown at him, he would be for heading home. However, he was far from giving in. His next stop would be National Grain's home office. Even if he didn't have proof of anything, guarding the road to the plant was reason enough to question them.

With the first gray light of early morning, the four men broke camp. Their breakfast was flat soybean cakes and dried fruit, washed down with a brew that tried to imitate coffee. The condensed foodstuff had the required nutrients, but Clay found it distasteful. It was hard to believe that much of the population lived on the stuff. Still, grain proved cheaper and easier to distribute than animal protein.

"I remember a time when we carried dried beef," Jeff said. "It was a lot tastier than this stuff."

As he rolled up his sleeping bag and took it to the Landmaster, Clay swallowed the last of the soybean cake. He would be happy to return home to Tillie's good cooking. Once again, he was grateful for his life on the farm. At least they were in a position to produce their own small amounts of beef and poultry. That, along with the kitchen garden, provided them with what most people would consider a feast.

The men were unusually silent. Clay supposed it was because they'd had the night to consider the situation. He had no doubt the other three had come to the same conclusions he had. With the campsite cleared, they climbed into the Landmaster, Doug started the engine and headed toward National Grain's main water station. They rolled over dry cracked ground that had once been producing fields. They were on National Grain land now, or land they had leased. Normally this time of year, spiky green shoots of perennial corn covered it. It was the crop assigned to the area when it had first come under irrigation. Jeff shook his head, the worry lines around his eyes deep in his dark face.

"Looks terrible, don't it?" he said.

"No worse than it did before they started working it," Doug commented. "Same as it was a couple of centuries ago, when it was nothing but desert badlands."

"I have to disagree with you; it is worse." Boyd spoke for the first time that morning. "Before the irrigation system, there was a whole ecology that held the place together. Coarse sand and rock stay put in high wind, and the plant life was adapted to dryness. Nature tries to reclaim desert and barren land. She starts with the tough, tiny vegetation and progresses to larger plants that can hold to the rough dry land. It takes a long time, but if the weather patterns change, everything is there to turn it into prairie grassland. If the rain increased, small trees would take root. This land is out of balance. With the natural vegetation plowed under and no cover crop, the land is defenseless."

No one answered Boyd because it was clear he was right. There were miles and miles of land flat as a tabletop, the big rocks removed to accommodate the giant machines that rolled across it, the pulverized dirt made even finer by the corn roots that helped turn the grit into soil. If the crops were still alive, the area would be a green sea stretching on forever. Now it wasn't even a respectable desert. The first good wind would take anything resembling soil into the air, heading wherever the current took it. Once the wind scoured it to bare rock, nothing could grow. Not even tough desert plants could reclaim it. Boyd was right, it was worse than before.

Sweat collected under Clay's arms and between his shoulder blades. It was a nervous reaction to the landscape. This was what their land would be by the end of summer if they couldn't get something growing on it. The long spell of dry weather hadn't seemed important with the water system in place. Without it, they were at the mercy of nature. He didn't know how to begin dealing with it. Farther north, the fields looked worse; they were driving through a nightmare landscape. They drove on, hoping to get close to the main water station, but before they came in sight of it, they found a fifteen-foot-high chain link fence. It stretched for miles in either direction.

Doug stopped the Landmaster and looked at the other three. "Well, what now? I suppose we could get through, if it doesn't have voltage on it. But we start destroying property and we might have more trouble than we want."

"What I want is a sample of the water," Boyd said. "It has to be as close to the original source as possible."

"Guess we go to Thompson's place. He's the only independent I know north of me," Doug offered.

Jeff gave a rough chuckle. "We could stop at one of old No Good Grain's operations and ask them real polite for a sample."

Heading south, the four men took turns driving, making no stops even at night. They had caught Boyd's desire for water to test. When they reached the long lane across Thompson's property and started driving toward the house, the farm seemed unnaturally silent. With the fields empty and bare, it was hard to remember what time of year it was. Doug had left his airplane near the barns, but it wasn't there now.

"Ira didn't tell me he wanted to use the plane while we were gone," Doug said, sounding puzzled. "I don't mind, but I doubt he'd do that."

Doug parked the Landmaster and they got out to stretch their arms and legs. Boyd took a while to work the kinks out of his lanky frame. When Clay stepped onto the front porch and started for the door, the curtain at a side window dropped into place. Someone was checking them before opening the door. When the door did open, Mrs. Thompson's anxious face greeted them. She was a small woman about sixty years old with a face that would have looked far more natural wearing a smile. The concerned, worried expression looked new and almost painful.

She rushed them inside the way a hen gathers her chicks before a storm. Doug removed his hat and looked at her questioningly.

"What's wrong with you, Dora? Where's Ira? That old hound run off with a young woman?"

Dora clapped her small hands to the sides of her face and shook her head. "Lordy, I wish he had, least I'd know he was having fun."

The men started to laugh, but the sound died in their throats seeing Dora's eyes dark with concern.

"Your airplane is behind the equipment barn. Ira had one of the fellows cover as much of it as he could with a tarp. When they came, they didn't ask anything about it." Dora kept shaking her head as she talked. "Guess they thought it belonged to us, or didn't see it. One or the other."

"I don't understand this. What is going on here?" Doug demanded.

Clay, Jeff, and Boyd kept silent. These people were Doug's friends and it was his place to ask the questions, but Clay could feel a current of apprehension circulating among them. Dora put her hand on Doug's arm and tried to smile.

"I don't know where my manners are, babbling away. You men must be hungry and dry as dust. Come into the kitchen and let me get you something. Maybe I can tell you what happened once I get my hands busy fixing some dinner."

Obediently, the men followed her to the bright yellow and white kitchen. They were nearly dancing with curiosity and puzzlement, but having women such as Dora in their families, they knew the only way to proceed was at Dora's speed. They arranged themselves at the long harvest table and Dora began opening cabinets, taking out plates and glasses.

"That second evening after you left, three men from National Grain came. They asked Ira what he was doing at the irrigation system station. He laughed and said any fool could see he hadn't been there. They did look foolish because Ira wouldn't have had time to get here judging from the time the Landmaster was at the check point."

Clay moaned. "Those guards took the license number and it brought them to you."

Dora nodded. "Well, anyway, Ira asked them what the fuss was about and they didn't say two words that made sense. Said something about repairs going on and didn't want anyone getting hurt. You could tell it wasn't the truth. Right away, I saw by Ira's face that he didn't intend to tell them the truth either. I kept still and let him handle it. They demanded to know who borrowed the truck. Ira cut his eyes toward me and calm as you please told them our son was using it and he didn't have any idea where Bob might have gone with it.

"You see, with nothing to do, Bob and his wife left last week to go visit her folks in Arizona. They might have been satisfied with that answer and gone off looking for Bob, but Ira couldn't let it go at that. He had to ask them what was wrong with the water in the system. Why didn't the agents give any straight answers? I guess the thoughts of our dry, dead land got the best of him. He told them he was getting ready to take some samples to an independent tester."

As Dora talked, the men ate, but Clay could tell none of them was tasting the cold chicken or potato salad.

"They tried to laugh it off and tell him that yes, there was definitely something wrong in the fields, that NG was experiencing difficulties, too. But it had absolutely nothing to do with the water. At that, Ira got raving mad. Told them he was going to call Washington, that something was rotten somewhere and if he didn't start getting answers from someplace, he would call everyone he knew and maybe a lawyer, too. That's when they decided to take him with them to the main offices. Said they could prove to him they had nothing to hide."

"And he fell for that?" Doug asked.

Dora shook her head. "Not by a long shot. He figured that as long as he kept them busy, they wouldn't be looking for you fellows. He was hoping by the time they found where Bob really was, you would have gone home. He'd pretend to be satisfied and they'd let him go, thinking he wouldn't make any trouble. I think they're treating him okay. Once you're on your way, I'll let him know and he can start acting convinced. Thank goodness he didn't mention his theory about that earthquake last year."

"But they checked that and there wasn't even an interruption in service," Clay said. "None of the pipes was damaged."

Dora sighed. "I know that. But Ira got this idea that it has something to do with our trouble now."

Boyd had finished eating sometime before and suddenly rose from the table.

"Mrs. Thompson, do you have the diagrams of your irrigation system, where the main pipe comes in?"

Dora dried her hands on a towel and started from the room. "They're in the office. I'll get them."

"You don't need to test that water," Jeff said to no one in particular. "I can tell you right now it's poisoned."

Boyd's mouth was a grim tight line. "I think it is, too, Jeff. But we can't decide what to do until we know what kind of poison it is."

When Dora returned with the diagram, they left the house and started for a far section where NG's main line connected with Ira Thompson's system. Clay wanted to head home immediately. He didn't need tests to prove the water was the problem. He had to go home and disconnect from the system as soon as possible. Perhaps whatever had contaminated the water would dissipate before next fall. Maybe it would rain, maybe their own wells could handle some of the fields. His head thundered with "maybes." Those bastards at National Grain had really stuck it to them this time. The bunch in Washington was as bad. No one else had the power to keep this from the news. They had spread a big black blanket over the whole thing. Any poor slob who had no connections had to sit in the dark wondering what had happened. For over a century, the small guy didn't have a chance. Not when the big grain distributors bought every crop and managed to set prices. At first, they didn't go in for any growing; they left that risk to the farmer.

When the government took more and more control, the big companies found they needed to get into the production end of it, too. The huge multinational grain conglomerates and the federal government formed an alliance. The conglomerates controlled things outside Washington. They sold seed, fertilizer, chemicals, machinery, anything needed to make the ground produce, plus the irrigation systems. It was a daily fight among Washington and the multinationals about who would finally control the entire U.S. production, with the few independent farmers caught in the middle.

Most a farmer ever wanted was to raise his crops, sell them at a decent price, and live on his land. Clay could see the day coming shortly when no family would work the land. Beyond that, he could even see the conglomerates finally losing to the government. They nationalized other industries at the rate of about one every three years. It was a bloody affair with big business fighting for its life. Sometimes Clay even felt sorry for them. Still, in a way, they had helped bring it on themselves. They had meddled in politics by pouring huge amounts of money into campaigns hoping to gain favor. They helped grow government to a size that finally didn't need their support. One by one, the government captured industries and made every decision for them.

A sour lump settled in Clay's stomach. There were times when farmers too had sent money to Washington to buy influence. Industries and individuals alike had clamored for laws and regulations favorable to them, subsidies, and government handouts. There was enough blame to go around. They had, every one of them, missed a most basic principle: The hand that feeds also controls.

There were three distinct classes of population: those employed by giant corporations and those working for the government. The third group lived on handouts from the government. No one voiced the concern, but government officials were beginning to fear the hordes of government-kept masses. With each riot or uprising, Washington squeezed more money from taxpayers to support the swelling tide of national wards. The government created jobs for people, but the work was senseless. It produced nothing and performed no service. Clay wondered how the rest of the people kept from losing their minds. He supposed they had remained sane by focusing upon their work, hoping that things would improve, but now it seemed impossible.

One year with no crop and some of them could still survive, but two years would finish them. National Grain could go on; they had huge reserves stockpiled from years of good harvests, reserved to force prices higher. Under government control, they would remain alive. Clay and the others wouldn't be able to sell their contaminated land. He remembered Frank's suggestion about selling to National, and a sneer came to his lips. He should go home and put Frank's sales ability to the test. Let him see how much National would pay for Sanderson land now. Oh, they would probably still buy the farm, but dirt-cheap. They were the only ones that were strong enough to wait for a cleanup. This final blow could kill the independent farmer.

After Boyd had collected his samples, the other three men followed him to the farmhouse like pallbearers at a funeral. In Dora's bright kitchen, Boyd arranged his portable lab. As he went to work, the others retreated to the front porch. Dora fussed around, pouring glasses of cool water for them.

"Wish the house was cooler," she apologized. "We've stopped using the generator for air conditioning to save on fuel expenses. Shouldn't be this danged hot in April anyway."

"Don't you worry about it, Mrs. Thompson," Jeff consoled her. "We're used to the outdoors. We'll be comfortable on this porch."

Jeff sat on the steps in the shade of a big, budding purple wisteria that twined around the porch railing and one side of the roof. It was a handsome plant, one of the largest Clay had ever seen.

"This sure is a fine-looking vine, how old is it?" Clay asked.

Dora beamed with pride. "Ira's mother planted it and it was a challenge for me to keep the blasted thing going. When we were first married, I used to carry buckets of water for it. Since we put in sprinklers it gets a share like the lawn and garden."

The three men turned their gaze over the green lawn with its border of spring flowers. There was also a freshly plowed garden. Light green lettuce, and dark green spinach were beginning to show. The area was in sharp contrast to the fields beyond. As if reading their minds, Dora spoke.

"Thank goodness my yard and garden are watered by our own wells. This winter was warm and I put seeds in early. Looks strange having it green now, don't it?"

The men nodded in agreement. Clay started to speak but didn't want to burden Mrs. Thompson with another fear that had begun to nip at him. If National's system had introduced something deadly into the fields, how long would it be until it seeped into private wells? It might creep through the soil, finally reaching Mrs. Thompson's prize wisteria.

When Boyd finally joined them, the men stood expectantly. It was like awaiting a jury verdict or for a doctor to give the final diagnosis. Boyd looked at them and his loose shoulders sagged.

"I'm sorry, fellows. You might as well know right off. Any land touched by this stuff won't be workable in our lifetime, our children's, or their children's." Boyd chewed at his thin mustache.

Clay's heart pounded; the sound beat in his ears. "You want to explain that?"

Boyd shrugged. "Sure, but it isn't going to help."

"Well, if we're dead," Doug growled, "I sure want to know what killed us."

"A combination of things," Boyd began. "Years ago, they declared Dytrom unsafe and took it off the market. They developed something called TR-456 to take its place. It was worse. They had to dispose of them both. Disposal has always been a problem. We have been churning out more junk than we know what to do with.

We got nuclear waste, pesticides, medical waste, and the everyday compounds we concoct. I'm not sure where they dump this stuff, but I happen to know they put Dytrom and its baby brother TR-456 in a site under the Bighorn Mountains. I don't know what's going on, but I've found definite traces of Dytrom and TR-456, plus some stuff I can't identify. Maybe there is a connection between the disposal site and the underground reservoir."

Clay knew about the site. It was supposed to be the ultimate in disposal sites. It was deep in the ground and the vaults reinforced with super strong, non-corrosive materials. It was supposed to be safe and last forever. There was no longer any question. The water from the NG system was poisoning the ground. However, he didn't know how the chemicals Boyd found got into the system.

Jeff hit his leg with his hat. "Well, that does it for me. I don't think Ira knew why, but he had it right. That earthquake probably split open both the dump and the reservoir. Now that stuff is mixing, and who knows what it'll create."

Doug turned pale. "If the reservoir is contaminated, they should have shut down the irrigation system."

"Maybe they found out too late," Dora said.

Clay couldn't stop the anger building in his chest. She was trying to give National the benefit of a doubt, but he had no such generous feelings.

"Can I use your comset, Mrs. Thompson?" he asked. "I have to talk to my dad."

Fourteen

Jan Brockman and Mark Sanderson had each taken a different part of town in their search for Evan. They had agreed to meet at the shopping center in Garden City when they finished. As Jan drove through the north entrance, her eyes scanned the parking lot looking for Mark's truck. She longed to see two men sitting in the cab. However, as she parked beside the truck, it was only Mark who looked out the window to greet her.

"No luck with you either, I see," he said.

Jan shook her head. "I can't imagine where he went. I stopped by Tom and Laurie's and he did see them, but left there a few hours ago."

"What do you want to do now?"

"Ryan's parents are gone on a county work detail; the meeting is being held at their house. We can go there and try to stop him before he goes in."

"Come ride with me," Mark ordered. "No use wasting more of your gas."

Mark started the truck and cut across the empty parking lot toward an exit leading into the street. Jan looked at the shabby storefronts. It was depressing to drive by the town's two shopping centers. She faintly remembered a time, maybe fifteen years ago, when the centers were busy, bustling places. Her mother had taken her there shopping and they always stopped at the Tobin's ice cream store. Those afternoons seemed long ago dreams. Everything had changed. The black asphalt lots were cracked and grass grew through the openings. Some of the plate glass windows were completely gone from a few of the stores, broken during one of the food riots. Men used to come by in trucks and put plastic slabs in the broken windows, but after the looters ripped away the shelving, they stopped protecting the stores. Now the only place to shop was downtown. The security was tighter and the sales were under control.

Ryan's neighborhood was as disheartening as the shopping centers. It was amazing how fast the town had crumbled. Because of its solid agriculture and oil-based economy, Garden City had survived longer than most towns. In the past, Garden City had a southern section with low-cost houses, while on the north edge of town stood the sprawling brick homes of the wealthy. In between lived a large middle-class population. Before, the town was mostly white, but had a large number of Blacks and even a few Asians. When the shortages became acute and looting began, the blame fell on the dark-skinned citizens. At first, many people objected until they grew hungry enough to agree. For it was better to send some away than for everyone to starve. Now the town had only two sections: the larger one filled with desperate, struggling people, while a few streets around Grandmother Fern's home still housed the wealthy. The lake addition, where Diana had insisted upon building, wasn't finished. After Diana's house, the developer built only two more. Building materials, especially wood, were in short supply and impossible to obtain unless you had political connections. It was clear the gap between rich and poor had reached dangerous proportions. Yet there were people, Diana for one, who refused to see reality and went on making plans for the future. Jan wondered if there would be one.

Ryan's neighborhood had once been middle-class, but with each passing year, it became more of a shantytown. The people who had jobs found their pay diminished by inflation. No one could afford home repairs or lawn care. Worse, owners who could no longer make payments left the houses empty. Ryan was lucky: his grandparents had owned their home and had left it to his mother. Things in Garden City were bad, but other areas of the country were much worse. For years, no news outlet had reported the world statistics on starvation. Governments restricted the type and amount of news citizens received; it was bad for their morale. However, Jan's father subscribed to special newsletters intended for the leaders in each community. She had read them and knew that these conditions had not happened overnight. Perhaps people were able to go on because it happened slowly. Some young people didn't question conditions. They knew no other way of life; hardship was normal.

Starting in her teens, Jan had wanted to help the less fortunate. She volunteered at a day care center evenings and weekends. When that didn't seem to be enough, she joined a youth action group. She spent long tedious hours organizing and managing the town's chapter of Youth for Social Improvements. There were tours, lectures, recruiting efforts, but she saw precious little improvement and grew impatient. When she met Evan, his message was a startling revelation. She had worked on external conditions, laws, rules, and regulations. Evan declared that progress only came after an internal transformation. When spirits were different, their circumstances changed. Jan was committed to Evan's work. She refused to let anything stop it.

A block away from Ryan's house, Mark pulled to the curb.

"Maybe we should watch for a while," he cautioned.

Jan nodded and they settled in to wait. It appeared Evan wasn't there. They hadn't seen his car or any of the farm's vehicles. Jan turned toward Mark with a sigh of relief.

"I think we're in time. We can wait for him," she said.

About fifteen minutes later, a dark blue sedan with a Church crest on the door roared past them and came to an abrupt halt in front of Ryan's house. Two men climbed from the car and hurried to the porch. When the door opened, they pushed it aside and entered. Jan stiffened, but then relaxed a bit.

"It's still okay," she said. "If Evan does come, he won't stop when he sees their car parked there."

Mark nodded. "Should we stay or try looking for Evan again?"

Before she could answer, Mark clutched her arm. "Look!" he cried.

Jan turned toward the house. The two officials were coming through the open front door with Evan wedged between them. Jan watched in horror as they shoved him into the sedan and drove away.

"I didn't think he was there. How could we have missed him?" Jan said.

"I don't know, but we'll find out."

Mark drove to the house and parked. They left the truck and hurried to the front door. A pale and shaky Ryan let them in. Two women and a middle-aged man stood in the living room looking equally scared.

"What happened?" Jan asked. "Why did you come? Didn't you get my message that they knew about the meeting?"

Ryan hung his head, perhaps to hide the tears she saw filling his eyes.

"Yes, but we knew if you didn't find Evan he would come. We didn't want him to face it alone."

"We were ready to go, too," the older man said in a thick voice.

Ryan raised his chin, defiance shining in his tearful eyes. "But they ignored us. They're going to do something awful to Evan. I know they are. They think the rest of us will be too scared to keep on with him gone."

"We could call the police," one of the women suggested. "They can't go jerking people from their houses."

"Yes, they can," the man said. "Local authorities aren't about to challenge the Church."

The other woman sat and buried her face in her hands. "I can't believe this has happened," she moaned.

"We didn't see a car...how did Evan get here?" Jan asked Ryan.

"It's in the garage; I thought if they didn't see any cars they wouldn't stop. People don't go far when they have to walk. I thought they'd think no one was home."

Jan patted Ryan's shoulder. "You did the best you could. Don't worry. We'll think of something."

Mark looked at her and raised his eyebrows. "Do you want me to take you to your car now?"

"What about Evan's car? We should take it to the farm, don't you think?"

"We can do that. I'll send someone to the center for your car."

Mark backed Evan's car from the garage and Jan drove Mark's truck. Following Mark to the farm, she began making plans. She would stay the night. She was too exhausted to drive home, even if one of the farmhands did deliver her car before morning. Tomorrow she would try to convince her father to represent Evan. He probably wouldn't want to, but he was good at bringing opposing parties together. When they arrived at the farm, they parked the vehicles and stepped into the late evening. As they walked to the house, Mark grinned at Jan and took her arm, leading her to the stairs.

"I'm glad you're going to stay the night. You'll have a good visit with your sister, and Eva always likes company. Don't worry about Evan; they're probably only talking to him. I'll go with you tomorrow. If your daddy won't help, maybe I can do something. I hope we haven't missed supper. I'm hungry, aren't you?"

Jan could have hugged Mark for his encouraging words. Her poor stupid sister had married into a warm, loving family and didn't have sense enough to appreciate it. In the foyer, Mark threw his hat onto the deer horn rack by the door.

"Eva," he called. "Your wandering man is home. Where are you, hon?"

Eva met them in the living room and immediately Jan saw something was terribly wrong. Mark seemed oblivious to anything but the big hug he gave his wife.

"Oh, have you been gone?" Eva said with a laugh.

"Don't tell me you didn't miss me," Mark teased in return.

As they walked through the dining room toward the kitchen, Jan wondered if they were fooling each other with the light banter. She knew Mark's news was bad, and even if he couldn't see it, she read trouble in Eva's eyes.

Jan and Mark sat at the kitchen table while Eva and Tillie bustled around reheating the evening meal. Eva turned toward Tillie.

"Tillie, buzz Diana and tell her Jan is here."

Jan raised her hand to stop Tillie. "No wait, I'll eat first and then go see her."

Eva gave Jan and Mark a sharp look; it was easy to see she sensed trouble. Mark lowered his head and Eva pulled a chair closer and sat beside him.

"You weren't able to catch Evan, were you?"

Mark shook his head. "But don't worry," he said quickly. "We'll get him home by tomorrow afternoon."

Tillie clicked her tongue as she set two large glasses of iced tea before them. "Mercy, what is this world coming to?"

Eva rubbed Mark's shoulder in a consoling way as he started on his salad.

"Sorry there isn't more in those greens," Tillie called from behind the refrigerator door. "Hot and dry as it's been, we're lucky to have the lettuce and radishes."

It was a small salad, but to Jan it tasted wonderful. There was nothing fresh in the markets yet. California and Mexico had been dry the past winter and only a trickle of produce found a path to market. Glenda had been complaining about there being nothing but canned and dehydrated fruit and vegetables. Again, Jan thought how lucky Diana was. Due to Eva and Tillie's perseverance, the family always managed to eat well. The greenhouse had performed wonders during the unusually warm winter and now with spring here, the two women were working in the large garden plot close to the house.

As they finished eating, Mark explained how they had missed Evan.

"I'll try to get my dad to represent him," Jan said.

Eva paid close attention and she was clearly interested, but Jan could tell that something else was wrong.

"How is Diana?" she asked quickly.

Eva smiled. "Fine, far as I know. After we ate, she went to her room to rest."

Mark blotted his lips with a napkin and scooted his chair away from the table.

"Well, Eva, we told you our story, now you tell us yours."

"I wanted you to relax some and have a peaceful meal first."

Jan had guessed right...it was a game. Two people that close could never fool each other. She was sure Eva had something unpleasant to tell and it worried her, but the compassion and caring between the two brought a sense of sweetness to the room.

"Clay called while you were gone."

"And?" Mark questioned.

"We're in real trouble, Mark."

Jan started to stand. "I'll go see Diana now," she offered.

"No, stay. You should hear this. Maybe you can explain it to Diana better than I did."

Jan sank onto the chair. Eva's expression gave a hint that things were not well between her and Diana. Jan flushed with shame. Eva was clearly asking for help in communicating with an unmanageable daughter-in-law. No one called Diana a spoiled brat; she was too old for that. Her demands and expectations had outgrown the childish phase. As an adult, she had developed a hard determination to have what she considered her due, no matter what the cost.

Jan listened closely as Eva told them what Clay had found. It was clear she was trying to soften the bad news.

"Maybe the weather will break," Eva offered, a hopeful look in her eyes. "Or perhaps we can drill more wells of our own."

"I don't know, sweetheart. If the ground is completely saturated, even clean water might not help. When did Clay say he'd be back?"

"By tomorrow evening."

Mark stood and pounded his fist on the table. "By God, Eva, what the hell is going to happen next? We've seen this place through drought, mortgages, government interference, and other pestilences, but this plague may be the worst yet."

Eva put her arm around his waist. "I know, dear. I know. Come sit in the living room, we'll think of something."

As they left the kitchen Eva called, "Tillie, bring Mark's coffee into the living room, will you please?"

Tillie nodded, her face set and stern. Jan left the table swallowing hard to keep away the tears. Eva and Mark had worked for years and now they could lose everything.

"I'll go to my sister now," she said softly.

Tillie gave Jan a smile and kept on with her work. Jan didn't know much about farming, but she had understood Clay's message. As she climbed the wide staircase to the second floor, her mind spun with the implications. She was accustomed to thinking in terms of national and world events, because of her father and her Uncle Avery's wide interests. Diana may have been right—she should have studied law, but if the land died, attorneys would starve the same as the next person. For years, the battle of overpopulation had raged; it seemed an incurable global disease. Along with more people came more garbage. Trash polluted the oceans and land did not escape. There had been warnings, but Jan knew the other side, too. Despite birth control and abortions, the world population grew, putting a strain on limited resources.

What was business supposed to do, refuse to supply them because the new technology wasn't proven completely safe? They needed to make profits and stay ahead of the competition, no matter the cost. With each depleted natural resource, corporations used substitutes and synthetics. They did this despite the heavy restrictions governments imposed. The nature of business is to find a need and fill it. Which was what National Grain did, and no one turned the gigantic water system away. It steadied the U.S. production and gave America a badly needed edge in dealing with other countries.

There would be years of endless lawsuits. Claims against National Grain, against the companies that had first manufactured the chemicals, against the government for providing what they thought would be a safe dump. Who would be the winner? No one, Jan thought glumly. National Grain would suffer the same as the rest. The poison affected their ground, too. If the government decided to pay off any claims against nationalized chemical companies, it would be in worthless scrip. People's taxes could never keep pace with the government's spending. It was hopeless, a snake swallowing its own tail.

Jan knocked softly on the bedroom door and called, "Diana, are you awake?" She waited a minute before carefully opening the door a crack. She put her head in and looked around. The bed was empty. Diana was on the longue in the sitting area, her arms on the windowsill, her head down, the window's drapes open to the night.

"There you are. Why didn't you answer me?"

Diana didn't turn or acknowledge her. Jan impatiently strode across the room.

"What's the matter with you now?"

Diana looked limp and languid, as she lay draped upon the longue, her folded arms hiding her face. She looked as though she might be crying. Still, Jan knew better than that. Diana didn't cry when she was alone; it would be a waste of talent. Diana's tears were a tool, something to use on people. Jan put her hand on Diana's shoulder.

"If you aren't going to talk to me, I'll go downstairs."

"Maybe you should." Diana spoke to the dark windowpane.

"What do you mean by that? I thought you would want company for the night. But I guess I was wrong."

Diana swiftly swung around and grasped Jan's hand. "I'm sorry, don't go. I do want you to stay. You've been downstairs with them for hours. Sometimes I think you're more concerned with Evan and the Sandersons than you are with your own family."

As Diana pouted, Jan took a seat on a small velvet chair.

"I was hungry; you could have joined us, you know. Besides, Eva wanted me to hear the horrible news from Clay. I'm sorry for them. Mark looked sick."

"What about me? Do you have any idea what this has done to my life?"

Jan studied her sister's distraught face and her emotions bounced from pity to anger. She was sorry for Diana. This calamity would bring her carefully made plans to ruins, but her selfishness was disgusting. Jan wished she could shake some sense or compassion into that self-centered head. Diana jumped to her feet, and wringing her hands, began to pace.

Calmly, almost with detachment, Jan watched.

"I've made the most horrible mistake. How could this have happened?" Diana wailed. "I thought it over carefully...farming seemed stable, and Clay is a simple man, no involvement with the hectic whirl of city business. Now the house is gone and I'll be stuck living with a bunch of country dirt farmers that don't even have the dirt to scratch in."

As she raved, the words came faster and faster, reaching a high pitch. Jan began to worry.

"Maybe you should sit down. Can I get you something to drink— tea, or coffee?"

Diana spun around. "A nice tall glass of arsenic; that would put me out of my misery."

"Oh please, Diana. Stop! It's not the end of the world. Clay isn't going to let you or the baby starve. It might help to start thinking about your son's future and how to provide for him."

Diana's gaze turned icy, chilling even Jan's practical bones. Diana dropped onto the bed and lifted her chin in defiance.

"My life hasn't even started. I'm not about to worry over some unborn bit of flesh. I'm not going to let this mess ruin me. I'm going home, Jan. I'll divorce Clay and start over. Fern knows dozens of fine families with sons and brothers that are extremely capable of providing a suitable life for me."

Wearily, Jan put her hand to her forehead, a dull ache starting above her eyes. She felt incredibly old, as if she had lived forever. She had spent too much time reading history, that was the trouble. She'd learned of ancient civilization in China, the old and new kingdoms of the Nile, the Mayan, and Toltec cities. She had followed the wars of conquest in every part of the world and the wars for independence. Nation rose against nation like the beating of the waves against the shore or the heaving of the earth's crust. One area rising to power, then shaken and overthrown by another. It was a broad, restless canvas where man and nature constantly painted new scenes. The past was a certain predictor of the future. Jan feared peace was impossible; people would never find the answer.

As she watched her sister, hope of a better world died, and the reason sat before her. The lovely Diana with the grasping hands and lust-filled eyes. Neither of which could be satisfied. No matter how much wealth and power, there were always unfilled desires. Jan's thoughts collapsed and her shoulders slumped. If it were not for these ambitious, hungry people, nothing would advance. Humanity would still be wearing skins and poking under rotten logs for grubs.

Before Jan met Evan, she had a clear idea of life. History repeated one generation after another. The details were different, but the pattern of a circle the same, mankind never changing. There would always be trouble and suffering, but in her short life span, she could make things better for the less fortunate. It would give her life meaning. Evan agreed that left to man's control, the earth would suffer the endless cycles of the past. His message was that God intervened. He put His hand into the affairs of man and lifted the circle into a spiral that would bring the world to its predestined place. This was the crux of his dispute with the Church. They taught that man's efforts would bring utopia. Evan swore on his soul that this was wrong.

"Jan?" Diana touched her arm. "Why didn't you answer me?"

Jan shook her head, clearing the maze of thoughts and cloud of memories.

"What? What did you say?"

"I said...you'll be glad to have me home, won't you? If it is going to disrupt everyone, I can stay with Fern. Yes, maybe that would be better anyway. She and I have wonderful times together. Maybe we'll go to Europe for a while."

"I wouldn't if I were you. It's worse over there. Haven't you been reading about their food strikes? No, of course you haven't. I'll bring you some of Dad's papers...you'll be glad to be where you are."

Diana waved her hand. "Don't be ridiculous. If you know the right places to stay, there will always be plenty. Fern has some very influential friends."

"Never mind. If you do travel, I doubt you'll go much farther than Dallas or New York. Grandma will have enough sense to stay in the states."

"I wouldn't go to either place. I pay enough attention to the news to know that Dallas is a scorched cinder with this horrid weather. And no one in his right mind would go to New York."

"Has it occurred to you there won't be money for trips? Daddy and Uncle Avery won't fare any better than Mark and Clay. Grandma Fern may have to settle for less, too. The law practice gives Daddy a place to go every day, but you know as well as I do the largest income is from the land."

For a second, a trace of fear flashed across Diana's lovely features. "Oh, wait. They lease the land. Daddy doesn't care what they do with it, as long as they pay the rent. If it doesn't produce anything, that's their problem. Too bad for them!"

"I'm afraid not. I've read the contracts. There is only a small base rent. The rest is on a percentage of what is harvested."

Diana's mouth flew open. "Why would Daddy do something that stupid?"

"It wasn't stupid when he did it. With prices going higher, no one locked into a set agreement. Profit sharing was the right thing to do at the time. Every Brockman contract reads the same."

It was late and Jan was tired of trying to make Diana understand. Their lives were going to be different. There were new rumblings in the world with more on the horizon. The shifting and washing over had started. Another cycle affecting the power centers, some new ones rising and old ones crumbling. Her belief in what Evan taught was growing stronger, but her position was the same. She would still fight for the good of the greatest number of people.

She was staying in Tracy's old room for the night. As she put on the nightgown borrowed from Diana, she nearly wilted with weariness. She had wanted to talk about Evan. It was possible Diana had some ideas about what to do for him. Lying there staring at the ceiling, she knew how foolish that hope had been. Self-centered Diana saw nothing but her impossible dream...none of Jan's words reached her. She couldn't do anything about Diana any more than she could about the dry, dead land. However, Evan was a different matter. She wasn't sure how to help him, but she knew her skills would be useful in his cause. He lacked organization and a proper plan. She could help bring his message to more people. It was an encouraging thought.

Fifteen

Diana did not sleep well. She tossed about on the wide bed until her body ached from the tense thrashing and her mind was feverish. She had firmly resolved that if the time came, she would take the capsules to terminate her pregnancy. Yet, it frightened her. Dr. Kruger had warned there would be some discomfort. The medication would kill the fetus and bring on labor pains to expel it. The method was the safest way for the mother; it followed more closely the natural abortion of a faulty fetus. In the early months, surgical procedures were harmless, but later on it became a major operation. Diana had also chosen this method because it gave the appearance of a spontaneous abortion, thus avoiding what would surely be a terrible fight with Clay.

Diana reviewed the instructions of how to take the pills. There should be no effects for a few hours, but when the pains began, she was to call Dr. Kruger and start for the hospital. From there on, it would resemble a normal birth except it would not produce a live child.

A faint pearl gray dawn pushed weakly through the curtains, filling the bedroom with a ghostly haze. Very shortly, the sun would be on the horizon sending long, piercing shafts of bright heat across the land and into her room. Clay was coming home today and she knew what that meant. He would bring the horrible details of the farm's financial collapse. But she would not be around to hear any of it. She intended to be in Garden City, having a drink with Glenda and waiting until it was time to start for the hospital. By evening it would be over, the mistake of starting the pregnancy corrected. By the following evening, she would have set in motion the process to terminate her marriage as well. If there wasn't a child to cloud the issue, Clay would have no claim on her. If he did attempt to complicate things, she would tell him the abortion was deliberate. His anger and disgust would make him glad for her to leave.

She needed to hurry. She was not anxious to encounter pain, but some physical discomfort was well worth her freedom.

Diana thought of the three other women in the house this morning. It was nauseating. Jan was probably dressed and already hurrying to do battle for Evan, while Eva was undoubtedly coddling and catering to Mark's every whim, ready to stand at his side and face their coming ordeal. Tillie hardly counted, a lump of a woman who knew nothing but pots and pans. How different they were from Glenda. Suddenly, Diana's opinion of her mother changed drastically. She almost laughed aloud. Why hadn't she seen how alike they were? Through the years it was the family opinion that Jan was the daughter who favored Glenda. Now Diana clearly saw reality. She was the one like their mother, knowing what she wanted from life and not being afraid to take it. It was she, not Jan, who was the independent woman.

Diana climbed from her bed and put on a pale pink summer robe. She ran her hands through her hair and tried to think. She could ride into town with Jan and Mark, but there would be endless questions about why she was taking several pieces of luggage. She intended to take everything. When she left the farm, it would be for the last time. Still, she didn't want to create a disturbance. She was nervous enough thinking about getting rid of the burden below her waistline. No, it was better to let Jan and Mark leave on their senseless mission; she'd have only Eva to avoid. With any luck, she could get her things in the car before Eva or Tillie noticed.

As she paced the room, she held her hands over her racing heart. She needed to remain calm. Being this excited made it hard to think straight. She went to the bathroom, took a tranquilizer, and on impulse swallowed another. When she stepped from the bathroom, it startled her to see Jan entering the bedroom.

"Oh good, you're awake," Jan said. "Breakfast is ready. I want to get an early start and Mark is still coming with me despite his own problems. Why don't you eat with us? Eva is going to need everyone's support today."

Diana started to refuse, but thought better of it. She didn't want any complications. Let them think nothing was about to happen.

"You go on; I'll be there in a minute. Let me get dressed."

Jan smiled and closed the door behind her. Diana began dressing and stopped in the middle of buttoning her smock. What was she thinking, where was her mind? She must call Glenda and tell her she was coming. She wasn't exactly sure what Dr. Kruger had meant when he said "discomfort." She should make certain Glenda was there when she arrived. This whole thing had to be over before she saw Clay. That meant starting the process now. She quickly finished dressing and went to the comset to call her mother.

Glenda was inquisitive. Diana thought the questions would never end. It seemed everyone knew about the land disaster.

"Your father left early this morning for Oklahoma City to meet with representatives of National Grain. I can't believe you don't want to be at the farm when Clay arrives."

"I told you, I need to be in town with you."

"You could at least stay long enough to hear what he has to say," Glenda argued. "We can use any information we can get about this thing. Thomas is very upset; he wouldn't have known if Ed's conscience hadn't gotten the better of him. He called last night."

Diana shook her head, trying to clear it. Ed, Ed who? What was Glenda talking about? Oh yes, Fern's brother who worked for National Grain. God, everyone was infected with this madness.

There was no chance to explain to Glenda about why she had to come home.

"Listen, Mother. I need to come home today." She was nearly shouting.

"Diana, what's wrong? You sound strange."

"I'm fine. I'll explain when I see you. You will be there, won't you?"

"Yes, I'll be waiting for you."

As she ended the call, Diana trembled from head to foot. She grew dizzy and for a minute couldn't think of what to do next. Her mouth was dry and the rest of her body damp with perspiration. This was ridiculous. She had to get hold of herself; it must be some animal instinct from the distant past. She wanted to eliminate the child she was carrying, but her body in its determination to reproduce was creating some sort of defense. It wouldn't work. She would not have her life ruined by some brood sow instincts. She jerked open the lingerie drawer and removed the packet. She tore open an end and three slim white capsules slid onto her palm. She had to clench her fist to keep from dropping the pills. The instructions said to take them two hours apart. Diana glanced at the clock; it was seven, she'd take the last pill at eleven. That should keep her on schedule. She would be in the hospital by mid-afternoon, about the time Clay would come hunting for her.

Diana swallowed the first pill and went downstairs.

Breakfast was a complete bore, everyone being solicitous of one another, speaking in soft tones. The entire house seemed wrapped in a funereal atmosphere. Diana covered her mouth to suppress a smile. They acted like something was dying, but she was the only one who knew what it was. When Jan and Mark finished eating, Jan stood and nodded at Mark.

"You don't have to go, you know."

Mark took a last drink of coffee, and standing, pushed his chair away. "I want to go. I can't sit around waiting for an answer."

After saying goodbye, they both hurried from the room. Jan always seemed to drag others into her lost causes. Still, at this particular time, it suited Diana to have Jan and Mark away from the farm. Two less to try to stop her departure. Tillie began clearing the table. Eva poured more coffee for herself and offered Diana some. Diana held out her cup.

"Thank you," she said primly.

Eva gave her a puzzled look and smiled. "I must say, you're looking well this morning. I'm glad. Clay is going to need someone cheerful when he gets home."

Demurely Diana lifted the cup to her lips. What a lot of drivel it was. Look at the two of them, Diana thought. Putting on an air of bravery, acting strong in the face of trouble. Eva finished her coffee and rose to help Tillie, who was putting away some clean dishes.

"When I'm done here," Tillie told Eva, "we can spend a few hours in the garden. Since it's hot early this year, I think we should go ahead with the rest of our planting."

"That's a good idea. No matter what,"—Eva sighed—"people have to eat. Clay and Jeff will be wanting something after those dry rations."

Diana excused herself, leaving the two women to their domestic chores. She nearly skipped up the stairs. Eva had said she was looking well, but it was nothing to what she was feeling. She looked at her watch: nearly nine. She would have to hurry. She got her suitcases from the hall closet, lugged them into the bedroom, and locked the door. No sense taking the chance of someone barging in. Time to take the second pill. Things were going perfectly; she felt fine. Dr. Kruger knew his stuff. The spacing of the capsules was working; three low dosages kept her feeling okay. Yet with the last pill, it was strong enough to do the job.

They expected Clay to arrive in late afternoon. She intended to be gone well before noon; there was no danger of their meeting. Even so, she needed to hurry. She couldn't wait to be in her parents' house. She wrinkled her nose at the thought of the afternoon...she didn't look forward to pain, but at the first sign, she would have Glenda rush her to Garden City General. They could sedate her immediately. With the wondrous drugs, there was no need for anyone to suffer.

Clay rarely took anything, even for recreation. Maybe that was why he was dull. It had been stupid of her not to have noticed before their marriage.

Diana finished packing and closed the last case. The four bags had taken over an hour and a half even with throwing her clothes into them. One by one, she carried the suitcases to the door and placed them in a line. It was more of a struggle than she had expected; the bulge in her middle made every move clumsy, but that would soon end. She intended to sneak downstairs and see if the way was clear. The garage was at the end of the house. To reach it, there was the risk of someone seeing her. No matter. If they did, no one could stop her. Still, it was safer to leave by the front door rather than go through the connection in back. Especially with Eva and Tillie in the garden behind the house.

Suddenly, as she stood deciding the best way to exit the house, a wave of nausea hit her. Sweat beaded across her forehead and upper lip, and her knees buckled. She reached for the doorframe to steady herself. She let her head drop forward and closed her eyes, but quickly opened them as it made the queasiness worse. When a sharp pain shot through her stomach, panic set in and brought on more trembling. Something must be wrong. She hadn't taken the third pill, and nothing should be happening this soon. She waited a minute and the feelings began to subside. There, that was better. She thought about resting for a while, but really didn't have time, and she was feeling fine now. Carefully she opened the door, and taking one suitcase, crept into the hallway. When she thought of how she must look, a fit of giggling threatened to overtake her. She could be mistaken for a pregnant girl running away from home.

In the garage, Diana put the suitcase in the backseat of the car she and Clay used and checked to make sure the keys were there. With people always coming and going on the farm, the rule was to leave a key with each vehicle. Diana appreciated the system; it made her departure much easier. Quickly she started toward the house. It was only eleven o'clock, and yet the air was as hot as heat from an oven. She shaded her eyes and looked toward the sky. It was pale yellow and cloudless.

The leaves that had started to unfold on some of the oaks in the yard were small and curled, almost parched. Just looking at the arid land made her thirsty. A small puff of wind blew around the south corner of the house, lifting dust from a flowerbed. It settled on her face and arms. She licked her lips and tried to spit out the grit that had landed on her teeth. As the wind died down, she turned her head away and hurried into the house. She reached her bedroom without seeing anyone. It was time to take the last pill, but she hesitated. Suppose she became too sick to leave, what would happen? Maybe she should wait and take it in town or at least wait until the bags were in the car. She entered the bathroom and stood looking at the slim, white capsule in her hand.

"Diana, what are you doing? Why are these bags at the door?"

She whirled around. Eva was standing in the bedroom holding a stack of clean sheets. Diana's hand closed over the pill.

"What are you doing here? I thought you were in the garden with Tillie."

"We decided she'd do the garden and I'd work in the house. I finished the laundry and thought you might need these for your bed."

"Don't you knock before coming into a person's room?"

Eva hesitated. "I'm sorry, the door was ajar. What are you doing with the suitcases?"

"I'm leaving. Why don't you go on with your bed making or whatever else a good farm wife does?"

Eva's mouth opened and closed. At the same time, anger flared in her eyes before dying away.

"I know you're upset. We are under a terrible strain. You'll feel differently when Clay is home. It isn't fun being pregnant, feeling alone. I even felt that way part of the time when Mark was right beside me. By the time the baby comes, we will have found a way to put this trouble behind us."

Upset, Diana thought. I wasn't upset before she came in. The damn baby again, a chain binding her to this family forever. The trembling started again and a black mist fogged her mind. She opened her hand, looked at the pill lying there sleek and white. It was the release from the messy, syrupy sentiment sloshing around her. She began to feel sick again. Maybe Eva could stop her from leaving, but she couldn't make her keep the revolting mass in her belly. Diana slapped her hand to her mouth and fought to swallow; the pill lodged in her throat and she grabbed the glass on the sink and filled it with water. As she gulped it, Eva dropped the sheets on the bed and rushed to her, grabbing her arm.

"Are you sick, what was that you took?"

Diana jerked away, her lips lifted in a sneer. "You want to know, don't you? But it's my business, now leave me alone."

Before she could say any more, she grew dizzy, making her feel faint. A darkness descended, clouding her eyes and hiding Eva's horrified face. As a ripping pain worked its way along her back and into her legs, she slid to the floor.

When she awoke, she was on the bed, with Eva in the hallway screaming for Tillie. When Eva came to the bedside, she looked worried. Diana rose on one elbow and tried to put her legs over the side of the bed, but Eva held her down.

"I can't find Tillie. I think she is still in the garden, but I've a call in for Dr. Kruger. Do keep still."

"Let me go, I'm fine. I need to leave. My mother is expecting me; I should have been there by now."

Diana still felt a bit dizzy, but her resolve hadn't weakened... she was strong enough to leave. She wanted to tell Eva what the pill was, what she had done. She would love to see the look on her face when she knew there would be no grandson. Diana was sure it was dead now, a mass of lifeless tissue waiting to be expelled. With her freedom close, it strengthened her further. Yes, it had been her fault, the marriage, the pregnancy, getting involved with this stupid family, all her fault. It should be her right to undo her mistake. If she could somehow get rid of this cow of a woman. Eva's face was set, stern, and her voice harsh.

"I don't know why you don't want this child, but Clay does! If you've done something to harm it you will answer to me."

Diana broke into gales of laughter; becoming lightheaded, she fought to control it.

"You're something from an old Western novel. This is my body; I say who stays inside me. You're too late, old woman. Get out of my way; I don't intend to kill myself, too."

Eva flinched as if struck, a stunned look on her face. Diana seized the opportunity and jumped to her feet. For a second, she was shaky and uncertain, but only from rising too fast. She was perfectly fine, not an ache or pain anywhere. She rushed across the room, grabbed one of the suitcases, and went through the doorway. Eva was right behind her, trying to take the bag from her hands. Diana jerked away and crossed the hallway to the landing at the top of the stairs.

"This is absurd," she screamed at Eva. "It's over, I'm leaving. Let me alone."

Eva lunged in front of her with surprising agility, stretching her arms wide to bar the way down the stairs. A fireball of anger exploded in Diana. She flung her arm toward Eva, hitting her square in the chest. The older woman uttered a cry of surprise mingled with fear, and she clutched at Diana, catching her hand. Diana dropped the suitcase and fought to make Eva let go of her hand. Eva tried to pull Diana away from the stairs, but with a cry of anger, Diana pushed Eva from her. As Eva fell backward, Diana shoved her harder. When Eva's foot hit the step, she reached for the newel post, but Diana knocked her hand away. Instead, Eva took hold of Diana's arm, dragging her forward. As they both started to fall, Diana gave Eva one last push.

Eva tumbled down the full length of the stairs, where she lay at the bottom in a crumpled heap, while Diana landed on the top two steps. She clung to the spindles under the handrail and painfully pulled herself up onto the landing.

Something was happening. When she fell, her tailbone had struck the edge of the top step. Pain shot through her lower body.

She lay flat on the floor, her head at the edge of the stairs. The first contraction had nearly caused her to lose consciousness. Now she wished she had, because a grinding pain gripped her, a tightening around her waist forcing everything downward. She rolled onto her side, trying to bring her legs toward her stomach to ease the sharp attacks. Her mind registered the pain, but it turned to agony that pushed her past reason and into panic. A wet stickiness coated her thighs; in a daze, she put her hand between her legs. When she withdrew it, the palm was red with blood. She began screaming.

~ * ~

The Brockman law office on Grand Avenue was an old silver stone building wedged between the bank and the new central communication center. The building had stood since the early 1900s, resisting the modernization the rest of downtown Garden City had undergone. As a child, Jan always looked forward to the times Thomas would take her to the office with him, mostly on Sundays when he had contracts and his personal investments to study. Jan would sit at the secretary's desk and pretend it was a weekday and she was a part of her father's exciting world of work.

It was a hushed place, muffled by thick maroon carpeting, heavy velvet drapes, and dark mahogany paneling. Two or three times in the past, they'd replaced carpeting and draperies, and each time the cost had soared, but Thomas and Avery had insisted upon keeping the offices in their original condition. The inch-thick paneling had only grown more lustrous and beautiful with the hundred years of rubbing and polishing, as had the immense desks, massive curved chairs, and heavy bookcases. It was still an intriguing place for Jan, even though as an adult she sometimes opposed the views held by her uncle and father.

The reception room was at street level where some concession to modern taste had crept in. The desk was a sweeping curve of chrome and plastic. On the walls were murals depicting Oklahoma history from settlement to mechanized fields and dome-topped cities. One wide painting showed giant men striding across the prairie with plows, followed by a sturdy looking family. Other pictures depicting modern days showed shining structures, buildings with tall spirals, and huge machines instead of people working the land. As Jan and Mark walked past the picture-filled wall, a sadness settled over her. She had no idea what the creator of this pictorial history intended, but to her it represented the disappearance of individuals.

Perhaps it was because of Evan and his fight for his right to teach as he pleased. It was enough to drive a person insane. The government claimed there was complete freedom...it encouraged people to do what they pleased, while at the same time, restrictions and regulations strangled any chance of personal choice. A push-pull situation that could end in complete stagnation.

In a second, the elevator took them to the second floor. They stepped from the brightness of the elevator into the familiar subdued elegance of her father's offices. Jewel Miller, sitting behind her desk in the outer office, smiled at them. Jewel had started working for the Brockman firm twenty-five years ago. During that time, her chestnut-colored hair had become white; it softened the creases in her face also brought on by the years. Yet, age seemed to have no effect upon her figure. She was still the trim, small woman Jan remembered from her childhood. Jewel stood to greet them.

"Jan, how nice to see you. My, don't you look pretty. And Mr. Sanderson," Jewel offered her hand to Mark. "I guess you are one of the family now with our Diana and Clay being an old married couple. I hear there will soon be a Sanderson baby on the farm. Oh, how I remember that wedding, a beautiful rosy, old-fashioned affair. Diana is certainly one for setting trends; several of the girls in town have followed her example."

Jewel stopped short and clicked her tongue. "Listen to me going on. Have you come to see your father, Jan?"

"Yes, I hope he isn't busy with something else."

"Well, I'm afraid he is. He won't be in today."

Jewel's face lost its softness and assumed an aloof, professional demeanor as the talk turned to business. "Is it something Avery or I could help you with, or is it personal?"

Jan turned toward Mark. "Uncle Avery could help as well, don't you think?"

"I don't see why not." Mark shrugged.

"Very well, I'll buzz him." Jewel stepped behind her desk and pressed the intercom button. Anyone not knowing Jewel Miller would have thought her abrupt, but Jan understood. Jewel was what her name implied. She had taken the entire Brockman family into her domain. She had been on the fringe of births, marriages, and deaths for years, remaining on the sidelines ready to offer help. Still, she kept personal matters and business affairs in two distinct compartments.

In a minute, Avery Brockman came through the double doors from his office. He was a tall man, straight and unbent by time and the years of untangling legal knots. His gray hair had grown thin. The deep lines from his nose to the corners of his mouth and the sharp look in his eyes made him appear stern when he was not smiling. As he strode forward to shake Mark's hand, he was smiling, his face relaxed and jovial.

"Mark, how are you? What happened, the sun and dust drive you in off the farm?"

"It almost has, Avery. I haven't seen such weather since eighty-two."

Avery shook his head. "Yes, seems we're in another long dry spell. But I'm sure you didn't come in to discuss the weather. Whatever it is, I'm glad you brought my niece; I don't see much of her. How are you, Jan?"

"Fine, Uncle Avery."

Jan liked her uncle. Since her grandfather was dead, Avery and her father were the last living generation. She hated to think of the time when they would be gone, too. Perhaps her brother, Tyler, would take over the firm if they could get him to give up his carefree lifestyle. However, it didn't seem likely he and his life partner, Warren, would return to the states any time soon. Maybe she should continue school and come to work in the firm. That would keep another generation of Brockmans in the business. In a way that would be a selfish decision, though, helping only her family. Whereas, Evan's cause could benefit many.

"Come into the office and tell me what I can do for you."

Avery extended his arm, letting them enter first, and followed, closing the heavy doors behind him. Jan and Mark sat on the leather chairs in front of Avery's desk. Mark looked at Jan.

"I'll let you explain. I can add my two cents later."

Jan took a deep breath and began. She watched Avery's face as she talked. Not a trace of emotion flicked across it as he listened. From long years of practice, he was noncommittal; his feelings and opinions did not matter, and the letter of the law was his strict guideline. He would only interrupt if something wasn't clear. Jan knew the law concerning infringing upon Church rights in religious matters. Still, even a tightly woven and worded law might come apart with sharp, careful study picking at it. Neither her father nor her uncle would bend or twist the law. Her hope was in discovering a weakness or loose wording that could work in Evan's behalf.

"Isn't this a clear infringement upon an individual's rights?" she asked. "Evan is being detained against his will. There is no one to present his side in the Church court."

Avery's hands rested calmly on the desktop; his clear eyes mirrored the same calm. There was almost the hint of a smile about the corners of his mouth. Jan wonder if he understood how serious this was. For a minute, Avery's gaze lingered on her. She knew what he was seeing. His young niece, the one overloaded with social conscience who was always battling whirlwinds, while the rest of the family waited for her to mature. Avery brought his hands together and turned his attention to Mark.

"Jan says you were with her last evening when Evan went away with the two men. Did you see any force being used?"

Mark slowly shook his head. "No, can't say that I did, but they were close on either side of him."

"And what is your opinion of this young man, what sort of fellow is Evan?"

Mark's forehead rolled into deep brown furrows. "I don't know what you're getting at, Avery."

"I mean, is he a trouble maker, is he starting a new cult? Is he an overzealous youth thinking he can do a better job than the organization? You're a logical man, Mark. What do you think of him?"

"Well," Mark drawled. "I like him. He is kind of a strange fellow; I don't know how to put it. Sort of other worldly, spiritual, yes that's it. He's more concerned with things going on in a realm that we can't see than he is with day to day living."

"You mean people could be starving, but as long as their immortal souls were saved, he would be happy?"

"No." Jan cut in sharply. "That is not it. Evan has a deep feeling for every aspect of human life."

"Yes, he does have that, too," Mark continued. "Maybe I put it wrong. He does care about the whole person. It's himself that he doesn't take much thought for."

"Humm, a truly selfless individual. The most dangerous kind. A young man with a vision," Avery said.

Anger made Jan's heart pound. "If you aren't going to help us, Uncle Avery, we might as well go." Tears threatened to spring to her eyes.

"Now, Jan. I'm trying to see Evan as the Church does. What is there about him that causes their reaction? They don't scoop up citizens and bring them before their council for no reason. We have to understand their views before we can find a way to defend him. If we know exactly what their fears are, we will know how to alleviate them. You know that," he chided. "I'm afraid you're too emotionally involved to see things in their proper perspective."

"Why would a powerful institution be afraid of one young man?" Mark asked. "I've heard him talking to Clay and he doesn't seem dangerous. Far as I can see, he only preaches peace and love. He's not the kind to lead a rebellion."

Avery sighed. "I know it must seem that way, but don't you remember the upheaval and actual destruction that took place before they formed the Unity Council? Cults everywhere, different religions demanding special rights, and we were on the verge of a religious war. In a changing world, people always look for something to save them. Thank God, the Council finally got itself together. The Council has helped avert conflict between nations, too. In knowing how to coexist, they are ahead of the European Federation and us.

"Unity Council is a mediator; it keeps us from ultimate destruction. That is why a single young man, if he has the power to enchant and draw people, can be dangerous. He can lead people away from a system that keeps us safe. The religions of the world are united and by cautiously following their example, who knows, this world might make it anyway."

"You should be representing the Council," Jan said dryly.

"You are right about uniting, Avery," Mark spoke. "But what about this boy? Jan seems to think he's in trouble. We took him in at the farm and I'm not going to fail him now. I'd go over and talk to Reverend Dewberry, except our family isn't in good standing with him right now. 'Course, Eva and I don't care, but I think it's caused trouble between Clay and Diana. Maybe you can find some way to fix this. It might solve part of Clay's trouble, too."

Avery seemed to consider the possibilities. "As I understand it, they want Evan to stop teaching outside the organization. If someone could convince him to agree to this, it could solve the problem." Avery looked at Jan.

She shook her head. "He won't, not for me or for anyone."

Avery drummed his fingers on the desktop. "That does make it difficult. Maybe before we do anything, we should know exactly what is happening."

Avery pushed a button on his console. "Jewel, get Reverend Dewberry for me, please."

Jan waited, tense and nervous, until Reverend Dewberry's face appeared on the video speaker. Jan and Mark could view the incoming caller, but it only transmitted Avery's image.

"Reverend," Avery said with a smile. They observed the usual formalities with comments concerning health and the weather before Avery stated the reason for his call.

"I'm sure this trivial matter can be cleared quickly. I wouldn't bother you, but as you probably know my niece has, shall we say, a personal interest."

Reverend Dewberry's face took on the proper look of amused compassion. Jan bit her lip in anger. She hated what the two men were implying, but if it oiled the slow-moving machinery that would release Evan, she was willing to tolerate it.

"Yes, yes," the reverend nodded. "I do understand and let me assure you, Mr. Brockman, that we share Jan's interest in Evan Hunter's welfare. Not in the same way"—he smirked at his own humor—"but we do have the boy's best interest at heart. It's a simple matter of some retraining. We do our best and yet sometimes our message misses the mark and sets off an undesired reaction in our brightest young protégés."

Jan motioned frantically at her uncle. "Ask if I can see him," she hissed.

"Still, Reverend," Avery replied, "if Evan is being detained against his wishes, there might arise some point of secular law."

"Come now, Mr. Brockman, surely you don't think we would overstep our bounds in that area. We have merely asked Mr. Hunter to spend a few days with us in reviewing our doctrine. I assure you he is perfectly willing to spend a few days with us."

"In that case, you won't mind if my niece drops by for a visit this afternoon. A few days does seem a long time to a young person."

Reverend Dewberry's eyes clouded for a second, and then brightened. "Of course not. A visit might be in order, perhaps help our young man regain his perspective. However, tomorrow will be better; we don't want to interrupt his reorientation classes today."

With a few more words, they concluded the conversation. And when Avery disconnected the communication console, he seemed pleased.

"Now, you see. It's a simple matter of some retraining. You will talk to Evan tomorrow and this whole thing will blow over as quickly as a summer storm."

Mark still looked skeptical. "But we haven't heard how Evan feels about this retraining thing. Maybe he doesn't want to stay there a few days."

"He can tell Jan that tomorrow and if there is a problem, which I doubt, we can talk again." Avery shook his finger in Jan's direction. "I don't want you running over there causing trouble. They have agreed to your seeing Evan tomorrow. Don't do anything that might change their minds. It is better to work through accepted channels."

Suddenly, Jewel burst through the double doors. Her normally professional face was filled with concern. "I'm sorry to interrupt, Mr. Brockman, but something terrible has come in over the news channel."

She stepped to the wide communication screen and flicked on the receiver. A newscaster, his voice steady, was giving a rapid-fire description as a scene of devastation flashed on the screen.

"Thirty minutes ago, at exactly twelve noon, Eastern Time, an earthquake shattered the calm tropical waters south of Cuba. The quake ran along the northern edge of the Caribbean Plate, shattering the island of Cuba. Parts of the island are submerged and our scanners have not found a standing building on the land that is still above water. As I am speaking, the quakes are continuing to spread destruction.

"The initial nine-point-eight shock did extensive damage in southern Florida and the Texas gulf coast. People must move inland as quickly as possible. There are reports of a gigantic tsunami rushing toward the Gulf of Mexico. The projected center of the wave lies in the delta region of Louisiana. It could bring extreme flood conditions to the Mississippi valley and mid-Arkansas."

The four people in the Brockman offices were stunned into silence. Finally, Mark spoke.

"There goes the rice land. Ohio better bring in one hell of a corn crop or there isn't going to be any grain produced this year."

Avery's hands nervously picked at the edge of a stack of papers on his desk. "It seems you may be right. Thomas is in Oklahoma City now seeing to our interest. And frankly, Mark, under the circumstances, I wonder why you are spending time on this Hunter matter."

Mark shrugged. "When you been a farmer long as I have, you know when things have hit rock bottom. There's nothing to do. I'm hoping Clay will have better information. But when the land is pumped full of poison and not even a skinny blade can live, there's nothing left but to ride it out."

"There must be some technology to clean the lines, pump fresh water, and flush the entire area. That would mean losing crops for only one year."

Mark drew his lower lip down and shook his head. "Wouldn't help. You'd be washing that stuff further into the soil and increasing the polluted area."

Avery's face looked pained. "What do you intend to do?"

"Nothing right now. Soon as Clay is rested, we'll try taking stock and see what we have. Maybe we'll have some clean land left, enough to raise cash crops and feed ourselves. As for the rest, maybe a miracle will come along. Those poor people in the path of that flood are going to be in one hell of a mess, but at least saltwater won't leave the land dead forever."

Jan felt cold; she wondered where the warm blood in her body had gone. The world was turning over. The situation in Garden City was horrible; most of the people depended on the production of wheat or corn to sustain the economy. This disaster was regional. With the earthquake and expected flooding, it spelled catastrophe for the entire country. Every nation was precariously balanced in the world trade market. When a country sustained this much damage, it could become a pauper in the global market. Power centers shifted in these circumstances. Strong, healthy nations could snatch the advantage.

Avery raised his hand as he turned toward the communication screen again. President Morris was speaking. He said the right words to inspire confidence and promised extensive aid in rebuilding. He didn't say one word, Jan thought bitterly, about the rupture in the Bighorn dumpsite. Where, she wondered, did he expect the large amounts of money to come from? More borrowing from the international fund, or simply print more scrip? Either way meant economic ruin, but what did it matter? No country was actually financially sound. The global chaos made her feel small and helpless. Yet it didn't lessen her resolve concerning Evan. He was the only one who spoke anything resembling reason. His message was a simple, straightforward truth that gave a golden light to follow in a world of darkness. Thinking of Evan calmed her.

Jewel had returned to her desk in the outer office, and Avery and Mark were still watching the news. Jan stood. She had heard enough. She was impatient to get through the day, hasten the time when she could see Evan, and hear his side.

"Are you ready, Mark? If you don't mind, I want to go to the farm with you. I want to hear the rest of Clay's report, and I need to talk to Jeff about Evan."

Mark quickly stood, shook hands with Avery, and they left the office. On the way to the farm, he smiled at her. She wondered why... there wasn't much to be happy about.

"Why are you smiling?"

"Just thinking, if I were a young man like Evan, I'd be glad to have someone like you on my side. Cheer up; I'm sure everything will be okay."

Sixteen

Clay's mind was numb and his body bone-tired as he drove onto Sanderson property. Jeff slumped in the seat beside him, his head turned toward the vacant fields. There was no need for more talk; both knew what they faced. Even the news they had heard on the radio failed to move them. Another earthquake and more farmland destroyed. They could identify and sympathize, but their own disaster held them fast. Hours ago, Jeff had voiced his black thoughts. For once Clay agreed. It was the most desperate, hopeless feeling he had ever known. In the past, they took measures to correct production problems, now there was nothing they could do. Clay had wrestled with every possibility and still found no solution.

They and the other independent farmers might file a class action suit against National, but the dumpsite's cracking open from an earthquake was a natural disaster. National would defend itself along those lines, saying it was not responsible for an Act of God. Yet there might be an angle in that it knew the system was contaminated and didn't shut it down or notify their customers. These facts should matter when cases came to court. Seemed the fate of the land was in the hands of attorneys, court processes, and the government.

Government relief money might be forthcoming, but even Clay doubted that. How could they justify paying farmers who had no farmable land? Still, despite the despair that threatened to overcome him, there was joy in coming home. He drove into the compound and parked in front of the lodge.

"Sure looks quiet," Clay said.

Jeff put his hand on the door handle and let it rest there. He looked too weary to open it.

"It does, but you got to remember there isn't much for anyone to do. Everyone is probably inside watching the news about that big wave."

Neither Clay nor Jeff had mentioned the twenty men the farm employed. Clay had purposely avoided thinking about them. Most of them would lose their jobs today or tomorrow, at the latest. Clay wished he didn't have to face them. He was tempted to let Mark handle that job, but their financial strain was enough for his father to face. No need to add an emotional burden as well. Jeff seemed to find the strength to open the door and step onto the parched ground.

"You go on to the house, Clay; I'll take our gear in."

Clay nodded and left Jeff to unload. As he strode across the dusty gravel heading toward the lawn that surrounded the house, he knew Jeff would be doing more than storing their equipment. The men would gather around, asking about the trip. Jeff in his concise way would give them the details. Clay sighed; having studied the situation, the men probably knew what was coming, but he still hated to be the one to drop the ax.

Clay kicked at a tuft of dried grass beside the brick walkway leading to the wide porch. He wondered how long Mrs. Thompson would be able to keep her prize wisteria alive if the weather didn't break soon. April was almost gone and it should have been a damp, misty month with a few heavy showers. There was still May to count on, but he didn't have much hope. Last summer had been dry, and winter hadn't been cold or wet enough to form even frost. With an overly warm spring and no moisture, he was ready to believe it would never rain again. And even if they did find some uncontaminated ground, there wouldn't be enough water to grow anything. As he crossed the porch, his boot heels thumped against the floor sounding as heavy as the news he carried. He hesitated, and then opened the big door.

Inside, the house was cool and dim after the glaring heat outside. He glanced at the deer horn hat rack and didn't see Mark's sweat-stained hat hanging there. He remembered his mother telling him that Mark had gone with Jan to see about Evan. A sharp twinge of guilt struck him. He and Jeff, caught in their own problems, had forgotten Evan's trouble. He was glad Mark had offered to help, but knowing what a generous man he was it didn't surprise him. Maybe if he tried hard, someday he'd be half the man his father was.

"Mother," Clay's shout rang as he stepped into the living room. "I'm home. Where is everyone?"

Perhaps she and Tillie were outside. Probably working in the garden, babying the tender young seedlings to provide the precious vegetables that kept them eating well. He turned, heading to the foyer and the wide staircase. He wouldn't have any trouble finding Diana. Not a chance of her being outside in the stifling heat trying to grow something. Still, what she was growing brought a smile to his lips. What the hell, he had known she wasn't the outdoor type when he married her.

"Clay. I thought I heard someone. I was in the kitchen."

Clay stopped with his foot on the first step of the staircase. With a smile, he turned toward Tillie. The instant he saw her white, puffy, tear-stained face, alarm struck like a fist to his chest. His first thought was of Diana and the baby.

"What's the matter? What's happened?"

Tillie sucked in her trembling lower lip and clasped her plump hands to her breast.

"I don't know if I can do this, my little fellow."

The blood pounded in Clay's ears; he knew the world was about to crumble. Tillie hadn't called him "her little fellow" for years. It was a term of endearment she had always used when trying to teach him something, or coax him to take some unpleasant medicine. Tillie lifted her quivering chin.

"You and I have a loathsome job. I have to talk, and you have to listen. The only way we can get through it is with determination and strength."

Clay looked at the polished floor between his boots. Someone was dead, he knew that much. Diana, Mark, something had happened to one of them. Black purple grief settled over him even before Tillie spoke the name.

"Your dear mother is dead."

Tillie's words hit with an unexpected impact. They stunned him. His mind reeled, his hand found the newel post and he grasped it.

"How? Why?"

Tillie took his arm. "Come, we'll sit."

Obediently, Clay followed Tillie into the living room and sat on the long sofa while she took the armchair. It seemed strange to see Tillie sitting. She was always in motion.

"Tell me, Tillie, go on." Clay was determined to help her deliver whatever horrible message she must. Tillie folded her hands in her lap and studied his face.

"There's no way, Clay, but to tell it as it happened. I was working in the garden and I came in to get a drink. I was in the kitchen and I heard some terrible commotion. I came through the dining room to see what the trouble was. It was your mother and Diana, at the top of the stairs, yelling at each other. Diana was fixing to leave. I didn't want to be caught listening, and I would never tell you this now except you have a right to know. Eva said Diana was doing something to get rid of the baby or was going into town to have it done…"

Clay quickly rose. "Is Diana okay? Where is she?"

He started for the living room door, but Tillie hurried to him.

"Stop. Listen to me. Diana is fine. You can go to her, but you have to hear the rest. Don't go off half-cocked."

Clay could barely restrain himself, but he knew Tillie was right. As the hard, sturdy stock in his bloodline kicked in, he returned to the sofa. They lived by the creed that if you were beat to your knees, but still breathing, you kept swinging.

"Okay, I'll listen."

Tillie, her face even whiter, stood before him. "I started to the kitchen door, getting ready to leave them in privacy; it wasn't my business. Then the arguing got worse. I hesitated in the doorway thinking I should stay. Eva might need me. They were at the top of the stairs. I saw them there. Eva was trying to stop Diana from going. They struggled, and when Diana shoved Eva away, it made them both fall, Eva to the bottom of the stairs and Diana at the top. I didn't know what to do, I ran to Eva..."

Tillie's steel resolve seemed to melt. Tears flooded her face and her shoulders shook as the tear-soaked words tumbled from her lips.

"...I got on the floor beside her. She looked into my eyes and said, 'Mark, tell Mark, I love him.' Then she was gone, Clay. She died wanting me to tell Mark that she loved him. But Lord above, Mark knows that." Tillie kept rocking with her round arms locked across her wide middle as if her stomach ached.

Clay had turned to wood. His mind worked with the clunky stiff action of wooden parts, badly chiseled gears haltingly delivering choppy words.

"What happened after that, Tillie?"

Tillie gulped twice, pulled a large white handkerchief from her pocket, and blew her nose. "I could see she was gone, Clay. I swear to God I would have given my own breath if it would have helped. I hadn't noticed before, I was too shocked over Eva, but I heard Diana screaming at the top of the stairs. She was on the landing. I suppose I should have run to her, but I couldn't have done anything. Instead, I ran to the intercom and called the lodge. I knew Terry and William were over there. I called the crisis center for emergency help and ran to Diana. When I got to her, it was over.

"The baby was dark blue, a poor bruised-looking little thing. Diana was bleeding. I feared she'd die. I got some towels, wrapped the baby, and did what I could for Diana. When William and Terry came, they saw the situation and took off to find Mark and Jan. When the medics came, they rushed Diana to the hospital. That is where everyone is now."

Clay wanted to bury his head in his hands and close his eyes tight enough to shut off everything. But he couldn't do it. When calamity struck, there was nowhere to hide unless you gave in to madness and completely lost your mind.

"Have you heard anything about Diana?" Clay couldn't think of his lost mother and tried to center on the living. Tillie nodded, causing a stray tear to drop off her quivering chin.

"Jan called me. Diana is okay. Eva had left a message for Dr. Kruger. She must have done it before Diana tried to leave." A fresh fountain flowed from Tillie's eyes. "I should have been the one to tell Mark. Eva would have wanted me to let him know right off that her only thoughts were of him. But I couldn't let you come home and not hear the straight story."

"Clay," Jeff called from the doorway. "The men at the lodge told me."

Clay stood and started toward Jeff, who looked bent and old, weathered and dark as a tanned hide. He was twisting the brim of his hat as it hung from his hands. His blue eyes were dark enough to seem black.

"Do you want me to go with you?" Jeff asked.

Clay didn't realize that he hadn't answered until he heard Tillie.

"You better do that, Jeff," she was saying. "No telling how Mark is taking this. I'll stay and keep things together the best I can."

Jeff went to Clay's side and started to guide him toward the front entrance. Clay kept looking over his shoulder at the living room with the huge fireplace, and the furnishings Eva had carefully gathered over the years. At the door, his gaze rested upon the staircase for a moment and then quickly shifted away.

~ * ~

When they came through the glass doors into the hospital lobby, Jan rushed toward them. She threw her arms around Clay and hugged him tight, crushing her face against his shoulder.

"Tillie called and said you were coming." Jan took Clay's hand, holding it while she reached over to touch Jeff's arm.

"I don't know what to say to console you. It's terrible."

"I know," Clay stuttered. "I better go see Diana. Is Dad with her?"

Jan's fingers tightened on his hand, her nails biting deep into his palm. A spasm of terror shot through him.

"Oh, God no! It's his heart when he heard about Mother, isn't it?"

"Take it easy, boy." Jeff's arm was around Clay's shoulders. Jeff's face, set and hard, turned toward Jan. "Mark is okay, isn't he?"

Jan nodded quickly. "Yes, yes he is. I'll tell you what happened before you go. The fellows from the farm radioed us as we were in the truck driving from town. They said to meet them at the hospital, something about Diana. When we arrived, the doctor told Mark about Eva. You were right, Clay, it was a big shock. Mark collapsed. It was good he heard the news with a doctor nearby. They started to work on him right away, and now he is stable."

Clay had been wooden and stiff, but suddenly his legs began to tremble and his whole body grew limp. The hammer that used to tap in Clay's head turned into a pounding iron mallet and the pressure became a crushing weight. His disjointed thoughts made it hard to speak, but words tumbled from his mouth anyway.

"Where is my mother, where did they take her?"

Jan lowered her head. "They are determining the exact way she died. Then I guess they'll take her to Resthaven Funeral Home."

"Tracy, has anyone called Tracy?"

"Yes, she and Frank are with your father now."

Clay looked toward the bank of elevators with the numbers above them. His feet felt stuck to the lobby's tile floor, his mind not sending a message to move. Jan seemed to sense his dilemma.

"Diana is in maternity on the seventh floor; Mark is on the fifth. Why don't you see Diana first? Your father isn't awake. The doctor is keeping him sedated until he is stronger and more able to cope with Eva being gone. Jeff and I will keep each other company."

Jeff gave Clay a reassuring pat on the shoulder before he and Jan headed for the waiting room. Somehow, Clay's legs found the strength to hold him and carry him into the elevator. A young medic shared the elevator with Clay. As it rose to the seventh floor, for one crazy second, Clay wanted to grab the medic and demand that he give him a sedative. A drug to make him unconscious, to relieve his unbearable misery. Clay was a simple man. He understood the basic emotions of fear, hate, love, and the commonly spoken words that expressed most outward actions. But he couldn't comprehend the complex emotions that made people do unacceptable things. Things that made people hurt others for no obvious reason.

Why didn't Diana want the baby, and if she didn't, why start it in the first place? This was as hard for Clay to grasp, as it would be for his thick, broad fingers to handle and weave fine, delicate thread into lace. He resented these complicated emotions in others. They had no right to cross and tangle their own feelings to create and caste a net ensnaring those around them. Clay yearned for the uncomplicated years of his childhood. A time when things were as plain as the blue sky, the yellow sun, and the green fields. He mourned the fact that those years had been short; now his world was a place of mixed colors where nothing was clear. Conditions swirled about him in somber browns, deep purples, and sharp piercing tongues of orange. It was hard to understand what was happening.

He stood outside Diana's room for long seconds trying to sort his feelings before facing his wife. The baby was gone, a fact that in another situation would have brought him great sadness. Yet, with this many losses at hand it seemed small, a tiny ghost that would linger on in wistful memory. The image of a small boy shimmered before him, but anger blurred and distorted the outline. Even with no proof of his mother's suspicions, Clay accepted them. It was a thing Diana could do. Life had too many twists and turns for a man who wanted to live in a straight line. Perhaps it was time to grab the serpent by both ends and snap it straight between his powerful outstretched arms.

Diana sat propped against white pillows. A simple green hospital gown covered her above the white sheet at her waist. Glenda was sitting beside the bed. It startled Clay; he had expected Diana to be alone. At his entrance, the two women looked toward him. They both had the same bright cheerful and unreadable smile. Practiced faces that certain types of people were, at an instant, able to present to the world. A bland mask that hid their devious thoughts. He wanted to strip those masks away and for once see the truth. This particular truth was as harsh as icy gall; yet he was certain nothing could make him more cold and bitter than he already was.

"Oh, Clay." Glenda stood and came to him. "We're sorry. How unfortunate this is, but at least we can be thankful that Diana is doing well."

She turned toward the bed with a fond smile. "Thomas will be home tomorrow, but I know I can speak for the entire Brockman family when I say we will be standing by to help in any way we can. Our deepest sympathy is with you."

Clay nodded.

Glenda raised a hand to fuss with her hair and gave another icy smile. "I suppose the decent thing for a mother-in-law to do is depart. I'll leave you two alone."

She took her purse and looked at Diana. "I'll stop later, dear. Remember, Clay, if you need anything be sure to let me know."

Diana reached to the nightstand and pulled a tissue from the dispenser.

"Thank you, Mother. I'm sure Clay knows how badly everyone feels."

Glenda stepped into the hallway, but hesitated and motioned Clay to follow her. When they were alone in the hallway, she put her hand on his arm.

"Clay, in case you haven't spoken to the doctor, you should know Diana is under strong medication. She may seem alert and calm, but she is not herself. Don't pay attention to anything she might say. You understand?"

When he reentered the room, Clay took Glenda's bedside seat and silently studied Diana. He couldn't tell if she was shedding tears or holding the tissue in a way as to hide the fact that she wasn't. She gave a last dab under each eye and met his gaze. Her face was sad and gave the appearance of being ready to crumple into crying. He remembered Tillie's bloated tear-torn face; it made him doubt that Diana had even cried. His cold, callous observations surprised him, for at the same time he wanted to take her in his arms. He hated dealing with two strong feelings at once. He should either hate her or love her. Nothing could be this evenly divided; one had to be stronger than the other was.

"Why did you do it?" Clay hadn't planned his first words...they came unbidden.

Diana clutched the front of the smooth gown, crimping it at her breast. "You blame me. I knew you would. It isn't fair; you don't care about me. I nearly bled to death. Don't you care about that?"

"Of course I care. At first, I thought Tillie was going to tell me something had happened to you and I wanted to die myself. Why can't you see how much I care, why can't you let our love be a sweet, flowing thing. Not something fouled and dirty with your schemes."

Clay lowered his head onto his hands and he felt her hand stroking his hair.

"I haven't done anything, Clay. Honest I haven't. You must understand. I've been as miserable as you have. It was a mistake for us to marry. I'm not blaming you. We didn't know it wasn't going to be the dream we'd both planned. Losing the baby seems terrible to you now, but you'll come to see it as a blessing. I have. If the child had lived, we might have felt ties neither of us could break. Now we're free to start again."

Clay lifted his head. "Are you saying you want to leave me?"

"Not right away, Clay. That would be unthinkable under the circumstances. I'll stand by you every minute until you're through the worst of losing your mother, and until Mark is stronger."

The colored waves of confusion threatened to engulf Clay. Things were badly out of focus. Diana had taken off on an unexpected track, leading him away from the important matter.

"Don't do me any favors. If you don't love me and think it was a mistake, we'll call it quits right now." Clay thought a trace of fear flickered in her eyes. "What's the matter? Didn't you think it would be this easy? I've lost nearly everything else that matters to me. What's one wife more or less?"

"A few minutes ago, you said you still loved me. I wanted to make things easier for you until you could see that you never really loved me. It was only some physical attraction we had."

Medication, his left foot. Diana was as much herself as she had ever been. Glenda knew it, too. She was afraid of what Diana might say and tried to cover for her. Afraid it would be a poor time to ask for a divorce. It was the wrong time to speak of something that serious... unless it was a diversion. Diana could well create a bad situation to hide something worse.

"Tell me what happened at the house today, Diana. How did this happen? Why are my mother and my baby dead?"

Diana turned her head aside and held her knuckles to her trembling lips. "I don't know, Clay. I wish I could give you some solid reason. Something to help relieve your sorrow. It was a terrible accident. Something went wrong with the baby. I went into labor. Your mother was trying to help me with my suitcase because we were going to drive right to the hospital. At the top of the stairs, I had another horrible pain and doubled over. She tried to help me and we both fell. Oh, Clay, I could have been at the bottom of those stairs, too."

"That isn't the way Tillie told it. Mother thought you were getting rid of the baby and she was trying to stop you. No one stops you, do they, Diana?"

"Clay, you can't believe that. You know Tillie has always hated me. You must stop her from spreading those stories. None of it was my fault."

~ * ~

That night, Tillie served three people at the large oak dining table. Clay sat in his usual place with Jan and Jeff across from him, each of them carefully keeping their eyes from straying to Mark's empty chair at the head of the table and Eva's at the far end. There had been no discussion about Jan coming to stay at the farm. It seemed natural. Sometimes, it seemed she was somehow more a Sanderson than a Brockman. Perhaps Diana was right and their marriage had been a mistake. He wondered if he had chosen the wrong sister, an error Evan had almost made. Suddenly he wished he could talk with Evan. Perhaps he'd have something to say that would help put the world right again, but that was an impossible task. The wheel of time kept on rolling, leaving indelible tracks upon their lives. Prints that no words could cover. It was strange how words could make things happen, but couldn't alter anything after it was done.

Mark had been awake long enough that evening to order Clay to "Get me out of this place. I've got to be with your mother." This was exactly what everyone was trying to prevent. However, the doctor did say they could release Mark in the morning. They thought he would be strong enough to handle the situation. Keeping him longer would only increase his agitation.

It was a relief to see how well Mark was reacting. His instructions to Clay were as direct and firm as ever. He didn't want them to take Eva to the funeral home. He wanted arrangements made to have her returned to the farm and buried at a spot they had both picked long ago. He wanted Evan to perform the service, and he'd already asked for Jan's help.

Mark had made it clear. "Jan is going to see Evan tomorrow. Let her tell those pigheaded men that if they don't send Evan, a good Christian woman is to be buried without the benefit of any words; I won't have one of them step foot on the place."

Tracy was no help. She was at either Mark's bedside crying, or in Frank's arms doing the same thing. However, Frank had been a complete surprise. He was extremely concerned over Mark's condition. Even more amazing was his interest in the activities at the farm. He offered to help with business there until Mark was able to take part. Frank had pulled Clay aside, voicing an earnestness that Clay had never before seen in him.

"We both know I'm no good in the agricultural end, but I could help in the office. I would have offered sooner, Clay, but it was only yesterday that I found what kind of trouble you have there. Does it mean the land is worthless?"

In a way, it made Clay feel guilty for not confiding in Frank when the problem first arose. He never thought Frank was interested. Although at Christmas, he had seemed attentive when they were discussing farm business. The offer touched Clay and he didn't bother to tell Frank there wasn't much work for anyone at this point. Let Frank come if he wanted; it might make him feel useful.

Clay ate from habit, shoveling each forkful of beef and rice into his mouth with short, jerky motions. No one had bothered to turn on the evening news. It wasn't hard to guess that conditions in the Gulf area were worsening. A flood was bad enough, but in a land with a depleted water table, seawater would be disastrous. The low groundwater was an invitation for the saltwater intrusion. Inch by inch as they pumped water to irrigate the rice, cotton, and soy crops, the ocean had seeped in. Farmers in the south and far southeast were aware of the problem. They had tried staggered pumping, installing catch basins for rainwater and recycled irrigation water, along with building desalination plants. As the national demand for food increased, and the government paid for higher production, companies and individuals pushed the land and water to their limits. It was risky, but it had worked. There was enough rainfall in the coastal areas to stay almost even as the water in the aquifer dropped. Now the balance was upset. It could be years before enough rain fell to raise the water table to a level sufficient to wash away the salt water.

Clay studied the grains of rice on his plate and pictures flashed in his mind of the grim faces of the farmers in the region that produced it. It was easy to imagine their expressions. They would be the same as the ones worn by the wheat and corn farmers in the high plains. When the full impact of the millions of lost farmland acres hit, it was going to be a horror story worse than any history had ever recorded. Two of the big grain conglomerates had some reserves, which gave the government a small advantage in dealing with non-food producing countries. This income kept the nation solvent. The question was, would the government feed people and suffer a crash in the world market, or struggle to hold its place and let their own people starve? On the other hand, it really didn't matter what the government did. Either way they would only be buying time. If it was not enough time to get the land into production, the entire society could collapse. In the south, man couldn't control the situation; in time nature could correct it. Heavy rains could sweep the south and the coastal land clean and supply them with fresh water again. The picture was not this promising for the plains. They never had enough water anyway, and even if the miracle of a heavy flushing did occur, it might spread the deadly chemicals.

"Clay, you've stopped eating," Jan said softly. "I know it's hard, but there's nothing to do but go on. Eva wouldn't want you to be this way."

With Jan's words, guilt and shame hit Clay. He hadn't been thinking of his mother; he couldn't. His mind shied away from the thought...it hurt too much. Instead, he had turned to physical problems. Terrible as they were, he was better able to cope with external disasters. Never seeing Eva again was something that cut too deep and painful. He was not equipped to deal with it. Maybe later, as the wound had time to heal, he could examine the damage. For now, he only knew how much he loved and missed her.

He would miss the love and comfort she had given him, but not only that. She had always handled any hard times that came. For years, Eva had moved away from actual management of the farm, leaving a place for her growing son to fill. Yet her opinions and advice had pulled them through more than one scrape. There was no one to fill the void she was leaving. Clay's anger with himself bit into his sorrow. He should have listened to Jeff and the softly dropped hints about Diana's suitability. Not that it would have made any difference, for he loved her. Maybe he still did in some strange way. Even though Diana would never be the farm wife his mother had been.

"I think Diana will be able to come home soon." Jan spoke in answer to his thoughts. "If not tomorrow, surely the day after."

Clay wasn't ready to deal with his feelings for Diana, any more than he was the grief over his mother. He fled to another subject.

"Speaking of coming home, are you going to have trouble getting Evan released?"

"I don't know."

"I offered to go with her," Jeff said.

Jan smiled at Jeff. "You know I appreciate the offer, Jeff. I honestly don't think it would do any good. Besides, the family needs you with Mark coming home. I think I heard Tracy say she and Frank would be bringing the children and moving in for a while. There will be more than enough for everyone to do. If Evan can leave tomorrow, do you want him on the farm? With your problems, are you sure you want to add another?"

Clay's mouth dropped in surprise. How could she even ask? She knew Mark had requested that Evan hold the service for Eva. It was insulting to imply that they would be less hospitable simply because of their own troubles.

"Sure, I want him." Clay's voice was sharper than he intended.

Jan ducked her head. "I'm sorry; I only thought it might be easier if he went somewhere else."

"I'm sorry, Jan. It was considerate of you to ask. The whole thing is confusing. What are they doing with him? Do they think preaching at him for a couple of days will help? How can they have authority over him now anyway? They already stripped him of everything. I know the education loan was paid. Mark took care of it. Evan was repaying him from his wages. What hold or claim do they have?"

"Ha," Jeff snorted. "You don't know much about religious fervor. There's nothing to beat a bunch of men set on their own gain, but hiding it under the banner of religion. It covers a multitude of sins. In the name of doing good, they can reach into places they never could on their own."

"I know it does go against all reasonable thinking," Jan tried to explain. "But they are within their rights to stop unauthorized meetings. They could prevent anyone from doing what Evan had been doing. You don't have to be an ex-employee of the Church. They are trying to stop groups from splintering off and heading for the hills crying doomsday. I've heard there are some small sects hiding away, keeping out of their reach, but Evan never advocated that. I want to take him away from there. Avery said it was sort of a retraining session. I have no idea what they will do to him if it doesn't work."

"Do you think it will?" Clay managed to soften his voice.

"No, not really."

Seventeen

In the northeast part of town stood the fifteen-acre estate once known as the Hampton Mansion. Around 1928, a wildcat oilman had struck it rich in a field near White Rock. He did what anyone swimming in the wealth that gushed from his wells would do. He chose a section of the young city and built a castle to rival those in Europe. In fact, the architect had come from England bringing plans, workmen, and even supplies on a ship chartered by Hampton. For a time, the parties in the new mansion set the town's tongues wagging. Hampton and the doings at the mansion were food enough for the hungriest gossip. The solid, but less wealthy, citizens shook their heads and cast reproachful glances at the excess. It seemed a rebuke against less successful, hard-working plainsmen. Yet, under the surface of their remarks was unmistakable pride that in their midst dwelt this highflying captain of industry. However, the passing years, like the winds sweeping across the prairie sands, erased the Hampton family and its fortune.

Bigger companies moved in, wells ran dry, and money gained in the heyday had long since been lost. Wade Hampton had two wives, but no children. When he died, old and broke, the only thing he left behind was the mansion. The high-walled estate with its maze of formal gardens, caretakers' quarters, and gatekeeper's cottage proved that stone and mortar are far more enduring than frail flesh. Sold to settle accumulated debts, the estate became a convent housing a cloistered order of nuns. With the past sins forgiven, the townspeople pointed with pride to a chaste, dignified monument, although not with the same enthusiasm as when the riotous living inside the walls had scandalized them. The mansion and grounds remained in the hands of the Church. After years of service, it became Unity Council's headquarters in Oklahoma. Huge oaks, older than the mansion, arched over the street leading to the entrance. The giant branches formed a leafy canopy, shading the pavement from the noon sun.

Jan drove through this cool, green tunnel to the tall iron gate set in a three-foot-wide wall of stone. From childhood, she had known the estate's history, its beginning and the mystery that surrounded the mansion. People said Hampton had a tunnel from inside the house, under the stone wall, and to the outside. A secret means of escape should he need it. Even after more than two hundred and fifty years, the town's teenagers still found the place fascinating. It was a gothic mystery set in the small town. Jan had been inside once when the grounds were open for a fundraising tour. The beauty of the stonework, marble floors, and great mahogany stairway was impressive. Yet she had felt a bit cheated and disappointed. The rooms were polished and bright, but there was not the slightest trace of a lingering ghost.

While Jan parked at the entrance waiting for the guard to admit her, some of the old fantasies returned. What did go on behind those high walls? Was it, as Simon insisted, something secret and suspicious, a tentacle of the monster that encircled the world? Jan smiled at the childish thoughts. Nothing could be more open than the working of the Church. They were a benevolent organization. If they guarded some of their procedures, it was for a good purpose. Evan, through his obstinacy, was in conflict with their rules. She had been worried about how he was being treated, but perhaps that too was flight of fantasy, for the gate swung open. A smiling guard directed her to follow the brick driveway to the mansion.

She pulled into the visitors' parking and walked across the graveled expanse to the entrance. Reverend Dewberry was waiting at the top of the marble steps.

"Jan Brockman, I believe. Your uncle said we could be expecting you today. Come in, my child, out of this heat." He pushed open the tall doors and coolness engulfed them as they stepped into the slate-floored foyer.

"There, that's better. Unbelievably hot for spring, isn't it?" the reverend commented. "If you will follow me to the study, we can discuss the purpose of your visit."

He led her past the grand mahogany staircase, along a side hall, and into a richly appointed room lined with bookcases. Despite her being accustomed to expensive surroundings, she was slightly awed at the lavish furnishings. Along with providing for underprivileged people, the Council had certainly provided for their members, too. The reverend seated her in a comfortable leather armchair before taking his seat behind a massive, carved wooden desk. For a moment, he smiled kindly, and pushed a button on a box sitting at his right hand. Jan didn't hear a buzzer or bell, but in seconds, a woman appeared at the side door.

"Hanna, bring us some refreshments. Miss Brockman looks as though she needs to relax a bit."

Jan raised her hand to stop him. "No, thank you very much, but I really can't stay long, and I did have a late breakfast."

The reverend looked a bit rebuffed, but quickly recovered. "As you wish. Hanna, you may leave now. I'll call if you're needed."

The woman nodded slightly and closed the door behind her.

"I understand from your uncle that you are concerned about Evan Hunter. I'm not sure how involved you are with this young man; I hope you are simply casual friends. At your age, we sometimes form unsuitable attachments. Therefore, in good conscience, I must warn you: he is not the sort of person with whom you should be involved. I'm afraid he has set his feet upon a rocky path." The reverend sighed.

"We are trying to help him. But I hasten to say we are not obliged to under the circumstances."

"I wasn't aware Evan needed help. I doubt he'd be willing to take it from you if he did."

A frosty look settled over the reverend's face. Jan immediately saw she was taking the wrong line with the man. She dipped her head slightly and sighed.

"You will have to excuse me, Reverend Dewberry. I don't know if you have heard, but my sister's mother-in-law passed away. And her husband is facing serious problems on his farm. To make things worse, Diana lost the baby she was carrying. I know it's not an excuse to be this abrupt, but both our families are upset."

A kindly expression returned to the reverend's face. "I do understand. It's enough to put anyone under a strain. I am aware of the Sandersons' plight and we have been praying for them. It's a sad thing," he said, slowly shaking his head. "I tried to explain the mistake they made in aligning themselves with this young man. It is always risky to give aid to an enemy of God."

Jan wasn't sure she had heard right. She blinked, and her shoulders stiffened. He couldn't possibly mean the Sandersons' misery was a punishment from God.

"You think that because they sheltered Evan it brought this upon them?"

He spread his soft hands in a conciliatory gesture. "Of course, we have no way of knowing for sure; however, the circumstances do speak loudly, do they not?"

Jan was inclined to argue the point, but she was not well versed in theology. Besides, it had nothing to do with her reason for speaking with him. Still, she wondered how he would explain the other farmers suffering from the break in the chemical dumpsite, and the weather failing them when they desperately needed rain. Had they sinned, too? Even with only a slight knowledge of God, her logic rejected his explanation.

"Yes, sometimes circumstances do seem to explain things, but in this case, I doubt it. I don't intend to defy fate or offend you by my coming on behalf of Evan. He is alone in the world except for a few friends. If you could tell me when he will be released, I would appreciate it."

The reverend laughed, showing surprisingly white teeth. "Released, you say. Why, my dear, he is free to go at any time. As you must know, he is a graduate of one of our finest seminaries. He was a most promising student. We had great hopes for him in the community. He could become a great Faith Leader. That is why we have extended ourselves in these few days of retraining. It is not unheard of for someone with a fine mind to become overzealous and somewhat fanatical." He sighed. "In these cases, we try to restore them."

"I see," Jan replied. "I can talk with him and if he wants to, we can leave together?"

"Of course." The reverend spread his tapered white hands.

As Jan followed him from the office, through the building, and into the yard, she saw they had added to the mansion. A long, low one-story building stretched behind the original house. It was the same stone construction, but when they entered, the inside was completely modern. The wide hallway had tile flooring above stark white walls and doors of either bold blue or green. There were rooms on either side of the hall. Some of them appeared to be classrooms, while others were lounges. Farther along, in a hallway to the right, most of the doors remained shut.

"These are the private quarters," Dewberry explained. He stopped in front of a closed door and knocked.

"Yes?" a voice replied.

Jan recognized Evan's voice and her heartbeat quickened. The reverend smiled.

"It's Reverend Dewberry, and your friend, Jan Brockman. May we come in?"

The reverend turned toward Jan and raised his eyebrows, confirming Evan's complete freedom. He might as well have said, "See? I told you."

In seconds, the door opened and Evan stood before them.

"May we come in?" the reverend repeated.

Evan stepped aside and Jan followed Dewberry into a small sitting room. Through a partly opened door beyond, there appeared to be a bedroom. The room was bright and clean as the hallway, and almost as sterile. The furnishings were sparse, but serviceable, with a built-in desk and bookcase on the longest wall. There was a small couch and one chair, both upholstered in a nubby orange material with blue and green stripes. Quickly, Jan studied Evan. He seemed to be fine, with a calm restful expression on his face. He was holding a book which he extended toward the reverend for his inspection.

"I've been rereading the last chapter in the Manual," he said.

"Good, my boy. I know Brother Barton took you through the entire book, but it never hurts to repeat the more complicated sections. There is no better place to rest and study than in our complex."

Jan was beginning to feel as numb as Evan looked. Possibly, it was the surroundings, for no sound from the outside penetrated the thick walls, and there were no windows. There were no light fixtures, yet the room was bright and there were no shadows, even in the corners or behind the furniture. The room seemed suspended in time and space, giving the impression that nothing existed outside the room. It was an almost hypnotic effect. To keep from sinking onto the couch and lapsing into a half-sleep, Jan cleared her throat and straightened her shoulders.

"May I speak to Evan alone, please?"

"Certainly." The reverend backed toward the door. "If you want anything, Evan can ring and someone will respond immediately."

"Thank you."

Jan didn't turn to watch him leave. She watched Evan's face, trying to catch the slightest trace of emotion, but he had virtually no expression. She wondered if talking to him alone would be of any use. When the door clicked shut behind her, she rushed to Evan and threw her arms around him. He neither stiffened nor yielded to the embrace. He seemed to feel nothing; she might as well have been hugging a post.

"Will you sit down?" he asked.

Jan nodded and moved away to sit on the couch. Evan put the book on the desk and sat in the armchair.

"It is nice of you to visit me," he said. "We don't get many visitors, but it's for the best. More time to study and meditate that way."

Evan's voice was as bland as his expression. He was a marble statue come to life, if you could call it life. He sat there, his face and form still perfect, the encompassing light brightening his skin and golden hair. If a beautiful work of art could become flesh, it would look as Evan did. Although, there was a certain spark missing; he didn't seem truly alive. Jan feared that something was drastically wrong with him. Her heart sank. She leaned forward and spoke softly.

"Evan, I want to take you home. They need you at the farm. Something has happened to Eva."

Evan nodded. "I know. The family must be in deep mourning. We have been praying for them. They said she fell down the stairs. I hope she didn't suffer."

She didn't know what to tell him. He seemed untouched; maybe she could shock him into some reaction. "I doubt her death was painless. Broken ribs puncturing vital organs had to be very painful."

For an instant, she thought something flickered in his eyes, but she was mistaken. His expression remained blank.

"I am sorry, but she is at peace now," he said.

Jan sighed. "They want you to perform the service. Will you do that?"

"I would like to. They were very kind to me. I will need to ask permission of the board at the meeting this evening. Harm can come from an unauthorized service. There is the matter of Eva's burial in sanctified ground. They may not allow it. The Sandersons were kind to me, but what they did in defying the Church was wrong."

Evan's loosely clasped hands rested on his knees. His head bowed, he didn't look at her. If he had not been speaking, Jan might have thought he was asleep. She swallowed hard, wondering what to say next. She wanted to grab him by the shoulders and shake him. To demand to know what they had done to him. Still, she hesitated. There was no way to be certain, but she suspected someone might be observing them. The main objective was to get him home, not cause more trouble.

"I understand, Evan, but that request isn't necessary. Mark wants Eva buried on the farm. You would be a great comfort to Clay. I told him I would bring you this afternoon. Can't we let Reverend Dewberry speak to the board? That way you can come with me now."

For the first time, Evan registered an expression. His forehead wrinkled, and his eyes shifted nervously as if he were confused.

"I probably should go to Clay. It would be my Christian duty, but I don't know if I am ready. I have much to learn. It could do more harm than good to give him false comfort. There are certain procedures we must observe in dealing with the bereaved. One of the more accomplished brothers would handle it better."

"But, Evan, Mark asked for you. Clay did, too."

Jan tried to hide her rising alarm. Of the things she had expected to encounter, Evan's reluctance to leave was not one of them. A tinge of sadness started to mingle with the alarm and fear. She suspected it was over for Evan, that he was forever changed. She didn't know what they had done to him, but it seemed effective. His fire and determination were gone. He looked the same, yet he was a different person. There was nothing of the magnetic quality left. He was still physically beautiful, but compared with the Evan of two days ago, the beauty was an empty shell. A perfect tool for the Church. She visualized him standing tall and gorgeous in the mauve and gold robes behind a polished walnut pulpit, everyone's eyes locked on him while he mouthed words approved by the Church.

Wherever they sent him, Evan would draw a crowd. No doubt, female attendance would double within a month. She wondered if there was any use in taking him with her now. It would only further depress everyone. She thought of going to her father or Avery and telling them the reverend was doing something awful to Evan. However, she saw the futility of it. Who would press charges? Evan was in no condition to do it, and she had no legal grounds to bring action. The only distant hope was that in time this would wear off, and that Evan would be himself again. She extended her hand to him.

"Please, Evan, go with me now. Even if you don't perform the service, they will want you to be there."

"I don't know," he said slowly. "Why don't you ask Reverend Dewberry? He'll know what's best."

Jan put her hand to her forehead and closed her eyes. Evan was no different from a mechanical doll going through a set of programmed actions. Maybe she was, too. Whatever freedom of choice she had, many times circumstances blocked it. Her life seemed a chain of events dictated by external forces. She had chosen to follow Evan. It was a good decision. She had thought she was in charge of her future. She remembered past choices that ended in disappointment, some by putting faith in the wrong person, others blocked by rules and restraints that drove her in a different direction. Now, she was powerless to help Evan, and with the loss of him, she was again, directionless. She pressed her lips together in silent mourning; Evan was as gone as Eva was.

"Are you two having a nice visit? I don't want to intrude, but we mustn't keep Evan from his books too long."

Jan had not noticed the door opening, and she jumped at the sound of Reverend Dewberry's voice. She turned and lifted her hands in a hopeless gesture.

"I've been trying to tell Evan how important it is for him to come with me, but he seems reluctant. I can't understand it. What have you done to him?"

She heard the spite in her words and wished they hadn't been as sharp. She also caught the momentary glint in the reverend's eye. They were playing a game, and she didn't observe the rules. His look said he meant to chasten her, but it only made her angry.

"Listen, Reverend, any fool can see Evan is not behaving normally. Something is terribly wrong with him. I know I'm supposed to close my eyes to it but—"

"Jan." Evan broke in sharply. "What are you saying? You have no reason to attack Reverend Dewberry. Please, we deal in Christian love and charity with one another." Evan turned to the reverend with a helpless look. "Tell her, Reverend."

He patted Evan's shoulder. "Now, now, don't upset yourself, my boy. She isn't accustomed to our ways. The world needs much teaching, that is why our work is important. It isn't easy to learn the way of love. Perhaps she is only angry because you don't want to leave with her."

Jan pressed her lips together tight enough to turn them white. The situation was indecent—more than that—it was evil. They had stripped Evan of his personality and done it under the guise of religion and love. She felt physically ill. Dewberry seemed to study her for a minute and then turned to Evan.

"Maybe you should go with her."

"But, sir, my work. I really don't know if I'm ready to be of service to the family."

"Perhaps not. We can send someone else, providing the family is ready to abide by the proper procedures. Still, I think you should put in an appearance. There seem to be some misconceptions concerning your feelings about this retraining course. Now, don't look worried. You need not stay long. I'm sure Miss Brockman will bring you back whenever you want to go. Isn't that right, Miss Brockman?"

Jan nodded, not trusting herself to speak. If the reverend was willing to allow Evan to leave, things were worse than she thought. Evan frowned, doubt filling his eyes, and the reverend was nearly glowing with satisfaction.

"Actually, Evan, it is very important for you to go. It will be good for you to practice something of what you have learned."

"Well, if you think it is best."

He went into the bedroom, took a brush from the shelf beneath a mirror, and began brushing his hair. His motions were stilted and jerky. Jan watched him through the open door. She whirled around to face Dewberry.

"I don't have words to say what I think of Evan's condition. I don't know what you expect to gain by letting everyone see him this way. They'll know in a minute. I did."

The reverend folded his hands and drew a long face meant to look pious and sad. "What a pity you don't understand, but this is what we face the world over. Our hope is to continue patiently teaching until we have wrapped the entire world in peace and love. Make no mistake, we will accomplish our aims. And a great deal more, as we recruit other fine young men along with Evan."

Evan stepped through the door. "I'm ready."

Jan walked Evan across the gravel toward the visitors' parking lot. It was like taking a patient home from the hospital. In this case, the weakness was mental not physical. She had to direct his every step. It wasn't difficult...Evan responded instantly to her voice.

"Open the door and get in, Evan."

Evan sat motionless while she slid behind the steering wheel and started the car. Perhaps she should have ordered him to smile; it would give expression to his blank face. She stopped at the gate and waited for the guard to open it. She should have been happy to have Evan beside her, both of them on the way to the farm and freedom. Instead, any joy in accomplishing her goal was as dry as roadside dust. That morning, she had imagined having trouble in taking him from the compound. She had pictured them speeding away down the tree-lined approach, escaping only by outrunning Unity's cars. How very unlike reality are our expectations, she thought with a sarcastic smile.

She had even suspected physical torture to bring Evan into submission. That was a childish fantasy, too. It was clear; they would never be that crude. They wouldn't run the risk of leaving marks, not with chemical means available. No wonder they allowed Evan to leave...what did they have to fear? She and Evan were babies, childish innocents, and absolutely no threat to the worldwide order of Unity Council. She didn't speak to Evan as she drove toward the farm. Conversation with him was useless. It filled her with despair. She intended to deliver him to Jeff; they could care for him in the lodge. Not that there would be much to do…give him a place to sleep and something to eat. No doubt the Church would be calling for their new toy in a day or two.

That should give everyone at the farm time enough to decide what to do. Would it be right to let Dewberry have Evan, or should they hide him and care for him because of what he once was? Jan sighed, glad she didn't need to make the decision alone. As she drove the long road to the farmhouse, a cloud of dust rose behind the car. The fields stretching away on either side were as parched and dry as the roadbed.

Occasionally, a light wind lifted some topsoil and whisked it into the air, creating a small whirlwind. The dried stubble from last fall's planting still held most of the soil, but the stunted frail growth made poor ground cover. It would not be long until even that cover decayed and turned into dirt. If no rain came before that happened, the slightest breeze would make the prairie move. In the last months, people rather than events had occupied most of her thoughts, because there was always some kind of crisis. The labor strikes, riots, shortages, and pollution usually affected other regions worse than they did Garden City. Still, for its size, the town had suffered its share of the nation's ills. However, the grain and oil the area produced had sheltered them a bit. Now, the dead land on either side of the road forced her to face the farmland disaster.

For years, certain food was in short supply, as were cloth and wood, anything taken directly from the earth, but people had managed. This could be far worse. The United States would join the rest of the world in the agonies of hunger, and the horror it brought. She glanced at Evan sitting complacently beside her; maybe he was the lucky one.

She parked in the large space between the main house and the lodge. Everyone was probably at the main house. If she left Evan at the lodge, it would give her a chance to explain before they saw him.

"Open your door, Evan." She sighed.

He stood beside the car until she walked around to his side.

"Okay, come with me," she said, with little expression. It made no difference, he responded to the meaning of the words, not any nuance.

As she headed for the lodge, Evan followed. When they were several yards from the car, Evan veered to the left and started toward the road. At first, Jan was annoyed, as she would have been at the malfunction of a machine. When Evan moved much faster and farther away, she became alarmed.

"Evan, wait."

She ran to catch him, but she was not fast enough. Evan crossed the road and with long, purposeful strides went into the field. As she ran harder, sweat dampened her face. Evan stopped and she rushed to grab him.

"I told you to stop. What do you think you're doing?" She was panting and the words came between gasps.

"You're a worse task master than the brothers," Evan said sternly. "Evan talk. Evan walk. Evan read. I did every one of those things and very well, I might add."

Jan shaded her eyes with her hand as she studied his face. For a second, the blank stare and slack jaw remained. When he suddenly laughed, it was startling. His teeth flashed in the bright sunlight and his eyes came to life, glittering with shine and vitality. For a moment, she thought he was mad, his mind breaking from some drug overload. When he took hold of her shoulders, she started to pull away.

"I fooled you, too. Didn't I?"

"Are you okay, Evan?" Jan finally found her voice.

"Yes, I'm fine."

"I don't get it. How were you able to withstand the effects of whatever they did to you? They were convinced you were completely under control. Why are we in the middle of this field? Are you sure you're okay?" She wasn't certain he was himself.

"I think I am, except for maybe being paranoid. I wanted to get far from your car and any buildings before I spoke. After what I've been through, I doubt I'll trust anything again. You were away from the car long enough; they could have put a transmitter in it. I don't think they would miss that opportunity, no matter how sure they are of me. I think the farm buildings will be safe. I don't believe the Council has had access to the farm. They don't have enough subversive action in our area to warrant long distance devices. I want to talk with you before seeing the others."

The sun made heat waves shimmer in the distance. The dirt under Jan's feet grew hot as did the top of her head; her blouse stuck to her, but the discomfort was nothing compared to her curiosity.

"Go on," she said. "How are you, really?"

Evan smiled. "The best I can determine, the only thing wrong with me is starvation. This has been some experience. When they took me, I was scared. I had no idea what they were going to do. I guess I had pictures of some medieval torture chamber under the mansion."

Jan laughed amid tears. The relief was too great to contain. "I did too, Evan; I thought the same thing."

"They're not that crude," he said as an ugly sneer settled over his face. "It's your mind they want, not your body. They acted calm, explaining they wanted to talk and go over my training again. Thank God, I didn't believe them. The first evening they put me in the room where you found me. I was puzzled. No one did a thing to me, but when a brother brought my supper, he stayed to watch me eat. They could have observed from the hidden viewers, but I suppose he was there to make sure I did."

"If there were drugs in the food, how..."

"I'll tell you. I wasn't sure it would work, but I didn't have a choice. He took the tray as soon as I finished and left. I was frantic. I wanted the stuff out of me, but I was sure they would be watching. I wasn't positive there had been anything wrong with the food, but there could have been. I went into the bathroom, stripped, and got into the shower enclosure. I turned on the hot water—it made a lot of steam and fogged the glass door—and I threw up. I don't think you care to hear how I used the shower drain to get rid of it."

"Ugh. You're right, I don't what to hear."

"I'm lucky they didn't use shots, or some other means. I suppose if I hadn't responded to the drugs that would have been next. That evening I was afraid I hadn't gotten away with it, afraid they knew what I'd done. I finally went to bed and in the morning when breakfast came, I did the same thing. I bet they thought I showered a lot. When they started the indoctrination, I kept mumbling about feeling dirty. Not worthy to carry the Word of God. I hoped that would explain the showers. I could get by with no food, but I needed water. I couldn't risk drinking anything they provided, even tap water. I took a chance on the water in the toilet tank. At least I didn't get thirsty."

"I'm amazed," Jan cried. "You actually fooled them. How did you know how to act, what response you were supposed to have? I didn't realize you were a good actor."

"I have hidden talents," he replied. "I know a great deal about acting. My parents were good teachers."

"Be serious, Evan. I still can't believe you're unaffected. You seemed completely changed."

"I'm sorry. I'm trying to talk straight, but I feel lightheaded, almost high. At first, I didn't know how they expected me to act, but I've seen enough people on drugs to fake it. I guessed they'd want me a complete blank; they could imprint a new mind on me. I thought my parents had given me a worthless childhood, but I became an actor without realizing it."

Jan pulled at his arm. "I don't care how you managed, I'm glad you did. Come on, let's get out of this sun and find you something to eat before you drop."

She could hardly wait to tell the others. Jeff and Simon would laugh when they heard how clever Evan had been.

"Jan, wait a minute. What are we going to tell everyone, that they simply let me go?"

Jan frowned. "No. Tell them the whole thing. Why not?"

"I gave you the highlights, Jan. They didn't do what they wanted with me, but something did happen to me. Maybe the same as when Simon went into the desert that time."

"You heard voices? The way Simon swore God spoke directly to him?"

Evan shook his head, a bead of sweat sliding down the side of his face. His eyes turned dark, the slate blue of a stormy sea. He looked as terrified as someone who'd witnessed a horror. He shut his eyes and wiped his forehead with the back of his hand.

"I can't explain. Something happened to me. I need time to think, get my mind straight. Let's tell everyone I came to an agreement with Reverend Dewberry."

Jan's mouth dropped. She couldn't believe Evan would deceive anyone.

"You would be lying. That isn't like you."

"How do you know it isn't? I don't know myself anymore, or that I ever did."

"Please, Evan, you scare me when you talk this way. Maybe some of the drugs did stay in your system."

The hard look in Evan's eyes matched the tight line of his jaw.

"No. I would have felt something. I was able to fool them because they underestimated me. They had no idea how suspicious I was of them. Part of my problem is I underestimated them, too. What I thought was wrong with the Council isn't a tenth of the real situation. I need time to understand."

"What is it? Did you hear or see something while you were there?"

He took Jan's arm and turned her toward the lodge.

"Look, there's Jeff. Don't say anything for now. Let me tell it my way."

Jeff walked toward them. At Evan's urging, they hurried to meet him. It was difficult to believe Evan wasn't suffering some effects of the drugs. He was different. It had to be his experience at the mansion, thought Jan. Jeff strode forward and clutched Evan's hand.

"It is good to see you. How are you?" Jeff's words were simple, yet his eyes, squinting against the sun, were asking a flurry of questions. Evan smiled at Jeff.

"I'm fine, Jeff, fine. And very glad to be here."

It was clear Jeff wanted more of an answer. She did, too. It seemed they would both have to be patient. Jeff patted Evan's shoulder and smiled at Jan.

"We'd better go in," he said. "The rest will be glad to see you. Clay brought Mark and Diana home and Tracy and her husband are here, too."

Eighteen

By the end of April, a strange eerie stillness had settled over the Sanderson farm. Each person carried about them an air of nervous calm. There were polite conversations that gave wide berth to serious topics. It was a touchy game; even the weather was an unsafe subject. It seemed everyone was barely balancing his burden. It was an exercise in agility to manage the heavy thoughts and at the same time be careful not to overturn those around them. Evan sympathized with everyone, yet he too was plagued with an inner turmoil. He wasn't the main cause of the family's problems, but he contributed to them. If he were certain that he should leave, he would, but it seemed wrong to run out on them. By staying, he might be of help, or serve some purpose in God's plans. Besides, something had happened to him in those days of confinement. Until he understood, he'd have to stay. He hesitated to call his experience a "vision," yet he'd seen something.

The day after Jan brought him to the farm he had presided over Eva's funeral. It was the first time he had performed this type of service and it was a wrenching experience. He had liked and respected Eva. Sorrow over her death produced tears that threatened to choke his words. The family honored Mark's wishes concerning her burial. The small party of mourners drove several miles across Sanderson land to a place where a ridge of low, gentle hills rose gracefully from the surrounding prairie. Short bur oaks and wild plum trees grew in the shallow, narrow valleys. The plums were white with spring blossoms clinging to the branches, while on the surrounding slopes, sparse patches of tall mesquite grass waved in the too warm breeze.

In a normal spring, the prairie turned a delicate light green with bits of white and yellow field flowers accented by blue bull nettles. In spring, the land usually gave the promise of becoming lush and bountiful. This April, even the flowering plum trees seemed to struggle. The area looked washed in amber, giving an even more somber note to the occasion. When they arrived, Mark had pointed to a spot on a low rise where some of the farmhands had prepared a gravesite.

"This is where we almost built our home," Mark said. "Eva loved this place. But the ground for her garden was better to the east and we didn't have to dig the well as deep." He stopped, as if reluctant to say more about water.

Since National Grain's irrigation system had developed a problem, they had to pay more attention to the wells on the farm. Some of them had gone dry years ago when the water table dropped. They guarded the deeper wells around the compound, rotating their use in hopes of conserving what was there. In earlier days, water and weather were the settlers' plague. They had been at the mercy of nature, which might be generous in some years and stingy in others. Technology brought powerful rigs that drilled deep into the earth and tapped the great Ogallala aquifer. When men became able to reach the great underground reservoir, they should have managed it as they did the land above. Perhaps the farmers thought the supply was limitless. However, it was not. By pumping more water than the scarce rainfall could replace, the wells went dry. Rescue came in the form of National's irrigation system. The company created a giant, manmade reservoir which they carefully managed. Since it had failed, there was nothing to replace it except natural rainfall. Now, nature withheld even the slightest moisture.

"How serious is this?" Evan had asked Jeff. Jeff had squinted his eyes against the sun, looked at the gray/brown dust between his boots, and said, "It's the worst I've ever known. Nature is like a woman— you ignore her, and when you need her, she won't be there."

Evan tried to stay out of the way, but he saw how the family suffered. For a couple of days after the funeral, Clay and Jeff didn't discuss business problems with Mark. He was lost in grief, unable to care about anything. Seemingly, his strength had died, too. Before they buried Eva, Mark was in control, giving instructions and orders, attending to the details of having her casket built in the farm's carpentry shop. Mark even took the telephone call from Reverend Dewberry. As Evan expected, the Council was not willing to let the Sanderson family ignore their orders. It would set a bad example for others...besides, Dewberry needed a reason to check on Evan. The reverend offered to perform the service for Eva, but Mark handled it with the diplomacy of an ambassador.

He explained how he and Eva had made these plans years ago. If he failed to carry them out, he would never rest. As for representing the Church, wouldn't Evan serve that purpose? Mark even asked the reverend to consider coming to the farm to consecrate the piece of land. For, as he explained, they intended it as a private family burial ground. Later, when Clay expressed dismay over his inviting this interference, Mark laughed.

"Look, son, once I'm in my place beside Eva, what do we care what mumbo jumbo some idiot says over us? We sure as hell aren't going to hear it."

The change in Mark after the service was startling. His body seemed to shrink; his face grew gray and somber under his permanent tan. It was a kind of withering process. Evan mentioned it to Clay, wondering if they should take Mark to see a doctor. Clay shook his head.

"He won't hear of it, Evan. He made me promise that he had spent his last time in a hospital. I'm worried, but how do you strip a man of his authority and dignity? He told me that it's his life and if I love him, I'll respect his wishes."

Evan couldn't argue with that. He had seen enough manipulated people denied their basic right of free will.

Still, Mark's health and emotions concerned everyone. Tracy hovered, treating him like a baby with a fever, and Frank was no less solicitous. If Mark stepped outside to stand on the porch and survey his dry, parched land, in seconds Frank was there, urging him to sit, and asking if Mark wanted a glass of tea or lemonade. Only Diana remained aloof. Evan wondered why she had even come to the farm, feeling as she did. Until one evening, he overheard Jan and Diana talking.

The sisters had taken a walk after supper. Evan had eaten in the lodge with Simon and was heading to the main house to find Clay. Sometimes they talked, and it seemed to help both of them, even though their problems were far different. It was dusk, and the western sky was alive with orange and pink, while the buildings and grounds turned a dusty lavender gray. Evan did not intend to eavesdrop, but the girls were standing beside Jan's car and in the dimness didn't see him approaching. When he drew near, he realized their conversation was private. Jan was asking the same question he wished he could ask.

"If you feel this way, why did you agree to come here?"

"Sometimes you're too simple, Jan. I had to. Don't you see? With that ignorant Tillie spreading her vicious rumor of how Eva died, I need to be around to defend myself. What if Clay began to believe her? He's a clod...no telling what he might decide to do. Maybe even charge me with something. But I promise you, Jan, it was an accident."

"And the baby?"

Evan heard Diana's harsh laugh. "I'd say that's my business. Wouldn't you, dear sister?"

He hurried on across the parking area and the lawn, hoping they wouldn't see him. As he entered the house, a sadness for Clay and a bitterness at Diana filled him. He had never heard Tillie accuse Diana of Eva's death. She had seemed to accept it as an accident. However, Tillie made it clear about the baby. When asked to elaborate upon her story, she would only say, "I didn't see anything. I can't tell any more than what I heard. It should be pretty plain that Eva is gone because of it."

At first, Clay tried to keep Tillie quiet about Eva when Mark was around. After a while he stopped. Nothing anyone said could reach Mark's grief; it was too deep. Eva was gone and with her went Mark's purpose in life. Evan was sure that half a man wouldn't live long, yet he kept this opinion to himself. There was no need to drop a match in a gasoline-drenched area.

Daily, Evan searched for some way to help the people living at the farm. However, nothing seemed suitable. Words of comfort and encouragement were hollow when everyone understood how serious the situation had become. Only Mark floated above it, wrapped in some cloud of sorrow making him deaf and blind to the growing disaster. There was no point in watching news broadcasts; they barely mentioned the crisis. Every branch of government enacted some form of censorship. President Morris justified it by claiming it kept the public from panic. Yet, the dead land and the rapidly rising commodity prices shouted the truth loud and clear.

The day Eva died was the same day Clay had brought home his terrible news. Evan had not been there, as he was at the mansion in the retraining program. Yet, he would remember that day because it was a day that affected everyone. He thought of it as a mountain of trouble dropping on them. He was standing at the peak, and every direction was downhill. There were no bright horizons, only dark valleys. He needed to talk with someone who would understand the thing that had happened to him in the mansion; that could only be Simon. Yet he hesitated going to Simon. Still, if he didn't tell someone, he might go mad. His personal crisis centered in a spiritual realm, but since the physical world continued to crumble, maybe his problem didn't matter.

The experts declared that food could now be officially added to the list of natural resources in short supply. As predicted, the tsunami from the Caribbean earthquake had swept into the coastal lands destroying rice, cotton, and other crops, while Florida lay under three feet of water. The Sandersons' farm suffering from drought and chemical poisoning was an example of what afflicted others. The damage stretched from Nebraska southward through eastern Colorado, Kansas, Oklahoma, northeastern New Mexico, and northwest Texas. None of the experts touched upon what would happen should the chemicals seep into the groundwater and begin spreading outside of National's system. Of course, they had closed the system and sealed the underground reservoir, but as Clay had said, it was a joke.

"Look at it this way," he told Evan. "You got this gigantic underground lake created by mountain runoff and several underground streams feeding into the catch basin. Maybe the earthquake did crack the dumpsite and National's reservoir, but both of them could have been leaking for years. Shutting down the system is fine, but they can never seal the reservoir tight enough, or the chemical dump either. When there is nothing to stop it, water flows. It finds cracks in the limestone and who knows where it spreads. There are hundreds of underground streams. Clean this spill? Not in our lifetimes. I doubt if any well in this area is safe. When the water from National's reservoir reaches the Ogallala aquifer, we're done for."

Evan didn't doubt Clay's conclusions.

The Environmental Control Agency was as active as dry leaves in a high wind, and as scattered in their efforts to place blame, or find solutions. Some companies that manufactured the poisonous compounds had been out of business for years. The factories that were still in operation had old permits issued by the government giving permission to use the dumpsite under the Bighorn range. The agreements stated that it was the government's duty to maintain the site. The suits and countersuits were mounting to the sky. In the meantime, the army was to seal off the area, attempt to find the leak, and repair it. The civilian inhabitants for a hundred miles surrounding the area had to evacuate for fear of drinking contaminated water. Occasionally, the government-controlled news network would broadcast a human-interest story of some old timer refusing to leave his home. What the newscasters never mentioned was the story of forced removal.

Conditions were too perilous, the nation in too much danger to allow consideration for individual feelings. Day by day, the greater good replaced the rights of any single person. When Thomas Brockman arrived in Oklahoma City to protect his family's interest, he found how few rights he had left. His long-standing as an attorney in the area and years of leasing land to National Grain meant nothing. Every attempt to collect damages, or terminate his agreement with National ended in failure. When Tom informed his brother, Avery, and asked for his help, Avery too engaged in the battle. He notified as many National Grain customers as he could reach. His plan was to file a class action suit. When Diana heard the news, she refused to believe the family income was in jeopardy. "Don't be ridiculous," she told Jan. "This may bother some people, but not us."

However, Jan knew that even her family could not escape this growing disaster. It affected every nation and every area of commerce.

Mexico had started ignoring some of their agreements with the United States. They refused payment in worthless scrip, and insisted upon payment in grain, clearly hoping to build a stockpile before there was none. Canada had no help to offer...the adverse weather had cut their production as well. Merchants in every country were rushing from one meeting to another, trying to establish new supply lines and trade agreements, while some cool-eyed national leaders were waiting, carefully assessing the situation. They searched for an advantage in the calamity shaking the earth. The picture of shifting world power grew clearer each day.

In the past, the nations seemed divided into three groups, unity achieved through common needs and interests. America, Canada, Mexico, Israel, Egypt, Japan, and parts of South America comprised a loose confederation. This enabled them to hold almost equal power with the more stabilized United Federation of Europe. These nations did not always agree, but common good kept them in loose accord. The alliance had, for fifteen shaky years, kept China, Russia, and her numerous satellites, in bounds. For some time, the United

Federation had been pressing for complete union among themselves and the other non-communist countries. For first one reason, then another, agreement could not be reached.

The Unity Council constantly chided the United States and the other holdouts for their lack of cooperation. The Council's position was that if two-thirds of the world united, they could stop the spread of Communism. Evan suspected the Council had more to gain from the merger than they wanted anyone to know. The waters were murky and clouded, but glimpsed from a certain angle, the real battle came into focus. It was between two giants: Communism and Unity Council. Unity's constantly growing power and structure was evident. Many of their reforms and policies were already in operation around the globe. However, it was a hindrance to deal with the many leaders of the individual nations. If political control were under one roof, as the religious community was, they could make fantastic strides.

Evan understood the power struggle between the two, but it wasn't good to give the Church this much control. He also knew there would never be peace between Unity Council and the Communist countries. Communism always demanded complete devotion to the State; it could not allow people to worship anything higher, while the Church, supposedly, put God first.

People seemed to believe the Council was primarily concerned with the spiritual realm: a conscience for the world. The truth was they were well informed and deeply concerned over world politics and commerce. During Evan's two days in the mansion, he'd overheard scraps of information passed between the brothers. They were aware of the looming food crisis. Unity had already chosen the role it wanted to play. At high levels, their priests and ministers had formed a food distribution plan. And their top advisors flew to Washington and other world capitals to present it. Who better to organize and control the buying and selling than those dedicated to ministering to the needs of mankind? The plan included individual identity stamps, creating strict controls to ensure everyone a fair share.

An icy chill swept over Evan as he envisioned the Council in charge of which hungry stomachs to fill. With the unsettled world conditions, he had no doubt that nations would accept Unity's proposal. Since governments had assumed more control of commerce and issued mountains of regulations, they might be happy to have this chore lifted from their heavy load. Like a foundering horse, government had taken in more than it could digest. It wobbled from side to side seeking any support, knowing that if it once fell, it would never rise again. This was an election year. As it had always been, it would be a fight on a double front: politicians promising lower taxes and to return control to the people, while at the same time guaranteeing more help from the government. The programs ranged from housing and healthcare to monthly allotments. To keep the two promises at the same time was impossible.

Every four years, the challenge was which side could hoodwink enough voters into believing they would deliver this impractical package. Meanwhile, Communism, like a giant python, slowly and methodically looped coil after coil around weaker nations. They waited for larger governments to grow top heavy and topple, making them easy prey. It was no wonder the European Federation kept screaming for consolidation. Size might be the only protection against being squeezed and swallowed.

~ * ~

The last morning in April, the sun rose with the wrath of August. By nine o'clock, the heat roasted anyone foolish enough to stand in the glare. Evan sat on the west-facing porch of the main house. He stared at the gravel road where, due to Eva's care, a few brave jonquils dared to bloom. Their yellow cups stood stiffly away from the already wilting leaves. Behind Evan, the house was closed tight and the drapes drawn against the heat. Those inside were still walking about in funereal silence. Only Frank Jr. and Robin, Tracy's two energetic children, showed signs of life. They raced around the yard and the lodge, their whoops and cries battering the dry air. The front door opened and Evan turned as Jan stepped outside. She leisurely crossed the porch, her hands hidden in the wide patch pockets of her tan smock. She took a seat beside him.

"Going to be another scorcher, isn't it?" She shook her head sadly.

"It looks that way."

"How are you feeling, Evan?"

"Fine." He shrugged.

"Well, I'm not. I feel we've been transported to a strange world where some unimaginable monster is lurking behind those hills."

Jan was looking across the miles of barren fields to the distant low ridge of smoke-gray hills. Irresistibly, the same view drew Evan's gaze.

"That seems spooky for someone as level-headed as you," he said. "It's probably because you aren't used to spending time in the open, not having the protection of buildings and pavement."

She shook her head and a tendril of hair fell loose and curled damply around her neck. With an impatient gesture, she whisked it aside and secured it beneath a pin.

"I don't think it's that. I'm as logical as I ever was. To feel any other way would be impractical. If you want to accuse someone of not being realistic, consider Diana."

"Have you two been at it again?" He tried to hide a smile.

The sisters were a study in contrast. Each one was actually the reverse of the image they wanted to project, Diana appearing feminine and sexy, flattering men's egos when it was to her advantage. Yet, underneath she was hard, calculating, determined to get her way. While Jan insisted on facts and keeping order. She used this to appear cool and logical, but beneath the surface, her emotions and instincts influenced her far more than she realized. Jan gave him a withering look.

"I didn't expect that from you, Evan."

"What did I say to upset you?"

"It was the implication. That Diana and I are the same. Two flighty sisters always bickering."

"I'm sorry."

She put her hand on his arm. It would have felt nice, except that it was warm and his arm was already hot.

"I know." She sighed. "I guess we do sound that way, but I can't stand by and watch her ruin her life any more than she has. She is determined to leave Clay. She thinks everything is the same, that she can go home or to Grandma Fern. She expects to have lace, crystal, and champagne surrounding her forever. She intends to launch some gay social whirl and find the perfect mate. She can't understand how different things are now. She refuses to think about what we might need to do to simply survive."

"Is that your monster behind the hills?"

Jan nodded. "You might say that. I've studied the situation and we're in trouble." Jan spread her hands toward the lodge and the main house behind them. "I don't mean only these people, or even Garden City. I'm beginning to worry about the world's survival."

Evan stood and shoved his hands into his back pockets and stared into the distance. He tried to focus on Jan's concerns, not his own.

"As bad as that, is it?" he offered with a slight smile.

"Now you're teasing me again. I thought you would understand."

Something in her words struck a spark in the bitter anger he had been trying to deny. Evan whirled to face her.

"Why should I understand? What makes you think I know any more about what's going on than anyone else? You think God takes me into His confidence? Shows me things no one else sees?"

Jan's startled, fear-filled look proved his expression mirrored his emotions. He began to pace, the heat of his body rivaling the sun's strong rays. In his agitation, a voice of calm assured him that he had seen something and it was the reason for his anger. Yes, he could admit he'd experienced something strange, but he didn't understand the meaning...it confused and angered him. Sweat covered his face and chest. His already damp shirt clung to him, but the heat was nothing to the burning in his stomach. The fire spread to his mind and threatened to explode.

"Anything I might have seen is a curse. It would be better to be ignorant. I would rather shut my eyes and put my faith in the Council. Go on peacefully secure in their false promises. I can't. It would mean turning away from God's Word." His voice cracked and his shoulders sagged.

The fear in Jan's eyes turned to pity. With tears welling, she stood and put her arms around him.

"Oh, Evan, my poor Evan. I don't know what you think you saw, but you're too intense. Maybe you saw reality and can't stand it. I know the suffering will be terrible, but some of us will survive. We'll be smarter and handle things better afterward. Technology will come to the rescue. We'll develop other food sources and find ways to control the climate. Even now, some of the cities under domes can control their weather."

Evan lowered his head and sat on the steps. Jan followed him. He appreciated her comforting words, but they proved how useless he was. After hearing him teach, Jan still believed mankind could save itself. It was hard to blame her. With the world growing dark and confusing, it was natural to hope in the physical future. Especially when things of the spirit were invisible. They had been to him, too... until now.

It seemed the Council, for the time being, was content to leave him on the farm. No doubt, they had other concerns. They had nothing to fear from him. Even if the drugs hadn't worked, he had stopped teaching. He reproached himself for this. What would he do when they came to claim his services? Would he use some other trick instead of standing square before them and denouncing the Council, no matter the consequences?

"...the only thing we can do," Jan was saying, "...is take each day as we find it and have faith things will get better."

She stopped and lifted her arm to wave at someone. Evan turned to see Mark walking across the lawn toward the garages. Mark waved in return and they watched as he climbed into a truck and backed away before heading toward the driveway.

Jan sighed. "There he goes again. Every day since the funeral, he's gone there. Clay says he sits by Eva's grave staring into space."

"Probably makes him feel better, but I doubt this heat is good for him."

As Jan nodded, they heard the door behind them open. Clay came onto the porch. "Is this private, or can anyone join you?" he asked.

Jan moved closer to Evan and patted the step on her other side. Clay smiled and sat beside her, resting his lanky wrists on top of his knees. He looked toward the prairie where Mark's truck was bumping along the lane toward the low hills. The truck was gone from sight, but the puff of dust marked its trail.

"I tried to stop him from spending too much time there, but he seems worse off sitting in the house. Maybe I'd rather have him away from the office."

"More bad news?" Evan asked.

Clay nodded. "You might say that. We turned this whole thing about National over to Thomas and Avery. They're going to battle with National Grain and possibly some government agencies. They'll handle the claims for the farms that want to join."

"That's the bad news? That my father and uncle are working on this?" Jan looked at Clay with mock indignation. Her expression made Evan and Clay smile.

"No, but it did sound that way, didn't it? The trouble is, it will take forever and cost a fortune, and we can't be sure we'll win."

Clay rolled his shoulders as if to ease the tension there. It was hard to watch him suffer.

"Is there nothing else you can do?" Evan asked.

"Jeff has a crew working on some of the old wells. I don't know how deep we'll have to go; we quit using them years ago. Even if there is water in them, I don't think we can pay for the electric power to run the pumps."

"If you could, you might get a crop in this year," Evan said.

"Maybe," Clay agreed. "Still, we have to waste time experimenting with the fields to find one that isn't completely contaminated. There are too many unknowns."

Jan had folded her hands in her lap and Evan could almost see the wheels turning in her mind.

"Can't the experimental station analyze samples for you and get a quicker answer?"

"I doubt it. Their terminal lines are always busy; they're searching for some neutralizing agent. The hell of it is, no one really knows what leaked from the dump."

"Didn't the guy who did the first testing give you the name of the chemicals?" Jan asked.

"A couple of the chemicals were identified, but that particular dump was considered safe and they put everything in it. Seems no one thought of what might happen by combining different wastes. Some of the tests are finding things no one has ever heard of. We're pretty much on our own, and if the contamination reaches the groundwater, it's over."

Jan wistfully surveyed the pale, cloudless sky. "Maybe it will rain," she said.

"Have you heard any more on the situation around the Gulf and southeast?" Evan tried to change the subject.

Clay shrugged and stood. "They aren't any better off than we are. Wiped out this year, for sure. The flood has tainted their wells, but the government is shipping in drinking water. Earthquakes, floods, pollution, and drought...we only need a volcano to finish us. Even China or Russia wouldn't want this piece of real estate after that."

Clay gave a harsh laugh. Jan and Evan tried to smile with him, but it was a weak effort. When Tillie stepped through the front door, Evan stood, and reaching for Jan's hand, helped her to stand. Tillie shook her head and frowned.

"You should come in...it isn't much cooler, but it's better than this heat."

The house was a few degrees cooler, but it was stuffy. The farm had quit using power for air conditioning. In case the old wells produced water, they would need as much energy as they could afford to run the pumps. Since the farm no longer qualified as a prime producer, their allotment of fuel was less. The three of them looked sheepishly at one another. They were foolish for ignoring the discomfort. Tillie stood with her hands on her wide hips and scowled at them.

"If there were a breeze, I'd sit with you, but there isn't. Clay, there's a man wanting you on the comset. Calling from some place in South America. What do you suppose he'd want with us?"

"Guess I better talk to him and see." Clay turned and started toward the north side of the long porch. "I'll take it in the office. You two better get inside before Tillie takes a whip to you," Clay called over his shoulder as he jumped off the porch and headed toward the office.

"I might," Tillie threatened as she reentered the house.

Jan started to follow her into the dim foyer.

"You coming, Evan?"

"No, I think I'll go to the lodge and talk to Simon for a while. Then I'll find Jeff and see if he can put me to work. I've been useless lately."

"No one thinks that, Evan. You needed a rest after what you went through. And"—Jan sighed—"speaking of going through, I might as well have another session with Diana. I'm beginning to worry about her. She isn't acting right. Even for her."

Nineteen

The farm's lodge had a large common area consisting of a long living room, a recreation room, and a spacious kitchen. The living room had a fieldstone fireplace and to the left of it a door to a wide hallway with sleeping rooms on either side. The lodge's furnishings were Old West rustic. Many of the tables, sofas, and chairs were cast-offs from the main house, but everything was in fine repair. Traces of Eva's capable hands showed in every room. A woven rug or picture bought on a Mexican vacation, a china pitcher and bowl set from an antique dealer in Maine, touches that made the farmhands feel they were part of the Sanderson family. Clay had talked with the men, explaining the situation, which most of them had already guessed. There wasn't much work to keep them on the farm, yet they were welcome to stay. Clay had to cut wages, but as long as there was food in the main house, he swore the men would eat, too. Some of the men lived off-site with their families. Clay promised to call them as soon as there was more work.

As Evan walked along the hall toward Simon's room, he thought of the satisfaction Mark and Clay must have felt in running the operation. The men they employed were also friends. He envied

Clay's life, even in the current circumstances. It was not only the large land holdings, sturdy buildings, and warmth of the people living there...it was the sense of belonging. Of having come into the world in one spot and knowing it was yours for life. A fitting into time and space. Something Evan had never known. He was not at home anywhere. The world didn't have a place for Evan Hunter. Perhaps it never would, because a sense of time running out constantly hung at the edge of his thoughts. It wasn't the morbid concern some people have about time, thinking they wouldn't live long; it was the nagging suspicion that time itself was ending.

Evan stood in the open door of Simon's room and smiled at the old man slumped in an armchair by the window, a book open on his lap. His glasses hung on the end of his nose. His frail chest rose and fell under the work shirt. Evan stepped closer and put his hand on Simon's thin shoulder.

"Are you asleep?"

"Not now." Simon peered over the rim of his glasses and sat straighter in the chair.

"I'm sorry. I hated to wake you, but I need to talk."

Simon moved around in the chair, shaking awake his limbs.

"Don't know what gets into me, sleeping this much. Must be getting old. Get that other chair and tell me what's on your mind."

Evan did as Simon suggested about the chair, but gathering his thoughts seemed almost beyond him. He struggled to put order to things he had trouble believing had happened. It seemed a lesson half-learned. The basic form was there, yet the details escaped him.

"Take your time, boy." Simon's laugh was sharp and broken. "I have plenty of time. Least I think I do, but at my age you never can be too sure."

Simon's body and face clearly showed the wear of his years, but his light blue eyes were alive, as youthful as young Ryan Lanier's were. Evan was amazed that after that many years of life's trials, Simon still had such vitality. His own twenty-seven years made him feel older than the prairie surrounding them. Slumping in the chair, Evan clasped his hands between his knees and voiced his first thoughts.

"I don't know what to do. I'm getting lost, Simon."

Simon chuckled. "Seems to me you got to know where it is you want to go before you can know you're lost."

Evan got the message. Simon was asking if Evan were a true believer. Did he really know where he wanted to go? Never mind that Evan had taught from the Word and tried to persuade others it was the only way; plenty of men before him had done likewise and still lost themselves. It frightened Evan more than he liked to think. Was he, in his own way, as bad as the men working in the Unity Council? It would be better to keep still and never give a direction than to point people in the wrong way.

"What is it you want me to say, Simon? Should I make a declaration of faith? You know I can say the right words. Even Satan can quote Scripture. I suppose he knows it better than we do. All I can say is I want to follow God."

Simon nodded and wiped the corners of his puckered mouth with his long fingers. "That's a sound enough destination. What makes you think you lost His trail?"

"Because I've developed double vision. I can't see straight."

It was a strange answer, yet it was the best way to describe what had happened to him. From the look on Simon's face, the old man was trying to understand. There was no shock or sneer, only kindness, and it encouraged Evan to continue.

"I used to see things in an ordinary way, or what I thought was ordinary. The standard story: God created the world, and us, then we rebelled. He provided a way to return to Him and right on through to His conclusion for this earth. I saw everything in physical terms. Solid ground with trees and plants, people moving about, and God's Word giving direction to those who chose to follow. When I was alone in the room at the mansion, something happened. It was like a pane of dark glass shattered. It broke some invisible barrier. Suddenly, another dimension came into focus. You're going to think I've lost my mind."

Evan put his hand to his forehead and shut his eyes. "How can I explain? I don't have words to express the things I saw."

"Keep talking, Evan. You're doing fine. Are you sure it wasn't some of that stuff they tried to give you?"

The old man bent forward, his eyes two lasers boring into him, waiting for an answer. It was a reasonable question. Simon knew of how Evan had tried to avoid the drugs. Evan had asked it of himself. It was possible, but still he was certain it had nothing to do with what he'd seen. He had also considered the effects of having no food, yet it had happened the first night.

"I'm sure, Simon. It happened too fast, before I ate anything."

"Tell me. Tell me exactly what you saw. Do you still see it?"

Evan exhaled a deep breath and tried to marshal his descriptive abilities. It would sound crazy, insane, yet he had to tell someone.

"It's some kind of split in reality. Everything around me is as it has always been, but there are other things, too. Shapes. Things I can see but can't touch. It doesn't follow any time pattern and it is not always there."

Evan stopped. This explanation sounded as if he had an eyesight problem. Still, he had to start somewhere, and work into it slowly. Maybe he was afraid speaking about it would make it real. Whereas now it was only he who knew about it.

Simon frowned. "When you get this...whatever it is...do you hear anything?"

Evan shut his eyes and shook his head. Would anyone ever understand? He had to explain it better.

"No, what I see is silent. At least they have been, and I pray they stay that way! When it first happened, I thought I was hallucinating. I saw these ghostly human forms, but they were transparent. There was a wickedness radiating from them, an evil force so intense, it almost paralyzed me. I saw them come and go as they pleased, at times merging into the bodies of the brothers. I cringed in the corner of the room, fearing one of them might enter my body. I sat on the floor drawn into a knot, and I prayed. I don't even know what I prayed. It took me the night to get a grip on my senses. If the brothers were watching, perhaps they thought my trembling and cowering was a reaction to the drugs."

Evan hesitated...how could Simon believe him? He was sure no one else would; Simon was his only hope. He studied the old man's face.

"Should I go on?" he asked.

Simon nodded and took Evan's hand in a comforting gesture.

"Okay, I fought to steady myself and keep acting for Dewberry. When the images swarmed around him, I must have looked horrified. He didn't seem to notice. When Jan arrived, I nearly panicked. What if the shapes harmed her? I have tried to convince myself they aren't real. Yet I can't. I know they are real. Do you think I'm crazy?"

A hiss of air escaped the old man's lips and he slumped in the armchair. "No, I don't think that. I don't blame you for being scared."

"If you believe me, what do you think it is, Simon?" Evan asked the question, but was fearful of the answer.

"I'm not sure. If God sends a vision, it has a purpose. Do you have any idea where they come from, what they are?"

Evan hung his head. "I know what they are, and they come from hell. When they appear I'm filled with disgust and loathing. They hover over some people. When they seem to direct their actions, it makes me physically sick. I'm outraged and at the same time horrified. They seem to have unlimited power, and I fear they will accomplish their aims with ease."

"What is it they want, Evan? What are their aims?"

"To own the earth, I think." He spoke slowly. "To make slaves of mankind. They seem to work through us by using our natural natures and turning them to their purposes. It must be easy for them, because our natures are weak. Even though I saw them clearly, I still stepped into the snare."

"What do you mean, son? Did you do something you shouldn't have?"

"Yes. Instead of turning to God, standing in faith, I used deception, lies, and trickery to save myself. I believe the evil shadows smoothed the way. They made it easy for me to fool the brothers. Now they know how far I'll go to save myself. I clearly saw the evil, but instead of fighting, I used the same means the enemy does. I should have trusted God to save me."

Simon slowly nodded his gray head. "Now you're getting into an area I can make sense of. Although, I never saw anything near what you have. Still, I caught glimpses of the spiritual struggle. I doubt the old stories have survived, but did you ever hear of the Lying Baptists?"

Evan shook his head and frowned. Simon smiled.

"I thought not. It was near the start of our nation, when settlers faced Indians. A group of Baptists, as the story goes, had gathered in a log cabin for a prayer meeting, when suddenly a young man burst through the door and begged them to hide him. A band of Indians was after him. Some of the Baptists had a truce with the natives and didn't want to break it; still, they couldn't turn the fellow away. Some of the men opened a trap door to the root cellar and pushed the young man into it. Then the arguments started.

"The Indians were riding at a gallop across the meadow toward the cabin. Inside, the Lying Baptists argued that giving the young fellow to the men was inhuman. In good conscience, the only thing to do was say they never saw him. It was worth the risk to save the boy. The Truthful Baptists declared there were no exceptions to being truthful. A lie was a lie no matter what the purpose. It would endanger their immortal souls to lie."

"What did they decide?" Evan asked.

Simon chuckled dryly. "I don't know. I pondered it many a time, trying to think what I would have done in their place. One day I'd be for saving the boy at any cost. The next, I'd rise on my spiritual haunches and decide truth had to be spoken, again at any cost."

"Well." Evan's mouth twisted in bitterness. "I guess I know which way I'd have voted. It would have been to lie."

Simon leaned forward and put his trembling hand on Evan's knee. "I can't tell you what to do, that is between you and God. I'll give you what I got and hope it helps. The way I see it, we're in the middle. It don't seem fair, but it's probably our fault for taking the reins in our own hands. Satan must have swelled and nearly bust with pride when he got us to take his bait. That's when it started: two invisible forces fighting for the souls of men. I suppose part of the rules is that we can't see either side. That's where faith comes in. We live by faith, which is a trust in things unseen. If some sort of crack has opened and you see the one side, I'd say that's strong proof of the other.

"Ever since I chose my side, I've been hoping I'd see the final outcome. I've watched the world heave, buckle, and suffer. Each time I'd run to the Bible and read, trying to find if we were closer to the conclusion, when Jesus would return. The truth is, we aren't going to know. We can read the signs, but no one knows. I'm wondering if this thing that is happening to you might be a signpost."

As Simon spoke, the old man's voice weakened, falling to a thin soft stream of words. The atmosphere in the room lightened and glowed with the mellow brightness of a hundred candles. He and Simon seemed inside an incandescent bubble, floating in dark space. Evan wanted to stay in this warm, safe place forever. His gaze shifted to the window. Outside, a darkness was forming. The semi-transparent shapes gathering beyond the glass dimmed the glare of the midday sun. Simon seemed unaware of this. Evan wondered if his mind were strong enough to bear living with this distorted vision.

For an instant, he feared the windowpane might break, allowing the forces to flood the soft, glowing haven surrounding them. Yet, the faces were neither angry nor impatient; they looked confident, powerful, and even haughty. They wore regal visages befitting rulers confident of their success. There was no vain or empty threat about them, only the self-assured expression of taking the enemy's measure, and finding it wanting.

Evan's flesh quivered. Silently, he claimed the promise that the gates of hell would not prevail against the true Church. Emboldened, he lifted his chin and leveled a piercing stare through the window. Perhaps a steadfast show of defiance would dispel the evil forces. However, slowly amused smiles spread across the crafty faces. Evan's hope evaporated. It seemed once the film between the two dimensions lifted, it was not easily restored. The suspicion that he might never be free of these shades shook his confidence even more. He knew exactly what Simon meant by choosing a side and sticking with it. He desperately wanted to persevere. He hoped Simon, with his years of experience, might give him some insight. It was a mystery as to why he should be plagued or blessed with this confounding revelation.

"And remember, Evan," Simon's voice flowed on. "God is in control. I know the suffering and trouble make us doubt, but He is."

Evan turned away from the window and tried to focus on the pale, lined face across from him. Simon was from an old, different age: the great waiting period, the long stretch of time between the ascension and the expected return. A time sustained by faith. Evan prayed for answers and hoped for understanding. The specters were a mystery. He didn't know their purpose. He could only press on through the strange, confusing situation. Evan grasped the old man's hand.

"Thank you, Simon. You're a comfort to me. I hope I haven't upset you with a lot of crazy nonsense that is probably my imagination."

Not for a minute did Evan believe the apparitions were imaginary. He wanted to leave room for doubt to keep Simon from worrying. No need for them both to slip over the edge.

"I'm sorry I can't help you more, boy. You got a rocky, lonesome road to travel. Don't worry about me thinking you might be crazy. It don't matter what I think. Real or not, it's something you got to deal with. If you're that certain you see it, it might as well be real."

Evan left Simon and walked into the blazing brightness. The ground and buildings looked sun-bleached to shades of brown, tan, and yellow. The pale sky stretched overhead with the look of taut, faded blue gauze. The compound lay deserted. Evan jammed his hands into his pockets and ambled toward the road. He looked from side to side, deliberately searching for the vague, thin outlines of his delusion. He saw nothing. He was not able to summon them at will. This reinforced his belief that they were not of his making. The world had always seemed a strange, almost unreal place; this added dimension confirmed the feeling. Talking with Simon had helped, but it changed nothing. He hadn't really expected it would.

Standing across the road next to the fence, he put one foot on the bottom rail and gazed toward the hills where Mark had gone earlier that morning. Thinking of Mark, he remembered the last call from Reverend Dewberry. The way Mark had handled it seemed to satisfy them for the moment, but it certainly was not the end of the matter. Every day he expected some contact or interference from them. It was strange not seeing the reverend or any of the brothers. Yet he knew they would, in some way, manage to control the lives in their district. Only the method was uncertain.

~ * ~

Inside the farm office, Clay stomped back and forth, his boot heels clacking heavily against the tile floor. He flashed hot and cold by turns, and a nervous sweat soaked the underarms of his shirt. Several times, he opened his mouth, but there were no words to express his anger. Instead, he hit the desk or tabletop, whichever he was near in his pacing, with his clenched fist.

With each thud of his fist, Clay shot murderous glances at Frank, who was slumped in a swivel chair in the corner. It had been several hours since Clay had taken the call from Señor Matoes in Colombia. What Matoes had said stunned him. As the man's words sank deeper, Clay became enraged. Occasionally, he was able to sputter, "Why? Why?" He nearly screamed.

Frank spread his hands and looked imploringly at his brother-in-law. "I've tried to explain, Clay, but you won't listen."

"Well, try again," Clay spat at him.

"You know how I have to operate, Clay. I need money to get things off the ground. In these conditions, no one is taking a flier into anything that isn't a sure thing. Tracy agreed with me. You have to admit we didn't take anything that wasn't hers. If you would have listened to me, I could have made the same deal for your half. You sure as hell wouldn't be in this mess now."

Clay's chest swelled with trembling anger. "I may be in a mess, Frank, but nothing compared to you. That Latino wants your scalp, and he doesn't care if your whole head comes off with it. He thinks you cheated him. That you knew how worthless this land has become."

"But I didn't," Frank protested.

"I know that." Clay snapped the words off, hating to give Frank any credit. "You still sold Tracy's inheritance. There's something indecent about it. Mom and Dad were not even dead."

Bile rose in Clay's throat while some half-formed, strange idea seemed to nibble at the fringes of his brain. Hints that perhaps in some way Frank's treachery had hastened Eva's death. Now only his father's life stood between him and Tracy coming into ownership. The thought was foggy and without foundation; Clay tried to brush it away. He had trouble separating one tragedy from another. Worse, it made him want to run, leave the land and get far away from the thing polluting their lives. The land he'd loved had turned against him.

He gripped the back of a chair and bowed his head, trying to steady himself. He wanted to pound Frank senseless, but his reason ruled. It wouldn't do any good and would only make things worse. His face was tight and stiff with control as he looked at Frank.

"Since you caused this mess, maybe you better fix it."

A flicker of suspicion lit Frank's eyes. "What do you mean?"

"Give the fellow his money. Maybe I'm stupid or something, but it seems right to me."

Frank's face was impassive, but Clay knew him well enough to know his crafty mind was busy. Once Frank had money in his hand, he'd fight the devil to keep it.

Frank began to fidget, but didn't move from his corner. Clay went to the desk, sat down, raised his legs, and propped his boots on the desktop. He folded his arms across his still heaving chest and waited. If Frank thought he was going to make it easy, he had another think coming. Clay put the blame where it clearly belonged. Tracy had her faults, always wanting more and trying to be part of the flashiest social set in town, but she would never have thought of this scheme. Frank couldn't deny this baby; it was the spitting image of him. Finally, Frank coughed and ran his fingertips across his fine brow as if wiping away a smudge. He coughed again and stood.

"Now you know I can't do that, Clay. I've been spreading it around, making investments. I got you from under your big house on the lake. Now don't get mad. Tracy wanted it and I did too, but you have to admit it was a piece of luck for you."

"Where's the rest of it?"

"I told you, I don't have it."

"I don't believe you, Frank. You haven't had time to lay off that much. You got it squirreled away somewhere."

Frank started toward the door. "Look, Clay, you're too upset. It would be better to let this rest. You have enough on your mind. Let me worry about it. I'll think of something, I promise."

Frank started to put his hand on the doorknob, but Clay sprang to his feet and sprinted across the room to stop him.

"We'll settle this right now. Go sit down, Frank."

For a minute, the two men stood glaring at each other; Frank shifted first and heaved a sigh.

"Okay, okay." He raised his hands in mock surrender. "But it isn't going to accomplish a thing."

They both returned to their seats. Frank smoothed the crease in his pants leg and assumed a nonchalant attitude. Clay drummed his square fingertips on the desktop and stared at Frank.

"It's very simple, Frank. Give Matoes what you have and let him take title to the lake house. He can put it on the market and when it sells, he might even make a profit. That might satisfy him and let him know our good faith for the rest. You don't have any other choice."

Frank shook his finger at Clay. "Wait a minute, I know what you think of me, small time wheeler dealer, but it's not true. Before, I never had anything to work with. If you think I'm going to let this get away, you're crazy. Tell me, how bad is this soil contamination... how long will it be before it's cleared?"

Clay's anger rekindled and his jaw tightened. He should cover his ears, not listen to a thing Frank said. Once he got talking, he could twist night into day. Clay heard the soft whir of the comset behind him and could visualize the constant lines of news sliding across the screen. It seemed the station told of new regulations or disasters every minute. Regulations and disasters! In Clay's mind, they were the same. The world was going to hell on a greased incline and men such as Frank were still trying to put deals together. The first ones on the spot in purgatory would probably make plans to subdivide.

"Well?" Frank insisted. "How long?"

"I don't know. If I did, maybe I'd have some idea how to weather it."

"Make a guess."

"Horse hockey, Frank. They got experts working on it and they don't even make guesses. What good is my opinion?"

Frank leaned across the desk, his eyes glittering mica chips. "Listen, Clay, there may be a way that will take care of us. Give me a guess."

"If they finally decide what it is and if they find an agent to flush the soil, maybe two years, possibly three. That's the optimistic guess. If nature handles it, twenty, thirty years, or maybe never."

Frank squared his shoulders and drew his eyebrows together. "Well, that gives me something to go on. Remember, this is the seed of an idea, but if it sprouts, you won't have to worry about growing anything else. Right now, you got what, maybe a twenty percent chance of the land being workable in three years? If it is, can you imagine the entanglements? There'll be a panic, setting new standards and tests for grain grown on this land. The requirements will be stiff. There won't be any profit when you do get into production. And that is the best projection."

"What kind of big idea is that, Frank? I know how hopeless it is."

"Now, wait. I told you this is only the beginning of an idea. We'll have to smooth it some and shape it, but it could work. First, you have to face facts and quit hoping for anything. I know you have the men working on some of the old wells, but I wouldn't count on them. Even if they manage to squeeze out a drop or two, how long before that's contaminated? There's also the matter of finding a patch of chemical-free ground. National irrigated ninety percent of this land. What good is less than ten percent going to do even if you get water for it? I hate to say it, Clay, but I've been figuring odds for a long time and I don't give you a ghost of a chance to survive this."

Listening to Frank made Clay's heart turn to lead, and he heard the death bell toll over the Sanderson holdings. A bitter metallic taste made his lips draw in at the corners. At that minute, he hated Frank. It wasn't Frank's fault, but Clay could well understand the desire to kill the bearer of bad news.

"Fantastic," Clay choked. "What am I supposed to do...roll over and die?"

"No, no." Frank radiated excitement. He was in his element. It was clear what made Frank's gears turn. It wasn't money alone, it was the game. The chase, the hunt, the outsmarting of an opponent. In a high fever, Frank continued.

"When you think you're backed into a corner, you turn and attack. Do the unexpected, take everyone off guard. Put yourself in the other fellow's shoes and try to guess what he plans to do. Matoes and his partner are in a fine fix. They want their investment money, but they don't have any legal recourse. Lawsuits take forever and as long as Mark is alive, they can't call in their note. It's a bluff on their part. They're trying to stampede us because they don't think the land will ever be worth anything again. The way I see it, they don't have any options. We plunge in and make them a deal. Sell them the rest of the farm, at a bargain price, of course. It's the only way you'll ever get anything for the place now."

Clay laughed despite his anguish. "Frank, I think you're crazy. Why under the sun would they do that?"

"Because," Frank explained patiently. "It's human nature. No one wants to feel duped or that he made a bad deal. I can convince them that buying your half for a song now will make them a killing later. Don't you see? I can tell them your misfortune is their gain. That you don't have capital to hang on, but they do. When it turns around, they will have more than they hoped for."

Clay slapped the desk with his open palm. "Forget it, Frank. I can't do it. I don't care if we starve. I'm not selling something that isn't mine. I'm sure as hell not going to bother Dad with some wild, stupid scheme. I don't know why I thought it my duty to get you to give them their money back. If Matoes, Santoes whatever his name is, calls again, I'm going to tell him to stuff it. I can't help what you've already done. It's nothing to me, or Dad."

Frank shrugged. "Thought I'd offer. It would give you enough money to settle somewhere else. Save you the pain of having only half the land, if it ever is usable. They'd probably lease their half to National Grain. I don't think they intend to operate it themselves."

Clay stomped from the office, leaving Frank to contemplate his failed proposal. Clay hated to admit it, but Frank's arrangement with Matoes really had put him in a bad situation. Half the land simply wouldn't be enough to keep things going. Clay had never considered selling any of the farm. With fewer acres, there were financial obligations he couldn't meet, no matter how good a yield or price. Maybe he should sell if the Colombians were dumb enough to take the chance. At this point, they had nothing to lose. By the time Tracy inherited her share, the land could be producing again. Matoes had panicked. Maybe once he thought it over, he'd be willing to wait. Clay was...even if he kept only half, he'd still stick with the land.

If Frank dared to mention any of this to Mark, he'd break the fool's neck. Mark had been too low lately. No telling what he'd do if he heard about Frank's deal. Clay started across the hot, dusty compound. He noticed Evan standing in the distance, one foot on the fence rail staring across the fields. It struck Clay what an odd assortment the people were on the farm, gathered there as if it were the last outpost.

As Clay neared the house, he kicked at the gravel and cursed the dust rising and falling on his boots. With less work to do, the days seemed endless, giving more time to despair and consider the loss. The tall farmhouse seemed to ride the wide prairie like a ship on the sea, and Clay wondered how long it would remain afloat. He had sworn he would never leave, but doubt and reality constantly plagued him. Still, if it came to leaving, they had nowhere to go. Of course, Diana and Jan could go home to their parents. He hated to think of Jan leaving. He missed his mother and Jan was the only female he was comfortable talking with. Tillie's hovering made him nervous. She was only trying to fill the void; it would hurt her to know how he felt. Tillie had eased off harping about Diana, but the sidelong looks and cold remarks were still in evidence. If Diana were gone, at least that would stop. Perhaps a hundred times Clay had tried to untangle his feelings. At first, he couldn't believe Tillie, or Diana's version of Eva's accident. He finally settled upon a combination. Diana probably did shove Eva, but Clay couldn't bring himself to think it was on purpose. The loss of the baby made his blood boil. Diana had no right to make that decision. For days, he hated looking at her.

However, lately he saw her in a different light. Something was definitely wrong with her. She seemed off center. Everything she said had a vague touch of strangeness to it. Clay remembered their conversation a few nights before. He had felt it was time for serious talking, to get to the bottom of their problems. Beset on every side, it would relieve part of the pressure if they came to an understanding. He had tried to start easy, not wanting to set her off again.

"We haven't had much time to ourselves," he'd said. "Can we have a talk now?"

Diana was lying on the lounge by the bedroom window. Her pale blue gown draped across her legs fell in graceful folds over the edge of the seat. The last light in the western sky came through the glass and edged her profile in gold.

"We can discuss whatever you want." She didn't look at him.

Clay sat on the side of the bed and took heart when her words were, if not kind, at least calm.

"I guess it's no secret I've been confused and really don't know how I feel toward you lately. I think I'm beginning to make some progress. Maybe I didn't take enough time to understand. Why don't we agree that perhaps we both made some mistakes and start from there?" His words were clumsy, he had trouble expressing what he meant, but it was a start.

"What do you say, Diana? Think we can put things together? It might be slow going, but don't you think it's worth a try?"

Diana turned toward him, tilted her head, and a sly smile crept across her face. "Now, now, Clayton Sanderson. You aren't going to trick me with soft words. I know what you're trying to do, saying you made mistakes, making me think everything is fine if I'll admit to some wrongdoing, too."

Clay slowly shook his head. "No, that isn't it. Look, let's forget the blame placing. We don't need to do that."

A tiny wrinkle settled across Diana's smooth forehead and her eyes clouded. "Why are you always talking about someone being to blame? What is it you think I've done?"

"You know, about the baby."

"Baby? What baby? I know you have always wanted children, but honestly, you mustn't let the subject obsess you." Diana cocked her head to one side and seemed to study his face for a second. "You know, I think Tillie is to blame, if there is any blame. Her talk of babies and childcare. I realize she is an old woman living in the past, a world where children were the center of everything. Poor old thing. Maybe you should apply to one of the reproduction centers. Perhaps they could arrange something. If you got a child from them for Tillie to play nursemaid to, it might set her right."

It was difficult to follow the twists and turns of Diana's mind. It was obvious she wanted to forget the baby she had aborted. Clay decided to drop the subject of the baby and try another angle.

"How do you feel about staying on the farm now?"

Diana laughed, waving her hand as if brushing away a gnat.

"Clay, dear. You know I can't stay forever. Fern is expecting me to come live with her. I'll wait until you are feeling more yourself." Diana sighed, a look of pity settling in her eyes. "I do understand what losing your mother did to you. Still,"—she brightened a bit— "we do get over these things."

The memory of their conversation made him walk slower. Their talk had settled nothing, and he hadn't tried again. He reached the front steps and stomped the dust off his boots as he crossed the wide porch. For a minute he hesitated...he hated going into the house, and it was a strange feeling. He had always loved his home, and now it was a place of gloom and confusing turmoil. He hoped no one was around; he wanted to be alone for a while. Quietly he opened the door and stepped into the dim interior. He crossed the foyer, slipped into the living room, and sank onto the long couch in front of the dead fireplace. He stretched his legs and his shoulders slumped with his chin touching his chest. He closed his eyes and tried to rest, but his mind raced on.

Maybe he should take Diana to a shrink; even Jan had noticed her strange behavior. Almost every morning, Diana packed a few clothes and told everyone she would be leaving that day. Except by evening, the clothes were again in the closet, ready for the ritual to start over the next day. Clay was weary of the charade and had offered to drive her into town, but she had become alarmed.

"Oh no, it wouldn't look right for me to leave you this soon. No one would understand. No, when I go to Fern's, it has to seem the reasonable thing to do."

After that, Clay let Jan deal with her. In a way, this new Diana was easier to be around, no harsh screaming and demands. It made him uneasy, like harboring a time bomb. A person didn't change this drastically without something blowing later.

Clay thought about the tasks he had given Jeff and the men who were still on the farm. He should be working beside them. Instead, a heavy sigh lifted his drooping shoulders; there was no energy to do more. Why should he keep fighting a losing battle? However, Clay knew the answer. It was for Mark. His father had caved in after the funeral. Mark had always been strong; now he withdrew from everything and everyone. All Clay could do was try to hold things together until Mark was well again.

The sudden sound of the doorbell sending its musical chimes throughout the house jolted Clay like an electrical charge. Tillie came bustling through the living room. As she started toward the foyer, Clay rose from the sofa. Tillie clasped her bosom and gave a small cry.

"Good grief, Clay, you startled me. I didn't know a soul was about."

"I'm sorry; you want me to get it?"

"No, I'll see to it."

Clay sank into his hiding place. Sometimes Tillie's protectiveness was a blessing. She made things easier, even with her bitterness toward Diana. Tillie ran the house and tended to the running of the lodge, and she fended off unwelcome intrusions. Clay felt bad letting her do this, but she seemed to be fulfilling some obligation she had to Eva.

Tillie stepped into the living room. "It's that Reverent Dewberry," she whispered. "You want me to get rid of him?"

"Oh crap," Clay hissed. He thought for a second before getting to his feet. "No, you better let him in. If I don't see him, he'll try to bother Dad."

Tillie nodded, and in a minute returned with the reverend in tow. Reverend Dewberry stretched forth his hand and came toward Clay.

"My boy, how are you?"

"Fine. And you?"

"Busy, very busy. The Lord's work is never done." The reverend chuckled and Clay tried to smile, hiding his dislike for this limp-handed, smug-faced servant of God.

"May we sit down?" the reverend asked.

"Sure, I'm sorry." Clay extended his arm, indicating a chair. "I forget my manners sometimes lately."

The reverend lowered himself to sit on the chair's cushion and a small smile rippled his tight-lipped mouth.

"Certainly, I understand. I hope it will help you to know we have been praying for you and your family." He shook his head and clicked his tongue. "Sometimes the chastening of the Lord is hard to bear, but if we follow His Will, the blessings will come."

Clay considered this sage bit of theological wisdom and decided he didn't understand it.

"What do you think the Will of the Lord is for the Sandersons?" Clay questioned, honestly wishing someone would explain it to him.

For an instant, the reverend narrowed his eyes, looking like he suspected Clay of being disrespectful. Clay stood his ground, his face as inquiring and open as he could make it. He evidently convinced Dewberry.

"Well." He cleared his throat. "Well now, Clay, that is sometimes a deep and hard thing to discern. However, one thing we can be positive of is that we must respect and support the Church."

Here it comes, Clay thought, another pitch for us to start chipping in more. "I guess you've heard, but I doubt we'll be in a position to support anything for a while."

The reverend gave a dry laugh. "It isn't always money the Church needs. No, my boy, there are other needs to be met."

"What might those be?"

"Like father, like son." The reverend chuckled good-naturedly. "Independent and to the point. I'm happy to deal with people who are ready to face what comes and do their part."

Clay didn't answer and waited for him to go on. The reverend cleared his throat again.

"Actually, my mission is twofold. First, how is Evan? Have you noticed his, well, unusual behavior returning? He isn't reverting to any of those rebellious practices, is he?"

"Not that I've noticed, but I don't keep that close a watch on him. He seems calm. What did you expect him to be doing?"

"Oh, nothing. As long as he remains quiet, I don't suppose there is much he can do. It's only that sometimes these obsessions have a way of flaring up. We in the Council are really too busy right now to give him any further help. I would appreciate it if you would let me know if he exhibits any tendency toward forming groups, that sort of thing. We don't want him starting trouble. Not during these times, now do we? This brings me to the second point.

"We have new responsibilities. Perhaps if you attended services, you'd be aware of this, but never mind...we'll discuss that small lapse later. This is more pressing. You know we minister to the needs of the people, both spiritual and physical. With the greater shortage of food, we certainly can't stand by and do nothing. President Morris has wisely decided to place the distribution of food in our hands, as did leaders of the other nations. They had to turn to us. Our organization is worldwide and highly efficient. What we need is storage. Your farm and several others are ideal.

"It is unfortunate the disaster hit, leaving your warehouses and storage bins empty. You can still contribute by donating this space for our use. As soon as the directive came down, I dropped my other work and began making plans for its operation in our section. To tell you the truth, it is thrilling to think of the vastness of this plan. Billions of people finally fed properly. With this distribution system, we can end hunger. I never cease to marvel at the ways of our Lord. What looks to be calamity turns to a miracle. I know you and your father will be proud to do your part in this great undertaking."

The reverend stopped to breathe. Clay could see that he was telling the truth about being excited over the new regulation. He had read the news as it came over the comset concerning the proposed food distribution plan; he wasn't aware it had actually passed. He hadn't given much thought to what it would mean, but as the reverend spoke, the far-flung effects of this measure alarmed him. What was that bonehead Morris thinking? Controlling the distribution of food would make religious leaders nearly invincible.

The newscast stressed that these were temporary measures, taken only to relieve the looming worldwide famine. Still, Clay had noticed that once an agency or other powerful body had taken more control, they never surrendered it. Governments and Unity Council had the people in a vise. As each organization grew larger, the common man suffered. There was no place to run. For a minute, Clay wished he were smarter, better able to think quickly and give a snappy answer. He envied Frank's devious mind. If he were standing in Clay's place, he would be thinking a mile a second of how to turn the situation to his advantage. Try as he might, Clay found it impossible to race his mind in that manner. If he refused, no telling what hardship the reverend would bring upon them. If he agreed, there would be brothers on the farm directing the storage. The last thing Clay wanted was a bunch of outsiders flooding the farm.

He preferred to be alone in his misery.

"Well, my boy, what do you say? This is a great opportunity for your family to take part in the Church's finest work."

"I don't know. I can't say anything before talking to Dad first. This is his place."

"I could speak with him now. I realize he must still be in mourning for his dear wife, but life does go on."

Alarmed, Clay was able to react swiftly. "He isn't home. He's been gone most of the day. I can explain it to him well enough."

Despite trying to appear calm and friendly, Clay's face grew warm and stiff. Dewberry gave him a look that plainly said he'd caught the meaning behind Clay's expression. He coughed again and his eyes turned hard.

"I hadn't wanted to insult you and your family by mentioning this, Clay, but we are authorized to pay for this space should anyone be less than charitable."

"Is that everything? I want all the details before I tell Dad about this."

"There is one other small thing. I hesitate to speak of it."

"Maybe you'd better."

"It's the law governing the greatest good for the greatest number of people. You can surely understand giving the Church this undertaking and not supplying the means to enforce it would be unwise."

"In other words, if you can't beg it, or buy it, you can take it."

On the surface, the reverend's departure was cordial. However, they both knew the family was far from being in the flock of the faithful.

Twenty

Jan sat on a stool at the kitchen counter with a cup of steaming herbal tea before her. Resting her elbow on the counter top, she cupped her chin in her hand and waited for the brew to cool. She stared at the brown tile floor. It was amazing how Tillie kept it spotless with everyone tracking over it, but that was Tillie. Her formula for curing a troubled mind was simple: work and more work. As she watched Tillie washing the window above the sink, Jan stifled a yawn. The brisk, vigorous circles going round and round in each pane made Jan tired. She felt wilted as the few drooping daises Tillie managed to keep growing at the border of the garden. Tillie had almost come to blows with Jeff over keeping her garden watered. He had to admit that the vegetables were a necessity, but how did the blasted daisies rate even a drop of the precious water? Tillie simply stared at Jeff and steadfastly went about her determined way to, as she put it, keep everyone's body and soul together. The flowers did help. Tillie put a small vase in the foyer and one on the dining table. She instinctively knew life was more than keeping stomachs full. When the last pane of glass gleamed, Tillie turned and wiped the sweat from her forehead with the back of her arm.

"Why, you haven't touched your tea," she admonished. "Now, you drink it and see if that mixture doesn't cool you off some."

Reluctantly, Jan lifted the cup and the steam, with its heavy herbal aroma, filled her head. As July boiled on into August, Jan was ready to try anything to keep cool, even Tillie's home remedies. It was easy to blame everything on the weather. But it wasn't only the hot, dry summer wearing her to the bone, sapping her energy, and leaving her limp and discouraged. She had never intended to stay on the farm this long...it had simply happened. One day dragged on into the next, and Jan saw the gratitude in Clay's eyes. As Diana withdrew deeper into her own strange world, Clay found it harder to make any connection with her. Jan had become the link between them.

Diana called for her constantly. She would hardly choose what to wear unless Jan approved. It was a sad, sick situation. In better times, Clay would have bundled her off to a doctor immediately. He had even reluctantly asked Jan to inquire about her parents' helping with the cost of treatment. It plainly hurt his pride, but Diana's health had to come before his feelings. When she inquired, she found their father was in no better position to pay than Clay was. Actually, Diana seemed happy enough and her physical health certainly hadn't suffered. Her complexion was creamy and flawless, a faint rose blush covered her cheeks, and her eyes glowed a soft sea green. Really, she had never looked better. Her mind seemed to have reached a peaceful plateau, leaving her body to bloom in a way as never before.

It was ironic. In the midst of trouble and turmoil, Diana slipped away, escaped while Jan worried more each day, and worked harder. She didn't mind taking care of Diana; it wasn't much trouble. However, Diana was not herself and that did trouble Jan. Some days she would have welcomed the old Diana, despite her former disagreeable disposition. Jan finished the last of the tea while Tillie concocted a meatloaf extended with soy meal. She put in one measure of meal, hesitated an instant, and dumped in a second.

"I wouldn't be stretching the meat this far," she said, her broad back toward Jan. "But with the way things are, Lord knows how long our supplies will last."

"Maybe I can speak to Reverend Dewberry about a few extra coupons. You are feeding a lot of people."

"Don't you ask that twit for a thing extra. We want no favors from him. You can bet your life there'd be strings attached and we'd never get free."

It was the truth, Jan thought. Ever since Clay unwillingly agreed to give the Church the use of the warehouse and storage bins, brothers were everywhere. You never knew when one of them would ask the loan of a vehicle, or use of the communication set in the farm office. Jan was proud of Clay for one thing. He had insisted upon payment for the use of the farm facilities. There wasn't any way to keep them off the farm, but landholders were entitled to compensation and Clay demanded they pay. The decision was purely Clay's; Mark didn't care one way or the other. Diana was not the only one slipping away from them. Mark was also of increasing concern.

He continued going to Eva's grave every day for a month after her funeral. Suddenly he stopped going. He also quit speaking about her. At first, his constant vigil at the gravesite worried everyone. Slowly they'd accepted it, reasoning that perhaps it was good to let him work through his grief in his own way. When his sitting at Eva's grave ceased, it had a jarring effect...the way a howling prairie wind left an uneasy calm when it abruptly stopped. Mark's new behavior was as unsettling as his last. He entrenched himself on the second floor, the way Diana had done.

Caring for her two charges, Jan shuttled from Diana's room to the huge corner master suite. Diana was serene, floating above everything, while Mark sank deeper into a dark silence. Jan worried that he was concentrating on ways to summon his death. Tillie coaxed him to eat by using her meager supplies to prepare tempting meals. Clay went to his room daily to discuss conditions on the farm. Neither Tillie nor Clay could rouse more than a weak smile or flicker of recognition in his dim eyes.

Tillie shoved the long dish containing the meatloaf into the oven, and sat on a stool across the counter from Jan. She took a handkerchief from her apron pocket and wiped it across the folds of her short neck.

"I can't help feeling things would take a turn for the better if this awful drought would break."

"Maybe it will," Jan offered. "Clay said they're having a cloudburst on the west coast. I haven't had time to catch much news."

"Isn't that the way of it? Enough rain there to wash them into the sea while we sit dry and parched."

Tillie's plump face sagged, exposing the deep hollows beneath her eyes. She sighed and Jan noticed how dark the blotches under her eyes were. Tillie's appearance was shocking, but it hadn't happened overnight. It was more startling to Jan to realize she hadn't noticed this before. For some time, Jan hadn't closely studied anyone's face. For each person carried a burden, and if you paid too much attention, you might absorb more than you could carry. She was ashamed. No matter how bad things were, they shouldn't withdraw from one another. They had to stay open and aware of others' needs. Her lack of sensitivity was surprising...she who was always intent upon helping people. Jan vowed to correct this.

"You look tired, Tillie. Is there anything I can do, maybe some chores in the kitchen, or more of the cleaning? It never takes me long to straighten the upstairs. Mark and Diana don't take much time. Diana does fuss if I leave her alone, but I could bring her with me. It would be good for her."

Tillie chuckled while a smile shoved her cheeks into their normal proportions.

"You're sweet to offer, but giving me more time to think won't help. No, what I need is more to do. Sometimes I wish I could turn my head off, same as that oven over there." Tillie jerked a thumb toward the other side of the kitchen. "See, it's turned itself off already. Did its job and now it'll set there nice and quiet till I need it again."

"I know. Sometimes I can't stop my thoughts either."

"Be thankful you're young. You don't have a great backlog in your head. I doubt you'd understand, but the last thirty years seem a hundred in relation to how things have changed. Sometimes I want to run away. 'Course I couldn't leave what's left of the family."

Tillie was partly right; Jan didn't understand. To her, the world hadn't changed much. Usually, she was impatient. Nothing happened fast enough to suit her. However, lately, lurking at the fringes of her awareness was a suspicion that something was drastically different. That some great force was actively at work. Evidently, Evan's teaching had more impact than she realized.

"I guess everyone wants to run at times. Where would you go, Tillie?"

Tillie held her head to one side and looked toward a corner of the ceiling. "Oh, I don't know. I have a sister, haven't seen much of her for years, but she's always said I'd be welcome. She married a microbiologist, studies bitsy living things. I always liked him. Bout ten years ago they went to live in Greenland where he works at a laboratory. My sister told me she'd be glad of my company. Still, I want to feel needed and Lord knows there is need enough since Eva is gone. She was as much a sister to me as my own."

Tillie dipped her head a bit and the glint of a tear glistened in the corner of her eye. Jan swallowed and pressed her lips tight. She had never decided what part in Eva's death her own sister had played. At a subconscious level, she kept backing away from the question, not wanting to know.

"I'm sorry, Tillie. Seems the Brockman and Sanderson families didn't mix well. This past year has been a nightmare for everyone."

Tillie reached across and patted Jan's hand. "Don't puzzle over it too hard. We're in a muddle; we grope around looking for reasons, putting the blame on ourselves or the other fellow. Truth is, we don't know. It isn't only us in the main house, either. I've been visiting Simon whenever I have a spare minute. Even that sweet old man is carrying a burden, and him near the end of his own time. Seems he, at least, should be left in peace."

"What's the matter with Simon? He isn't sick, is he?"

"No. He's strong as you could expect. It's something else. Every time I go there, he's sitting with his Bible, thumbing through the pages muttering. He must be looking for something he can't find. It has to do with Evan, I think. Speaking of troubled people, that boy looks a ghost of his former self."

Jan knew about Evan's trouble. Many evenings after supper, they took long walks, or sat on the porch; it was inevitable he would confide in her. She had tried to reason with him about his guilt, explaining there was nothing he could do. One evening she even tried to shame him.

"Evan," she had said. "How can you behave this way? What about the victorious Christian life you talk about to others? That no matter what, God is in charge and we are to rest in that faith."

A look of anguish was enough to make her wish she had never spoken.

"Don't you think I know," he had cried. "But I'm weak, my courage and faith fail me. Sometimes I'm ready to stand and fight, and then the fear overcomes me. I despise my weakness."

"What is it you're afraid of? Surely not death, if it came to that."

His caustic laugh had rattled in the dry, warm night air. He raised an eyebrow and the moonlight slanting across his handsome face changed his angelic appearance to a satanic one.

"Death would be a welcome release from the life I live now."

Evan's fight was on a spiritual level, where no one could help or reach him. He was alone with his God and his demons. Evan never questioned his salvation. Instead, he struggled with some impurity. At times, it seemed the cure would kill him. It was his personal trial, a testing and refining. To Jan's dim understanding of things concerning God, it seemed those in His vanguard were tried and tested harder. She could only offer compassion and companionship.

Evan had been getting stronger after coming to the farm, making plans to start the meetings again, but then the Church moved in, controlling the storage on the farm. The constant presence of the brothers seemed to undermine Evan's progress. In front of them, he kept the pretense of compliance, but Jan saw that denying his true beliefs weakened and wounded him. At times, she wished he would find the courage to face Dewberry and tell him his views were as strong as ever. That he intended to start teaching again. Of course, that would put Evan in danger, and this time, he might not survive. Wearily, Jan lifted herself off the stool and leaned against the counter.

"Thanks for the tea. I think it did help. I should go upstairs and see why Diana isn't calling for me."

Tillie chuckled her silent laugh and Jan gave her a knowing look. It felt good to have some relief, even at Diana's expense. As Jan started toward the dining room, she called over her shoulder.

"I'll look in on Mark, too. Maybe I can get him to come for lunch."

"We can only hope." Tillie sighed.

Going through the darkened dining room, its drapes drawn against the noonday sun, Jan brushed a few wisps of hair off her neck and bent her head forward as she fastened them to the clump of curls on top of her head. As she entered the long, wide living room, her mind was a thousand miles away, thinking of the icy white coldness where Tillie's sister lived. How wonderful it would be to awake one morning and find a great mountain of sparkling cold snow piled in the front yard. She was halfway across the living room before she heard the soft sobbing.

It was coming from the entry hall where the stairs led to the second floor. Jan ran across the living room and into the foyer. What she saw nearly stopped her heart and breath. Mark was sitting crumpled on the bottom step, his shoulders and head leaning back against the stairs above. His eyes were closed and his mouth hung open. Crouched beside him, Diana was patting his face and moaning tearful words.

"Get up now, please do. Oh, don't do this. You can't sit here, stand up."

Diana's hair hung across her forehead hiding her face, but the agonized tone of her voice was enough to freeze Jan's blood.

Diana continued to pat Mark and coax him with soft words. "No one must see you. This is wrong, now get up. Oh please, get up."

Jan's body turned to hot lead; she felt heavy and flushed, and her heart pounded hard enough to choke her. For a second, she started to turn toward the kitchen for help, but instead she ran to Diana, calling over her shoulder.

"Tillie. Tillie. Come quick," she shouted.

She grabbed Diana and tried to move her away from Mark. Diana stiffened and clutched at Mark's shoulders, her fingers locking in the material of his shirt.

"Let go," Jan cried.

"Go away. Leave me alone!" Diana screamed, turning wild, fiery eyes on her sister.

As Jan wrestled with Diana, she heard the heavy thud of Tillie running toward them.

"Oh, no!" came Tillie's anguished cry.

Jan's mind cleared a bit and she looked over her shoulder at Tillie.

"Quick, call for help. I'll try to get Diana away."

Stricken to silence, Tillie nodded once, her face a sick gray-white, and spun on her heel to hurry away.

"Come on, Diana," Jan pleaded. "Let go, you might be hurting him."

Diana threw her head to the side, hitting Jan's jaw with a thumping crack. The blow stunned Jan for an instant and her hands relaxed. Seizing the opportunity, Diana fell forward across Mark's body and began a high-pitched scream. It echoed through the house and sent chills along Jan's spine.

Quickly, Jan recovered and, using what force she could muster, began pulling Diana away from Mark. Diana fought harder and continued the eerie sound that turned from scream to long, sharp wailing. Jan worked on in silence, her sore jaw set hard and tight. It was no good reasoning with Diana. She was past hearing. Suddenly, Diana weakened and Jan jerked her to her feet. As they staggered away from the foot of the stairs, Jan got a good look at Mark. She hadn't seen many dead people, but the limpness of his body and the empty face along with ash-pale skin made her sure his life was gone.

She and Diana were alone.

The human form slumped at the bottom of the stairs was as void of life as the polished wood it rested upon. The emptiness and strangeness of a body with its animating spark gone awed Jan. She felt Diana twisting and turning in her arms. She heard Diana's frantic wail turning to a whimper, but the spectacle of a life simply vanishing held her in shocked wonder. She stared at the crumpled body. She wanted to call to Mark. Where are you? Where have you gone?

The impulse was so overpoweringly strong, Jan thought she had spoken. For a bit, she'd lost sense of time. She knew it had been only minutes before Clay, Jeff, Frank, and Tillie burst in, but with Diana held in her tightly locked arms, it could have been days. Diana's torture became her own; she could feel the convulsions racking Diana's body and the vibrations of the moan rising from her throat. For weeks, something had been at work in Diana, akin to a virus destroying her link with reality, a low-grade infection slowly burning away rational thought. Now Mark's death seemed to break the last weak strand of reason.

Jan watched Clay and Jeff working furiously over the body trying to restore some sign of life. Tillie clasped and unclasped her hands, repeating to unhearing ears that the doctor was on his way with the rescue unit.

Jan, with her practical turn of mind, was already mourning Mark. She quickly absorbed the shock, knowing she needed to gain control. Mark's passing added another layer of sorrow to the year's growing accumulation. With his death a fact, she turned her efforts to the living. Diana was slipping further away with each passing minute. If Jan didn't reach her soon, it would be too late. The others took no notice as Jan carefully guided Diana from the entry hall and into the living room. Diana moved easily as a feather; only a touch swept her past a chair and brought her to rest on the couch. Jan sat beside her and with her arm around Diana's shoulders, began a soft questioning.

"What happened, Diana? Did Mark fall down the stairs? Why didn't you call for help?"

Diana's eyes were the dull, murky green of a flat oily sea. Studying her sister's face, Jan despaired of getting any answers. Still, the flicker of an expression rippled Diana's marble features.

"I told him to get up."

"Yes, sweetheart, I know you did."

"You make him get up, Jan."

Diana grasped Jan's hand in an icy vise while her mouth worked in a futile effort. Panic was building a violent storm behind her turbulent eyes.

"Easy, Diana." Jan tried to calm her. "It wasn't your fault. Mark's heart was bad."

"No. Not my fault," Diana muttered. "She did it. Yes, I saw her. She left him for me to find when I came looking for you."

"Who left him?" Jan asked.

Diana turned a little girl's face to Jan. "She's smart, but I saw her. They were both at the bottom of the stairs. When I came toward them, she left. She wanted you to think I'd done it."

"You were coming to find me and found Mark instead? Is that it?" Jan prodded gently.

Diana gave a quick nod, but a dark, crafty look settled over her face.

"Why did you stay away that long? She doesn't come when you are with me. Eva only comes when I'm alone. I don't want to be alone," Diana began to whisper. "Now there are two of them. I told him to leave, but he wants to stay with her. Take me home. I want to go to Fern's."

Jan closed her eyes and slumped against the couch, pity for Diana threatening to bring her to tears. It was too much to bear. Diana always sparkled hard as crystal. Why hadn't they realized she would shatter as easily. What was worse, it was Diana's own maneuvering that had sent her crashing over the edge. Diana never should have returned to the farm from the hospital, yet that was another of her games. She probably thought leaving Clay as a friend rather than a bitter ex-husband would work to her advantage. Besides, with Eva's recent death, leaving at this time could make Diana look bad. Jan knew most of her sister's tricks. It was hard to believe Diana felt enough guilt to crush her, but maybe she had changed. Jan wasn't sure what went on in Diana's mind now. What would they do with her if she were beyond repair? Still, time changes everything; perhaps it would mend her sister in its passing.

The sound of activity in the entryway rousted Jan from the gray wasteland of speculation.

"You stay here, Diana." Jan patted her sister's hand. "I'll be right back."

As Jan stood, Diana clutched at her skirt. "No, no," she shrieked.

"Come with me." Jan tried to help her stand.

"No, no." Diana buried her head against Jan's legs, covering her eyes with Jan's skirt. There was no hope of untangling herself. She watched the medics carry Mark's covered body past the wide arch connecting the living room with the entry hall. She heard the front door open and the trampling feet as they moved with their burden across the wooden porch. Shortly engines started, the sound of several cars and the rescue unit pulling away.

When Tillie entered the living room, her body sagged. She shuffled across the room and stood silent before Jan.

"There was no hope, was there?" Jan asked.

"No." Tillie shook her head once, her voice dry and colorless as the parched earth outside. Tillie looked at Diana hovering beside Jan.

"Did she tell you how it happened?"

"More or less." Jan sighed. "I guess she came looking for me and found Mark."

Tillie's expression was a jumble of emotions; it was painful watching her try to arrange them. Where did pity for Diana fit into the distrust and anger of before? Finally, her visage settled into compassion and sorrowful acceptance of the unchangeable.

"We should have had the doctor look at her. I'm sorry, I didn't think."

"It probably wouldn't have helped anyway," Jan answered. "He would have given her a sedative and recommended we get her to a psychiatrist. There are pills in the bathroom that should put her to sleep for a while. If you'll help me, we'll take her upstairs."

As they stood on either side and began to move Diana toward the entry hall, she gave them a searching look. Near the archway, Diana dug her heels into the carpet. She began to tremble and shook her head, bumping first Jan and then Tillie. Jan tightened her grip on Diana's arm and pushed harder, while Diana's struggles increased.

"Now, now." Tillie's soothing tone startled Jan and stopped Diana's twisting. "Don't you worry, Tillie will help. Lean on me, that's right. Poor tired child."

Tillie smoothed Diana's hair and held her against her plump side as she moved toward the doorway. Tillie continued her comforting words.

"Won't those clean, cool sheets feel good? After your nap, I'll bring you some chilled broth, and maybe one of those tiny sandwiches you asked me to make. Now won't that be nice?"

Jan stumbled along behind them, blinded by a film of tears. She wondered if she were crying for Diana and Clay, or perhaps even Tillie. As the drops gathered on her cheeks, the sorrow broadened to encompass everyone. It was hard to see much hope for the future, but somehow they must pull together and find a way. There was no choice...giving in to adversity was not an option.

Twenty-one

They put Mark's body into the earth from which he always said it had come. Clay tried to grieve, but instead, a numb, heavy, sorrowful acceptance settled over him. His father's oneness with nature was now complete. The vital energy that once powered the robust Mark would blend into the soil, giving strength to the sick, depleted ground he loved. Perhaps what steadied Clay in this final and complete loss of his parents was the knowledge of Mark's wanting to go. He was tired of battling the elements, praying for favorable wind, rain, and sun. It had been a lifetime of love/hate. Now, in final surrender, Mark was at peace with the land.

Conquest by merger.

Clay watched Evan take a handful of the dry prairie dust and let it fall upon the casket. A hot, light wind blew some of it past the oblong cut in the ground and scattered a fine silt across the mourners' shoes. The same dust-laden breeze carried Evan's words past Clay's ears. Some bits and pieces of his message settled into Clay's mind, where they scratched and irritated his thoughts.

The past was over, dead and done, same as the lives of his parents. He couldn't let memories stick and clog the process of reasoning. There was no guilt in his determination to get on with the job of living. Mark and Eva would have wanted him to plow ahead. Evan kept the ritual mercifully short and as the others walked through the brown grass toward the cars, Clay stood for a last moment alone between the two fresh graves.

Now, if any Sanderson were to endure upon this piece of land, it was his responsibility. His thoughts, thin as frail hands, tried to gather pieces of the broken, scattered family. The tiny son that should have been sleeping and growing in a nursery at the farm was gone, really never had been. Accepting the loss of Diana was perhaps harder than the loss of Mark and Eva. He had known they wouldn't be with him forever. Still, there were Tracy, Robin, and Frank Jr. They were Sandersons, even though they carried the Ivers name. Although Tracy had cut her ties with the land by going along with Frank. Clay closed his eyes and fought the leaden shroud of weariness hanging about him. He lifted his head and looked across the rolling fields. The view brought no great surge of strength or inspiration. Only a solid, steadfast determination to put one foot in front of the other and each day do those tasks before him.

Clay had thought his sorrow at the gravesite was the extent of his grieving, but returning to the big house proved him wrong. Even though others were there, it seemed a place devoid of personality, as lifeless as the barren fields surrounding it. He had no idea how to bring it to life again.

Jan was upstairs seeing to Diana while Tillie and Tracy worked in the kitchen preparing a meal no one seemed eager to eat. Jeff had taken the two children to the lodge, where Simon kept them entertained with stories of days long gone by. Leaning against the fireplace mantle holding a glass of scotch and water, Clay wished he too could sit at Simon's knee and become lost in the safe, dead past. Evan sat silently in a big corner chair, never speaking, but his eyes gave comfort and encouragement when Clay glanced at him. Frank was the one full of talk and restless energy. He had emptied and refilled his glass several times, downing the liquor as if it were more necessary than the gulps of air he drew between sentences.

"I guess you know we've run out of time on this Matoes thing," Frank was saying. "It may be a poor time to talk about it, but Mark being gone does bring us to the deadline. If you'll pardon the expression."

Clay almost smiled despite his mood. Mark wouldn't have minded; in fact, it had amused him to see his son-in-law wiggling in and out of tight places. This time Frank had pulled Clay into that tight spot with him, and there was nothing funny about it.

"I told you what to do, Frank. Now you'll have to shit or get off the pot."

"Hey." Frank spread his hands in an appeal. "I'm trying to help you. Far as I'm concerned, those two Colombians can whistle for their money, and it won't come. They made the bargain. Tracy's half for the gems. If you don't want to figure some way to pay them off, let them take title to their half."

Clay glanced at Evan and saw he too knew Frank was trying to shift the problem to Clay's shoulders. Clay didn't intend to let Frank get away with it.

"No, Frank, you have things wrong. Don't you remember? The agreement reads that the gems were a loan against her inheritance, due and payable upon her receiving half the farm. The farm is only the security for the loan. Maybe they would have wanted the land, but not now. They want payment in something of value, not worthless land."

Frank took another swallow of his drink and gave Clay an indulgent look. It said Clay was in over his head, not understanding how to conduct big business. For the first time, what Frank had planned from the start dawned upon Clay.

"Now I get it." Clay nodded. "You were counting on me not being able to stand having strangers as partners. You know I can't make it on a place half this size. You figured when the loan came due, I'd find the money to keep the farm in one piece—in effect forcing me to buy Tracy's part. Isn't that what it amounts to?"

"Clay, honest to God, I never thought of it that way."

"Well, that's the way it is. You never figured on the land being worthless. I wouldn't give two cents for Tracy's share and I bet Matoes isn't going to either."

"Why didn't you let me make the deal I suggested? Sell them the whole thing at a bargain rate. No, you'll hang onto the patch of dust and grit until it buries you, too. You don't want to part with an acre of it to anyone except another Sanderson."

For the first time that day, Clay felt a hard, solid emotion. Anger burned across his brain and sent flames racing to his arms and his tightened fist. He clenched his teeth to keep his jaw from trembling. The truth of Frank's statement enraged him. The farm belonged to the family; selling even part of it was unthinkable. Frank drained the last of his drink and set the glass firmly on the end of the mantle.

"I have to go to town. I'm meeting a couple of fellows at four. They have a deal going that might be interesting. Let me know if you decide on anything I can help with."

Frank stopped in the entry hall and turned as if he'd had an afterthought.

"Oh yes, tell Tracy I might not make it home tonight. She'll probably want to stay anyway."

The front door closed with a heavy thud, and Clay smashed his fist into the open palm of his other hand.

"That slimy son of a bitch. If it weren't for Tracy and the kids, I'd kill him. Why do I stand him?" Clay paced in front of Evan.

"You just said it," Evan replied. "Because of your sister."

"Maybe, but this time tears it. The only thing worse than having nothing is having half of nothing."

"Sometimes," Evan said slowly, "you have to give some to make a gain."

Clay studied Evan and frowned, trying to make sense of what he'd said. "What do you mean by that?"

Evan's eyebrows drew into a deep pucker, his eyes narrowed, and his lips tightened, all evidence of his concern for Clay.

"Would it be that terrible having new neighbors? How do you know Tracy wouldn't have sold her part later on, even if things were normal? You wouldn't have liked that any better. Frank brought it on sooner. It's a clear choice, Clay. Either find a way to pay off the debt or find some way to work with the Colombians. They are in a bad spot, too. You have to make a decision or it will be made for you."

Evan had stated the facts clearly. It never would have worked, even if the farm had been bringing in money. Frank wouldn't have rested until he got Tracy's part in cash. What did it matter? Now or later, the situation was the same.

"You have to decide what is more important," Evan continued. "Fighting a losing battle or settling for what circumstance lets you have."

Clay smiled, but it seemed more like a sneer. "I guess you've already decided what I should do."

"No. I'm not trying to tell you what to do. You have to decide what you can live with."

Clay nodded. Evan was right. Still, if he didn't mind offending Evan, Clay wanted to ask why he didn't take his own advice. Clay had half-understood Evan's fight with the Church. When it started, he thought how they were both battling things larger than they were. Even now, their conflicts ran parallel. They could both fight, or settle for what others were willing to let them have. Thus far, Evan had ducked the issue of making a stand. He might have fooled Dewberry into thinking the drugs had worked, but it didn't make any difference. The Church had gotten its desired results. Drugs or fear, one or the other kept Evan silent and obeying the rules.

Those close to Evan could see the struggle in him. They knew that if he didn't act soon, it would destroy him. Clay wasn't sure he wanted Evan to become active again, in open opposition to the Church. He feared for his friend's safety. On the other hand, it was as Evan had said, a person had to make a decision they could live with. Clay didn't think Evan could live with the decision to keep silent. It would be only a matter of time until he came to the crossroads. He would either follow his convictions or knuckle under to the beliefs of others. The thought of Evan giving in turned Clay's stomach. If he couldn't stand it in his friend, how could he tolerate the same in himself?

Evan sat quietly, giving Clay time for his thoughts. They seemed connected by a thin vibrating wire, each sharing the other's feelings. Suddenly, Clay felt better. He should be making plans, not crying over the circumstances. He still had half the land, more than Mark had when he started. Sure, times were different, but Clay was different, too. He'd find a way to survive this. He held his empty glass and glanced at Evan's half-finished drink.

"You want some more ice in that?" he asked.

"Maybe a bit. You look better. Are you over being mad at Frank?"

Clay smiled. "I can always find a reason to be angry with Frank. Maybe I should thank him. He pushed me into seeing things the way they really are." Clay hesitated in pouring from the decanter. "No, maybe it's you I should thank, Evan. You helped me."

Evan laughed and Clay was glad to hear it.

"How did I help? For over a year you have helped me."

Clay waved his hand, brushing aside the thanks. "I don't want to hear that, Evan. I told you at the first, I did it as much for myself as for you."

Evan raised his head and smiled. A stray beam of light seemed to catch in his eyes, making the pale blue turn to crystal. It startled Clay, and he understood people's reactions to Evan. The strangeness about him was hard to define. Despite Evan's inner battle, there was still a solid core to him. Something that either drew or repelled a person.

"I wish I could repay you," Evan said.

"Don't worry about it; there's nothing to repay."

From the dining room came the clattering sound of silverware and the softer clunk of pottery plates as someone set the table. Tracy stepped through the living room door.

"Clay, call Jan and Diana. We're ready to eat now."

She looked around, a frown wrinkling her forehead. "Where did Frank go?"

Clay and Evan exchanged glances, each giving the other the opportunity to tell Tracy her husband would not be having dinner with them.

~ * ~

Later that evening, Clay left the main house to walk the compound, visiting the lodge and checking the buildings. It was a simple, useless task, but one Mark had always done. It was the last chore of the day, a time of taking account...an almost tucking-in procedure. It was also a pleasant and fulfilling part of the day. Even though the warehouse, storage bins, and barns were full of someone else's grain, from long habit Clay still made the rounds, checking each building.

The night was warm, only slightly cooler than the day. The moonlight shone a hazy blue-gray over the landscape and painted long, inky shadows at the bases of trees and buildings. The nighttime prairie was entirely different from the bright open face of day. In the sun's glare, the land hid nothing. However, the night, with dark and clouded images, gave a hint of a great mystery...a glimpse into things beyond man's control, a process ongoing and unfolding that swept on no matter what men did during the day.

Light and dark, one following upon the other, a miniature version of the larger seasonal cycle. The ebb and flow of time washing over the land. To Clay, it was the breath and pulse of a living earth. The relentless, inevitable working of nature might be daunting to some, but to Clay it brought comfort. It put boundaries to his life. Nature's cycles created problems, but they were familiar hardships, and men who loved the land welcomed the challenges. There were fat years and lean years. There was satisfaction, even joy, in overcoming the obstacles. Clay was at peace with nature, even the blistering heat of a rainless summer. The thing that frightened him was outside interference. He didn't know how to handle rules and regulations when they became overpowering. When others took control of his land.

Clay shoved his hands deep into his pockets, and with his head lowered, walked slowly across the wide, graveled space between the office and the house. Under the blanket of night, the farm was at peace. The brothers had gone to town and the men in the lodge were playing cards or watching television. The lodge windows threw blocks of yellow light onto the black ground. Occasionally, a laugh rode the night breeze, punctuating the rusty ratchet of locusts in the trees and dry grass. The tiny blink of fireflies, like stray bits of light from the windows, randomly flashed and disappeared. For a second, the scene fooled Clay into thinking nothing had changed, that tomorrow the fall planting would continue. Soon the cold white of winter would return, the land soaking under a snowy cover of nitrogen-rich moisture. To his left loomed the tall silent elevators holding wheat and corn trucked in from distant farms. The foreign grain in the silos broke the spell. Nothing would be the same until they held grain grown on his own land.

"Clay," Jan called, her voice floating softly through the night.

She was walking from the house, her dark form outlined by the brightness cast by the long side windows. As she drew nearer, her light shirt took on the moon's bluish hue and her dark hair shadowed her face.

"I've been watching for you. I wanted to catch you before you went inside."

As they met, Clay took her hand...it felt small and cool in the warm air. "You could have walked with me. I wasn't doing anything important."

"I know, but I thought you might want to be alone for a while."

"Maybe I did," Clay answered quietly. "You want to go for a walk now?"

"If you want to, but mainly I wanted a chance to talk about Diana."

Involuntarily, Clay stiffened. "What's wrong? Is she worse? When she didn't come to dinner, I knew I should have gone to sit with her."

Clay squeezed Jan's hand until he felt her flinch. He stopped walking and turned toward her.

"What's wrong with me? I know how confused she is, and yet I can't stand to spend time with her."

"Don't blame yourself. It's something in her, something that's always been there, I guess."

Clay looked away, wanting to say something that had been on his mind for some time, but it was an unworthy thing. Perhaps he was looking for a way to lighten his own guilt. Yet the words pushed at the roof of his mouth, demanding he speak. He swallowed hard.

"Jan?"

"Yes?"

"Do you think Diana knows what she is doing? Is this another game she's playing?" Clay paused a second, his breath coming in short jerks. "I know I shouldn't say it, but sometimes I suspect her of doing it on purpose. Maybe to get something she wants. This is awful of me, isn't it?"

Jan was silent for a minute, seeming to weigh her answer. "No, I understand. If you know Diana well, you come to suspect everything she does. I don't know why she would do this either. Perhaps to win pity. When she leaves you, it will seem she is the injured party. Don't frown at me. You started this, and it doesn't mean I don't love her. I'm only trying to help you understand."

"I don't know how she can keep on with this act. This can't be normal, can it?"

"We could talk forever and we'd never understand how Diana's mind works."

"What are we supposed to do? How do we deal with her? You know, now I've changed my mind again. She's not clever, she's sick."

Jan's laughter broke the still night. She put her arm through his and they resumed their walk.

"You must stop trying to figure her out or you'll really go crazy," Jan advised. "The only thing to do is accept what we see, take her at face value. Whether it is some scheme, or if she really is sick, it makes no difference. We must take care of her."

Jan's reasoning made sense. If Diana were playing some game, he didn't want to play. If she were truly sick, they had to find help for her. Either way, his marriage was finished.

"Yes, we have to take care of her. I don't think staying is good for her...she hates the farm."

"I know. I hope you don't mind, but I've already talked with the rest of the family. I called Mother. She isn't interested in having Diana at home, even if I stay there and help with her."

"Glenda won't take her?"

"She didn't exactly refuse, but I got the idea. A damaged daughter would be an inconvenience. She said things about Daddy's financial problems. How she wasn't at home much. I know that if we send Diana there, it wouldn't be three weeks before they'd have her in some hospital."

Clay swallowed the rock in his throat. "Maybe that would be better for her; doctors could help her."

"It won't work. My dad is in no better cash position than you are. He's lost his income from National, and with inflation eroding every dollar, he couldn't afford a suitable place. They'd send her to a state home that would release her in a month. You know the treatment people get there. Pills, brain probes, and if that doesn't work, a complete personality purge. She might become a functioning person, but she'd never be herself again. I don't think you want that for her, do you?"

Clay shook his head as they continued walking along the moonlit driveway. He was grateful for Jan's help. Even though Diana was her sister, she could have left him to deal with the problem. He knew what she meant about the state institutions. They never gave a person a chance to get well. One, two, three, and if no response, right into the recycling ward and bang, a few days later an entirely new person. Only they wouldn't fit into the family anymore. They didn't know what to do with themselves. The institute bragged about their cure rate, but Clay suspected it wasn't the truth.

As they neared the road, Clay slowed and stopped. He looked across the white rock lane to the ghostly fields, as he considered what Jan had said. What he wanted for Diana was short, private sessions, and with a doctor who didn't demand complete authority over the patient. However, that type of treatment took more money than he, or his in-laws, had at this point.

"I should have gotten help for her right away. But honest to God, Jan, I couldn't find the cash."

"It may be better you didn't. At least Diana is still herself. In time, she'll thank us for leaving her personality intact. I know I would if this had happened to me. Fern and I have talked about it. If Diana is going to heal, Fern's house is the place for it. She is sure Diana only needs to have time and to be away from her problems. How does that sound?"

"This means Diana is going to get exactly what she wants." It was hard to keep the bitterness from his voice. Sane or insane, Diana would outsmart everyone.

"What do you propose?" Jan asked.

"Nothing. I don't think we have a choice. The longer she stays, the worse she seems to be. If Fern will take her, it's fine with me. What will you do when Diana is settled? Will you stay there, too?"

Jan sighed. "Spend more time with Evan, I guess. I think he is ready to start moving again. He could surely use my help."

"Since I've known you, Jan, your causes and crusades are other people's fights. Don't you have a goal of your own? What do you want out of life?"

"Of course I have a goal," she snapped. "I'm a helper. I help in causes I think are good. It may seem second rate, but only a few are equipped to be a spearhead, the sharp point cutting new trails. There must be a body of followers to give strength to a movement. As unglamorous as it may seem, I happen to think it is important work." Jan cocked her head to one side and looked at him. "I haven't seen you objecting much to my taking care of Diana. It isn't any great cause, but I saw a need and tried to fill it."

Clay took a deep breath. She had him there. He couldn't deny she had carried part of his responsibility; still, she hadn't answered his question.

"I'm sorry if I haven't shown enough appreciation...you've helped me more than I deserve. You made it easy to let you. What I'm trying to get at is what does the real Jan Brockman want? I mean, you can't live vicariously. One day you'll wonder why people aren't giving you the credit you deserve. Sure, you'll help them achieve their goals, but you'll be left with an empty basket."

Jan's shoulders stiffened and her face turned pink in the white moonlight.

"I don't need praise when I know I'm doing a good job. You don't understand, and neither does Evan."

"Has Evan given you this talk, too?"

"Not exactly, but almost the same. He keeps trying to shoo me away, saying don't follow him, that I can't find my own path walking in his footsteps. Sometimes I wonder if Evan will ever get his mission off the ground, thinking the way he does. He has no concept of organization. He keeps telling me how many others there are in this great body of Christ, as he puts it." She shook her head, looking disgusted. "A more loose-jointed body I've never seen. He should be making contact with those small groups, welding them into one strong unit. Doing that, he'd see some progress."

Clay laughed. "Well, I struck sparks there. Still, think about it. You can work with him, side by side, but the cause has to be yours as much as his. Do you think you would be as committed if an ugly old man were heading it?"

"You're disgusting, Clay. Couldn't it be possible I judge people more for what they are than how they look?"

"Don't get hot at me. I'm only trying to make you take a good look at yourself. How about it, you got something going with Evan or not?"

The expression on her face softened, her shoulders slumped. "You won't understand, but yes, I love Evan. He's good and pure. Oh, he doesn't think he is. He feels unworthy and weak, searching for the right course, and thinking he is failing. But once he realizes what power he really has, there won't be any holding him."

"Pardon me, but that doesn't sound like the sort of love I was thinking about. You know the plain old man and woman stuff? Maybe if your vision wasn't misted over with his high calling, you'd find someone able to give you some earthly pleasure."

Jan narrowed her eyes, turned on her heel, and started toward the compound.

"Thanks for the advice," she threw over her shoulder. "But if you and Diana are an example, no thanks. I think I can control my physical desire until Evan solves his problems."

Clay hurried to catch her. He flinched from the sting of her criticism. There was also a tinge of jealousy at Evan's good fortune, but pity softened him. He was sure Evan didn't share her feelings; if he did, he would have acted by now. No matter how busy a man is with other things, he would find time to make love to a woman if he really wanted her.

"Has Evan told you he loves you and asked you to be patient?"

"Isn't that too personal, Clayton?"

"Well, has he? I'm trying to help you."

"Not directly," she said slowly.

"Even indirectly?" he pushed.

"No, but I know how he feels. When the time comes, you'll see."

"Jan, can't you see? Evan isn't the sort of man to put a woman first in his life. His mystical calling will always hold that place. I don't want you to be hurt."

Jan's laugh was weak and a little too high. "I guess there are different kinds of love, aren't there? But we're not talking about my love life or the lack of it. Do you think what I've suggested for Diana is right or not?"

Clay shuffled his feet and tilted his head. "I think it's the only thing we can do. She always hated this place...the sooner she gets away the better."

"That's the way I see it, too. Fern is getting a room ready, in case you agreed. She said we could bring Diana anytime."

As they headed toward the house, they walked faster. Jan seemed in control as they discussed the time and manner in which to move Diana. She could have Diana's things packed by the next day. Both of them would deliver her to Fern. That way the trip should be friendly and pleasant, making sure Diana felt secure in leaving. Jan was a whiz at making plans, organizing things. Evan should make use of her abilities. With the details settled, Jan said goodnight and hurried to the house.

Clay watched Jan disappear into the shadows and emerge into the brightness surrounding the front porch. She was a strange girl, firm in her conviction that her purpose was to help those around her. However, he thought emptiness and disappointment awaited if she didn't find a new direction. She should listen to him. It was a waste and a pity for her to become someone's acidy, old maid aunt. Thinking about Jan, his conscience objected; his wife should be the one laying claim to his pity and concern.

When he reached the porch, he stopped and sat on the steps, pondering his latest loss. He'd known for weeks that Diana was no longer his, but this move made it final. Something was certainly wrong with her and he hadn't been much help or consolation. Yet, he felt almost nothing when he thought about her. He had tried to be forgiving and generous and to consider their union in a fair light, but it hadn't worked. No matter how he rearranged the facts, it came to the same answer: if he hadn't married Diana and brought her to the farm, both his parents might still be alive. He had no proof, yet he knew she had somehow caused his mother's death, which made his father's weak heart fail sooner.

He decided Diana's condition stemmed from guilt, or some other twist of her mind. Whatever the cause, it didn't arouse his pity. As he stood and entered the house, he wondered exactly when it was that he had stopped loving her.

Twenty-two

By the first of October, Diana had been at her grandmother's home for over a month. During that time, the farm had taken on the atmosphere of an armed camp on the eve of battle. Evan worked with Jeff and the small crew of men trying to repair and put into use the old wells. The bare shoulders of the workers glistened with sweat and Evan felt the moisture on his back, too. It soaked into the waist of his pants and his leather belt grew musty and stained with white salt lines. After weeks of toiling in the hot fall sun, the men were dark and hard as carved mahogany. While Evan's body darkened, his hair bleached from gold to near white, making his aquamarine eyes even more piercing. He became a startling apparition; he hardly recognized himself in the mirror. Everyone worked on in determined silence. The importance of their task gave them grim, unsmiling faces, broken only by an occasional success when the pipes would gurgle and bring up a hopeful stream. It caused the men to break into wild, excessive whoops and laughter before gathering their tools and trudging on to the next location.

Clay, stationed in his office, designed one strategy after another. He contacted drilling companies with their powerful rigs to arrange for new, deeper wells in different locations. The hope was that they could strike a pocket brimming with fresh, pure water, but with no ready cash, it was impossible to entice a drilling company. The drillers were in high demand. The Sanderson farm was not the only one engaged in the desperate search for a new water supply. The best Clay could pry from any of them were vague promises of possible dates, and none would even discuss methods of payment other than cash. Taking the only course open, the men labored over the old wells. There was no talk of failure; the search was single-minded. Water was their salvation.

One evening after supper in the lodge, Evan dropped wearily into an armchair and asked Jeff the question no one else seemed to dare voice. Perhaps they knew the answer.

"What good is the water if the land is still contaminated?"

Jeff fixed him with a stern look. He would tolerate no defection in the ranks, but a crooked smile cracked his weatherworn face. He cast a glance around the room to include the other men. They didn't seem surprised at a city boy asking the question.

"Well, this is the way of it," Jeff began patiently. "If the land was good and there was no water, we'd be worse off than we are now. Someone may find a cure for the land, but I've never heard of anyone producing water where there is none. We have to be prepared."

The other men nodded and from the corner of the room Simon muttered, "That's a fact for certain. It's the same as a body not having blood." He looked around at the brown faces, accepting their unspoken praise for his bit of wisdom.

"We need to get the holding tanks full," Jeff went on. "Make sure the pumps and lines are in order and keep charts of how much each well can produce. It may be we'd need to give it a rest in order to refill. It will help us know how much land we can water, if we find a patch to grow on. In the meantime, we better be begging, praying, or whatever it takes to break this drought."

When Evan wasn't working for Clay, he spent time seeking a cure for his own private contamination. It slowly became clear that he could partially control the visions and the icy fear which paralyzed him. There was a formula for dispelling those soul-shriveling demons. He tightened his lifeline to God. Most of the day and even in the night, God dwelt with him, almost a second conscience. Each time he saw the evil outlines of his enemy, Evan silently cried for help. His constant stream of communication kept the line open.

After several weeks, he began to notice a strange thing. He was sending and something came in return. It was not vocal or a surge of emotional experience. It was a steady, natural inflowing of a life-giving substance. He compared it to a tree, its taproot deep in the earth drinking in health-restoring, mineral-filled waters. Not for a second did he take credit for this healing. Bible study and constant prayer were not his inventions; they were instructions from God. He began to see life as a lesson. He was powerless, but could accomplish things with God's help. As this knowledge grew, an abiding peace wrapped his spirit. It brought his splinted parts into one vital healthy being. He no longer felt abject terror when he beheld the dreadful images. Instead, he was calm. When the time came, he would know what to do.

Evan was glad for the work that kept him in the fields most of the time. If Reverend Dewberry should come looking for him, he might be spared that encounter. However, Dewberry hadn't called at the farm for well over a month. He was too busy with his new duties. Daily, orders and regulations came over the comset instructing citizens as to the location of distribution centers. Advising them about the identification they must show, and other requirements they'd have to meet to obtain their allotments. There was constant assurance that the new system would work once the citizens fully cooperated. Thus far, there were no penalties for failure to cooperate, but Evan caught the veiled threats. The Church's dictates, enforced by civil law, made it clear people must obey or go hungry. There were not many brothers at the farm now, only the ones left to receive new shipments and record the withdrawals. The farm workers ignored them. The crew went about their chores barely speaking to the Church staff. They were no different from the blowing sand, an irritant the men could ignore.

One afternoon, Evan stopped by Clay's office when he was speaking to Señor Matoes. It reminded him of two bulldogs tugging on the same bone. Clay paced in front of the screen stopping only when speaking to Matoes.

"If you don't mind my asking, what were your intentions when you made this deal?" Clay asked.

"Strictly an investment. The production of food is of the highest priority in these times. My partner and I certainly view it that way. What better investment could there be than in land which provides this valuable commodity? As we understood it, your sister never intended to have any part of actually running the operation and neither did we. We would, in effect, become your partners and, of course, compensate you for your efforts in managing our interest." Señor Matoes sighed and waved a beringed hand. "That is now a plan of no importance. It seems we are now in the same leaky boat."

"What are you going to do?" Clay said.

The corners of Matoes' mouth drew up and he shrugged. "For the time being, nothing. We have spoken with our attorney and he advised that it would be difficult to prove Mr. Ivers knew the worthlessness of the land at the time of our transaction. We prefer not to call attention to ourselves. Naturally we would be glad to sell." Matoes laughed gruffly. "But where would we find a buyer?"

For an instant, Clay froze. Evan could almost hear the name of National Grain forming in Clay's mind. They were the only ones with enough capital to buy the Colombians' interest and wait for the land to heal. Clay wiped sweat from his upper lip. If National gained possession of the land, it would never be in the hands of an independent again. Between the Colombians and National, it was no contest whom Clay would pick.

"Listen," Clay spoke earnestly. "You must be in a position to wait. You didn't expect to gain title this soon."

Matoes frowned and shook his head slowly. "No, we're deeply sorry over the passing of your father. We had assumed it would be years yet."

"Then wait, don't sell now. I'm working night and day on a water supply. Any day we may find a way to clear the land of the contaminants. Please, don't let the land go for a while."

Señor Matoes studied the plea for a moment. "Very well. We will wait. You must inform us of every development. Your faith is encouraging; we will hope it is justified."

When the screen returned to dull gray, Clay pushed the button breaking his connection and looked toward Evan.

"Whew, things get tougher and tougher. For a minute, I thought we'd lost him. If National gets part of this land, it wouldn't be a year until they squeezed me out. I keep thinking things can't get any worse, but they do."

"Yes, it seems that way," Evan agreed. "Clay, have you thought how it would be if Tracy still had her share of the land?"

"What do you mean?"

"I was thinking, Frank may have accidentally done you a favor."

"That'll be the day. How do you figure that?"

"With you and Tracy being partners, the money is coming from the same pocket. There is no new capital. It could take a big investment to get into operation. Matoes seemed to be a reasonable person, maybe he'd be willing to help. You could arrange to repay him with a larger share of future profits. Think about it. You could have a worse partner."

"That's a thought." Clay looked longingly toward the fields. "You know, he isn't a bad fellow. He did agree to wait; maybe he would take a chance on me." Clay turned around, a bitter smile twisting his lips. "But that doesn't make it rain, now does it?"

As he listened to Clay, Evan thought of how suspended they were, as they waited on cooler weather, rain, and a way to clean the land. It was a puzzle with the pieces locked tight one into another. If they solved one problem, maybe it would lead to a solution for others.

"Has there been any progress in finding a way to clean the land?" he asked.

"No." Clay grimaced. "They have tried neutralizers, washing action—now they have some sponge-like fungus that is supposed to thrive on toxic waste. I wonder how they get rid of the fungus after it's done the job. It's a waiting game. If you can't wait long enough, you lose."

"Don't despair, things might turn around tomorrow."

Clay ran his hand through his hair and his eyes clouded with worry. "I don't know, Evan. I work hard at being optimistic but sometimes I do want to quit. We have big problems and yet small things get to me. I can't stand having those brothers marching around like they own the place. Crazy, isn't it? With everything else I have to think about."

Evan wanted to say something to help, but words seemed frail. What Clay needed was rich, fertile fields to work. Nothing could replace the family he'd lost, but if the land were healthy, it would speed Clay's healing. When the plains were again ripe with grain, the Church would have to return the barns and storage bins. Unity Council would still find a way to retain part of the control the disaster had given them, but Clay would be free of them.

Clay began to laugh. The sound startled Evan, almost as much as Clay's raised eyebrow and wide smile.

"Evan," he said. "You should see your face; it is a mirror of how I feel. Can it really be this bad? Maybe in the morning we'll find it's a wild, mass illusion. That's more of my craziness, isn't it? Maybe I'm laughing because it's driving me over the edge. Is this the way madness gets a start, feeling so helpless and hopeless it makes you laugh?"

"No," Evan answered. "You're not going mad. Your problem is similar to mine...you see too clearly. I wonder if anyone can stand that. Still, there is this to count on...nothing ever stays the same."

"You're right." Clay pursed his lips and gave a solemn nod. "It will probably get a whole lot worse."

Clay burst into laughter again, and this time Evan joined him. Sometimes when work and prayer didn't seem to make a difference, there was nothing to do but laugh.

The only progress Evan saw was that made by the Church. With each week, its control grew stronger. It was hard to bite the hand feeding you. Attendance at Sunday services was at a record high, and the Church instituted rewards for reports of illegal food operations. The longer the crisis continued, the more power the Church gained over the lives of people. As Evan grew spiritually stronger, he struggled with impatience. He wanted to move on, take some action against the Church, begin the meetings again. He longed to teach what he knew to be mankind's only hope of salvation. However, he had matured since his last encounter with representatives of the Unity Council. He no longer leaned upon his own strength...he was learning to wait.

He was not the only impatient one at the farm. Most days, Jan viewed him in tight-lipped silence, her eyes always filled with one question. When? She had stayed on to be near him, ready to help in whatever he asked her to do. As she waited, she filled the time by visiting Diana and working with Tillie. Evan marveled at her patience, for she was waiting on a mere man while he was waiting on God. He tried to direct her attention to God, explaining how they must wait for His Spirit.

Early one morning, he and Jan were in the greenhouse where she was starting a new seedbed for the rotating lettuce and spinach Tillie kept growing year-round. Even though she didn't work in the direct sun, Jan's arms were tan and with her dark hair wound into braids, she could pass for an Indian maid. She didn't demand an answer, but her dark eyes constantly questioned him.

"Christian," he told her. "The name means follower of Christ. Don't look to me; don't you see how I stumble at every turn? You must establish your own relationship with God. Who knows, He might have a purpose for you far more important than anything I'll ever do. I'm not always going to be around."

"Are you thinking of going away, Evan?"

"I don't know. It's possible my work will take me to a different area."

Not looking at him, Jan sprinkled seeds over the pulverized growing medium.

"That would be fine with me; I'm ready to go anytime," she said.

"Maybe you should consider—"

"There is nothing holding me," she interrupted with a confident tone. "Frankly, I don't know what you're waiting on. We could find another town or city where the Church isn't this aware of you. Get a small group of believers and build from there. Let's do it, Evan. At least we would be accomplishing something."

"I can't," he said. "Not yet."

"Why not?"

"I'm not sure; I think it's something I have to do for Clay."

Jan rolled her eyes and shook her head, meaning she thought it was another stall to keep from getting to work. He wished he could explain, make her understand, but it was difficult when he himself wasn't sure. Perhaps it was pity for Clay that made him think he should find a way to help. Maybe it was gratitude. What could he possibly do? Clay had title to half the worthless land and was partners with some disgruntled Colombians. A bad situation for everyone.

For the next few days, he found his mind turning more and more to the idea of helping Clay. He ate absentmindedly, went to bed when the other men did, spoke when spoken to, but his thoughts were always on something else. There was an answer, he was sure of it. It seemed locked away in some secret compartment slightly beyond his grasp. He argued with himself that Jan was right—he should be on about his business. Perhaps the obsession to do something for Clay was simply another clever ruse of the enemy to keep him from the work.

Yet the pull was strong enough to defeat any argument to the contrary. How could he do anything when the experts could not? Even the suggestion that it was hopeless faded before his growing determination. No one seemed to notice his preoccupation. Only once did Simon come close to asking him about it. Evan could see the question forming in the old man's mind. However, he must have thought better of it. Simon shut his mouth and simply nodded at Evan.

In pondering the problem, his reasoning stretched beyond the farm and the present time; the world itself was a great festering problem waiting for a healing solution. The entire history of man had been one long series of ordeals and rescues. The only possible answer was that there was a plan. There simply had to be, otherwise the endless reoccurring events were merely the restless circles of a madman in an asylum. Round and round, constantly on the move, but never getting anywhere. Mankind had no choice but to follow the dictates of nature. Death following birth, each season following the other, a never-ending chain...no purpose or destination.

With the revelation of God came reason and conclusion. The endless circles became a spiral, everything rotating in a way natural to man. Yet the drawing, pulling power of the creator would lift life upward to the ending He had planned from the beginning, thus providing a meaning and purpose to life that man could only long for. Evan didn't bother trying to understand why the weather had turned perverse, giving no rain to the dry areas and drowning others, bringing chaos to world markets and making bold already aggressive nations. It was a waste of energy to ponder what no one could change. It was better to accept and move ahead.

Men had questioned adverse conditions from the time they learned to speak. Evan remembered the Israelites' tortured wanderings, their jubilation in times of blessing and their despair and disappointment in times of trial. Still, there was a plan. It was to make them recognize God and give Him praise, no matter the circumstances. Now, it was every race suffering and cursing their luck. Perhaps it was for the same purpose: to show them their weakness and need.

Evan was tired; he went to his small bedroom across the hall from Jeff's room. It was late and the lodge was silent. He removed his boots, intending to take a shower, grateful for the one well supplying the compound. Instead, he dropped upon the bed, turned on the lamp, took his Bible, and began to read. The time slipped by and soon a faint gray light came through the window. His eyes were dry and scratchy, his neck stiff. It reminded him of his days in the seminary and the late hours of study. He had been sure he was not learning a thing. Later, to his joy, he found his mind retained more than he'd thought.

Evan arched his back and stretched his arms toward the ceiling. Relief from the cramped position felt good. He lay on the bed, the pillow under his head, and closed his eyes. Visions of what he had read played in colorful scenes on the backs of his eyelids. The exodus out of Egypt, Moses on the mountain, the burning bush, Abraham telling Isaac to gather wood for the sacrifice, Aaron becoming the priest, the burnt offerings of the people, Moses striking the rock to bring forth water. Evan chuckled. God's children, how predictable they were. Eager for release from Egypt, yet when nearly dying of thirst in the desert, they turned on Moses. "You've dragged us into the desert to die of thirst," they'd cried.

He could almost see the expression on Moses' face as he hurried to God. "Quick, tell me what to do. These people are ready to stone me."

Too bad he didn't have Moses' rod to strike a boulder and create a whole river for Clay. Even if he did, in this flat prairie land, God would have to provide the boulder, too. Fire and water, Evan thought. The whole world was full of the two. Cool, soothing, life-giving water...the importance of it was overwhelming. There were dances to the rain god, certain tribes that prayed to the lord of their particular rivers. The Egyptians had a god of the Nile, and Romans a sea god, Neptune. Yet, the huge burning ball in the sky ruled. The fire god. The great giver of light and heat. It was the light ancient man had prized the most, for night brought danger and fear. The fire in the sky purged the demons of the night, cleansing the earth for one more day. No wonder burnt offerings were necessary to purge the evil.

Unable to sleep even after spending the night reading, Evan sat on the edge of his narrow bed and stared at the far wall. He let his mind float free, following a torch of fire through the ages. Sodom and Gomorrah had burned to the ground, purified and cleansed by fire. God's final judgment, the refining fire. To be worthy, a man's deeds must stand the test of fire. The crackle and roar of leaping tongues of orange and red, licking and devouring, leaving behind a clean, purified land.

Could it be possible?

Evan sat straighter, excitement tingling through him. No, he must be wrong, surely someone would have thought of it sooner. Still, what would it hurt to try? He could take a small patch of ground, confine the fire to that area, and make it as hot as possible. The dried stubble would catch in a minute...maybe he could find something else to burn on the spot, making the fire last longer. Evan stopped. What was he hoping for, that the heat would somehow change the chemicals, render them harmless? Destroy them? That didn't seem possible, for nothing was ever lost. It only changed forms. Fire might cause an even more dangerous mutation of the chemicals. Still, he wouldn't risk much, only a small area. His first impulse was to wake Clay and tell him. Any hope was better than no hope at all. On second thought, he decided to wait. It would be a better gift after testing. If it didn't work, he would have spared Clay the disappointment.

It was almost dawn and the others in the lodge were not stirring. Evan moved silently along the hall toward the bathroom. As the shower water flowed over his chest, he ducked his head under the stream and turned his face to the relaxing flow. If he had lived six thousand years ago, water would have gotten his vote as reigning god. Fire was harsh and painful, a judge unmoved by cries of mercy, while water claimed its victims with a soft smothering embrace. Water couldn't wash away the sickness in the fields, even if they had enough to try. As Evan bathed and gave the idea more thought, it still seemed worth trying. He would need help; he couldn't risk losing control of a fire.

He and Jeff could handle it. Jeff knew where to send the samples for testing after the experiment.

By the time Evan was in his room and dressed, he had made a decision. He would tell Jeff about his wild idea and hope he would agree to try it. Evan left his room and went onto the long veranda stretching across the front of the lodge. He drew in a deep breath; the air was only slightly refreshing, the nights not cool or damp enough to overcome the burning days. Humans were limited in controlling life, but they tried. Perhaps the builders of the domed communities had the right idea. They called them Crystal Cities. The air and temperature were perfect and the children born there were healthier than the ones in cities exposed to the polluted environment. People certainly tried, but they were still bound to the earth and shared its fate. Domed cities still needed outside support.

The first rays of the sun turned the sky pink and shot streaks of yellow and orange along the horizon. Across the compound, the grayness near the ground faded. In the morning silence, the sound of crunching gravel caught his attention. It came from the corner of the lodge. As he turned toward it, a voice called softly.

"Evan, over here."

Evan crossed the length of the porch. "Who is it?"

"Shhh, be quiet."

Evan stepped off the veranda and turned the corner. Ryan Lanier was crouched against the side of the lodge, his young face clenched with anxiety, his body drawn into a tight knot as he hid there.

"Ryan. What are you doing here?"

"Shhh, I told you, keep still."

"Okay," Evan whispered. "What happened?"

"They nearly caught me. They'd have put me in jail."

"What were you doing?"

"I wasn't doing anything."

Evan studied the short, stocky boy huddled before him. The pinched face and darting eyes revealed Ryan's fear. Evan couldn't imagine what had happened. The last time he had seen Ryan was the evening of the meeting at Ryan's house. Surely, he was too young to have done anything that could bring him to the Church's attention. Jan had assured him that people suspected of attending meetings only received light warning letters. The Church had no interest in calling attention to the matter. Still, he was sure Ryan's flight had something to do with the Unity Council's regulations.

"It is the Church, isn't it?" Evan questioned.

A tremor rippled Ryan's body. "It wasn't my fault, I swear it. I won't stay long, I wanted to say goodbye to you and Simon. I stayed hidden yesterday. I walked most of the night. Are you mad at me for coming?"

Ryan's hair was as rumpled as the brown jacket he was wearing. As the daylight brightened, it revealed a face covered with dust and cheeks lined with streaks. Evan suspected tears had washed away part of the dirt during the long night. Ryan was a pitiful sight. Evan pictured the boy alone and frightened, making his way to the only friends he had.

Evan put his arm around the boy's shoulders and drew him toward the side of the porch. A cord tightened in Evan's throat, making it hard to speak.

"I'm not mad at you. Come on now, we better get you washed and see what's for breakfast."

Ryan stiffened and pulled away. "What about the other men living in there? I heard the Church is using the storage on this place. You've got to believe me. If they find me, I'll be taken away."

Ryan's fear made him shiver. Evan needed to do something to calm him. There was no hurry; the brothers never arrived before eight o'clock. By that time, he'd have Ryan settled in a safe place.

"Tell me what happened. Sit on the steps; no one can see us from inside."

Ryan seemed satisfied and sat beside Evan.

"After the night they took you away," Ryan began, "I asked around and learned you were in the mansion. I was trying to find a way to help, but before I could, one of the fellows who works in the kitchen there told me Jan got you loose. I would have come to see you sooner, but I didn't have a way. Evan, you don't know how it is in town. They've started rationing things. People pushing and grabbing in the lines. The stores still have some unregulated stuff, but there isn't much. People are scared they might lose their right to buy food. They don't say or do anything the Church wouldn't approve of. It's really bad for them."

Ryan tugged at the collar of the brown jacket he was wearing. "You know where I got this? Found it behind the recycling plant; it must have fallen off a load they were taking in. I don't need it in this heat, but I'm going north. I'll need it and I didn't have anything that was as good."

"Why do you think they are after you? What did you do?"

"I told you, nothing. With you gone, I kept low. I didn't go around spouting off about my beliefs or anything. Besides, with things in a mess, I began to think the Church was doing the right thing. Someone has to help the people. The Council is getting food to them, but people seem to go crazy thinking there won't be enough. The Church has tight guidelines; they know everything about each person. That's the way they decide who gets coupons. There are five groups: five is the lowest, but you can work your way up by doing work for the Church. My family had a five rating, the lowest. They got a letter saying they could move to a four or three."

"That must have been encouraging. What would you need to do?"

"If I started going to meetings and they reported me, they'd get credit."

"Is someone holding meetings?" Evan asked.

"Not that I know of. I couldn't convince my mom and dad of that. They kept glaring at me, always blaming me for our shortage. It made me feel bad, but I couldn't do anything about it. I never thought they'd do what they did, though."

Ryan lowered his head, and for a minute, Evan thought he was crying. When he lifted his face, his chin trembled but he went on.

"My mom and dad turned me in. They told the committee I was talking to kids at school, trying to start a group."

"You're a child, what would they have done to you?"

Ryan laughed. It was a chilling sound.

"Can't you guess? My folks signed the papers giving their permission. They declared me defective, mental problems. They were going to recycle me." Ryan plucked at the sleeve of his jacket. "Same as they'd do to this old coat. I'd have been a new person. They might have put me to work for the Church. Even before they turned me in, I thought about trying to work for them; you did. But not now. My parents fixed that."

Evan swallowed the bile rising in his throat. The Church was moving much faster than he realized; maybe it was already too late. He'd thought that if the land produced again, it would break the Church's hold. For the sake of the miserable looking boy at his side, he tried to sound confident.

"You'll be safe. We can hide you somehow."

As he offered Ryan this reassurance, his mind raced. He didn't have the right to cause Clay more trouble. Clay wouldn't turn the boy away; therefore, it would be better if he didn't know. Evan tried to form a plan where only he and Simon would know about Ryan.

Ryan squared his shoulders. "I didn't come for help. I only wanted to tell you and Simon goodbye. I heard of a group of Christians close to the Canadian border. They move around some, but I think I can find them. This may sound crazy, but I have this feeling. I know there is a place for me. A place where I can work for the good of the people. I'm not sure where it is."

"Ryan, you can't take off across country. How would you live?"

Ryan's chest swelled and he tossed his head. "I've got ways. Sometimes a kid can get by better than someone old as you."

Evan smiled. To Ryan he was an old man already. Well, the boy might be right; he certainly felt he had aged in the last two years.

"Look," Evan said. "Stay for a while, until we can arrange to get you away safely. If you still want to go north, maybe we can arrange it. Simon keeps to his room most of the time. If he pulled the shades during the day, everyone would think he was sleeping. The other men are working during the day. How about it, only until you are rested?"

He could see the boy weaken, weighing a long hard journey against the comfort of food and rest.

"Okay. But only for a while."

With full daylight, the men were moving around in the lodge. He didn't dare take Ryan through the front door.

"Go around this side of the building," Evan told him. "The long wing is the bedrooms. The third set of windows is Simon's room. I'll meet you there and open the window."

Ryan nodded and quietly slipped away. When Evan went into the lodge, he met Jeff heading toward the dining room.

"Jeff, I want to talk with you this morning. I'm going to see Simon, but I'll be right back."

Evan hurried down the hall and knocked on Simon's door. The old man called for him to come in. He explained about Ryan, went to the window, and opened it. Ryan scampered in quickly as a young squirrel, his eyes darting from side to side, the look of fear still on him. Simon calmly listened as Ryan explained his situation. He agreed that Ryan should stay hidden in his room until it was time for him to leave. The first day would be no trouble. As tired as he was, Ryan would probably sleep until evening. Later, they could make plans for sending him from the area.

With Simon and Ryan settled, Evan headed for the dining room. Jeff was seated with several of the men, each digging into a breakfast of eggs and tea. It had been close to six months since they had any type of meat for breakfast. The Church had taken control of the few animals on the farm. They missed having bread the most. The men understood how few reserves the ranch had left, and were grateful to eat as well as they did. Evan went to the sideboard, filled his own plate, and took a seat beside Jeff. As it had for the past few weeks, the talk around the table concerned the water wells. The men were eager for the work and glad to have it; others were not as lucky. They were men living one day at a time, their minds, and backs occupied with the task before them, never looking or thinking beyond that. There were a few crude jokes aimed at the Church and the brothers who were overseeing the grain storage. Still, even in the safety of the lodge, surrounded by men who they had worked with for years, their comments lacked real confidence.

Evan kept his eyes on his plate; he knew if he looked, he would see traces of suspicion and fear in the leathery faces. His heart grew heavy over the spreading poison. He could well imagine how people in town were reacting if even these rugged, free-natured men were intimidated.

Jeff ate the last of his eggs and turned to Evan with a grin.

"There, that ought to hold me till noon anyway. What was it you wanted to talk about?"

Evan glanced around the table; most of the men were through, some pushing their chairs away and lifting their lean frames to their feet. Others were still eating.

"Let me finish; we can talk outside."

Evan shoveled in the last of his breakfast while Jeff frowned. Jeff always spoke openly before the men. He'd said before that no good came of keeping secrets from a crew. Doing that meant only one thing: trouble. Evan finished and headed for the front door with Jeff behind him. Swiftly, Evan crossed the veranda, went down the steps, and walked to the center of the compound. Jeff hurried to keep pace.

"What's got into you this morning?" Jeff growled. "You were around pretty early; you better not tell me we got trouble of some kind."

For a second Evan considered telling Jeff about Ryan, but that could wait. The important thing was to see Jeff's reaction to his idea. It was hard to keep the excitement from his voice.

"Whatever stuff is in the ground ought to burn...chemicals burn, don't they? We could do a small test patch. Fire purifies. What do you think?"

Jeff rubbed his chin and wrinkled his forehead, hiding his eyes beneath his bushy eyebrows.

"Fire might do it," he muttered. "It would have to be hotter than hell. You'd have to get that dirt heated something fierce. I doubt we can get it hot enough."

"I know." Evan nodded. "Could we pour gasoline or oil on it maybe?"

"Gas maybe, not oil. Burnt oil could leave the ground in worse shape. I doubt we can get much gas."

"We could get enough for a test, couldn't we?"

"I guess we could. When you want to try it?"

"Anytime you're ready."

"Now is okay with me. I'll get the men started and be with you soon as I can."

Evan paced nervously about the compound, excited over the test and at the same time worried. It was crazy. It would never work. Jeff had spotted the flaw right off. It was doubtful they could get temperatures high enough to detoxify the dirt. The government had people working on the problem. They'd have the equipment in a lab to incinerate a soil sample, if possible. They must have thought of high heat. Since there had been no word of such a test, either it didn't work or there was some reason for keeping it secret. There was no trust between the government and those it governed. This seemed an even better reason for doing the test. If it didn't work, there was nothing lost. If it did, they could spread the word to other farmers.

He ran his hand through his hair and shook his head. Jeff was the only one he'd dare tell. Jeff's being willing to try showed how desperate the situation was. As he waited for Jeff to return, a dark blue sedan turned off the gravel road and pulled in by the warehouse. Reverend Dewberry and his whippet of a lackey, Mr. Carter, stepped from the car. They started for the warehouse door, but stopped to stare at Evan. He thought about walking away or even running, but that would seem strange. Instead, he stood firm and watched as the two men approached.

Suddenly, along with them, the transparent images made their first appearance of the day. Evan steeled himself against the effects they always produced. His body tingled with revulsion; it took great strength to stand steady. The reverend had a benevolent smile, but the watchdog, Carter, looked ready to snap. His dark eyes were small, glittering slits in the glaring early morning sun. The men stopped a few paces from him while the dark shapes formed, dissolved, and reformed. Dewberry extended his hand.

"Well, well, Evan Hunter. How are you, my boy? No need to answer that, anyone can see you're in fine condition. Look at him, Mr. Carter, brown as a heathen and lean as a whip."

Evan tried to ignore the dancing shades with their leering faces and obscene gestures. He made his smile as friendly as possible and shook the reverend's hand.

"It's the outside work," he said.

Dewberry nodded. "Certainly no denying it seems to agree with you. Aren't you wasting your abilities in the fields? Really, Evan, your duty is to be doing the work we trained you to do. When are you going to quit playing farmer and stay where you belong?"

Evan's mind spun as he searched for the right answer. He was once again in Simon's story situation of the Lying Baptists. If he revealed his true feelings, the reverend would see him as a threat and take him away immediately. Continuing the pretense was the same as lying. Still, he needed time with Jeff to put his idea to the test. Perhaps it wasn't justification enough, he wasn't sure, but he still played the role that would keep the reverend at bay for a while longer.

"I know. I've been thinking about where I belong. But Clay is my friend and I hate to leave him in his time of need."

The reverend studied the dust at his feet, apparently considering what Evan had said. Beside him, Carter wore a smug smirk. He looked certain that he knew exactly what Dewberry would answer.

"Admirable, my boy. We must always show consideration for those we serve. Still, we must face facts, and the bitter fact is that Clay's farming days are finished. I hate to see these farmers struggle against the Will of God."

The statement startled Evan. "What do you mean?"

"I'm surprised you don't see it, Evan. Perhaps you have been away from the real world too long, toiling in a hopeless effort. Two thirds of the country's land is useless. Thank God for the clean land we have left. Where do you think most of our grain is coming from? I'll tell you. We're importing. Canada, Australia, even Russia; we buy wherever we can. The weather pattern affects them, but their water source is untouched. Why the grim look? This is a blessing. It forces the countries to depend upon one another. Now they see the brilliance of the Church's plan. A united world. Sometimes a people have to be brought to their knees before they will do the right thing."

Evan tried to stop frowning, but it took an effort to control his expression. He managed a small smile.

"Surely we wouldn't want to be dependent upon other countries for an extended time. Clay's information is that our top men are working night and day to find a solution."

A thin smile played at the corners of the reverend's lips. "Of course, and God willing, in time they will find one. In the meantime, our new system will be established and great strides will have been made in uniting the nations."

"Well, good," Evan said, hoping to end the conversation. "At least our people aren't starving."

Mr. Carter fingered the tip of his small mustache. "Of course they're not. I've already been to five ranches this morning, checking storage bins. New shipments are due to arrive anytime. I think you'd find far greater satisfaction working within the Church's efficient structure than flitting around chasing rainbows."

Dewberry patted Evan's shoulder. "I'm sure Evan knows that and we'll be expecting him shortly. You won't disappoint us, will you?"

Evan mustered a smile, but couldn't bring himself to answer. When the men turned to leave, Carter suddenly whirled around.

"By the way, we have a watch out for a young boy named Ryan Lanier. Didn't you know him when you were living in town?"

Evan cast about in his mind, wondering how much of his life before the drugs he should remember. Everything or nothing? He put his head to one side and studied the distant horizon. For a few minutes, there was an awkward silence.

"Now, Mr. Carter," the reverend spoke. "We can't trouble Evan with these details."

"I only thought the young scoundrel might have headed this way."

"What has he done?" Evan asked, hoping to gain some information about how seriously they were looking for Ryan.

"Defiance," Carter barked. "Spreading defiance against the Church. We will find him."

Reverend Dewberry took his assistant's arm and walked toward the warehouse. The hovering dark shapes clustered around the two men. Evan watched them go; Ryan had reason to fear if they caught him. After listening to Dewberry, Evan had no hope of deterring the Unity Council's growing control. He'd do the small things. If he could, he'd see that Ryan reached a safe haven. If his idea worked, the land might start producing again. That would stop the Church for a while. He had no illusions that the setback would be permanent. Any group with great power was a menace to freedom. However, when the group claimed to be an instrument of God, it meant certain disaster. People could be deceived into losing their freedom. In the blazing sun, a chill rippled across Evan's shoulders. He felt small and alone. Deserted, even.

Deserted. The word settled dark and heavy in his mind. He struggled to remember the promise. God never left His people. His prayer was quick and silent. *Help me, Lord. I'm weak and don't understand.* Doubt clouded his mind and with it came guilt. Doubt meant lack of faith and with no faith, a relationship with God was impossible. The doubt grew. Members of the Council were supremely confident and secure in their position with God. Could it be they were right and he was wrong? Why didn't God send him a sign? A revelation. Anything to strengthen his sagging faith. Some vision instead of the vague impression that he was to wait. As he struggled, trying to understand, a wave of shame washed over him. What was the matter with him? Who was he to question God?

At the same time, realization hit him that he already had the vision he begged to see. Poor, struggling human that he was, too blind to understand. The shapes that had invaded his sight were his revelation.

Those transparent wicked images. Each dim face conveyed pure evil and they always surrounded the Council members. Hovering guides and advisors clearly showing the iniquity that infected the Church. What more could he want in the way of a signpost? Again, he marveled at God's wisdom. If he had seen visions of heavenly beings, it might have been comforting, but it would have done nothing to show him the way. Of the ability to see the horrors of the enemy, there could be no doubt. To stay on the right road, he only need go in the opposite direction from the Church. Nothing could be clearer.

The first visions had shattered him, brought days of confusion and terror. However, he had slowly learned to live with the double vision, to live in a world where solid and transparent combined. At first, he had feared for his life. When no harm came to him, the fear lessened. He should have used that to his advantage and understood exactly what power the shades had. Did these beings transmit information about him to the Council? It was a chilling thought. Was Carter's mentioning Ryan an accident, or had one of the specters planted the idea? If that was happening, how could he conceal anything from them?

As Evan waited for Jeff to return, the October sun penetrated the light material of his shirt and burned into his already dark skin. He looked toward the sky, noting the sun's lowered position. The rays were certainly not as strong as they had been in July, but they were harsh enough to keep the land baked hard and dry. For two and a half long years there had been no rain, and it was sixteen unbearable months since the irrigation system had become a poison stream. It meant the prairie was turning into desert. Some of the more stubborn scrub oak and ragged, tough plants and grasses were still clinging to the gritty parched ground. Even with Tillie's persistent care, the garden flowers and shrubs had finally died.

Evan wiped the sweat above his eyebrows and resettled his straw hat. He tried to shake his despair and summon a bit of hope. He remembered what Jeff and the men had said about their work in finding a water supply. He didn't doubt they were right; even if the ground were pure, the water counted the most. He wasn't Moses and he couldn't produce water from a rock. He could only offer a farfetched scheme.

The blare of a car horn startled him. He saw Clay's car parked in the road near the house. It looked as if Jan were with him. Evan hurried across the compound to them. As he came near, Jan called to him.

"What are you doing standing there alone?"

Clay leaned across the seat, putting his arm around Jan's shoulders, and yelled through the open window. "We haven't interrupted some divine revelation, have we?" he teased.

Evan lifted an eyebrow; it was surprising how close Clay had come to the truth. He reached the car and smiled. "Where are you going?"

Clay shifted his gaze toward the windshield and away from Evan's face. "A visit with Diana. It's never easy."

Jan pressed her lips together, a wrinkle rippling her smooth forehead. "Would you want to go with us?" she asked. "Maybe you could say something to her that would help."

Evan didn't know what to do with his hands, and they hung loosely at his sides. "I doubt it. Even before what's happened, she wasn't fond of me."

"She doesn't think that much of me either," Clay remarked. "She's still set on the divorce."

Evan leaned his arm on the hot windowsill. "Is a divorce what you want, too?"

Clay ran his fingers nervously across the back of the seat. "I guess it is the right thing. Fern has taken Diana to a doctor, an old friend of theirs. He said Diana might turn around once she has the papers in her hand. I'm supposed to see Avery about getting the divorce started." Clay gave a harsh laugh. "Isn't that a hell of a note? Getting rid of me could be the cure. I must be one sorry bastard."

Jan patted his arm. "Stop it. You know it's not that way."

Clay straightened and gripped the wheel with both hands. "That's what you keep telling me." He turned toward Evan. "We better go. I should be back late this afternoon. Try to keep the place from blowing away while we're gone."

Clay smiled as he started the engine. When they pulled away, Jan turned to wave at Evan. He thought her expression was strange and hard to read. It was sadness mixed with questioning, and bewilderment rolled together. He watched them drive toward the farm's main entrance. Diana would finally be free to start again. He doubted she would ever find happiness. He had seen too many of her kind, like the women who had been friends of his parents. Beautiful creatures, searching for the one situation or person to make their lives as beautiful as they were. Jan had said shock and guilt had driven Diana over the edge. He had tried to be sympathetic, but he couldn't believe it. It was easier to think it was a scheme she had devised to escape an unpleasant situation. Still, perhaps Diana was as disturbed as she seemed. There were many ways of seeing things. He grew dizzy with the twists and turns in trying to reach the truth.

As he turned away and started toward the buildings, Jeff drove in from the well site.

Twenty-three

By the time Jan and Clay reached town, she was windblown, hot, and sticky, her face caked with dried makeup. Her mascara was smeared, and wisps of hair were straggling from the cluster of curls at the nape of her neck. She remembered a time when cars were air-conditioned; she supposed some still were, perhaps for the upper one percent of the population. For others, when the feature broke down, there were no materials for repair. Impatiently, she tucked the tendrils into place and fastened them. She knew she looked a sight and firmly decided it was the last time she would use cosmetics. If her unadorned face was too repulsive for others to view, that was their problem. It was crazy. For years women had fought to gain equal footing with men and they were still smearing paint on their faces. She smiled, thinking that it wasn't an exclusively feminine trait. At various stages in history and in certain cultures, men too altered their appearance. Even now, many men out for an evening wore eye shadow or lip gloss. Perhaps it was a sort of shield or confidence builder men needed.

She glanced at Clay's clean, smooth face and decided she liked plain men better. Before living on the farm, away from the confines of society, she never gave much thought to the cosmetics she used. She had accepted many of the values she now questioned. Evan had something to do with her changing social habits, although he never commented on the outward appearance of a person.

As Clay turned a corner onto Main Street, heading for the Brockman offices, she studied the buildings. Everything had changed; it was no longer the Garden City of her youth. Each time she came into town it was in worse condition. The farm was no paradise with the water shortage, electric, and fuel rationing, but it was better than being in town. People had turned their lawns into gardens, hoping to grow a few scrawny vegetables. More than one house had ramshackle chicken pens at the side or in the backyard. Everywhere people were afoot. The dry warm weather was a curse, but in another way a boon. Shoes were an item not easily made by hand and materials to make them were practically nonexistent. Dry ground was much better for the poorly shod population.

Garden City was a small town, but it still held more misery than she could bear. Cities, particularly on the east or west coast, were in near-riot conditions. People daring to leave a shelter after dark must be equipped to defend themselves. Even if they carried no money, the clothes they wore were enough to get them killed. For over ten years, most nations had been in an economic decline. The last two years of crop failures had destroyed the last bit of stability.

As the situation continued to worsen, the world's population declined. Perhaps the overthrow of existing governments was the answer. Destroy them and start over. She was sure that greater minds than hers were working on a solution. She wondered if they could find one in time to save mankind. Jan smiled and Clay looked at her and frowned.

"I'm glad one of us has something to smile about. What is it?"

Jan sighed. "Nothing really. I was thinking of something Evan said."

"Yeah? Something encouraging?"

"I'm not sure. I'll have to think about it."

Clay shrugged and drove on in silence while she thought about Evan. He had a theory of world salvation. With him, everything was divine intervention, something called the second coming. When she questioned him, he had to admit it had been a long time since their Savior had left, and there was no set time for His return. Jan had difficulty believing this part of Evan's message. Besides, she had decided it wasn't necessary to accept every part of the doctrine. If Evan and other believers would simply work at making more converts, they could eventually win the world. The basic concepts of love, sharing, and caring for others were enough to bring in a new order. Selfless people could achieve a better world. She'd have a talk with Evan when she returned to the farm. It was time he stopped meditating and took action. It would be a hard fight—the Church was already making great strides—but she had faith in Evan.

When Jan thought of the great struggle ahead, a tremor made her heart flutter. She wasn't sure if it was fear or excitement. She couldn't accept the Bible literally, but she was sure that Unity Council spelled the death of individual freedoms, something against which everyone should fight. Three weeks ago, she had been home and read some of her father's bulletins and special publications. The information in them was disturbing. The Council had met in Rome with most of the world leaders. The success of the food distribution project gave them credibility in pushing for nations to unite in other areas, to put more programs under centralized control. Their proposals sounded good, yet giving unbridled authority to one organization seem questionable. Jan wondered if the nations' leaders had considered this. They must have. Perhaps they thought the Council was right. Since they had brought every religious group under Unity's wings, maybe the same could work in the secular world.

One paragraph in the *Global Reporter* had caught Jan's attention. It concerned a fellow named Justin Denovo. He had a most unimpressive background and held a small position in the Church, yet the Council described him as "brilliant with a magnetic personality." Amazingly, the president of the Council had given him thirty minutes to address the meeting. The article continued with Denovo's methods for converting individual currencies into a united monetary system. He also presented a plan to bring the divided

Middle East into total harmony. In Jan's opinion, Denovo was nothing special. What concerned her was that heads of state would listen to him; it meant they were grasping at straws, and that was frightening.

As they drove through the center of town, she noticed how few vehicles there were on the streets. Most of them belonged to companies and city officials; the real traffic was on the sidewalks. Women hurrying to poorly stocked markets while the money in their purses became increasingly worthless. Nearly every woman had a small child at her side and some had another one in their arms. Jan wondered how many of them carried babies hidden in their bellies. Maybe when faced with starvation and death, the urge to procreate became over powering: a drive to ensure the continuance of the race. Even though, in the circumstances it made more sense to comply with the regulations and limit their families. However, if conditions didn't improve, women could lose the ability to conceive, making their current instinct correct. She doubted the increased birthrate indicated faith in the future. It was probably more of a natural instinct, a reaction to the population decline.

When Clay drove into the parking lot next to the Brockman law offices, he said, "I hope Avery can see us right away."

"I'm sure he can," Jan answered. "It won't take long. I explained and he'll have the papers in order."

Clay hadn't spoken much since they left the farm and there was no need for words between them. Too many times, they had worried the problem of Diana back and forth until they were exhausted with the discussion. Jan was satisfied they were doing the best thing for Diana, and it was best for Clay, too. When neither of them was happy with the other, it was time to correct the situation.

As Jan had predicted, the meeting with Avery was over in a matter of minutes and they started for Fern's home. Waiting for a red light at the intersection of Main and Eighth Street, Jan looked toward the south, the direction of her parents' home.

"Do you want to swing by and see your mother?" Clay asked.

She shook her head. "No. Daddy is in Oklahoma City today and Mother is probably busy as usual."

"You don't see much of them lately."

"No reason to."

"You haven't argued with them, have you?"

"Of course not, what would we have to argue about?"

"I don't know. Diana maybe. Or you're spending too much time at the farm."

He had said the farm, but she thought he meant her parents might be angry about her association with Evan, or even Clay, for that matter. Since Diana's separation, the ties between the two families had nearly evaporated. The Brockmans were still representing the Sandersons' interest with National Grain, but that didn't foster any social contact.

When Fern's three-story house with the tall white pillars came into view, Jan marveled at how it never changed. The lawn was green, despite the drought, and the boxwood hedges were trimmed. Not a single leaf from the two tall oak trees littered the white gravel drive. As they climbed the wide steps onto the shaded porch, Jan looked toward the ceiling. The sparkling crystal porch light hanging from four swag chains looked as clean as the day Fern had it installed. It was hard to understand Fern's obsession with her home. It seemed a shallow concern...still, the perfect place for Diana. Jan quickly banished these thoughts; she had no right to judge.

Clay pulled a tasseled cord beside the door and chimes sounded inside the house. Instantly, Clarence swung the door open to admit them. The foyer was cool and the hardwood floor polished to a mirror shine around the edges of the Persian rug. In a second, Fern came sweeping in from the den to greet them. She smiled and planted a soft, cool kiss on Jan's cheek, and turned to clasp Clay's hand between her slender fingers.

"How nice to see you both. Come, Nora has arranged a tea for us in the sitting room."

Not waiting for their response, Fern floated ahead of them through the double doors into a sundrenched room that opened onto the garden. She spread her hands toward a small table in front of a long, silk couch.

"There now, doesn't that look lovely? Nora never fails to arrange an attractive setting."

Fern indicated a large comfortable-looking armchair for Clay. She sat on the couch and patted the seat beside her.

"You sit with me, Jan. My, don't you look pretty today. I never see enough of you. You're always busy. But you never were one to sit still very long."

Fern leaned forward and began pouring tea from the china pot into three delicate cups.

"Isn't Diana joining us?" Jan asked, taking note of only three cups.

"Oh, I'm sure she will later, dear." Fern lifted her head and looked toward the large windows across the far side of the room. "Right now, she's walking in the garden. She seems to take comfort from it. It calms her."

Fern extended a cup and saucer toward Clay. "Now tell me, what have you been doing today? I hope things are going better at the farm."

Clay had been looking over his shoulder at Diana's slender figure as she strolled along the garden path. He returned his attention to Fern and accepted the cup of tea. "I'm sorry, what did you say, Fern?"

Fern laughed softly. "Nothing, nothing of importance. Diana is looking lovely, isn't she? From this distance, you would never suspect a disturbing thought ever crossed her mind."

Jan balanced her cup and saucer, noticing how unkempt her hands looked in comparison to those of her grandmother. Maybe it wouldn't hurt to pay more attention to them.

"How is she?" Jan asked. "Has there been much change since we last visited?"

"Oh yes, dear. I must say Dr. Kruger was right. The minute I told her Clay had agreed to the divorce, she seemed to shed a load of care." A pained expression flashed across Fern's smooth brow as she quickly looked at Clay. "I'm sorry, Clayton. I didn't mean to make it sound that leaving you is the answer to every one of her problems."

Clay shrugged awkwardly. "That's okay, I understand. I'm having a hard time admitting it, but I suppose I'm relieved, too. I'm not deserting her," he added with a tight edge to his voice. "I'll be around anytime she needs me, or if there's anything I can provide for her."

Fern leaned forward to pat his knee. "I know you will, and you mustn't let this cloud your own future. No one can lay a bit of blame at your doorstep over this. I'm sure when things are normal again, you will be the best of friends."

Fern gave Jan a look that said she expected her to be a good girl and not give her sister any trouble over the situation. For a second, it angered Jan. Nothing had changed. Their grandmother would never blame Diana for anything, no matter how bizarre her actions. Even when Fern assured Clay he was not to blame, she still sounded as if he were. It was the same thing Fern had done to Jan when comparing her to Diana. Diana was the shining example; Jan was a rebel, causing disturbances and discord. The family seemed blind to the crises Diana created when she didn't get what she wanted. Jan tried to dispel the bitter thoughts. What did it matter anyway? She wouldn't trade a minute of her life in exchange for Diana's way of living.

She tried to think well of her sister, but she couldn't help suspecting this was another of Diana's complicated schemes. This wasn't the first time the thought had crossed her mind. Still, how could even Diana sustain the performance this long? She had to put the question aside. There was nothing to do except deal with Diana on her terms. That never changed; she should be used to it by now.

"Have you been to see Avery yet?" Fern asked.

"Yes," Clay answered. "There was nothing to it. He'll file the papers tomorrow and we'll receive the termination in a week to ten days."

"That is fine. I know Diana will be relieved it went well."

"Why don't we call her in and tell her?" Jan suggested.

Fern frowned slightly. "To tell you the truth—now don't let this upset you, Clay—she's been nervous about facing you. You know, after seeing Avery and signing the final papers. Maybe it would be better for Jan to pave the way. Jan, you go talk to her and explain. Tell her everything is fine. That will make it easier for her to come in and visit with Clay."

Jan raised her eyebrows questioningly at Clay. He nodded in agreement. "It's okay; you handled her better at the farm. I seem to make her nervous."

Conscious of her rumpled appearance, Jan set her teacup on the table, stood, and smoothed the front of her skirt. Old habits were hard to break. Her grandmother's home had always made her feel grubby, never meeting the expected standard. As a child, she was the one to lose the ribbons off her braids and manage to dribble ice cream on her best dress. While Diana moved about, a tiny duplicate of Fern, every hair in place and never wrinkling her dress, even when she sat. It was irritating to feel this way. She should be mature enough to put this childish hangover aside.

Stepping onto the flagstone terrace, Jan closed the French doors behind her. Diana was at the far end of the garden sitting on a bench beside the roses, a large sunhat shading her face. She looked toward Jan, but made no move to come and meet her. Jan followed the gravel path to where Diana awaited her. When she stood before Diana, she smiled.

"How are you?"

Diana extended her hand. "Jan, how nice to see you."

It was startling how she and Fern sounded alike. Still, there were worse people to imitate. Jan took Diana's hand and held it for a second before sitting beside her sister.

"I'm glad to see you looking this well, Diana. I hear Dr. Kruger has high hopes for your complete recovery."

Diana sighed. "Yes, I know. I hope I don't disappoint him."

"Why should you? There's no reason you can't be in circulation by Christmas. I don't think you want to miss the parties, especially the one Fern will surely have this year with you available and eager."

The corners of Diana's satiny lips tightened and she gave Jan a reproachful look. "You act like I can turn this off and on at will.

Honestly, Jan, no one knows what I've suffered. First Eva tried to throw me down the stairs hoping I'd lose the child, which I did, even though she didn't live to see it. It was her fault she died instead. Then I find Mark that way." Diana put a trembling hand to her forehead and sighed again. "I'll never be the same."

"Sure you will. You will bounce back."

"You know Eva never liked me, not really. Mark didn't either. If they were alive, they would be happy to know Clay is divorcing me. I don't see how he can do it after what has happened."

Jan's mouth dropped open and she made an effort to close it. What kind of new twist was Diana putting to the facts this time? When she had last seen Diana, she'd said the incident on the stairs was an accident, a story Diana told with trembling hands and fear-filled eyes. Now she had worked it around to the point that Eva had wanted to kill the baby. Even saying Clay demanded the divorce. It was hard to keep things straight, but Diana had told her that she did not want the baby! She asked for the divorce. Diana made her head swim. Sitting beside her, Jan took Diana's hand.

"Diana, Clay is in the house. Do you think you can manage to speak to him and not make him feel worse than he does?"

For an instant, a trace of merriment shot thought Diana's sea-green eyes before a sad look of bewilderment replaced it. "Why should he feel bad? He is getting everything his way. In ten short days, he'll be completely free of me."

"How do you know the divorce is filed? Did Uncle Avery call you when we left his office?"

"I didn't talk to him. Fern mentioned his call."

Jan stood, put her hand on her hip, and shook her head. "Boy, what a bunch of winners we have in this family. Can't anyone simply say something without hedging around? Why didn't Fern say Avery had called, instead of letting us think we were breaking the news? If you already knew, why did I need to ease the way for Clay?"

Jan's face grew even warmer than it had been from the sun. The longer she talked, the angrier she became. Diana stared at her from under the brim of her sunhat.

"Sit down, Jan. Stop playing the injured child. You know how perfect Fern's manners are. It would be impolite to rob you of telling your little story. If you must know, I don't relish spending any more time with Clay than I have to. But I do miss you. Now tell me, what's going on at the farm? I was right, wasn't I? Clay is going to lose the whole thing, isn't he?"

Jan lowered her head in defeat and sank onto the bench. If they both lived to be a hundred, she would never understand how she continued to care about Diana.

"I don't know why it should concern you anymore, but things might not be as bad for Clay as you think. There is a Señor Matoes in the picture now because of what Frank did. It happens that he may be a blessing in disguise."

"How nice for Clay."

"I can see how overjoyed you are at his having a bit of luck."

Diana waved her hand. "Don't be a righteous ass, Jan. Tell me about it."

"At first Matoes and his partner thought they had made a bad bargain. Now that they know Clay better, and understand how intent he is upon getting the land into production again, they're willing to pay for sinking some deeper wells. They will invest more to get the farm in working order, something Clay couldn't have done even if he'd had the entire farm. This may save him."

"And what about Evan? Is he still the love of your life or is Clay filling that spot now?"

"You know, Diana, if you weren't certifiably insane, I might take offense."

Diana tilted her head and gave a full, rich laugh. "Oh, Jan. You're precious. I once thought you might grow up and finally understand what life is about. Now I realize you'll always be a serious, but lovable child. Do you want to know a secret?"

"Would it make any difference? I know you'll tell me anyway." She sighed, resigned to Diana's chatter. "Who is doing what to whom in Garden City's high society now?"

"Not exactly society, my dear. It's the Iverses. My soon to be forgotten in-laws. Tracy has been coming to visit me. Not exciting company, but she does help pass the time. Have you seen her recently?"

Jan shook her head. Lately, Tracy and Frank had not been very welcome on the farm.

Diana narrowed her eyes and leaned forward. "You're missing a real show. She's wearing the most expensive clothes and jewelry, very gaudy due to her abominable taste, but very expensive nevertheless. It seems wily old Frank has finally hit his stride. He has made connections in some commodity trading and somehow wormed his way into the food distribution operation. Can you see Frank doing business with the Church?"

Jan was puzzled. She could understand Diana's distaste concerning Tracy's clothes and her amusement in Frank's connection with a Church operation, but it didn't rank as a choice piece of news.

"Not really, but what does it matter?"

Diana leaned closer. "Here's the really killing part. Frank and his associates bought carloads of corn and soy. It's due to arrive in the area anytime. The Church has authority over the actual distribution, but Frank profits from the sales. And where do you think this shipment is going to be stored?"

Before Jan could speak, Diana gushed, "On the farm, that's where! How could you ever top that? Frank used the money from Tracy's inheritance to buy into this market. Now Clay is providing the facilities that will make Frank even more money. I wish I could see Clay's expression if he ever finds out."

Jan managed a weak smile, really more of a sneer.

Diana straightened her hat impatiently. "I guess the irony of it is lost on you, but take my word for it, it is funny."

Jan looked at the expertly cared for rose bushes near the bench. Some were still bravely in bloom, past their season and looking wilted due to the heat. Jan reached behind Diana and broke off a small, stunted red bud.

"I see Fern managed to keep her roses despite the weather. Everything at the farm is wilted or dead."

"Yes, they are lovely. A bit bedraggled, but I'm glad to see them before they're completely gone for the winter."

Jan studied her sister's face and thought she saw an honest emotion. Diana was grateful to be living in Fern's house. Perhaps, Jan reasoned, it was exactly where she belonged. Jan hated to think ahead to a time when even this oasis might be gone. What would happen to Diana? She dropped the rosebud in a sand-filled urn.

"We should go in now. Clay is probably getting tired of waiting. Out of curiosity, how are you going to act toward him?"

"Why, my dear, I'm surprised at you. I'll simply be myself, as I always am. There is no need to act. He is still my husband, and I hope my future friend."

Diana swept along the flagstone walk ahead of Jan and lowered her head demurely as she placed her hands on the knobs of the French doors.

Later that afternoon, as Jan and Clay drove to the farm, Clay seemed actually happy, or perhaps relieved was more accurate. Diana had been civil and, to Jan's surprise, didn't explode her bomb concerning Frank's grain deal. She knew Clay would probably learn of it, but she wouldn't tell him. He needed some rest from his problems; he needed one day away from any new complications. Besides, he might even be glad for Frank's good fortune. If not for him, he'd be happy for Tracy's sake.

~ * ~

As Jeff turned off the section line road, he drove bouncing across the field. Evan braced himself against the seat and the pickup's door. He turned and looked through the rear window into the truck bed where the equipment he and Jeff had gathered rattled and shifted under a huge tarpaulin. It was a good thing he had asked Jeff's help. He never realized it would take this many tools to accomplish the job. He had supposed they'd pile some flammable material on the ground, toss a match into it, and let it take off from there.

Jeff thought differently.

"If we're going to give this thing a fair trial, we better do it right," he had said.

With that, he'd marched toward the equipment shed. They loaded anything that looked as though it would make a hot fire. Jeff also slung a hundred-foot length of hose into the truck bed. He hesitated a minute and went back for more.

"Don't want this thing to get away from us," he'd muttered. "If it burns at all."

Evan had watched as Jeff checked the tool chest to make sure the right sized wrenches and adapters were there. He had decided upon a spot close to a wellhead that had produced a respectable flow of water. Setting a field on fire in these dry conditions needed many precautions. Jeff added a few glass jars and a wooden tray to hold them.

"In case we get lucky and have samples to carry," he'd said.

The last things Jeff collected to complete their supplies were two five-gallon cans of gasoline.

As they bounced toward the site, Evan studied Jeff's profile. The weather-beaten hat sat low on his forehead above his piercing bird of prey eyes where a delta of lines deeply scored the corners. His nose and chin jutted forward as he hunched over the steering wheel, his gaze locked on the land stretching before them. His expression was that of a normally practical man driven to extreme measures. They both knew it was dangerous to start a fire in a dry, stubbly field. The constant wind could spread the flames faster than either of them could spit. It would race over a dozen acres in a flash. Still, it seemed worth the risk. They had shovels and rakes to make a firebreak and with the hose connected to the wellhead, it should stay under control.

When they reached the spot, Jeff began working on connecting the hoses to the well. Evan paced off a patch of ground and began clearing a wide path around it with the rake. He made a bare six-foot-wide swath around the selected ground. Next, he dug a shallow trench in the middle of the firebreak. If the flames tried to cross, they could fill the small ditch with water. Jeff finished with the hoses and they both carried tinder and kindling to the center of the test plot before placing a few heavier pieces on top. Jeff pulled a handful of straw from the stack, twisted it into a long bundle, and put it aside. Jeff squared his shoulders and gave a hitch to his jeans.

"You ready?" he asked.

"I guess."

"You want to man the water, or set the fire?"

"Doesn't make any difference to me."

Jeff had connected both lengths of hose and had them stretched out on either side of the test patch. He walked to the one on the left, reached for it, and nodded at Evan.

"Since it was your idea, I'll let you do the honors."

The gas cans were still in the truck. As Evan lifted the first one and brought it to the pile of straw, kindling, and wood, his heart pounded. He trembled like a racehorse at the starting gate and felt foolish for it. Reason told him it wouldn't work, a bonfire on a small patch of ground, adding more heat to an already hot day. He tipped the can and watched the vapors rise in wavy lines as the liquid sank into the pile. The oily, flammable smell stung his nose and he stepped away, holding his hand to his face.

"Get the other can," Jeff ordered.

Evan frowned, but followed Jeff's instructions. Jeff usually knew what he was doing. The farm was an extension of his body and he knew exactly what it would take. Carefully, Evan walked around the pile emptying the second can. The dry soil soaked it in as greedily as it would have water. He threw both cans some distance away and looked at Jeff. Jeff stood ready with a hose and gave him a sharp nod. Evan walked to the straw bundle Jeff had made, stooped over, and picked it up. Striking a match, he lit the straw and held the burning torch away from his body. He hesitated a second before advancing toward the gasoline-soaked pile. When he tossed the flaming straw into the center of the pile, he spun on his heel and ran.

Almost the instant he turned, there was a deep thump, a push of air at his back, and the swoosh of igniting gasoline. At a safe distance, he whirled around to watch their experiment. Red and orange flames were pyramiding over the pile of wood. Through the flames, he saw

Jeff holding the hose, keeping guard at the edge of the firebreak, his face filled with caution. The bonfire crackled and roared, leaping higher as the heavier pieces of wood caught. Fire spread like a dancing mantel over the surrounding dried stubble where it quickly consumed the short, dead plants, causing plumes of gray smoke to twist above the ash. It was a good strong fire whipped and fanned by the prairie breeze. It gave no sign of jumping the cleared space or getting away from them, and Evan's pulse slowed. The hope was that under the middle of the pile it would burn hot enough to destroy the foreign substance in the soil. He moved closer to Jeff.

"What do you think?" he asked.

Jeff shrugged. "I don't know, have to wait till it's burnt out and we can take a sample."

The excitement of setting the fire had worn off and Evan was impatient for it to end. The true test would come when they took the glass jars of dirt to a laboratory. Again, he was glad they hadn't told anyone. No point in raising hope if the content of the jars was the same as the rest of the section.

"Evan," Jeff yelled. "Look, there."

"What? Is it getting away?" Evan ran to grab the other hose, his eyes darting around the edge of the fire. "Where? I don't see anything."

Jeff wasn't shooting water on the flames. He was waving wildly. "Come look at this. I don't know what the hell is happening."

Evan dropped the hose and ran to Jeff's side.

"See? Right there," Jeff pointed to a spot where stubble had already burned.

Evan leaned forward searching the ground. He quickly saw it.

A strange blue and green fire was shooting from of an already burnt area. The flames were three or four inches high, flickering among the wisp of blue-gray smoke. It was a slow creeping fire, but steady and strong. He watched in amazement as it crawled across inch after inch of ground. Occasionally, a yellow-white tongue flared higher and longer than the blue or green. When that happened, the spread quickened as a different accelerant fueled the fire.

They stepped forward and bent over to study their strange fire at close range. Evan narrowed his eyes and squinted at one small section. The charred bristle of burnt stubble was not involved in this burning. It was ash or black brittle stalks, while the jewel-colored flames flickered and danced along. Evan looked harder; it seemed the soil itself was on fire. The dazzling carpet crept to the edge of the firebreak, leaving the ordinary hissing and spitting red and yellow bonfire to burn alone. The fire they had set, fed by wood and straw, looked bland and dull.

"Isn't that the damnedest thing you ever saw," Jeff muttered. "Seems the dirt is burning."

"Not the dirt, Jeff, what's in it. I think the chemicals caught fire."

Jeff looked greatly puzzled. "Nothing burns underground without air."

"Must be getting enough, or doesn't need it."

Suddenly, Evan realized they were watching a fire no cleared area would stop. Already the short bright flames were jumping along into the bare dirt of the firebreak. If anything, it grew more intense in the stirred soil. From Jeff's startled look, he'd reached the same conclusion. Evan grabbed the shovel and started to scoop dirt to smoother the fire, but instantly stopped. Whatever fed the flame was in that dirt, too. He would be adding fuel. He dropped the shovel and raced for the other hose.

Jeff was quickly dousing the area closest to him. As Evan released the nozzle at the end of the second line, the water pressure on Jeff's hose weakened. Jeff shot him a troubled look, but didn't speak. Evan continued to flood the far side of their test area. As the water hit the flames, they seemed to duck and dodge, dying under the direct flow, but the instant the spray moved to another spot, they flared again. There was no smoke, but a biting, acidy odor stung their noses and made tears stream from their eyes. Silently, they frantically continued to battle the short, brilliant flames with the steady, but weak streams of water.

Evan felt like a giant fighting a miniature blaze with a toy hose; both were slow and small yet the tiny shafts stabbing the air were more threatening than a roaring house fire. It was the lack of knowledge about the odd smokeless fire and fumes filling the air. They may have started something no one could stop. Evan's throat tightened and his eyes stung, while his body stiffened with tension. The sharp clear blue and green spears were strange and frightening enough, but as the burning continued, a new color appeared: a ruby-red flame that sporadically flared. Through tear-blurred vision, he saw the shifting bright colors; the ground appeared covered in sparkling sapphires, emeralds, and brilliant rubies. The chemical fire was a beautiful sight, except for the tears and fear it caused.

"The water isn't going to quench this!" he shouted at Jeff.

"I know," Jeff yelled as he kept spraying the ankle high flames.

Evan dropped his hose and ran to the truck. He grabbed the large, heavy tarp they had used to cover the equipment. As he ran to the fire, he tripped and stumbled over the dangling ropes hanging from the corners. When he reached Jeff, he dropped the tarp at his feet and grabbed the hose from his hands.

"I'm going to try to kill the wood fire," he cried, and dodging the chemical flames came as close as he could to the test patch. The burning wood quickly turned into a heap of wet, black boards with rising steam and smoke. With the pile soaked thoroughly, Evan dropped the hose and hurried to Jeff, who had started spreading the tarp. He had needed no explanation...he understood Evan's idea. Quickly they pulled the tarp to full size and stretched the heavy cloth between them.

"I hope it's big enough," Evan said.

He worried that it too might catch and start burning, but there was nothing else at hand. Something had to smother the dancing flames or they could go on forever. He and Jeff held the tarp high and advanced on the burning patch. They dropped one edge at the side of the fire and, each taking an end, spread the gray tarp over the brilliant-colored flames. It covered everything except a long a strip that looked about eighteen inches wide. They ignored this area and went to work stamping the tarp tight to the ground. The process didn't take long considering the amount of time they had wasted trying the water. After a bit, Evan cautiously raised one corner and peered under the tarpaulin. The flames were gone, and he gave a long whistle. The last small section that was still merrily burning didn't worry him as much now.

"How is it over there?" he asked.

Jeff looked under his side of the covering. "Looks dead to me," he called.

"Do you think it is safe to move it now?"

"We can give it a try."

Gingerly, they lifted the top edges and pulled the covering forward over the remaining fire. After smothering the last area, they stopped to rest. Jeff pulled a large handkerchief from his pocket and mopped his brow.

"There for a minute, I thought we'd had it," he said.

"It scared me, too. But I think we're on to something."

Jeff nodded slowly as he stuffed the handkerchief into his pocket.

"You have to admit this wasn't your everyday kind of fire. Whatever was burning in the dirt had to do something to the soil."

They stood on the edge of the burnt area and studied the ground. Evan wished he could read the soil's composition. Maybe Jeff could.

"My best guess," Evan said, "is either the chemicals burnt out, or the burning made a new reaction. No telling what the mix is now."

Jeff knelt and started brushing away the ash and bits of burnt stubble, quickly pulling his hand away as he hit hot spots. He dug into the earth and lifted a handful of brownish gray dirt. He brought it to his face and sniffed, and extended his tongue to lick the soil.

"Hey," Evan yelled. "Don't do that. We don't know what's in there."

Jeff hesitated and his face cracked into a rare grin, revealing short, worn tobacco-stained teeth.

"I been eating this stuff one way or the other. What do you think we been breathing? The wind carries it and I swear it seeps through the pores of my skin. To say nothing of how much I swallow every time I open my mouth."

Jeff was right. The chemical-coated soil had blown around them ever since the spill. It was on the clothes they wore and in the food they ate. Evan wondered if the environmental agencies had thought of that. There hadn't been any warnings about the hazard. There was panic enough. Instead, the authorities assured everyone that the chemicals were not harmful.

Jeff extended his tongue and licked his fingers. He worked his lips with a thoughtful expression as Evan waited for the diagnosis.

"Can you really tell anything by tasting it?" he asked.

Jeff tightened his throat and brought a glob of spit. With a hawking sound he spat a dirt-speckled blob. "Most often I can." Jeff spat again. "It doesn't taste strange."

As they shook the tarp and folded it, Evan began to hope again. Perhaps they had stumbled on a cure. Jeff's taste test was encouraging, but they needed an official opinion. In a short time, the truck was packed and they were bouncing across the field toward the road. On the floor at Evan's feet sat a square box containing the sterilized jars now full of soil from the burnt patch. He couldn't stop looking at them.

"You still want to keep quiet about this?" Jeff asked.

"We don't have anything to tell yet."

"Pretty cautious fellow, aren't you? Don't know as I can keep it to myself."

Jeff didn't smile, but his eyes twinkled. Evan shrugged; it might be a good thing if the others knew. Even a false alarm could bring relief. He would let Jeff decide. Evan had Ryan to deal with; he couldn't hide the boy forever. If the Church discovered Ryan, even Clay couldn't protect him. Clay liked to think the farm was a haven, but Evan knew better. Clay did too, if he would admit it. The taking over of his barns proved he'd lost control.

The wind whipped through the open windows, catching at Evan's hair and drying his sweat-soaked shirt. The sun was still strong, but not as hot as summer. Even the dry wind had a different feel. It was still too warm for this time of year, but winter was on the way. From reports, it would be another dry one, but still cold. Not a good time to head north. The thin jacket Ryan had pulled from the trash wouldn't provide enough protection for even a mild winter. It would be much colder in Canada; maybe they should go south instead.

Evan's thoughts shocked him. When had he decided to go with Ryan? What purpose would it serve? Maybe he was looking for an escape. Some excuse to move across country where he could get lost in time and distance. Going with Ryan might be the right move. If they found the group of Christians Ryan spoke of, perhaps he'd be of more service there.

When Jeff parked in the compound, Evan put his thoughts to rest. Each day was enough to deal with; what he should do would unfold when the time came. He helped Jeff put the tools into the equipment shed. Carrying the rake and shovel toward the wide double doors, he saw the reverend's sedan still across the road between the warehouse and the storage bins. Evidently, the grain delivery had not arrived yet. Even if he hadn't seen their vehicle, he would have known churchmen were there. There were transparent shapes weaving their silent way through the buildings. They appeared to be dark evening shadows gliding through the glare of midday. It was hard to believe he was the only one who saw them. He glanced at Jeff, but Jeff continued the unloading, evidently unaware of the dark shades.

Twenty-four

Jeff leaned against the tailgate of the truck, took off his worn hat, and wiped the sweat from his forehead. He cleared his throat and spat, making a dark spot in the dust. Tilting his head, he looked across the compound to where the reverend and Mr. Carter were impatiently pacing.

"Look at those two," Jeff growled. "Acting like they own the place. No better than vultures feeding off misery and death. If it weren't for this trouble, they'd still be sitting behind their walls reading psalms and figuring new ways to be pious. I'm as God-fearing as the next man, Evan, but I can't see these pulpit-pounders as anything but leeches."

Jeff paused to spit again; it seemed even speaking of them left a bad taste. Evan was mildly surprised at Jeff's outburst. He knew Jeff held a bad opinion of the Church's activities, but he usually kept it to himself.

"Yes sir, if I had my way, those profiteers would be sent away with their tails between their legs. By damn, it might happen yet, 'cause between you and me, I think we got the answer to cleaning this land."

"You think there is a chance?"

Jeff nodded slowly. "I may be getting carried away, but I can't tell you how happy I'll be when this is over. When the farms start producing, everybody will get their storage back. The Council might still find a way to keep hold of the distribution system, but they won't be stomping around on private land."

Jeff removed his hat and slapped it against his leg, knocking off some of the dust.

"I better get to work. The boys will think I'm taking the day off. First, though, think I'll amble over and needle the reverend a bit. Let him get a look at these sample jars." Jeff chuckled as he settled his hat on his head and lifted the wooden box with the glass jars. "You coming? Might be fun watching them squirm if they think we found a way to clean the fields."

"No. I have to do something at the lodge. I'll meet you at the drilling. They still working on number eight?"

"Yes, should finish there tomorrow. You can bring that boy Ryan, if you want to. We can find something for him to do."

Evan flinched in surprise. "How'd you know about him?"

"You aren't as sneaky as you think. I saw you two this morning."

"Don't say anything, Jeff. The Church is looking for him."

"Stop right there. I don't want to know any more. Be sure to keep him hidden till the vultures are off the place."

Jeff hoisted the box a bit higher and started toward the warehouse. Evan headed in the opposite direction toward the lodge, wondering how many others knew Ryan was there. It wasn't easy to keep secrets on the farm. One thing was sure; he couldn't ask Clay to harbor Ryan, too. It would be better if he and Ryan left as soon as possible. He had no reason to stay. He'd given his one plan for helping Clay to Jeff. If it worked, Jeff and the men could clean the fields. If it seemed he was deserting Clay, he couldn't help it. It was time to move on, shake the dust of Garden City off his feet. There would be other Dewberries in other towns; however, the chance remained that he could get a group established before they stopped him. Maybe he could accomplish more by moving around. Stay in a town long enough to explain the true message and find someone to continue the teaching, while he went to the next place. It was something to consider.

Evan found Simon and Ryan in the old man's room. They were getting along fine. Other than the cook, they were the only ones in the lodge. Ryan was thrilled when Evan said he was thinking of leaving with him.

"Still," Evan added, "I can't simply take off. I want some time with Clay and Jan; they've been good to me. I need to explain before leaving."

"I wish I were younger," Simon said wistfully. "I'd be going with you."

Ryan's face wrinkled in disbelief. "Don't even think of it, Mr. Taylor. We aren't going to have any place to sleep and who knows where we'll find food."

They smiled at the boy's story of hardships, for he couldn't disguise his excitement and eagerness for what he obviously considered a great adventure.

"You trying to tell me I'm too old and scrawny to travel with you and Evan?" Simon said with mock sternness. "Listen, I'd be in the field working if it wouldn't give Jeff a stroke."

"Speaking of Jeff and work," Evan put in. "I should go to the well site and see if I can help. Stay in Simon's room and we'll make our plans later tonight."

When Evan left the lodge and started for the equipment shed, he noticed two big tandem trailers parked near the storage bins. Evidently, the reverend's shipment had arrived. Evan was relieved. That meant he would be gone by late afternoon. Maybe by the next time it was necessary for Dewberry to be at the farm, he and Ryan would be gone. It seemed strange to think of going away; still, this was not his home. He didn't belong to this land. Not as Clay, Jeff, and the men who worked the farm did. His field lay further away and his harvest was of a different sort.

The truck he and Jeff had used that morning still stood beside the shed. Evan poked his head into the building's shady interior.

"Jeff," he called.

There was no answer and he could see the shed was empty. It puzzled him for a bit as to how Jeff had gotten to the work site. Although, one of the men might have come in for something and Jeff could have ridden with him. The keys were still in the truck. Evan climbed in and headed toward the road. There wasn't much left of the afternoon; the men would be tired and welcome a fresh hand.

Heading south on a small dirt road, a soft peacefulness descended upon him. Gritty dust rose in swirling clouds under the rear wheels, powdering the dead grass on either side of the road, but in front the air was clear. The stark sky seemed to stretch on forever above a tan and yellow land. Not a living creature was in sight and the only sounds were the engine's rumble and the tires crunching an occasional rock. Time and space were suspended; even the movement of the truck seemed to lose meaning. The vast land encouraged solitude. Its peace and emptiness lowered the fences of the mind. Thoughts were free to roam on forever. Freed from intruding ideas, restrictions, and rules, his vision cleared. There were no shady forms or shapes in view. It gave a preview of a possible evil-free future. Evan took a deep breath. The tightness in his throat and shoulders melted.

Perhaps it was deciding to leave and begin a traveling ministry that had brought the release, but the solitude helped calm him, too. He eased off the gas, no need to rush the enjoyable drive. The silence was a soothing salve on the raw stinging wound of past indecision. With nothing but land and sky, it was easy to forget the world's troubles. He should bring Simon for an afternoon drive; it would help renew the old man's spirit. Simon seemed fine, but sometimes he caught a quick glimpse of Simon's weariness.

Once Simon had looked at him and with a tired voice said, "I don't know what good I am anymore. I'm ready to go home." Still, a light had shone from the old eyes, brightening his softly wrinkled face. "But since God hasn't seen fit to ask my opinion, I'll do well to keep my place and abide by His Will."

It was hard to keep from questioning God, but Evan hoped he had learned to trust rather than question. Yet he understood why others did. Eva and Mark, both needed by their family, were gone, while Simon remained. Many people never looked for a reason...they simply accepted events. Maybe that satisfied some, but to believe there was no purpose or plan was beyond Evan's ability. He knew evil existed, and its presence proved the existence of good. Sometimes he yearned for the final revelation that would fill in the unknowns. Waiting called for patience and gratitude for the knowledge he did possess. There was nothing to do except warn whose who would listen, and wait for the day of answers to come.

Evan parked where the men were working on the number eight well. It had been years since the farm had needed water from these wells. National Grain's system had supplied the area for longer than most of these men had worked on the farm. The old number eight well was in bad shape with corroded pipes, and some shifted sections that let in dirt. It was hard to tell the extent of the damage, and repair parts were difficult to find. When Clay had found a source for new lengths of pipe, they decided to sink a new well. Drilling near the old one, they expected to hit water at the same depth. If they were successful, they could pull pipe from the old well and perhaps reuse the good lengths in other wells.

The drilling rig was outdated and broken down, much of it patched and reworked. They had even adapted some parts from other types of equipment. The rig crouched like a huge insect, poking its splinted and bandaged mandible into a hole in the ground. Close beside it sat the companion vehicle with the water tank for cooling the bit and carrying the lengths of pipe. Three of the men were standing some distance away, protecting their ears from the clattering roar of the engine. Two others, wearing ear protectors, were taking their turns at the actual drilling. If one of the commercial rigs had been available, they could drill the well in no time. However, with every farm in six states looking for water, there was no chance of hiring a crew.

Evan walked across the trampled work area to the three resting men.

"How's it going?" he asked.

"Fair, I suppose," William answered. "We find wet sand and some water, but nothing to brag about."

Evan scanned the area looking for Jeff. "Where's Jeff? When I left him, he was headed this way."

"Haven't seen him since breakfast," William said.

Evan glanced around, trying to find a way to be useful, but with more than enough men for the job, there wasn't much to do. The men stood in the hot sun or squatted in the shade of the truck and passed the time with the other workers. Watching the sweating, grim-faced men, Evan was tempted to tell them what he and Jeff had done, but Clay should be the first to know. That was probably what Jeff was doing, explaining to Clay about their experiment. Either that or taking the samples to be tested.

Yet, when he and the men returned to the main compound, Evan found he was wrong on both counts. Clay hadn't seen Jeff that afternoon and neither had Jan. Upon further checking, Evan discovered he was the last one to have seen Jeff. None of the vehicles was missing; if Jeff had left the farm, he had done it on foot. Evan continued to wonder where Jeff had disappeared to, but others didn't seem concerned. After dinner, as dusk enveloped the area, Evan left the lodge. The lighted windows in the farm office gave a warm yellow glow, and Evan stepped onto the porch. When he opened the door, Clay rose from his desk chair, an eager expression on his face.

"Oh, it's you," Clay said.

"Are you expecting someone? I can leave if you're busy."

"No, I thought you might be Jeff."

"You haven't heard from him?"

Clay frowned and shook his head. "Guess he must have gone into town for something."

Evan sat in a chair by Clay's desk. "I doubt that. The cars and trucks are still here."

The lines across Clay's forehead deepened and he straightened his shoulders, giving them a shake like someone throwing off his worry. He smiled at Evan.

"Hey, it's nothing serious. Jeff's an old tiger; he can take care of himself. He'll be okay."

Despite his words, Jeff's disappearance clearly upset him. Evan wanted to let Jeff tell Clay about their experiment, and maybe he had gone into town, despite the lack of transportation. He might have caught a ride with someone. Still, Evan doubted Jeff would have left before telling someone. Weighing their secret against Jeff's disappearance, Evan decided to tell Clay what they had done. Jeff would understand.

"I wasn't going to mention this, Clay, it was going to be Jeff's surprise, but now I think I should tell you."

Evan recounted his and Jeff's midday adventure. Clay listened eagerly. "That's it, he's taken the samples to a test station," Clay exclaimed.

"Would he have started in mid-afternoon? What did he use for transportation?"

For a minute, the two sat in silence, each trying to find a reason for Jeff's absence. Clay stood and slapped the top of his desk with both hands.

"It's a mystery for sure, but we'll know sooner or later. I'm sure Jeff is fine. In the meantime, I need some air. I can't break the habit of my nightly rounds even when there isn't any need."

Evan rose from his chair. "I'll go with you, if you don't mind."

The October night was dark navy, the stars glimmered, and a quarter moon hung low in the west. A tiny breeze rippled the shirts on their backs and brought a dusty smell to the air. The darkness was deceptive; it made the land seem to hold some moisture. Clay tilted his head and gazed at the heavens.

"What I wouldn't give for some rain. It's been too long; I'm beginning to think we'll never see a rain cloud again."

Evan hated to add to Clay's concerns, especially with the nagging worry over Jeff, but he had decided to tell him about Ryan. Clay had a right to know and it was better to tell him than run the risk of his finding out some other way. If all went well, they'd both be gone soon anyway. As they stood at the corner of the main house, Evan explained.

"Ryan didn't have any place to go. He doesn't intend to stay. I'll leave as soon as possible and take him with me. We are both grateful to you for harboring us this long. I doubt any of the men will give us away. I don't want you to have trouble with the Church."

Clay listened quietly.

"You're both welcome to stay," he said. "I don't give a damn for what the Church says. Besides, if you and Jeff are right, we'll be getting rid of them. But if you're set on going, have you thought of how Jan will take to traveling?"

The mention of Jan startled Evan. Since she had been spending time with Clay and seemed to fit in well at the farm, he had supposed she would remain.

"I hadn't planned on Jan going along."

Clay chuckled. "You'd better ask her about that."

"I thought maybe the two of you were forming some sort of understanding."

"That would be fine with me. But she seems committed to furthering your crusade. If it comes to it, I couldn't say which way she'll go."

Clay and Evan finished making the nightly rounds in silence. They ended at the lodge, where Clay came in and talked with the men about the drilling that day. Preparing to leave, he added,

"Does anyone happen to know where Jeff might have taken off to?"

Several of them shook their heads. Terry said, "It is kind of strange. He usually says where he's going."

Most of the men nodded in agreement.

"He'll probably be around by morning," William offered.

After Clay left, Evan went to Simon's room, where he spoke with Ryan.

"I've told Clay about you," Evan said. "But it wouldn't hurt to stay away from him. That way he can honestly say he's never seen you."

Simon frowned and Evan raised his hand. "I know, but Clay isn't a good liar. This gives him a chance to get by if questioned."

"He doesn't need to worry. We'll be gone in the morning," Ryan said.

Evan shook his head. "I'm not ready to leave that soon."

"Why not? I'm not waiting around," Ryan insisted.

"I can't stop you from going if you are in a hurry, but there may be a way to clean the land. I want to see if it works. It shouldn't take long for the test. Only a day or two."

Ryan ducked his head and muttered, "I don't know, maybe I can wait."

Later, alone in his room, Evan listened to the muffled nighttime sounds of the lodge. The rising and falling tones of the men's conversation as they played cards and the soft music from a radio in the background. Some of the windows were open and an occasional breeze rippled the curtains. Familiar odors accompanied the familiar sounds of life in the lodge. There was the smell of stale tobacco smoke mingled with that of over-boiled coffee, and the scent of the men. The husky smell of well-worn shirts and pants, an odor that even many washings did not purge. The leather boots and sweat-stained hats added to the aroma. Evan had grown comfortable with these sounds and smells. Though it was temporary, and he didn't belong, it was as much a home as he had ever known. These were simple, strong and sturdy men. Perhaps they were grim warriors in the last great battle, the ongoing fight many people refused to acknowledge.

Evan lay on his narrow bed, his hands clasped beneath his head as he stared at the ceiling thinking about the men. In their hard work and grim determination, they were copies of their ancestors. The ones who had conquered lands, built great cities, and dreamed dreams that spurred them forward. They hoped for their children to have better lives, yet they were born with the same strengths and weaknesses as the parents. The tide of humanity rolled across the earth, each surging generation sucked under, and the next rising to continue the useless cycle. Evan yearned for the perfection of God, a conclusion to bring meaning to the constant ebb and flow.

The world could never satisfy his longing for peace, harmony, and joy. It was certain that humans would never change. There was a balance of sorts between selfishness and selflessness, but never enough of the latter to elevate the race. He had to include himself in the mix. His emotions ranged from self-preservation to sacrifice for others...he was an example of the common man. At first, he'd had the illusion that he could attain a higher spiritual level and lift others to the same understanding. It was a naïve idea. He was merely a signpost, not a conveyance for elevating anyone.

That night there were no floating, shifting shapes in view, yet their presence was strong. He could almost point to their locations. However, his fear of them was gone, replaced by scorn and disdain. In time to come, banished, they would return to the evil realm from which they had come. For a minute, assurance washed over him, yet experience proved these periods of confidence never lasted. He wondered what traps awaited him in his next time of weakness. The forces of darkness constantly changed their method of attack. It rarely came directly from them. They were too cunning for that. Instead, they created situations where an individual's natural tendencies usually led to his destruction.

As he drifted into sleep, hazy dreams warned him to be on guard, for the enemy was clever. The most innocent circumstance could quickly turn into a horror. There were times when he thought he was prepared, had rehearsed the right words or actions, and still his mind or body betrayed him. Half asleep, Evan nodded in agreement with the apostle Paul. "For the good that I would, I do not: but the evil which I would not, that I do."

Twenty-five

The next morning, Jeff was still missing, and Simon no longer tried to hide his worry. He left the lodge to roam aimlessly about the compound; his grim, tight-lipped face kept anyone from discussing the situation with him. The men stayed a respectable distance, honoring the old man's privacy. However, Jan walked across the wide graveled driveway to intercept Simon on his third pass by the four-vehicle garage. Apparently, Jan felt Simon needed company and comfort. She took Simon's arm, and with their heads bent closely together, she continued the slow walk with him.

Clay, Evan, and several of the farmhands standing at the foot of the veranda steps watched Simon's pacing. Clay wore a worried expression, as did the men waiting for his instructions. He settled his broad-brimmed hat more firmly on his head and turned to the men.

"We may be jumping the gun," he said grimly, "but I don't see anything to do but start looking for him."

The sober-faced farmhands nodded in full agreement. Evan was as concerned and puzzled as the others were. It would ease his mind if one of the vehicles were gone. The more he considered the situation the more he worried.

Clay smiled, obviously trying to be optimistic. "He'll probably be here shortly and make us feel foolish," he said.

It was clear none of them believed this, yet they were quick to join in adding bits of encouragement, like ants scurrying about, each carrying a grain of sand to rebuild a destroyed nest.

"Yes sir," William threw in. "You can bet there's some important reason for Jeff to take off. Still, don't suppose it would do any harm to look."

After making his decision to have the men start searching, Clay seemed undecided as to how they should go about it. People had already been through the house, the office, the lodge, and equipment shed. The warehouse and storage bins were under the control of the Church. That left the huge expanse of farmland. Several of the men narrowed their eyes as they stared across the road, past the warehouse, and on to the never-ending stretch of land. There was no talk for a bit, the unspoken thought circulating that if Jeff was on the farm, it left only the empty fields and low hills. Acres of land safe enough for men and machines when working, it was still not a place for a man to be afoot and alone.

"You fellows probably know where to look as well as I do," Clay said. "Terry, you and William take a run into town and see if you learn anything. If you do, give me a call. The rest of us will search the farm. We can meet at noon and compare notes."

It wasn't a brilliant idea, but no one had any other suggestions. Terry and William set off with long, purposeful strides toward a pickup. The rest of the men left by twos and threes to look in areas of their own choosing.

By afternoon when the searchers again gathered outside the lodge, the situation was the same. Clay had heard nothing from William. There was a slim hope Jeff was in town, but most everyone doubted it.

"We'll need to call for outside help," Clay said.

When he made the reluctant statement, the men looked as hesitant and wary as his voice sounded. It was common knowledge that no one relished the idea of police probing and poking into life on the farm. Even though there was nothing to hide, farmers knew the less a person had to do with institutions and authorities the better off they were. It put everyone in the awkward position of inviting strangers to snoop around in return for help in locating Jeff.

"Maybe we could give Jeff until tomorrow," a man suggested quietly.

With one accord, everyone turned to Simon. The answer should come from him. Simon glanced at Ryan, who was sitting at the edge of the lodge veranda.

Clay cleared his throat and said, "Don't worry about him, Simon. We can keep one young boy out of sight."

Ryan stood, jutting his chin in an independent attitude. "Don't anyone need to worry about me. I can take care of myself. Nobody will see me."

A weak smile flickered across Simon's pale lips as he turned an inquiring face toward Evan. Simon's silent plea for help sent a chill through him. This had to be the old man's decision.

Evan shrugged. "I don't know what to say. Simon, it's your call."

Simon patted Evan's arm. "Yes, it is. If Jeff is some place on the farm, he's hurt and can't come in, and you boys can find him faster than a troop of strangers. If you don't, he must be off on business of his own. If that's the case, I doubt he'd thank us for having the police mix in." Simon's frail shoulders heaved once under his cotton shirt. "I don't see the harm in waiting till morning to call in help."

"Don't worry, Mr. Taylor, we'll keep looking," one man assured him.

"That's right. We'll turn this place end over end," another added.

With that, the men, wearing determined expressions, started again. Jan took charge of Simon and the reluctant Ryan. She herded them into the lodge, as she continued a cheerful, encouraging line of chatter.

Clay headed for the office, telling the others he would join them later. Evan waited and was soon standing alone in the glaring sun. He squinted against the brightness and looked toward the warehouses and elevators with the squat storage bins huddled at their sides. The storage units bulged with sacks of wheat, corn, and soybeans since the Church had taken control. The elevators contained grain from many different sources. Evan had heard some of it came from other countries, creating another link in the Church's efforts to unite the nations. He remembered the day before, when the reverend's dark blue sedan stood near the warehouse; he and Carter had been waiting for a shipment to arrive. Not knowing exactly why, Evan headed toward the storage buildings. He crossed the road and stopped in front of the towering grain elevators. He tilted his head, gazing up at the smooth concrete sides of the two cylinders. Then he walked to one of the long warehouses and stood in front of the four-foot-high wooden platform where the trucks unloaded sacks of grain. The door beside the platform had a yard-long iron pole propped against it. The pole was holding the door shut, for the latch was broken. Evan removed the bar and leaned it on the wall, shaking his head in disgust. If Clay were in charge of the building, it would be in much better shape, but since the Church had commandeered the facilities, the farmhands had strict instructions to keep their distance. Dewberry had made it clear there would be consequences if anyone other than a Church employee entered the storage units. The silos, grain bins, and warehouse needed constant maintenance, something the Church ignored.

Evan stepped across the threshold into the dirt-floored metal building. Light filtered from the two long skylights on either side of the roof's ridgepole. There was a path through the center of the building; the sacks of grain were stacked head-high on both sides of it. The warehouse was crammed full, and the dry mash smell of grain dust filled his nose. It was a good, clean, earthy smell but it made him cough. He backed out of the warehouse and replaced the heavy iron bar against the door. He didn't know what he was looking for or what he could expect to find. These were simply buildings packed with grain.

Outside, he returned to the loading platform, leaned against it, and put one foot on the bottom rail. The last time he'd seen Jeff, he'd been heading toward this warehouse. As he stood considering possibilities, his throat, dry from the grain dust, tightened and a coughing fit stuck him. He bent over, trying to summon enough moisture to stop it. With his head down, he caught sight of a box on the ground under the corner of the platform. As he stopped coughing, he straightened and walked to the end of the platform. He knelt and reached under the decking to retrieve the box.

As he examined the box, it looked familiar. It was the same as others on the farm. They served many uses; they held tools, and any small item that would be awkward without a container. Tillie had some she used as flats in her greenhouse. There wasn't anything unusual about finding one tossed aside under the edge of the platform. Except when he'd last seen Jeff, he was carrying one of these boxes, holding the glass containers with the soil samples. Evan stooped over and squatted to put his head and shoulders under the platform. The weeds that had tried to grow in early spring had died during the summer. They stood stiff and brown, breaking under his hands as he probed farther under the deck. Something pierced the palm of his hand and he jerked it away to see a drop of blood welling on the skin. Instinctively, he looked to the place where his hand had been to see what had punctured him. Instead of rocks or bits of metal, broken glass littered a small area.

Inspecting the ground closer, he found jar lids. Evan frowned and his heart pounded. The discarded box along with the broken sample jars worried him. Unless Jeff had gone crazy, he'd never have dumped the dirt samples. Sunlight coming through the cracks in the boards put yellow stripes on the dirt and made the pieces of glass sparkle. He tried to stay calm and think rationally. These bits of debris didn't mean anything; they could have been here for years. He struggled to dismiss his first fears, but his mind wasn't having it. Thoughts flashed in bright colored lights—red, green, and purple—until they flowed together, forming a vile vision of what he suspected. If these broken bottles and the cast away box were what Jeff had been carrying, where was Jeff?

Evan scooted from under the deck and stood staring at the box. With the late afternoon sun shining behind him, his thoughts turned as dark as the shadow that stretched before him. He fought to find a logical explanation. Questions flooded his mind, confusing him; he blinked, fighting to control the wild thoughts. What was worse was the hot anger building in his chest. The more he tried to be reasonable, the larger the feeling became, reaching a low-grade rage. Something had happened to Jeff and Dewberry was responsible. If they had arrested Jeff for entering the warehouse to talk with them, Evan would make sure they paid! He had never felt this angry. His thoughts ran together creating a morass where there was only suspicion and hate.

He stood stiff and frantic, looking around for an expected attack. However, there was no one in sight. Still, he sensed the hovering presence of evil. He wanted to shout at the dark spirits to show themselves. Even if they were not around now, he was certain they had been. Most certainly accompanied by the humans who executed their wicked plans. Unable to calm his churning mind, he was slipping over into uncontrollable anger. He understood the compulsion to destroy; it was a loathsome feeling, yet it had a powerful allure. Overcome with fury, a certainty burst full-blown into his mind.

They had killed Jeff; he needed no proof. The unspeakable abominations had thought to silence Jeff. Stop him and put an end to the discovery that might clean the land and endanger their growing control. As a memory formed before him, Evan clenched his teeth in a bitter grimace. Jeff, the box in his arms, striding toward the black-garbed pillars of the church. The men Jeff had called vultures. Jeff's face smug with the idea of goading the profiteers a bit. Evan should have stopped him, kept Jeff from confronting them; he knew the evil that surrounded Dewberry and Carter. How he wished he had shouted a warning to him.

"Jeff, Jeff." Evan's cry rang with anger and pain. Now it was too late!

He whirled around, searching the compound. Had they taken the body with them? Again, reason tried to balance the horror; maybe they *had* arrested Jeff, locked him away to prevent testing the samples. Still, the over-powering certainty of his death extinguished the tiny flare of hope.

A cloud of dust rising in the long road from the highway caught Evan's attention. As he watched, a navy blue sedan rapidly approached the compound. He spun and raced for the warehouse, obeying an instinct to hide. He grabbed the iron bar holding the door shut and hurried inside. In the dusky amber light, he leaned against a tall stack of grain sacks, the iron bar clasped in his hand. In the grip of a growing sense of evil, he grew breathless. Gasping for air, he clenched his eyes against the colored lights flashing behind his eyelids. As the car pulled to a stop, gravel crunched under the tires, then two doors slammed. Evan trembled with the anger filling his body.

The growing rage expanded, unlocking Evan's spirit to float above the towering piles of grain where it absorbed sounds, odors, and sights. He was one with the dust-covered soil, the fat bags against which he leaned, and he was the aluminum of the building towering aloft. He drew energy from the surroundings, even the inanimate objects seeming to seek answers. A sense of power infused him and he opened his mind, ready to receive a revelation.

The wood, stone, and metal of the building, hovering and hushed, holding a secret it needed to share, urging him to voice what it could not. The grain, the fruit of the earth, filled him with strength. In exchange, his anger and rage promised justice. He barely noticed the heat until sweat stung his eyes and made the golden air turn hazy. Yet his senses turned sharper, and rising in the dusty air came the coppery odor of blood and dead flesh. The sensation lodged a scream in his throat. He wanted to open his mouth and let the dreadful sound fill the world; instead it threatened to strangle him. He could no more issue a sound than he could release the roar of rage in his head.

A dead silence prevailed.

Until broken by Reverend Dewberry's voice, low and solemn, and the higher whine of Carter's reply as they neared the warehouse. Before they reached the door, Evan started backing away. He moved along the long corridor formed by the high walls of the grain sacks. He turned into a side aisle and crouched there, letting the iron bar rest against the pile of grain sacks. When the warehouse door opened, fear ripped through him. It was a sharp, piercing fear that stiffened his body, and a vile, bitter taste flooded his mouth. For a second the emotion paralyzed him, before he realized he was not afraid of the two churchmen. He was terrified of himself. The burning rage roaring through him was overpowering. A small voice kept whispering a warning. He must act with calm reason. The conflict made him tremble, but the pounding fury destroyed any hope of rational thoughts.

On a sudden instinct, he swung his head toward the far right corner of the warehouse and leaned forward. He saw through the mountain of heavy grain sacks as if they were transparent. He listened for a voice that he would never hear again. While he heard nothing, his eyes widened in horror at the clear vision of Jeff's body. The ability to see through a pile of grain sacks seemed natural; it was the same as viewing the evil shapes. Jeff lay on his side with arms and legs crossed at awkward angles, his face smashed into the earthen floor. As Evan stared, the blood in his veins turned to venom. A powerful vengeance enveloped him; it was a force akin to a turbulent, boiling storm. A fury, a wind, gathering to rip across the land. He became nature's instrument reacting to an unnatural act.

The reverend and his assistant entered the building and walked down the wide center path. A cluster of the dark shades shifted and hovered around both men. The reverend walked briskly past the aisle where Evan was hiding. Carter scurried beside him carrying a pick and shovel.

"You were a fool," The reverend said angrily.

"He had to be stopped," Carter insisted.

"But not before learning if anyone else knew what he was doing. We could have dealt with it in another way."

"I don't see how," Carter whined. "He had to be stopped before he could do those tests."

"The reports, you idiot. We could have influenced someone at the testing station. Some fool always needs money."

"Perhaps." Carter sounded injured. "Still, that wouldn't have stopped them. Once the other farmers got wind of a solution, no matter how farfetched, they would have tried it. Proven or not."

"No matter. We'll deal with the situation as it is, not as it might have been. Do stop dragging that shovel, you're raising a dust."

They turned between two rows and started for the far right corner of the building, as Evan knew they would. His hand closed over the iron bar at his side and he stepped into the center aisle. As he did, the ghastly gray shapes gathered. Some were tall and thin, their faces set in leering smiles, while others were fat, bloated with conceit. They came close, taunting him with obscene gestures. Four of the larger forms blocked his way. The normal world turned into an alien, unhealthy place for humans, yet he wasn't afraid. His fierce anger solidified into a powerful protection. Coming face to face with the unspeakable, he became the untouchable. With shocking clarity, he knew that nothing in the universe could touch him unless God approved. Evan walked forward with measured steps, the shapes flowing aside making a foggy mist.

When he turned the corner into the path the two men had taken, there was the thud and chunk of a pick breaking the ground. Near the corner of the building, there was an expanded area clear of sacks. Except for the ones hiding Jeff's body. There was the start of a hole in the ground a couple of feet away from the body. Carter swung the pick while the reverend used the shovel to scoop away the dirt. When they became aware of Evan they stopped, their faces filled with alarm. The reverend quickly recovered and dropped his shovel on the pile of sacks covering Jeff's body.

"Evan, you startled us. What are you doing here, my boy?"

Carter's small dark eyes glistened in the subdued light filtering in from the warehouse skylights. He fingered the pick handle nervously.

"What's wrong, why the strange look, Evan?"

The reverend spoke, but Evan watched Carter. They expected him to speak, yet he stood mute, dumb as the sacks of grain. The reverend started toward him and Evan drew away as if from something vile and slimy.

"Are you sick? You're white as paste and your eyes look feverish. Let us help you to the lodge."

The reverend stepped closer to Evan and beckoned to Carter.

"Come, help me with him. He must be having some sort of delayed reaction, although I don't know why it should happen now."

Evan pulled back a bit farther, but they still advanced, both looking puzzled. When he found his voice, it surprised him, as he'd taken no thought of what to say.

"Why are you digging?" His words were hard and sharp.

The question halted both men in mid-step. The reverend drew a deep breath.

"It's nothing for you to be concerned about," he said softly. "But if it will satisfy you, we're taking care of a small drainage problem. You see, the footing along the side of the building has a slight crack. When it rains, water can seep in and damage the grain. We are trying to bank it with dirt."

Carter nodded vigorously and scuttled to the spot he had started digging.

"Yes, look. I'm going to take the dirt from this hole and pack it against the side over there."

"That's a strange job for the two of you."

The reverend laughed. "You think we should have sent some of the brothers. Evan, Evan, don't you realize by now that we don't hold ourselves above any task, however menial?"

"It hasn't rained for months. Did you receive some divine message of a coming storm? If you did, I'm sure the farmers would be delighted to know."

The reverend tilted his head to one side and gave Evan a searching look.

"I think it would be better if you went to the lodge, Evan. Or better yet, go sit in the car and wait for us."

For a long minute, Evan returned the reverend's steady gaze, making no move to leave.

"You heard him," Carter squeaked. "Go to the car, that is a direct order."

Evan stared at the two standing before him. He glared at them, the gaze strong as a laser shooting fire.

"You are trying to bury Jeff. To hide him forever." His words seemed thunderous in the metal building. The statement hung dark and heavy around them.

Slowly Evan raised the iron bar above his head while the two men looked startled. The reverend lifted his hand in defense.

"Listen to me, my son. Your mind is tricking you. You are having some fantasy. Let us help you."

"The way you helped me before?"

Carter quickly stepped forward, lifting the pick, ready to strike. Instantly, Evan swung the iron bar crashing it into Carter's head. As the small man fell, the bar continued its deadly arc smashing into the terrified face of Reverend Dewberry. Evan saw it happen, yet was a bystander. He was oddly detached, untouched by the carnage the weapon in his hand created. Blood poured from the heads of the two fallen men, across their necks, and soaked into the black fabric covering their shoulders. There was no need to examine the battered bodies at his feet. The life was gone from them.

The iron bar slipped from his hand and fell to the dirt floor. A tremor went through Evan, shaking him from head to foot—a shock wave, and the aftermath of his extreme emotions. He stepped across the bodies and turned his head aside to gasp for air to fill his starved lungs. He began coughing; moisture filled his mouth, and his nose ran. Using the tail of his shirt to wipe his face, he walked past the shallow hole in the dirt and stood before the grain sacks hiding Jeff. The top bags, filled with grain, made a normal looking mound, as if it were nothing more than another pile of sacks.

As he removed the last sack and stood above Jeff's crumpled body, tears scalded his face. Jeff had died in the same manner as his killers, one side of his head smashed and broken, the flesh, bone and blood now hard and set in a gory death mask. Carter must have come up behind Jeff while he talked with Dewberry. Jeff had disliked the clergymen, but never thought they were physically dangerous. He had let his guard down; their cloak of religiosity protected them.

Evan bent over, took the body in his arms, and left the building. Outside beside the car, he carefully put the remains of his friend on the ground, removed his dirty, sweat-soaked shirt, and covered Jeff's head with it. His steps were stiff and mechanical as he started across the compound to the lodge. Simon would have to be the first to know. He couldn't think of the right words to tell Simon about the evil way his son had died. Remorse and sorrow for his friend filled him, but he was devoid of any feeling for the two men he had killed. The act felt natural and meant nothing. Yet the religious community and secular law would not share this view. For every action, there is a reaction. Perhaps something equally serious would balance the killing. What that might be didn't concern him. Unexpected events filled every life. The only way to survive was to believe in an Almighty Plan. Otherwise, there was nothing but chaos, a jumble of unrelated occurrences. Faith that there is reason in the universe would keep him sane.

Even late in the day, the October sun stung his bare shoulders. Weather patterns were shifting; if this continued, the prairies would turn to desert. However, the changing world meant nothing compared with finding some gentle way to tell Simon about Jeff. He walked on, intent upon forming the message, when a speeding pickup entering the compound broke his concentration. The truck halted in a cloud of dust. William and Terry jumped from the truck and ran toward him. With fear-marked faces and heaving chests, they stopped at Evan's side.

"Where's Clay?" William demanded.

"In the office, I think. What's wrong?"

Terry gestured wildly, pointing across the road past the warehouse and storage bins.

"The fields. They are aflame, burning. It is coming this way, moving fast."

Before Evan could speak, the men turned and ran toward the office. Evan quickly went to the rear side of the warehouse. The proof of what William and Terry said was in plain sight. Not far from the buildings, the fields were burning in the same manner he and Jeff had seen them the day before. The accompanying fumes rose into the air, creating shimmering waves above the short multi-colored flames. He watched for a second before grimly resuming his mission. Head down, he stalked past the car hiding Jeff's body. Across the road, Clay and the men burst from the office door. Perhaps the burning fields would hold their attention until he could explain about the two dead men in the warehouse. Along with the one outside near the car.

Evan could also explain the fire in the fields.

He and Jeff had started something beyond their understanding. They were foolish to think unknown elements would stay extinguished in the same way as normal fire. Moreover, there was no reason to believe the fumes filling the air were safe to breathe. A harsh laugh hung in Evan's throat. Evidently, the evil shapes and powers guiding the reverend were as unable to tell the future as any human was. Killing Jeff had served no purpose. They silenced the man but not the flames, which might possibly burn forever. Life was a strange game with the players stumbling and fumbling in the dark. He knew he could not have killed if he had never seen the evil shapes. He would not have felt justified. Perhaps he wasn't, and the shades had won. God would judge him.

In the lodge, Evan went to his room, put on a shirt, and continued wondering how to tell Simon about Jeff. He found Simon, Jan, and Ryan in the lodge's large living room. Ryan was telling them about conditions in town. Jan probably kept the unpleasant conversation going to keep Simon's thoughts off his missing son. Although Simon was too old and wise to be distracted for long. As Jan and Ryan kept talking, Simon's eyes studied Evan's face. They shared a communication needing no words. Simon lifted a trembling hand.

"Evan, you've found Jeff."

Jan and Ryan turned expectant faces toward him, young faces not yet made grim by years of disappointments, while Simon, seasoned by time, sat with the patience of old age. He looked neither hopeful nor fearful, simply ready to hear what he must. Evan sat beside Simon and delivered his message, although he didn't think it was the right time to explain how he had avenged Jeff. Jan gasped and covered her mouth while Ryan turned pale, a stunned dullness veiling his eyes. Simon slumped and pressed his wrinkled lips together. He opened his mouth several times before a sound emerged.

"Take me to him, Evan. I'll see my boy."

As Simon started to stand, Jan rushed forward to stop him.

"Do you think you should, Simon? It may be too much for you. There is no need for you to see him this way."

Simon patted her hand and slowly rose to his feet. "I must."

Evan put his arm around Simon and helped him through the lodge door onto the porch. With Jan and Ryan walking solemnly behind them, the small sad group started across the compound.

Clay and some of the men were gathered near the car, where they had obviously found Jeff's body. None of them seemed to know what to deal with first, Jeff's death, or the fire in the fields. The longer they stood mourning Jeff, while casting anxious glances at the advancing flames, the faster an expression of helplessness appeared on their faces. In the presence of death, there is nothing to do. No word or deed can alter the reality. They could do nothing about Jeff. They surely suspected there was nothing they could do about the flaming fields. As the men looked at one another, this knowledge seemed to pass from man to man.

Clay finally began giving orders. He sent Jan to the main house to tell Tillie. William and Terry were to take Jeff's body to the house to prepare it for burial. Simon and Ryan followed Jan, Ryan's arm protectively about the old man's shoulders. As the rest of the men went to face the advancing fire, Evan and Clay stood beside the car.

"Where is the reverend? Does he know how this happened?" Clay asked.

Evan shivered slightly despite the dry shirt that now covered him. "Yes, he knew. He and Carter did it. They're inside."

Alarm mixed with confusion flashed across Clay's face.

"What are you talking about?"

"I'll show you. And I'll show you what I did."

Evan walked toward the warehouse and entered the dim interior. Immediately, his eyes began to water, and behind him, Clay coughed. The grain dust seemed thicker. Wiping his eyes, he moved along the center aisle and on to the far corner of the building. Clay followed and when Evan stopped, Clay stepped to his side. At the sight of the two forms crumpled on the ground, Clay's only sound was a quick gasp. He grabbed Evan's arm, his fingers biting into the firm muscle.

"You did this?" Clay rasped.

Evan nodded.

"Does anyone else know?" Clay whispered.

Evan shook his head. "I didn't tell Simon. I only told him I found Jeff. I wish you didn't have to know either."

"Did they attack you? What happened?"

It was hard for him to remember what had happened, but he told Clay as clearly as he could. Clay coughed and swallowed several times as he listened, his eyes shifting nervously.

"I don't know what to do, Evan. The only thing I'm sure of is that we have to hide them. We have to get rid of that car, too. We need to hide it right away. Put it in one of the garages for now; we can decide where to take it later."

"Clay, the only reason I had to show you this is because you would have found out later. We need to protect you. I can't let you be involved."

"Involved? Churchmen killed on my property— how can I not be involved?"

Evan's heart shriveled. He still wasn't sorry the men were dead, but he was extremely sorry for putting Clay in jeopardy.

"I'll make it right; I'll keep you out of this."

Clay's expression lost the nervousness and turned to anger. "What do you intend to do, confess you killed them? Sometimes I think you, Simon, and the few others are the only ones that really understand what's happening to us. You have been fighting the Church ever since I met you; you'd be crazy to submit to them now. You can't admit to doing this."

"No, I don't intend to confess, unless there is no other way. I'll handle it on my own. For everyone's good, I'll move on. I'll take the car and bodies with me. No one will find them."

Clay had turned away from the bodies to face Evan.

"Okay, I'll leave this to you, but there won't be much time. The fire will attract attention, if it hasn't already. I don't think we can stop it; it will have to burn itself out. I'm going to the office to start notifying people. We both know what's burning. It must be that weird mixture of chemicals, and it will follow the irrigation lines. That will involve nearly every piece of land from Texas clear to the reservoir and dump site in Montana."

For some reason unknown to Evan, and he supposed to Clay as well, they extended their hands and performed a firm, steady handshake.

"Come on," Clay said. "We need to get out of here before we both choke."

Evan nodded. "You go. I'll finish up here. It won't take long."

He watched Clay leave the warehouse, feeling they had sealed a bargain. Not once had Clay been angry with him concerning the fire. He hadn't even questioned why Evan and Jeff tried the test before asking him. Perhaps Clay knew he would have agreed to it and the result would have been the same.

Evan put his hand to his forehead, where a dull ache began building behind his eyes. He saw the shovel Carter had used. He wished he could bury the two men under the warehouse the way they had intended to do with Jeff. However, he wouldn't do that. He couldn't leave anything to incriminate Clay. For now, he had to hide them and the car. Later he could use it to take the bodies away from the farm. The grain sacks had served to hide one body; they could do the same for two. Evan grasped the bodies by their heels, one at a time, and dragged them into a side aisle where he piled grain sacks on top of them. He was sweating from every pore, as much from nervousness as from heat and exertion. His eyes were stinging; tears mingled with the sweat on his cheeks. It was becoming difficult to breathe, and he stopped several times to catch a breath. He knew he was in better shape than this. It was surely the pressure of the situation.

With the bodies covered, he took the shovel and began turning the dirt where their blood had left dark, caked patches. After smoothing the area, he walked across it several times until it looked the same as the rest of the floor. It didn't take long to fill the hole Carter had started. When he finished, he threw the shovel to one side and started to leave, but suddenly the iron bar caught his eye. Even if he tried to clean it, there could be traces of blood. He'd put it in the car and get rid of it along with the bodies and the car.

Evan bent over and grabbed the bar. As he did, blood rushed to his head and he dropped the bar. Dizziness and darkness swirled around him. As he started to lose consciousness, he struggled to stand straight. The dark began to gather into shapes, and fear froze him. This time they could kill him because he had killed.

He had broken God and man's law. He needed to move, get away from the threatening images, be they demons or angels. Yet his body refused to obey until a tiny voice said, *the spirit can move the body*. It was a reminder of the spirit that lived within him, and in a flash, he regained control. He glared at the hovering apparitions, denying them any influence over him. For that which was within him was stronger than that which was within the world. With renewed strength, Evan hurried from the warehouse, closing the door behind him.

Twenty-six

Hiding the car in one of the garages didn't seem the best plan, but for the time being it was the only thing Evan could do. Later that night he would drive it, with the bodies, as far away as possible and find a place to dispose of them. As he walked to the lodge, the lengthening shadows signaled the approaching evening. In a few hours, it would be dark enough to leave. He wasn't sure what was happening in the rest of the world, or even in Garden City, but on this once prosperous farm, the end seemed near. The end of what, he wasn't sure and he might never know, for by morning he would be gone. There was nothing more he could do for Clay, and his staying would harm him.

In his room, Evan changed his clothes and began packing his few possessions. As he put the last of his books into a bag, a bitter smile played at the corners of his mouth. He had wanted to help Clay, but he had only brought problems and plagues. A sorry way to repay Clay's kindness. He went through the room carefully, removing every trace of his having been there. When the Church began their search for the two missing men, the farm would come under scrutiny. It was no secret Evan had been staying there, but there was no need to leave anything behind to complicate matters. With the car and bodies gone, Clay could claim that the reverend had driven away, no one on the farm knowing where he went. Evan checked the room again and set his bags in the hallway. He'd stay until full darkness when he could take his loathsome cargo to some isolated spot. If he carefully hid the bodies, there was a chance no one would ever find them. It was a slim chance—bodies rarely stayed hidden forever— still it gave him a bit of hope. However, he couldn't think about it now; he had to finish what he had started.

Evan sat on the couch in the long living room and bowed his head, intending to pray for forgiveness and guidance, but he couldn't concentrate. His life had been a series of leaving, running away, and escaping; in his wake, he'd left destruction, wreckage, and anger. When he started his journey, he had left behind a mother hardly recognizable as a human being; he left a totally distorted Church, and he fled from town leaving those who had listened to him to suffer persecution from the Church. Ryan was an example of that. Now he was leaving the farm in a total ruin. How much of the tragedy was his fault he couldn't say, but he had been there.

Searching through the past, he looked for situations where he was to blame. He couldn't have helped his mother's condition; she was too far-gone. Staying to watch over her would have been useless. A waste of time. The errors of the Church made it impossible for him to stay there, and he did not regret leaving. Holding meetings in Garden City and revealing the biblical truth to people could not be wrong. Even if it brought them trouble. Raking through and sifting the events of his life, Evan discovered the serious flaw buried within him. His guilt was in straying from his only purpose in life. He was to preach the Gospel to people who might otherwise never hear. It wasn't his role to become involved in secular problems. In trying to help Clay, he had put aside his rightful duty. He had tried to solve things his way, instead of relying upon God. If he hadn't tried to cleanse the fields, they wouldn't be burning. Jeff would be alive, and he would not have killed two men.

When the front door opened, he quickly stood, tense and alert. As Jan entered, he relaxed.

"It's you," he said with a smile.

There was no corresponding smile from Jan. "You were probably expecting the police or at least someone from the Church, right?"

"What makes you say that?" he asked, even though he was sure he knew.

"Because that is what usually follows when there are three murders."

He frowned and searched her face for some indication that she was not feeling as hostile as she sounded. Jan nodded toward his bags in the small pile by the hall door.

"I see you are ready to leave. Clay told me you would be going. He told me how it happened. I promised him I'd keep still, but I had to talk to you. What went wrong? Finding Jeff that way I can understand your anger, but what happened? Didn't you know you had them right where you wanted them? You only had to call someone. Even the Unity Council would have to acknowledge the crime. It was the first crack in their armor. Your teaching would have gained more notice; their persecution of you would have come out in the investigation. Now that the gain is on their side, there probably won't even be a mention of Jeff's death!"

She was right, but it had not occurred to him to turn Jeff's death to an advantage. He'd acted in vengeful rage. Jan was well equipped to operate in the world; she was quick thinking and she knew how to play the game. Jan shook her head and sighed.

"I'm not blaming you. You didn't think; you simply reacted. It's such a waste. You could have used it to turn the tables. Now I don't know what will happen. I don't know if there will ever be much hope of advancing your cause."

"How many times have I tried to explain? I have no cause other than to speak the truth. You're looking for some emerging new order that I'm not suited to lead."

Jan looked bored, a child hearing the same old rules she had heard a hundred times before.

"We can't go over that again, Evan. We've more immediate problems. Simon wants Jeff buried now, right now. We tried to explain that we must report the death and receive a certificate. He won't have any of it. He says it isn't anyone's business, and if we are his friends, we will help him put Jeff to rest and never mention it again."

"Is Clay willing to do this?"

Jan lowered her head and chewed at the corner of her lips. "Clay is willing to go along with whatever Simon wants. Tillie is backing him. Poor Clay, he is trying to stay strong but I don't know how long he will. We are in a mess. Ryan was telling about the conditions in town; the prices change every day, sometimes twice a day, and people are getting rid of their money as fast as they get it. There are guards at every store.

"Now," she continued, "there is a rumor that the chemical spill has gotten into the drinking water. If it is this bad in Garden City, think what it is like in larger cities. I called my father and he said it was unbelievable. I asked if he wanted me to come home, and he laughed. They may need to come here for refuge. Of course, Clay won't refuse them. He called Tracy and told her to bring her family if it gets too bad. But she has heard about the fires and is scared of the fumes, thinks it would be wrong to expose the children."

Jan stopped for a second and gave a dry laugh. "I don't know what makes her think the fumes won't spread to town once they're in the air."

Evan thought for a bit. "Maybe she should take them to the nearest domed city."

"They are sealed; no one is allowed to enter," Jan said. "The citizens there feared a horde of people trying to rush in. There doesn't seem to be anything we can do now. Clay has called everyone he can think of for help. He asked me to bring you and said we'd hold a short service for Jeff before any official arrives."

Evan gave a curt nod. He would stay with Simon and pay his last respects to Jeff. He could remove the bodies later. He should have time before the farm swarmed with strangers.

When Jan and Evan left the lodge, they found the farmhands, along with Clay, Simon, Ryan, and Tillie, gathered by the workshop. Some of the men had quickly built a coffin while Jan and Tillie had prepared Jeff's body.

"I never thought I could do that," Jan said. "But Tillie is a rock and somehow it wasn't difficult caring for the remains of a dear friend."

Evan glanced at the sky. A thin orange stripe hung on the western horizon; it was growing thinner by the minute while a few barren clouds drifted away, dissolving in the dry air. It would soon be dark; at best, they had an hour. The gravesite was on the far side of the compound. The fires had reached the gently rolling hills where Mark and Eva were buried, making it impossible to bury Jeff there. It seemed the farm was a huge burial ground. Evan walked to Simon and put an arm around his shoulders. Simon wiped his lips with a trembling hand and tried to smile.

"You don't think I'm a crazy old coot do you, Evan?"

Evan shook his head. "No. You should have the right to bury your son as you please."

A single tear slipped from Simon's eye. "Can't be born or live and die in your own way. Well, my boy is free now, and I won't have his body put in the ground by anybody's rules but my own."

The others standing within hearing lowered their heads and tears glistened in several eyes. William, Terry, and four others went into the workshop and returned carrying the coffin. Everyone moved aside as they walked by and then fell into step behind, forming a silent respectful procession. They buried Jeff at the edge of the garden where flowers once grew. It was a short ceremony and Tillie put some carved, wooden roses she had used as a table centerpiece on the top of the coffin.

"They are the nearest I could come to real flowers," she said to Simon.

No one made a move to leave after Simon had said a few words and sprinkled a handful of dirt onto the coffin. Clay nodded at two of his men and they, with their shovels, began filling the grave. It was a symbolic act, one meant to give the last personal touch to the burial. In the distance, a man sat ready on a small tractor. Shortly, he would come forward and quickly finish filling the grave. As the first shovelfuls dropped into the grave, an evening wind freshened and dry powdery dust settled on the shoes of those standing nearby. Tillie was the first to move.

"We best go now. There is nothing more we can do."

Across the road from the compound, the jewel-colored flames had total possession of the land, creeping and licking to within several hundred feet of the warehouse and storage bins. The only comforting fact was that the contaminated irrigation water had never touched the ground within the compound. The buildings should be safe, but Evan had another worry. With everyone watching the burning fields and beginning to talk of ways to save the warehouse and storage bins if necessary, he wouldn't have a chance to remove the bodies.

Suddenly a terrific boom sounded, followed by a great shock wave. The earth seemed to move, shaking the compound and the people clustered there. It was a second before anyone understood that the warehouse had exploded. Perhaps imploded was more accurate. In quick succession, a second and third whopping thump rocked the area. The elevators cracked in several places and pieces of the concrete flew off the tops. The explosions sent everyone running to the far side of the compound, away from the buildings. Clouds of dust and black smoke billowed high into the air, further darkening the early night sky. The group of shocked, coughing people huddled together by the fence about thirty yards from the end of the lodge. Clay had his arm about Jan and she leaned against him.

"What happened?" she stammered.

Clay stared straight ahead at the buildings while the debris settled and a fire roared inside the warehouse. Clay didn't answer her; he only shook his head, an amazed look on his face.

"Lord a mercy," Tillie gasped.

"Will you look at that," Terry said with awe.

"What the hell is going on? We never had a grain fire," William growled.

Some of the other men edged closer to the fence, looking tense and fearful, instinctively withdrawing from the explosions.

"Wonder what happened?" one of them asked.

"How could we know? None of us been allowed in there," another answered.

"There is no water, we can't fight it," a man said, shaking his head. Nervously, everyone looked toward the other buildings in the compound.

"I think I know how it started," Evan cried. "My eyes and throat were burning when I was in the warehouse. There is gas rising from the fields. It must be collecting in the closed buildings."

It seemed a logical explanation, but Clay shook his head.

"Maybe it served as an ignition source, but Dewberry wouldn't listen to me about how to maintain stored grain. The accumulated dust in that confined space could have been enough. That doesn't matter now. If gas from the chemical fires had something to do with it, we better open the other buildings."

With the deep gray of night settling over the farm, the flames from the warehouse and storage buildings were torches lighting the darkness. The men rushed away in different directions, becoming black figures moving against a backdrop of orange and red. Evan headed for the garages, where he threw open the doors, while Tillie, Jan, and Clay ran for the main house and the office building. Soon the lodge stood open to the night breeze, curtains trailing from the open windows. There wasn't any question of trying to save the grain; it burned too quickly and soon filled the air with the nutty smell of roasting wheat, corn, and soy. Under that pleasant odor, Evan was sure there was the scent of charred, burnt flesh.

He'd forgotten to take the iron bar with him after hiding the bodies; the dizzy spell had left him confused. He had intended to get it. Now it didn't matter; the fire should cleanse it. However, he doubted bones would burn. There would be skeletons to explain. Was it Divine intervention, or simply another strange happening in a confusing world? With the remaining buildings standing open, the men returned and gathered in small groups. Some of them shook their heads in stunned silence, seemingly unable to find words strong enough to describe the destruction around them.

In the distance a siren sounded, the high whining whirl growing louder as it came closer. Every head turned toward the road where headlights were visible. At first, a feeling of hope rippled through the group. When they saw it was a single vehicle, the feeling faded. Yet, it was someone from the outside. The farm was no longer isolated, a place sealed off as if under a glass dome. No one had mentioned it, but there had been a growing sense of isolation. The farm was alone and helpless in a crumbling world because Clay's messages and calls for assistance had gone unanswered. Now there was no hope that even an entire regiment could save them, but any sign of help was encouraging.

When the Landmaster slammed to a stop, gravel spitting from under the wheels, Clay ran toward it, the others following him. Two men stepped from the vehicle. They were dressed in the dark green and tan of the Emergency Service Corps. The light from the warehouse fires flickered off their shiny tan helmets with the green triangle on the front. Neither man gave a second look to the buildings or the fields on the far side of the road. Their faces were blank and expressionless, the masks of authority men wore when taking control of others. Everyone pressed closer to listen.

"Are you Clay Sanderson?" The taller one spoke to Clay.

"Yes," he answered, nodding toward the road. "Are the others on the way?"

"I'm sorry, Mr. Sanderson, but there won't be anyone coming," said the man who seemed to be the senior of the two. Upon hearing this, a chorus of disgusted exclamations rippled through the small group.

"What do you mean?" Clay demanded. "Surely there will be help in fighting this thing."

"I'm afraid not. We're part of the survey and assessment crew. Our job is to assess the situation and advise you and your people in the evacuation process."

This brought shouts of objection from everyone. They made no attempt to soften their surprise and outrage.

"That's a fine response to a cry for help." William spoke from between clenched teeth.

"What did you expect?" Terry nudged him. "Nobody gives a damn about us."

Clay raised his hand, silencing the men behind him. "It won't take long to assess our situation." Clay waved his arm toward the fields. "We're ruined. Now what the hell do you mean, 'evacuation?'"

The spokesman gave his companion a weary look; they had obviously heard this question before.

"Sanderson, do you suppose you are the only farm in this fix? Since noon, we have been on the road going from one place to the next. It's the same story at every operation that was on National's pipeline. For one reason or another the chemicals caught fire."

"There's been no news bulletin," Jan cried. "Why weren't we told how widespread this is?"

"It's for everyone's safety. We don't need a panic."

"Is every field burning?" Clay asked with amazement.

"Most of them." The agent nodded. "Those that didn't catch on their own are starting as the fire spreads. There seems to be a buildup of gas in any closed building, but you must already know that from the condition of your buildings. No civilian population is to remain in the area. There are staging points arranged for the temporary relocation, until this is controlled and the danger eliminated. We are to instruct you in how, and where, to go."

Evan, Ryan, and Simon edged to the rear of the group. Ryan nudged Evan but kept his eyes on the two men.

"Likely they are going to take us someplace," he whispered.

"Not you and me," Evan answered.

"Not me neither," Simon said.

The taller official turned in a half circle, surveying the group. "You are allowed one small suitcase of personal belongings. My assistant will answer any questions while I fill in the report. We won't be long; you'll have approximately thirty minutes, and we must leave together. At the main road, you are to proceed to the armory at the south end of Garden City while we continue on to the next farm. You will receive further instructions at the armory."

"What if some of us don't choose to be herded about the same as a bunch of cattle?" A voice rose from the middle of the group.

"When we report that our area has been assessed," the man went on addressing the group, "clearance troops will arrive to sweep the counties, making sure the citizens are safely removed. Test stations will be built and scientists can determine what action is needed for the restoration of the land."

"How long will that take?" Jan demanded.

"We have no timetable at present, but you can be assured your land and homes will be returned to you in working order as soon as possible. We ask your full cooperation in this."

Clay, standing in front of his farmhands, looked angry. The confusion and even fear circulating through the group was painful to watch. Evan wished to help, but he couldn't think of a way. Although, it seemed Clay was willing to try. He stepped closer to the emergency services agent.

"Look," Clay began. "Our other buildings are clear. We opened them. We'd be of more help staying. We can manage."

The officer gave a smile that was half sneer. "That isn't possible. You will follow orders; otherwise, we have no alternative but to remove you by force. Now if you will please hurry, this operation is on a tight schedule."

Clay hung his head and motioned the others to disperse. The official took Clay aside to answer questions on the forms concerning the farm. William and Terry lingered at the rear of the group near Evan.

William narrowed his eyes. "When did the government ever give back anything once they got their hands on it?"

Terry shook his head. "Never happens, not once they got control. What're we going to do?"

"Nothing right now. Let's go into town, we can't stay. We'll figure out something."

Tillie and Jan hurried away toward the house evidently wanting to make good use of the time allowed for packing. They were practical enough to know there was no point in fighting the order. Most of the men grumbled, but slowly started for the lodge. Evan grabbed Ryan's arm and pulled him along at the back of the group while Simon hurried to stay with them.

"Keep with the others until we're inside," Evan told Ryan. "These officers probably have no connection with the Church and won't be looking for you, but there is no use taking chances."

"What about you?" Ryan asked. "When you opened the garage, I saw Reverend Dewberry's car. Where is he? What's going on, Evan?"

This wasn't the time to answer him; instead, Evan rushed Ryan and Simon into the lodge with the other men. The minute he'd heard the explosion and saw the warehouse burning, he thought about the hidden bodies. There was no way to retrieve them. The men wouldn't allow him to stay long enough to sift through the burnt rubble. He needed desperately to talk with Clay. At some point, someone would find the bodies. He had intended to leave; now he would have to go into town and accept blame for the killings. He couldn't let Clay face it alone.

Ryan had nothing to pack. Instead, he helped Simon, who was having difficulty choosing which of his books to leave behind. He cast Evan a pained look.

"It's hard to part with even one of them," Simon muttered.

"They'll be okay until you return," Evan tried to reassure him.

"But I'm not coming back. I'm going with you and the boy, that is if you can suffer the burden of having an old man with you."

"I'm not going," Evan answered. "Ryan will have to go alone."

Ryan frowned. "I don't understand. Have you lost your nerve? You've been acting strange." He turned to Simon. "You can go with me; I'll take care of you."

Clay and Jan came into Simon's room, cutting the discussion short. Evan stepped aside to let them in, and Clay shut the door behind him.

"Evan, I'm guessing you and Ryan won't be going to the armory with the rest of us, am I right? Once you are in town, even with the confusion, someone is bound to spot you."

Ryan stepped forward. "You're right; I'm not going. I don't know about Evan." He gave Evan a sharp glance.

Clay raised an eyebrow. "Now listen, okay? I have a plan for you to slip away."

"Wait," Evan cut in. "I can't leave you to explain what's in the warehouse ash."

Clay smiled, a triumphant light in his eyes. "I took care of that! While we were completing the assessment report, the fellow from emergency services spotted the Church's car in the garage. I said how the reverend and his man were checking supplies in the warehouse when it exploded. I told him we couldn't do anything. How sorry we are that they are still in there, victims of this terrible calamity."

"He didn't seem a bit surprised," Jan added. "He said there had been other deaths in connection with the fires. He wants one of us to drive the Church's car to town when we leave the farm."

Ryan and Simon looked puzzled.

"Don't worry, I'll explain later," Evan said to them, and turned toward Clay. "Won't there be more questions?"

Clay broke into a laugh and put his hand to his forehead. "Questions? There will be nothing but questions. No one knows what this gas in the air is doing to us. Those two officials they sent are nervous about their own safety. The younger one is edgy as a mouse in a room full of cats. Keeps putting his handkerchief over his nose and mouth. I figure they wouldn't let them wear protective gear on this job. It might panic the people they're trying to round up. Far as I'm concerned, you and anyone else that wants to can go your own way."

"Are you sure? I can't leave you to take the blame if there's trouble," Evan said.

"No one is going to doubt my story. It makes perfect sense. You can have my car and I'll drive the reverend's. After we leave the farm and the emergency services guys split off, you can be on your way.

With the pickups and the dump truck, we'll make a big convoy. I don't think anyone will notice one less in our group."

Clay's plan sounded fine, except what if something went wrong? Would there be evidence of what happened to the Churchmen in the reverend's car? Evan tried to remember; there'd been blood on his hands when he put Jeff on the ground. He didn't think he'd touched anything outside. It was a blessing he'd not put the iron bar in the car.

"Evan? What's wrong, don't you think my plan will work?"

"What? No, I mean yes. Yes, it's a good plan. Thank you for thinking of it."

"Where will you be heading?" Jan asked him.

"North, I suppose. That's what Ryan had in mind. I'm sorry if I've disappointed you, Jan. I hope you don't forget the important things I tried to teach."

"I won't. You know I fully intended to go with you, but Clay needs me. I honestly think I can be of more use staying with him. When this is over there is going to be a tremendous amount of rebuilding. This thing has ruined everyone. Even poor Frank has lost again."

Clay looked at her in surprise. "Frank? He got his money and ran. I'd say he's the only one that did okay for once."

Jan shook her head. "No. That last shipment of grain in your storage was his. He put the money from the sale of Tracy's inheritance into grain. He thought food was the safest investment: high demand, and low supply. Now the supply is going a lot lower than even he expected. And since his grain is gone, he'll have nothing to sell."

Clay gave a half snort. "Don't worry about him. It's like I always said about Frank—if he gets to hell first, he'll meet you at the gate with a layout of parcels that get the coolest breezes."

Jan looked around the room. "Have you packed everything you want, Simon? Clay and I will take you and Tillie with us. I can't imagine what they intend to do with everyone once they are collected. Probably ship them to unaffected states. If it is safe in town we can go to my parents, or to Fern."

Simon straightened his frail shoulders. "I appreciate the offer, my dear, but if Evan and Ryan will let me, I intend to push on with them."

Evan winced. "I'd welcome you, Simon, but there are things you don't know. I have the mark of Cain on me. I may not get by with it. Do you understand?"

Simon shrugged. "No, I don't. You can tell me about it later. The only thing I can see is that you are still taking too much importance to yourself. If the boy and I choose to travel with you, it's on our heads."

~ * ~

Ryan was silent as he listened, but his mind was quick and he caught what Evan meant, even if Simon didn't. Evan had done something terrible that Clay and Jan were helping to cover. Since being at the farm, Ryan had seen Evan in a different way. At first, he was sure Evan's teaching was the beginning of a pure, perfect new order, but now he wondered. Not because of anything Evan might have done, but because he hadn't done more. It was impossible to help people unless there was a solid power base. He'd heard some of the things Jan had said, and she was right. When they reached the others in the north, this movement should gain strength. With more support, they could grow and bring hope to thousands, maybe millions, of desperate people.

Clay extended his hand toward Evan.

"Guess this is where we part company. Don't worry about any of us. Take care of yourselves. Keep in touch. When things get settled and we're on this farm again, you'll always be welcome."

After a few words with Simon, Clay and Jan went to the center of the compound where the others stood around the trucks and cars. Ryan and Simon climbed into Clay's car, with Evan behind the wheel. It was good of Clay to let them have it. It was much better than anything Ryan had expected. He'd thought most of their travel would be on foot. The emergency services Landmaster was in the lead as the vehicles prepared to leave. The engines and headlights came on, and like some giant brightly lit caterpillar, they began to weave down the road. Behind them, the farm lay deserted, already taking on the air of a ghost town. The big main house stood white against the night, reflecting the flames of the dwindling warehouse fires across the road, while small jewel-colored flames continued to dance across the fields.

The land with its silent flickering fire seemed endless as it stretched into the distance. The hot bright color of the burning ground was a stark contrast to the black heaven with its scattered icy-white stars. Even the sound of the cars and trucks barely disturbed the great silence of the barren land. As the humans retreated from a ruined prairie, the noise of life faded amazingly fast.

At the highway, the Landmaster turned to the left and its siren began to shrill through the dark. The other vehicles from the farm went to the right toward Garden City. Ryan, Evan, and Simon were in the last car. Three miles outside of town, Evan drove slower, letting the others pull farther ahead. When the last taillights became ruby dots in the distance, Evan wordlessly swung onto the interstate ramp, heading north. Ryan tingled with excitement thinking of the adventure ahead. He wanted to do something to mark this beginning. They needed to keep a record.

"Simon, do you have a tablet with you?"

Epilogue

From the private journal of Ryan Lanier
Age, thirty-one
Rome, Italy
September 10, 2212

I am alone in my apartment. In the morning, I will be on Unity Council's Falcon flight to Jerusalem with Justin Denovo. He is to speak there before the Knesset. I have spent the evening sorting through my papers and electronic storage devices. I will leave nothing behind in case we do not return. There are those who would sabotage our mission. I have destroyed the secret documents and incriminating letters. Only the writing I have done over the last ten years, most of which has been published in one form or another, remains. However, I have kept one thing private: the journal I began fifteen years ago and, alas, never continued. A sixteen-year-old boy rarely has the perseverance to carry on with his good intentions. Perhaps I should discard these pages. They tell of my innocent youth, before I learned the truth. Still, as misguided as I was, they are my past and I find it hard to dispose of them. I will leave the tablet with

Father Roushman; he will understand this sentimental flaw. How optimistic I was at that age, taking everything in stride and certain that tomorrow would be better. I pity the children of today; they have no memories free of hunger, war, plague, and natural disaster. The years of constant upheaval have made me cautious. Even Unity Council's valiant efforts made only a small improvement in conditions. Yet, a spark of that old hope still glows within me.

Justin Denovo is responsible for my optimism. His fervent devotion to a united world burns brightly; light and reason come to every project he touches. When he approached the Council fifteen years ago, they recognized his astounding abilities. Indeed, he is our last hope. For years, the World Assembly held the nations in a loose coalition based upon trade, but there were still hostilities. One by one, Justin has convinced countries that war is not the answer. That if different religions could unite and retain their identities, nations could do the same. Our mission tomorrow is vitally important. Justin has secured concessions for Israel that, if agreed to, will bring complete unity. Israel is the final link in forging a strong, lasting worldwide peace.

No nation is willing to give total power to another, but Justin's great plan assures equal representation for every country. We are on the eve of achieving the only possible solution for a world in chaos. If nothing intervenes, the first election of an International Council President will take place at the end of the month. There is no doubt Justin will win. Not only does he have Unity Council's strong backing, but in addition, a great wave of public support is swelling across the globe.

Nothing would please me more, not because of my position as his personal assistant—I have already received more satisfaction and pleasure working with him in his glorious cause than I ever dreamed possible, but because he is the only answer. I am in awe of his plans, the wonderful things he intends to accomplish once he is in power. If the nations had united sooner, we would have avoided years of war and other dire conditions. Even the forces of nature have seemed bent upon the destruction of mankind. Every year there is invading debris from space, while the ground below twists and cracks open in a new spot. The comet that tore through our atmosphere five years ago disrupted the weather patterns even more, and again disabled much of our electronics.

In order to survive, mankind must unite. I have raged in fury against the shortsighted self-interest groups, hanging onto their puny authority at the expense of others. That will change under the new order. It reminds me of my childhood in a small prairie town, where there was lack of organization in the face of calamity. Of course, it was minor compared to what has followed. I have no idea what became of my parents, or the others left there. It would be sheer luck if they survived. The economy of the area is dead; nothing grows on the dry, brown land. The nation lost a full third of its grain production to poisonous waste. Still, with the global weather growing hotter and drier each year, none of the other countries fares much better. The myth of adversity drawing people closer and bringing out their best has proven entirely false. The only stable organization to survive is the Council. Justin must have known this would be the case when he went to them with his plan.

I wonder if Evan Hunter or Simon Taylor would now admit their error? They were strongly opposed to the Council, yet millions more would have died without its wise guidance and excellent food management programs. I admit I too was once blind to the true order, but while assisting Evan in his traveling ministry, I did have doubts. I will never denounce his sincerity, but as I explained to the Council upon joining their effort, it is possible to be sincerely wrong.

Evan and Simon are gone, taken ten years ago by the malady which killed hundreds of millions. No one knew the exact death toll. It struck the scattered renegade groups, the ones defying the Church and government directives. Before the mysterious plague, the authorities begged the dissenters to go to the nearest survival center. There they could receive a number and be given care, but few of them did. Living on starvation rations and with inadequate shelter, it is no wonder they died when the new disease struck. There was no pity for those isolated groups. Many felt it just punishment for their lack of cooperation. At the time, I thought Evan and Simon had died of some delayed effects from the chemicals at the Sanderson farm. However, that didn't explain the millions of others who also died.

From governmental accounts, it seems the disease struck everywhere at the same time, in the same manner. There was no sign of illness, only an instant disintegration caused by the strange virus. It destroyed every atom of the body, leaving no remains to examine. The World Health Center's official report stated a combination of possibilities. Those who died were in poor physical condition from their practice of using unapproved water sources. As our years of drought continue, the contamination of the water grows worse. The only safe sources are under the control of each country's Ministry of Water. The WHC also believes the rebels' limited communication with those outside their faith contributed to their weakness. They even refused to keep in touch with the 'gray skies' units which broadcast the air hazard alerts. I think it was perhaps a combination of those things. I was with them and know how they ignored every government effort to protect them.

That day, even if there was no sky alert, it was obvious we would be under heavy contamination. The first light of day came with bloody streaks across an oily dark sky. Later the colors merged and hung close to the ground. It was dusk the entire day. As those around me died, or actually disappeared, I remained untouched. Suddenly I understood. Evan and his kind were wayward branches sapping strength from the true vine. Pruning them made way for healthy growth. The lesson was clear; I knew which direction to take.

We were near Winnipeg at the time, sheltered by a family of the Society of Friends. They, children included, suffered the same fate as other similar groups. Their destruction was a definite sign. It was time to apply the knowledge I'd absorbed from Evan and Simon. My education was far more complete than it would have been if I had stayed within the Council's system. Being on the outside, I had firsthand knowledge of the terror about to destroy our world.

Uniting is the only hope.

The day Justin spoke before the World Commerce Commission in New York City, I knew I must go to him. There was not a trace of doubt; my destiny was to labor in his vineyard. From the years of hunger, I was reed thin, my raw wrists and ankles protruding from tattered clothes. Yet, even in this condition, I felt a strength surge through me. Failing to reach him never occurred to me. The courage of my convictions drove me. When I stood outside the great metal doors waiting for the meeting to adjourn, I was bold beyond reason. I would wait as long as necessary to see him.

An immense crowd, ragged as myself, gathered in the street around the building and armed guards lined the sidewalk. I pressed forward until I hung over the ropes cordoning off the area from the doors to the armored cars. As the tall bronze doors swung open, a great cheer arose from the throng. There he stood, magnificent in his flowing red robe and a black cape edged in gold draped over his wide shoulders. For a second, I could only gape at this splendid, royal man. Everything I had heard was true. Peace, love, and wisdom fairly radiated from him. He swept through the door and raised his hand to bless the shouting mob as he glided toward a massive armored vehicle. He was nearly past me before I found my voice.

"Justin," I cried.

He stopped and turned. Instantly, his ebony eyes found mine. His gaze pierced my soul. Silently, he motioned me forward. I stood before him, unaware of the war-torn city or the hushed crowd.

"I see you are here at last," he stated.

I simply nodded. It was a moment wrapped in a mysticism transcending every explanation. An instant of total revelation. From that day, I became his assistant, working as an appendage needing no instruction; his will became mine. Even now, thinking upon our work, my heart thrills. As a boy, I admired Evan, recognizing the surrounding glow which seemed to make him some special being. Now I realize what a pale, temporary light he had shed. He was a faint flicker in the darkness compared to Justin's blazing sun, which illuminates the entire world and will shortly burn away the long midnight of mankind. Lately I have noticed myself growing aggressively protective of Justin. At times, I feel I could actually kill for him, but upon careful study of this growing emotion, I am satisfied it stems from the threats of a few scattered political fringe groups. Justin assures me I shouldn't take them seriously, yet if harm came to him, I could not be responsible for my reaction. I do not intend to boast, but my abilities have become considerable in the last few years. In Justin's presence, I can perform miracles. He empowers me to an extent I never thought possible.

It is growing late and I must rest in preparation for our journey tomorrow. We shall not fail. I am completely confident victory will be ours. Justin will win the office of International Council President. When his full power becomes evident, a new position will be created for him, that of World President. Finally, the earth will rest in the care of he who is worthy. I will work even harder to ensure that people everywhere learn to worship this miraculous man, for if they do, it will bring about their own salvation.

Meet H. L. Chandler

H. L Chandler writes in several genres: thrillers, paranormal, adventure, and mysteries. She has also written stories for children. She has lived across the U.S. and for a short time in Canada.

Other Works From The Pen Of
H. L. Chandler

The Keepers - A story of a family torn apart by an insidious force intent on using each member for its own evil purpose.

Evil Intent - Gary married for money. When the money ran out, it was time to collect Janet's life insurance. Yet, *something* at the mountain cabin where Janet takes refuge has other plans.

Lost in Fear – In childhood, Julie Taylor survived a family massacre. As an educated young woman, she strives to live a normal life. She might succeed if it were not for the evil which plagues her.

Song of the Sparrow - Living with a cruel stepfather, Lugene and Harley grow up fast. But not fast enough to escape the dangers that face them as run-away teens in New Orleans.

Legion's Land – In a post holocaustic world Nora lived a comfortable life. She never questioned the system until it threatened her children. How far will she go to save them?

Hoodoo Murder – A murder and kidnapping put Private Investigator Ladonna Rose in the middle of a case that merges with a tragedy from her past.

Mystery at Sunset Ridge – Is the missing real estate developer a murderer, or a victim? When P. I. Billie Ross gets too close to an answer, she disappears as well.

Murder Bayou – Was Ross Delroque worth more dead than alive? Or was he about to report a toxic waste dump? To arrive at the truth P.I. Ladonna Rose searches for answers among his sadly dysfunctional family.

Sure and Certain Shadows – Ingrid grew up on rough Kansas City streets, proud to have survived. Thrown into an alien world, she fights to stay alive and return to her own planet.

Rest Beyond the River – The story of Micah Hanson's personal tragedy played out against a great natural disaster in the center of the United States.

Shattered Illusions – Kate's quiet life ended with her brother's murder. Determined to find his killer she uncovers a shocking past that puts her life in danger.

Letter to Our Readers

Enjoy this book?

You can make a difference

As an independent publisher, Wings ePress, Inc. does not have the financial clout of the large New York Publishers. We can't afford large magazine spreads or subway posters to tell people about our quality books.

But, we do have something much more effective and powerful than ads. We have a large base of loyal readers.

Honest Reviews help bring the attention of new readers to our books.

If you enjoyed this book, we would appreciate it if you would spend a few minutes posting a review on the site where you purchased this book or on the Wings ePress, Inc. webpages at:

https://wingsepress.com/

Thank You

Visit Our Website

For The Full Inventory
Of Quality Books:

Wings ePress.Inc
https://wingsepress.com/

Quality trade paperbacks and downloads
in multiple formats,
in genres ranging from light romantic comedy
to general fiction and horror.
Wings has something for every reader's taste.
Visit the website, then bookmark it.
We add new titles each month!

Wings ePress Inc.
3000 N. Rock Road
Newton, KS 67114